TEMPORARY DEATHS

A NOVEL

GUILLERMO INFANTE

A MALOCA PRESS ORIGINAL JULY 2022

Published in the United States by Maloca Press, LLC, Cherry Hill, New Jersey.

Library of Congress Cataloging -in Publication Data
Infante, Guillermo A.
LCCN: 2022905366

Temporary Deaths – A Novel / by Guillermo A. Infante

ISBN 979-8-9863907-0-3 (alk. Paper)
1..Fiction

Interior Design by www.formatting4U.com
Author photograph ©Nathan Silvers
Cover design:
Illustration ©Diego Pombo
Cover ©quetengoenlanevera

www.malocapress.com

Printed in the United States of America

Prologue

It happened during the month of the winds. August. Lázaro was about six years old. Halfway through dinner the earth began to tremble; the lit candles in the candlestick and some plates that were on the long dining room table fell to the floor. Lázaro's grandfather stood up from his chair and rushed to stand in the door frame.

"Come!" he yelled.

"It's an earthquake, m'hijo! Don't worry," Lázaro's mother said, but he knew she was afraid.

Lázaro and his mother hurried to stand with Señor Villamayor.

"Josefina, come!" Lázaro said.

Josefina, a young maid who was about ten years old, picked up the candles that were still burning and tried to join them, but Señor Villamayor pushed her away.

"Not you!"

Josefina went to a corner of the dining room and crouched protectively.

When the ground stopped shaking, they returned to the table.

Josefina set the candlestick back on the table and started to pick up the broken plates, but she cut her hand. Lázaro stared at the red blood that contrasted with the whiteness of the porcelain plate.

"What's the matter? What's wrong with the child?" his grandfather asked, alarmed.

Lázaro's hands tingled; he lifted them up to his face. He was dizzy, trembling, and his heart pounded inside his chest.

Someone tapped him on his shoulder.

"Niño Lázaro, come," Josefina said, but her voice sounded strange, as though she were talking inside an amphora. His heart kept racing. Something was pulling him down into the earth. He resisted, but the more he resisted, the deeper he sank into a shadowy hole that reminded him of a septic tank. A monster's mouth had engulfed him.

His heart started fibrillating, then stopped. He knew he was dead, but his mind wasn't foggy like during the previous death—as far as he could remember. He was alert—pulseless, but alert.

"Mom!" Lázaro screamed, but the shrill sound of his voice reverberated only inside his own head.

He tried to grab onto something, but he kept sinking until his feet hit a hard surface. The impact shook his body and the momentum launched him forward; he stumbled until he stopped. And he was able to see again.

He'd returned to the dining room, as it had been before the earthquake, but something had changed; he was in a corner of the dining room observing. His mother, his grandfather, and another Lázaro sat at the table. Josefina was standing at a prudent distance

"Mom, what's going on?" he asked. The sound of his voice was so painful that he swore someone was stabbing his head with a knife, and he had to cover his ears with his hands.

Once again, his grandfather rushed to the doorway. "Come!" he yelled.

The earth trembled again.

"It's an earthquake, m'hijo! Don't worry," his mother said.

Lázaro and his mother hurried to meet Señor Villamayor in the door frame. The plates and the candlestick with the burning candles fell to the floor.

"Josefina, come!" Lázaro yelled.

Josefina tried to join them, but Señor Villamayor pushed her away, "Not you!"

After they returned to the table, Josefina picked up the candlestick, the candles, and the broken plates, but she cut her hand.

"What's the matter? What's wrong with the child?" his grandfather asked.

Lázaro lifted his hands to his face; they were trembling, and his skin was changing colors, like a chameleon: waves of black unfurled from the tips of his fingers and turned purple as they descended to his wrists; the purple turned to pink as the waves reached his elbows, and the pink turned pale, almost white, the color of death, as the waves disappeared beneath his short-sleeved shirt. His arm muscles quivered. The chair he sat on broke and, in a cloud of dust, he sank down below the floor, as though something had exploded underneath him.

The dust dissipated; his grandfather knelt at the edge of the hole Lázaro was in and tried to lift him out by his hands, but he couldn't.

"Oh God, what's happening! This child must weigh more than a ton!!" his grandfather cried.

"Hey, Lazy," another voice said.

It was Ramiro. He was standing next to a majestic tree.

"I didn't want to. I didn't do it on purpose!" Lázaro yelled and started to run.

"I know," Ramiro yelled back.

Lázaro stopped and turned around. "Honest?"

"Yes."

"Are you still dead?"

"Yes."

"I am lost," Lázaro said.

"You're not lost, just dead."

"No!" Lázaro said.

Ramiro shrugged.

"I don't want to be dead," Lázaro said.

A noise made them turn around. A girl with two long braids hanging down her back was playing marbles with someone.

"Who's that girl?" Lázaro asked.

"Josefina. Don't you recognize her?"

"Nope. And who's she playing with?" Lazaro asked.

"With you, of course."

"Me? I don't believe you."

They tried to approach her, but the girl slid a couple of feet farther away from them as if she were on a slanted slippery surface.

"You can't get closer, but I can," Ramiro said.

Josefina and this other Lázaro continued to play marbles. He looked bigger than he did in the living room mirror, but his two different colored eyes, just like his grandfather's, his black wavy hair, his hands, his face, were exactly the same.

"And you? What are you doing here?" Lázaro asked Ramiro.

Another noise made them turn around again. A couple of steps away from them, an Indian woman held a younger girl's hand while a man stood in front of them.

"Who's that man?" Lázaro asked. "He looks familiar."

"Your grandpa, don't you recognize him, Lazy?"

"I told you not to call me Lazy. Do you want me to push you over the cliff again?"

"That's not funny," Ramiro said.

The Indian woman glanced at Lázaro's grandfather and said, "Patrón, she's your daughter."

"So you say," the man said.

"Who's the girl?" Lázaro asked.

"That's Josefina when she was little," Ramiro said, pointing at her.

"But she was just there a moment ago," Lázaro said looking around. The older, marble-playing Josefina had disappeared. "Where'd she go?" Lázaro asked.

"I don't know," Ramiro said, "pay attention. I am confused too. Since I'm dead I see many people, and I see what they do. Time isn't the same here either. Yesterday went fast, and today's going on and on."

"Patrón, please, take care of her," the Indian woman said, and pushed the little girl toward Lázaro's grandfather.

Josefina cried and clung to her mother.

"Josefina, Señor Villamayor is your father, and you're staying with him," the woman said.

"See? I told ya," Ramiro said. "I ain't no liar."

"Get away from here. And don't tell anybody," Lázaro's grandfather yelled at the woman.

"Goodbye, Lázaro," Ramiro said, "I know you didn't mean to kill me."

At that moment, Lázaro's heart resumed beating again. One beat and then a pause; one more beat and a shorter pause, until it was palpitating with all its mighty strength.

"Wait," Lázaro said, but Ramiro was gone.

The soft patch of grass Lázaro had been standing on disappeared and he was back in the hole in the dining room. He stood. His head was barely above the floor. His grandfather was still kneeling at the edge of the hole, pale and trembling, drenched in sweat.

"Grandpa," Lázaro said, extending his hands so his grandfather could reach them, but his grandfather didn't answer; his eyes looked somewhere in the distance as though nothing else existed.

"Grandpa," Lázaro repeated.

"I'll find a cure," his grandfather said, his hands on top of his knees, motionless.

His grandfather's words echoed inside his head. Cure-cure-cure. It made Lázaro sick. He covered his ears.

"You'll see."

See-see-see.

"I'll do anything… There's nothing I wouldn't do to help you. Nothing."

Nothing-nothing-nothing.

Chapter 1

The smell of formaldehyde reminded Doctor Lázaro de Jesús Villamayor of the room in which his grandfather kept his collection of snakes. He placed the corpse of the nun on the concrete slab in the middle of the autopsy room, and the corpse of the nurse on top of a metal table next to a wall. From a storage cabinet, he took out a couple of candles—the kind used for first communions, tall and thick—and a box of matches. He lit the candles and put them in the candlesticks he had arranged around the room. The yellowish light danced on the walls. He took out his pocket watch; it was almost midnight. Five hours had elapsed since the women had been killed.

Time was running out. If he didn't start the autopsy immediately, the language the organs spoke would vanish forever, and he would be left without knowing why the nun had asked him to perform her autopsy.

The victrola, like an ear, sat on top of a table in one of the corners. He turned the crank several times and set the needle down on the record. The sound of the guitar in the Concierto de Aranjuez, with its sad chords, filled the room and entered his ear canals, climbed the white walls of his temporal bones, traveled to his temporal lobes, and dripped like melted caramel onto his auditory cortex.

Lázaro moved to the cabinet and took out some materials and tools: a well-worn rubber apron, a pair of rubber gloves, a couple of knives, a scalpel, and a saw. He pulled on the apron and gloves, and removed the nun's habit from her corpse; underneath, she wore a white silk slip. The blood had dried in some places, leaving almost black spots, but the most recent drops had stained the silk with the brightest reds. In between, soft pinks appeared here and there, dispersed like little flowers. What a beautiful and at the same time terrible landscape, Lázaro thought. He took off the slip. The nun was becoming stiff, cold, and pale. The bullet had entered her body through her chest on the right side, and left through her back. When he tilted the body to the side to unbuckle her brassiere, a gush of blood came out with a wheezing sound. He removed her brassiere, her underpants. Beside her hips, her hands rested on the slab, her fingernails impeccable.

She had the face of a Madonna and was the most beautiful dead woman he'd ever seen. She resembled the woman in the photo Bermúdez had given him, which had been taken at least thirty years earlier. The half-torn photograph matched the half-torn photograph of his grandfather that Lázaro had found years ago after the mudslide.

Regarding her request, his mind played out several possibilities, one of them terrifying. The nun had known what Lázaro was capable of. Who'd told her? Not that it mattered. Everybody knew. Didn't they?

For a moment, he thought she was breathing and he put his ear close to her mouth. Silence. The smell of fresh blood entered his nostrils, and the air returned to his lungs filled with her death.

He hoped it wasn't too late. Straightening his back, he picked up the scalpel. She was a stranger at his mercy, and he was ready for an intimate encounter.

The hairs made a popping sound as he incised the scalp, like crumbs crushed on a table. The incision went from behind one ear to the other, following an arc. Lázaro exposed the skull the same way he'd peel a mango. Her face disappeared, covered by a mass of bright flesh crossed by tiny blood vessels. He incised the flat muscles attached to the cranium and inserted the handle of the scalpel between the muscles and the bones to scrape the bones clean.

He took the saw and started to cut the front of her skull, above the eye sockets. The smell of burnt bone filled the air. Lázaro followed a horizontal line with the saw until one end met the other. He removed the top of the cranium and set it on a metal tray. The brain was protected by a pearled and resistant membrane

The brain was offered like a pear in a bowl.

Another transparent membrane enveloped the brain; it reminded him of the transparent paper that separated the pages of his grandfather's album of photographs. Papel de araña. Spiderweb paper. Lázaro slid a finger over the folded surface of the brain and closed his eyes, waiting. She'd wanted Lázaro to know her story, and he had the feeling of something growing inside his chest, like a premonition of an impending disaster.

He slid the fingers of one hand underneath the brain, over the hard membrane stuck to the bone, until they reached the brain stem and using the other hand, he cut the stem with the knife.

The pear came out of the bowl.

He grabbed the brain with both hands and turned it upside down; the severed cranial nerves of the brain steam quivered like thin worms.

Lázaro put the brain on the metal tray.

Silence.

"I am ready," he said.

Once before he'd done an autopsy several hours after the death had occurred, only to discover the organs had already gone mute. No extraordinary revelations. Just what the flesh and bone would tell any surgeon with a knife.

Silence.

Perhaps it was better this way.

But sometimes, touching an organ or separating it from the body wasn't enough for the organ to tell the story contained within it. He had to dissect the organ.

So, he split the brain in half in a single cut from top to bottom.

Nothing.

He put the two halves together and made another cut, at the level of the frontal lobe. No revelations. He waited a little longer. Impatience. Silence. More silence. He was soaked in sweat. The heat of the night was mortiferous. He wondered where to make the next cut; he would cut the brain inch by inch if necessary. The auditory cortex? Would sounds, words, pour out?

He made a cut at the level of the auditory cortex.

More silence. There was a past.... To know was dangerous. Since she had asked him to perform her autopsy, why hadn't she been able to wait?

He sliced the back of the brain, into the occipital lobe, cutting through the visual cortex.

Nothing happened. It was too late. The door to her past had been closed forever and he'd been left in limbo. He looked around; the autopsy room reminded him that this was no little room of dreams. The music of Enrique Granados had abandoned the air.

He collected the slices, put the brain back together on top of the metallic tray, and then decided to try one more thing, something he had not tried before: he took off the rubber gloves and threw them on top of the slab next to her body, set his bare hands on top of her brain, like the hands of a clairvoyant on top of a divination ball. Not to see the future, in this case, but the past.

The autopsy room vanished from his sight, and he heard, and he saw.

The nun's memories were revealed under Lázaro's hands, on top of her brain, that lay on the cold, bright metal tray.

Chapter 2

The autopsy room vanished from his sight and he heard the voice of the brain that resembled the sound of a drum. ***BOOM!***

And it said: *There are things that adhere to us like a shadow, like a faithful dog, even if we don't want them to, things we do not always realize are there: the way we walk, the way we smile, the way we talk, the way we are.*

A shadow crossed in front of him, and he followed it until it slid under a door. He opened that door; multiple cubicles formed a grid, like a map, an unknown city.

He stepped inside the nearest.

A girl was in a kitchen, in front of a wood stove where water boiled in a pot. Wooden hooks hung from the ceiling, and pots hung from the hooks. She grabbed a big wooden ladle, filled it with scalding broth, walked carefully toward the kitchen door, and stepped onto a patio, where a pig was tied to a small tree by a short rope knotted at its neck. The girl dumped the scalding broth onto the pig's rump. The pig squealed and bucked like a rodeo horse. The girl laughed her heart out.

Poor little pig, he thought.

A tall man with broad shoulders stepped in front of the girl. His figure was blurred, like an overexposed image, or a ghost.

"Forgive me, Papá," the girl said. Her voice was a mix of a girl's voice and the sound of the drum.

BOOM.

"You should've thought about it before…" the man said. The sound of the drum mixed with the man's voice, distorting it.

BOOM.

"You're going to pay for this! You-will-be-sorry," the man said.

The girl and her father disappeared and the cubicles reappeared.

He hesitated before stepping into another one.

The same girl was tied to the tree on the patio by the same rope, now knotted around her neck. Her father was standing in front of her.

"Why didn't you think twice before doing it?" her father said. The drumming was fading, and the voice had become more human. "Let's see how you like it." The man went to the kitchen. When he came out, he held the wooden ladle as though he were going to feed a sick person; he grabbed one of the girl's hands; she resisted, but he poured the scalding liquid over it.

Smoke rose from her hand, and her flesh sizzled.

He had to cover his ears. The cubicle disappeared and he was by the slab again in the autopsy room. Lázaro looked at the nun's hand. The scar was subtle: a pinkish and corrugated area on the dorsum. Poor girl. He ran a finger along the scar, but the time to ponder was over, he was back in the cubicle. It was morning. The girl had spent the night tied to the tree on the patio, and now a servant peon came and untied her. She started to shuffle, but soon, she was on the run.

A woman's voice called from behind, "Araminta! Sister, sister!" The voice also held the vibration of the drum. ***BOOM***.

The girl ran by him, followed by her sister. Araminta's sister's figure was blurred, like an organism under a microscope that wasn't in focus.

The sisters continued to run until they came to the bank of a river. Their father caught up with them. Araminta's face was well defined, and although her sister had come more into focus, and he could see some details, like her sandals, her face was unrecognizable. Araminta looked strong, athletic, while her sister was tiny, almost insignificant.

Sometimes, he would find the reasons the apparitions didn't show their faces: shame, guilt, regret, shyness, oblivion, ambivalence. Or they just didn't want to. Others, showed themselves in close-up fashion, to acquire relevance in a story where they were minor characters; eventually, they disappeared in a mass of faces, bodies, colors, textures, landscapes, movements.

"I'm going to throw myself in the river," Araminta said.

"Go ahead!" her father said and laughed. "You can't swim." His voice had continued to lose its booming quality.

A pair of dogs arrived wagging their tails. Araminta knelt; the dogs licked her face, while her sister caressed her head.

"I'm sorry, Father, I don't know what's going on with me," Araminta said.

"Forgive her, Father. She'll never do it again," Araminta's sister said.

"Shut up," the father said, lifting his hand in a menacing manner. "I've had enough of both of you." His voice was now completely human.

While their father's voice faded, he wanted to get closer, but he knew if he tried, they would slip away. Yet, he stepped forward. The trio disappeared into darkness. A small point of light appeared in another cubicle. Lázaro went in. There was a multicolored burst of light from a small point in the distance. He put his hands in front of his face, trying to shield himself. The light dispersed like shattered glass, and the multicolored rays became flowers.

Araminta was in the middle of a garden, next to a jasmine bush. Her sister sat on top of a stone wall at one end of the garden.

The jasmine bush trembled and exhaled a mouthful of perfume.

Araminta said, "Good morning Victor, my son," and caressed the jasmine bush. "You must be thirsty, but you know that giving you water at noon could be fatal. Water in this heat will make you boil. Let's wait until the end of the afternoon, and then I'll give you all the water you want."

Her sister laughed.

Araminta pointed to the right, "Those rose bushes are aspiring ballerinas, Maria, Rebeca, and Rosa."

Her sister laughed again.

"Milagros… you are so quiet," Araminta continued as she pointed at a group of white, red, and pink impatiens to her left.

Araminta walked to meet her sister at the stone wall and looked up to the sky. Birds flew by, among them a flock of macaws and white herons.

"Let's go back to the house, I'm tired," Araminta said.

Her sister climbed down the stone wall. They passed by a small tree full of orchids. A sweet scent penetrated the air.

"Orchids' names are the hardest to choose," Araminta said, "Eulalia, Agripina, Dominga."

"Those are horrible names!" her sister said.

"Well, I read them in the newspaper, a beauty queen, an actress, and a recent bride," Araminta said and stuck her tongue out.

"You look like a beauty queen," her sister said. "A mad beauty queen."

"What did you say?"

"Come on. Don't be mad, little nut," her sister said and covered her mouth.

"Little nut? Your mother!" Araminta said.

"Same as yours. Do you remember her?"

"No. My dear Marcelina, you are the most beautiful daughter," Araminta said, ignoring her sister and pointing at a rare orchid. "That's my favorite orchid." Araminta kissed the flower.

Her sister held Araminta's hand. "They say our father made her kill herself."

"I wouldn't be surprised… Eulalia, my daughter, I would like to have tea with you when you come back from your trip to London," Araminta continued. "Sister, did you know that Marcela returned from a very long trip with her handsome husband and two of her daughters?"

Araminta's sister rolled her eyes, "No, but let me help you choose the names of your girls," she said mimicking her sister's way of speaking when she pretended to be a señorita from the Capital City. "They are so lovely. What do you think? Mara? Juanita?"

The sisters laughed and continued to walk holding hands among the dahlias, lilies, and azaleas. Federicas, Isabelas, Eugenias.

"Now let's walk with our eyes closed," Araminta said.

"Here we go again. You and your weird games. I don't like them," her sister said, but she closed her eyes first.

They took several steps until a yap was heard. Araminta opened her eyes. It was dark; they'd tripped over one of the dogs that lay on the ground.

"It's an eclipse!" Araminta's sister said.

The bluish light that had descended in the middle of the day made the blood-colored flowers almost imperceptible and the white ones, iridescent.

Their father came out of the house. One eye was bigger than the other; his nose was too small for his face, his fleshy lips, out of place, tilted to one side. He resembled a collage that had been made out of many different pictures and put together with no attention to proportions.

"Get in the house!" their father hollered.

"Come! Mariscal," Araminta's sister called to the dog.

"Leave the damn dog alone!" he yelled.

The sisters ran inside the house and reappeared on the balcony. Several pots of geraniums hung from the balcony railing.

"Look at the pond," Araminta said, "the water lilies, Roberto, Pablo, Juan, Nicolás, and Arturo, are opening their corollas." She looked at a solitary flower. "Oh, you poor little thing, what's your name?"

He thought she was asking him what his name was. Who? Me? But he didn't remember his name. He laughed silently. It didn't matter. A first: he was witnessing her life, but he remembered nothing about his.

The eclipse ended, the roosters started to crow, and Araminta began singing a lullaby with an angelic voice. Perhaps she's an angel, he thought as he closed his eyes and tilted his head. He felt a rocking motion, so comforting, so peaceful.

Araminta's sister said, "I wish I could sing like that, sister. Sing a little more."

He wanted to sleep. The voice faded. One, two, three seconds passed.

He woke up in the autopsy room, wearing the worn-out rubber apron, standing next to the metal tray, scalpel in hand.

"My name is Lázaro," he said and made another cut into the occipital lobe, the visual area.

Araminta and her sister were sitting on the grass, in front of a mango tree.

My name is… He couldn't remember. He tried to remember something else, but he couldn't; he didn't care.

Araminta had her head in her sister's lap; her sister lowered her head and whispered in Araminta's ear. "I wish I had your beauty and your voice."

"But you are beautiful, sister."

"Next to you, everybody is ugly."

The sisters laughed.

Although he didn't know why, he started to laugh as well.

A pebble rolled next to the sisters' feet; they stopped laughing and Araminta turned her head to see their father hiding behind a tree.

She said, "It's Father trying to scare us."

Another pebble rolled next to the sisters.

"Don't pay attention," Araminta said.

The sun was almost below the horizon. Little pieces of flame from the sun detached and fell to earth, surrounding the sisters.

"You know what I was thinking?" Araminta said.

"What?"

"I was thinking that these candles were little pieces of the sun that have fallen to earth."

"You, silly girl, you've been reading my poetry!" her sister said.

"No, I haven't."

"Yes, you have." She pointed at Araminta's face and then removed a little notebook from a pocket in her dress. "See? 'Little pieces of sun have fallen to earth,'" she read.

"You've got me."

The sisters laughed again.

He was perplexed. He could see Araminta's thoughts as scenes that were happening right in front of his eyes. A first, too.

"Do you want to know something else, Chiquita?" Araminta asked.

Seeing the sisters next to each other, it was clear. Araminta's sister was tiny. Chiquita.

"Tell me," Chiquita said.

"Everybody thinks I'm crazy."

"That's not true!" Chiquita said.

"If only they could be in my shoes, they would understand."

"I understand."

Araminta pouted and nodded.

"I want to tell you what I dreamed last night," Araminta said.

Chiquita listened.

"I walked around a circular dresser that had hundreds of drawers. I flicked the knobs with my fingernails, then I stopped and tried to open one, but it was stuck, so I pulled it harder. When I finally opened it, a bunch of doves flew out."

Chiquita said, "But then, the doves started to fall, killed by invisible bullets?"

"Correct."

"Araamiiintaaaa, write your own poetry!"

"All right, but seriously, I dreamed that I was dead."

"Oh my god!"

"I ended up naked and on top of a slab."

"That's why people say you're crazy!"

A chill run down his spine. Lázaro shook his head. The autopsy room reappeared. The likelihood of one's corpse ending up on top of a cold slab wasn't small, especially if one had been murdered.

Araminta lay on the slab, her brain on the metal tray; Lázaro turned it up. The arteries at the base of the brain formed a geometric figure, the Circle of Willis. Some described it as a spider; he could discern its legs. He ran a finger through its center.

Another cubicle appeared. In it, a black car, like a spider with luminescent eyes, traveled along a meandering road illuminated by the light of the moon. The car entered a town and Araminta, her sister, and their father stepped out of the back in front of a church. One of Araminta's cheeks was swollen.

"Wait here," their father told the chauffeur, "it's too early to see the dentist."

The church was deserted. Massive clusters of lit candles gave the impression that the walls were melting. They sat in one of the pews, in front of the body of the crucified Jesus Christ that hung from the ceiling. A group of women dressed in black came in right after them, veils covering their heads; they sat together and began to pray. Their hands moved rhythmically, counting the rosaries' beads while their lips recited litanies without seeming to emit a sound.

"Chiquita, I feel worse. I feel as though Jesus' crown of thorns is circling my tooth," Araminta said.

From her tooth, the thorns walked on tip toes across her cheek and traveled to her brain. Inside her skull something exploded like firecrackers popping in an empty eggshell. This time, the vision of her thoughts made him feel pain. He shook his head and he was back in the autopsy room again. Lázaro rubbed his cheek; it was sore.

"This pain is not mine," he said, and debated: either he didn't go back and gave up the dissection, or he went back and faced physical pain. It was his choice. Nobody had given him an ultimatum. Except for Bermúdez.

He touched the brain again in the frontal lobe, the commander of humanity, (the area that specializes in predictions about rewards and punishments). Another cubicle appeared.

"Holy-father-forgive-me," Araminta said, and without pausing, "Hijueputa!"

The ladies dressed in black turned around with piercing eyes and crossed themselves.

Father and daughters left the church right before dawn, climbed back inside the car, left the square, and drove along a narrow street, until they stopped in front of a small building. On the wall next to the door, a sign read: "Dr. Rodriguez—Dentist. Extracción sin dolor. Painless extraction."

The father knocked on the door.

They heard noises inside the building, and after a while a woman asked: "Who's there?"

"Open the door, we need to see the dentist," their father said.

The woman opened the door. Including the chauffeur, they all entered the building through the wooden door.

"Sit down please," the woman said.

They sat on a long wooden bench, next to a desk.

From a dark room, a man trying to arrange his disheveled hair came through a door.

"My daughter has a toothache," Araminta's father said.

"Would you like coffee?" the woman asked.

Nobody answered.

The dentist asked them to follow him and opened a door into another room; he must have been at least forty, and the woman around twenty. The woman followed with a lit lamp.

Araminta's eyes grew wide and she ran for the door.

The chauffer, the dentist, and her father had to drag Araminta to the dentist's chair and force her to sit down. She turned her head away from the dentist. On the floor next to the chair was a rusty bucket with remnants of blood, black, dry, and thick.

The sight of blood nauseated him. Cows emerged from the darkness as though someone were running after them, until they came to a halt, trapped by a wire fence. Somebody opened a gate in a corner of the fence and the cows entered a long, narrow corridor, one by one. At the end of the corridor, over an elevated platform, a peasant stood above the cows and hit each one on the head with an enormous hammer. One by one, the cows dropped to the ground, quivering, their eyes rolling up beneath long and curly eyelashes, until they became immobile. Men placed a hook into the cow's neck flesh and pulled them up, one by one. The cows hung from the hooks attached to long metal chains. The butcher, knife in hand, cut their necks where the jugular vein protruded under the soft hair. The blood cascaded until it filled metal buckets.

Araminta's father placed a tumbler beneath the open vein so that the blood poured into it and asked Araminta to drink. She didn't want to drink the blood, but raising her eyes to the sky, and holding her breath, she drank it. She gagged.

Lázaro retched; the autopsy room reappeared briefly and then vanished as he heard their father's voice: "Drink, m'hija, it's for your own good. It will cure your madness." He collected blood directly from the jugular vein of a cow and filled a tumbler.

Lázaro ran to the sink in the autopsy room and threw up. After he washed his face and hands with soap, he went to the autopsy room's door and opened it. He stepped outside, took a deep breath, and looked at his pocket watch. It was fifteen minutes past one in the morning. Lázaro looked into the autopsy room; Araminta was waiting. What if he didn't finish the autopsy, he wondered. But he'd never left unfinished business; he stepped inside and went back to the brain on the metal tray. He slid a finger on a sulcus with caution, as though when one suspects the surface of an object is hot.

Araminta grabbed the leather armrests, but her hands were drenched in sweat and slid, like soap on porcelain.

The dentist buckled Araminta into the chair with hairy leather straps around her waist, wrists, ankles. Her ample skirt fell along the sides of the chair.

The dentist's wife opened an autoclave. Steam scented with menthol spread in the air.

The dentist took out a steel syringe and said, "Please, open your mouth, señorita."

"I'm not in pain any longer," she said.

The dentist's pelvis, pressed against Araminta's arm, made her shake even more.

"Please, open your mouth, señorita," the dentist repeated in a soft voice.

"I said I'm not in pain anymore," Araminta said and closed her mouth even more tightly.

Her father signaled the chauffeur to get closer and said, "Pinch her nose."

The chauffeur obeyed while Araminta's father held her head with both hands. Running out of air, Araminta opened her mouth and gasped. The steel syringe shone under the harsh light of the lamp. Despite the restraints and the chauffeur's and her father's grip, Araminta was still able to writhe. The dentist's wife and Chiquita helped.

"Hold her tighter," the dentist said, almost singing.

They did.

She closed her eyes. Darkness. The pain of the needle made her moan.

The dentist said, "We have to wait until the anesthetic works."

Araminta opened her eyes and fought tooth and nail, but in the end the dentist won. He raised the tooth between the pincers. She spat a thick mouthful of saliva and blood that dangled from her lips over the rusty bucket. She cut it with a harsh movement of her hand.

The dentist bent over and unbuckled Araminta; his face was so close to hers; his green thick glasses slid down the bridge of his nose, and she noticed his pretty blue eyes.

The cubicles began to disappear in a domino effect, and Lázaro was back in the autopsy room. He waited to be sure the brain had said the last word. Nothingness. The Victrola was silent. The nothingness had a sustained sound. Like tinnitus. In B flat.

Lázaro picked up her brain, put it back inside her skull, replaced the top of the cranium, and pulled the flesh of her face to cover the anterior portion of the head. Araminta's face reappeared. He did the same in the back and pressed the thick mass of muscle, skin, and hair against the roundness of the cranial bones and rearranged her hair.

Araminta's eyes were half-open; they reminded him of his mother's eyes when she pretended to be dead.

"Abelapetaluloonoñoa."

"Open the door of your eyes, señora," he'd say in baby talk, while he pressed his index finger and thumb against her eyelids to force them open.

Chapter 3

"Abelapetaluloonõnoa."

Lázaro's mother didn't answer.

"Open the door of your eyes, señora!" he repeated.

There was still no answer, so he climbed up into the tall four-poster bed. "Mom, are you dead?" He waited. "Abelapetaluloonõnoa," he said while he tried to open her eyes.

She opened them, laughing, "I love the way you talk, like a baby," she said. "Why did you want me to open the door of my eyes?"

"I thought you were dead."

"Of course I'm not dead, son. I'm taking a siesta."

"Don't die, Mom. Don't die," he said, "Nochimera, nochimera."

"I'm not going to die."

Lázaro ran down the stairs, left the house, wandered in the garden that never knew the absence of flowers, until he ended up under the stone arch with big carved letters that read EL EDEN. His friend Ramiro was waiting for him. The two boys sprinted and laughed. Lázaro wore brown leather boots and Ramiro was barefoot. Since Ramiro ran faster, Lázaro pulled from his pocket a slingshot that his grandfather had made for him out of a branch of an orange tree. He took aim at Ramiro's back and released a pebble. The pebble hit Ramiro in the middle of his back and he fell forward, almost flying, and crashed to the ground. Lázaro ran to his friend and knelt next to him.

"Ramiro, Ramiro," he said, but the boy didn't answer. Blood dripped from Ramiro's head. Lázaro's eyes fixed on the blood. Somebody touched his shoulder and a voice called him. Lázarooo. Something strange was happening to the ground under his feet. The ground tremored. His heart raced inside his chest and stopped. He was about to fall and tried to look for something to grab onto. After that, he couldn't remember anything else.

When Lázaro opened his eyes, he was in a hole in the ground up to his waist. Ramiro was still on the ground, moaning. Lázaro climbed out of the hole. The blood on Ramiro's head had dried. Lázaro retreated as though Ramiro were a poisonous germ.

Ramiro sat up, laughing. "I fell, Lázaro. I fell." He stood up. "What the heck, who made this hole?" he asked.

"It wasn't me," Lázaro was quick to say.

"I feel funny," Ramiro said, "like I'm drunk." He stumbled and stopped. "Let's go to the swing."

The boys walked side by side. Lázaro helped Ramiro. They stopped at a majestic tree at the edge of a canyon. A rope forming a loop hung from a branch.

"When my godfather pay me, I'm gonna buy a spinning top," Ramiro said. "I don't like this one I made." Ramiro had made a top that looked like an ugly rock.

Lázaro snatched it from his friend's hand and threw it into the canyon.

"Why'd you do that, Lazy crazy?" Ramiro asked with watery eyes.

"Don't call me that," Lázaro said, "it was an ugly one. Here, play with this one." Lázaro took a colorful and polished spinning top from one of his pockets.

The pair played with the top for a while, until Lázaro decided to shoot rocks with the sling shot. He said, "I bet I can kill that bird over there," and pointed at the tree that held the swing.

"I bet you can't," Ramiro said.

Lázaro aimed at a blue bird and shot. It fell to the ground. He ran over to it, picked it up, and stuffed it into his pocket. Ramiro was already by the swing.

"Push me," Ramiro said, opening the loop and sitting in the swing. "Come on, Niño Lázaro, push me."

The tree grew at the edge of a precipice. Lázaro looked down. At the bottom of the canyon, the river looked so small. Lázaro pushed Ramiro on the swing, and after a while, he said, "Enough! My turn."

"Nooo, niño Lázaro. One more time. One more time!"

Lázaro watched as Ramiro swung. He rose against the blue sky, leaning forward; for a moment, he was suspended. Then he descended, his dirty head upside-down, with his straw-like hair and his rotten teeth smiling.

"Weeeee!" Ramiro laughed, "Push me harder."

Lázaro positioned himself so that when Ramiro returned, he could jump and push Ramiro from behind, propelling him into the air.

"Higher. Higher," Ramiro laughed.

Lázaro heard a snap.

A moment later, the torn rope almost hit him in the face. He peered over the edge of the precipice. Down the side of the mountain, green trees alternated with barren ground and rocks. At the bottom, the river moved slowly. Lázaro felt the wind on his face. The bird in his pocket moved. He took it out and flung it away. It fell to the ground and hopped, tilted its head to one side, and tried to fly, but it couldn't. Its breathing was fast and shallow, like Lázaro's.

It was dark when Lázaro returned home.

"Where were you?" his mother asked grabbing Lázaro by an arm and shaking him. "I was worried! You already know I don't like it when you're out for very long."

"There's a monster inside me," Lázaro muttered.

"What?"

"There's a monster inside me."

"Why would you say that?" Leonor asked and embraced him, but he pushed her away and ran to his room.

For the next three days, he didn't talk.

Leonor made him dulce de leche, his favorite dessert, but he barely touched it.

"If you don't eat, you're going to die. Please," she begged.

She tried to play with him, but Lázaro sat reticent at the kitchen table.

"Go and look for Ramiro—"

Lázaro didn't let her finish; he ran upstairs to his room again.

After dinner, Leonor put him to bed.

"Am I sick, Mom?" he asked. "Am I going to die?"

"No, my sweet little angel," she said, "why are you saying that?" Leonor caressed her son's head. "Good night, my son," she said and kissed him on his forehead, pulling the blankets up to his chin. She waited a few seconds and blew out the candle.

The sound of her steps going to the door and the click of the door closing vibrated in Lázaro's head.

A month later Christmas arrived. The presents didn't interest him.

Six days later, his grandfather told him: "I want to take you someplace," and summoned Alirio, one of the servants.

"Have the horses ready," he ordered.

"Where are we going, Grandpa?"

"Up there," Señor Villamayor said pointing with his finger.

"I don't want to go there," Lázaro said.

"Why?" his grandfather asked.

"I just don't want to go."

"We go wherever I say," his grandfather said. "I want to show you something."

Grandfather and grandson mounted the horses along with Alirio and Manuel and they started off. Lázaro was quiet. They rode for some time until Lázaro smelled something fetid. "What's that, Grandpa?"

"Cover your nose and your mouth," Lázaro's grandfather said.

Lázaro obeyed.

In the middle of the path, there was a decomposed corpse.

Lázaro yelled, "I didn't do it! I didn't do it!"

"Dumb-dumb, of course you didn't," his grandfather said.

They stopped. Señor Villamayor dismounted and helped Lázaro down. Alirio dismounted too.

Lázaro backed away from the corpse and started to run.

"Grab him," Señor Villamayor ordered.

Alirio ran after Lázaro and brought him back; while Manuel held the child, Señor Villamayor forced Lázaro to open his eyes.

"It's an old man, a peasant," Señor Villamayor said. "Why do you care?"

Lázaro opened his eyes and looked. The dead man was old, purple, swollen, and covered in maggots. It couldn't be Ramiro. Ramiro was tiny, Lázaro thought.

They stood contemplating the corpse for a couple of minutes.

"All right," Lázaro's grandfather said, "it's enough. You better get used to it." And they continued to ride.

When they got to the edge of the canyon, his grandfather again helped Lázaro to dismount. Lázaro's eyes were at the level of his grandfather's hand. As he traced the path of its veins, his grandfather lifted his hand and set it on top of Lázaro's head. Lázaro felt its weight pushing him down. He thought he was going to sink, and the thought of a temporary death shook him; he tried to shake the hand off. Lázaro looked at the ground. He wasn't sinking. His grandfather lifted his hand, swept it in an arc, and said, "Happy Birthday, Lázaro, this is my present to you."

Lázaro had his eyes fixed on the bottom of the canyon.

"Look!" his grandfather said, forcing him to raise his head.

Lázaro saw the mountains on the right. In the middle, a portion of the jungle had been turned into pasture dotted with innumerable cows that seemed so small they looked like toys. To the left, the jungle continued.

Lázaro grabbed his grandfather's hand, which felt like the bark of a tree.

"Why are you trembling?" his grandfather asked. "It was just a dead body."

"Please, let's go, Grandpa. Let's go."

"What's the rush? Do you see that tree?" his grandfather said, pointing at the majestic tree Lázaro knew well. "Let's carve our names on it."

Lázaro resisted.

"What's wrong with you?" his grandfather asked as he dragged Lázaro to the tree.

"Who put this thing here?" his grandfather asked, gesturing to the rope.

"I didn't do it," Lázaro said.

"Why are you trembling?" his grandfather asked.

"I didn't do it!" Lázaro continue to tremble.

"Stop it," his grandfather said, and pulled on the rope. The rope hit Lázaro on the head. Lázaro flailed and shook himself as if trying to get rid of a snake.

His grandfather grabbed his arm. "Lázaro, Lázaro!"

Lázaro opened his eyes.

"Calm down, calm down," his grandfather said.

Lázaro sobbed. His grandfather took out a handkerchief and cleaned Lázaro's tears and snot.

From a little distance away, Alirio said, "An animal must be dead."

Lázaro looked to where Manuel pointed; vultures soared above the canyon.

The following day, his mother dressed Lázaro up with black leather boots above the ankle, long black socks that stretched up to his knees, short white pants, white shirt, and a white and blue jacket that made him look like a sailor. "Son, you look handsome," she said. Lázaro kissed her hand and raised his head. An emerald hairpin in the shape of a frog sparkled in the black pond that was his mother's hair.

"Why are you wearing your pin?"

"Because it's your birthday! It was my mother's. Your grandfather gave it to me."

They left the room. Josefina was outside. How old are you?" Josefina asked.

"Six," he said.

"I'm ten, I think," the maid said.

They all headed downstairs. In the kitchen, Leonor started to make a cake. Three maids were helping her. Lázaro sat on the floor and started to play with marbles.

"Happy birthday!" his mother said, and removed her hand from the bowl in which she was mixing the ingredients and offered Lazaro a finger. Lázaro licked her finger. She transferred the batter to the cake pan, opened the oven door, and pushed the cake pan in.

Lázaro threw a marble and followed its path with his eyes. The marble rolled across the tile floor until it stopped against the coal stove, right beside a serpent.

Lázaro lifted his hand to signal his mother but didn't have time to warn her. The snake struck Leonor on the calf; the maids screamed and gathered in a corner. The snake slithered away through a crack in the door.

"Bring me a knife, Josefina," she ordered.

Josefina did as she was told, with her skirt hiked up as she walked.

Leonor took the knife and slashed her calf where the fang marks were. Her blood ran down to her ankle.

Lázaro heard his mother calling him: "Lázaro, come." The tile floor disappeared as he shivered. His heart raced and stopped. He sank into the ground. He wanted to call his mother, but he couldn't utter a word. He kept sinking. The gravel around him squeezed his body, until his feet hit a hard surface; his body jerked and he fell onto a cement floor. He didn't know where he was, but it was a world in black and white, like a photograph, static, without sounds. In the photograph, his mother sat on a chair holding a baby while another woman stood behind her with her arms wrapped around his mother. His mother's face was clear, the woman's, blurred.

His

"Mom?" he whispered, but his voice sounded earsplitting. He covered his ears with both hands and kept silent.

Another picture appeared. The woman who had been wrapping her arms around his mother was now holding a letter. He read: Name my son... He tried to read more, but the letters became blurred, then everything disappeared.

Lázaro called from the bottom of the hole. He stood in tip-toe, and yet, he couldn't see outside the hole. Leonor's face appeared up there. He raised his arms; his mother knelt and took him out of the hole; her eyes were swollen and red. The others were gone but the oldest maid had remained in the kitchen.

"Vírgen Santísima. I thought niño Lázaro was dead," the maid said.

Leonor gave the maid a stern look and she fell silent.

"Are you all right, son?

Lázaro's grandfather ran into the kitchen and looked perplexed. "What kind of a joke is this?" Lázaro's not dead!"

"I'm sorry for making you come back, Father, I thought he was dead, I swear!" Leonor said.

Señor Hipólito Villamayor slapped Leonor across the face with his enormous calloused hand. She lost her balance and landed on the floor. Lázaro ran to help her, but his grandfather seized him. Señor Villamayor lifted Lázaro and held him firmly. Lázaro tried to push his grandfather away, but he was trapped like defenseless prey.

His grandfather told Leonor through clenched teeth: "Next time you want to play a trick on me, you'd better think twice. You'll be sorry." He released Lázaro.

The child ran to his mother.

"Do you think I have time for games?" Señor Villamayor said, and turned to leave.

Lázaro took out his slingshot and aimed at his grandfather's back, but Leonor grabbed his arm as Señor Villamayor disappeared through the door.

"It's hot in here," Leonor said.

Lázaro grabbed the lid of a pot that sat on a table and fanned Leonor, "Don't die, Mom. Don't die."

Leonor's foot was becoming so swollen that it no longer fit in her sandal.

"Cut the straps," Leonor ordered the maid.

The old maid took the same knife Leonor had used to slash her leg and cut the straps.

Leonor took a few steps and stopped. "Take me to my room," she said, "I am dizzy."

"I'm gonna make a poultice," the old maid said, "I'm gonna look for some herbs in the garden."

"Please, take care of Lázaro," Leonor said, "and tell Josefina to come to my room."

Lázaro followed his mother to her room, climbed onto the bed, and lay next to her. Josefina came into the room and stood by the bed on the other side.

"Promise me that you will take care of him, too," Leonor said while foam came out of her mouth; she had started to shake.

After a brief period, Leonor fell still.

"Is she dead?" Lázaro asked.

Josefina was playing with her two long braids and shrugged.

The oldest maid returned with a poultice. "Patrona, these are medicinal herbs. If you don't die in two hours, you'll survive."

Leonor didn't respond, so the maid put a mirror close to Leonor's nose, "She's not dead yet," she said, applied the poultice to Leonor's leg, and left the room.

Lázaro grabbed the mirror and lay next to Leonor, looking at her face. An hour elapsed. Then two hours. The maid returned.

"So, she's not gonna die?" Lázaro asked her while he set the mirror close to Leonor's face, unsure of what he was supposed to see.

The maid took the mirror and said, "No." She cleaned the mirror with a rag, changed the poultice, and ordered Josefina to bring more cool water.

Josefina returned with a clay pot filled with water. The maid soaked a cloth in it and laid it across Leonor's forehead. After a while, she told Josefina, "Do it like I did. I'm going to do some other chores and I'll be back. Stay here with la Patrona and niño Lázaro."

Leonor's leg was turning black up to her knee.

Josefina sat on the bed after the maid left. "Your mother did this to you when you were dead," she said to Lázaro, and set her ear on Leonor's chest. She waited a couple of seconds. "She's not dead."

"How do you know?"

"Her heart is jumping."

Lázaro set his ear on top of his mother's chest.

"Your mother said you were dead. And she said you were like stone, too."

Lázaro rolled his eyes. "Liar-liar-pants-on-fire."

"Niño Lázaro, it was horrible."

"I didn't have time to tell her the snake was in the kitchen," Lázaro said.

"No. It was horrible when you were dead."

Lázaro looked at her in disbelief. "When did I die?"

"You don't remember?"

"Nope."

"Ask the servants. They came in the kitchen and you were stiff, like a stick. And they tried to lift you, but they couldn't. They said you were too heavy!"

Lázaro yelled. "Liar-liar-pants-on-fire," and went running down to the kitchen.

The deep hole in the kitchen floor was still there.

Chapter 4

After a month, the snake's bite had left a hole in Leonor's leg and an extensive area of discoloration. Lázaro sat on top of a boulder by the road. A boy and a girl passed by.

"Where are you going?" Lázaro asked.

"School."

Lázaro followed them. The boy and the girl were carrying boards under their arms.

"Don't you have a board?" the girl asked.

He shrugged. "Nope."

"I can share mine," the boy said.

"What's your name?" Lázaro asked.

"Alfredo."

"And I'm Matilde," the girl said.

"My name is Lázaro."

"We know," they said in unison.

"You were Ramiro's friend," Alfredo said.

Lázaro froze.

"Do you know what happened to him?" Matilde asked.

Lázaro shook his head, then said, "Your school is an awful shack."

Alfredo and Matilde shrugged and kept walking. Lázaro followed them. The kids were barefoot.

"Why don't you have shoes?" Lázaro asked.

"Why do you care?" Alfredo said.

They kept walking. When they arrived at the school, Lazaro said, "See? I told you, an awful hut, even though, my grandfather gave away the glass for the window."

"So what?" Matilde said before stepping inside the shack. Alfredo trailed.

When Lázaro tried to get in, the teacher blocked his entrance.

"I'm going to tell my grandfather," Lázaro said.

"Precisely. It's because of him I cannot let you in. If I do that, I'll be in trouble," the teacher said.

Lázaro waited outside, looking through the only glass window there was in the shack.

Later on, his grandfather came, holding a belt in his hands. Lázaro started to run. His grandfather ran after him. They circled the adobe hut twice, but Lázaro ran faster and started to see his grandfather in front of him. His grandfather stopped, turned, and ran after him. Lázaro got to the door and knocked, Alfredo opened it, and Lázaro ducked inside. His grandfather ran around the school a couple of more times before the teacher opened the door.

"He's inside," the teacher said.

Lázaro was behind a pile of students.

The teacher pointed at the group.

"Move!" Señor Villamayor ordered.

They moved away.

Lázaro was hiding behind a wobbly desk with books on top.

"Why do you want to be here with these peasants?" his grandfather asked.

Lázaro didn't answer and stayed put. His grandfather got closer and started to lash him.

"One," Lázaro said, "two, three." Lázaro counted up to ten.

"Well, at least you know how to count," his grandfather said.

Lázaro stopped counting, but Alfredo continued, and Matilde and the other kids joined in.

His grandfather whipped Lázaro until blood began to drip down Lázaro's legs. Lázaro looked at his own blood with a mixture of fear and more desire than ever to die; but no death came to his aid. At the count of twenty-five, there was a brief silence; the kids looked at each other and said, "Patrón, please, stop. No more."

Lázaro's grandfather was drenched in sweat. "All right," he said. "Let's go.

Lázaro looked back to see the children behind the window. Their hands left greasy marks on the glass.

Grandfather and child walked back to the house where Leonor used a clean rag to wipe his wounds.

"My sweet little angel. I cannot believe he did this to you —"

"Señora Leonor, I swear Niño Lázaro's cuts smell like dulce de leche," Josefina said.

Leonor sniffed the air. "I told Doña Joaquina to make dulce de leche."

Lázaro raised one of his hands and brought it close to his nose, "It hurts," he said, and licked his hand, blood staining his lips.

"Disgusting!" Josefina said.

"Don't do that," his mother said.

His own blood tasted like dulce de leche.

After his wounds healed, eight days later, Lázaro went back to sit on the boulder by the side of the road. Before long, three peasants hurried by, fear in their voices. Hemorrhagic dengue had arrived in town.

A peasant passed in the company of another man who, judging by the way he dressed, was not a local. Despite the heat, he was wearing a tie and a jacket. The peasant's skin was mottled and yellow, and blood was dripping from his nose, ears, and mouth.

Lázaro turned his head to see who had tapped him on his shoulder; no one was there; a voice asked him to come. The boulder Lázaro sat on broke under his weight and he sank, sliding into the entrails of the earth. The gravel around him trapped his body so that he couldn't breathe. His heart stopped. The deeper he slid, the colder he felt, and the more pressure there was against his body. He kept sliding into the abyss until he heard a splash; he opened his eyes wide and looked at his feet. He was standing, without sinking, on the surface of a river.

The peasant he'd just seen with the man in the tie was fishing, but his nose wasn't bleeding. The water flowed, and its sound was soothing.

The peasant caught a fish on his hook. The fish struggled. The colors intensified. The scales were iridescent.

The man wearing the tie said to the peasant, "I need a favor." The words sounded clear. No distortions. "I need a phenomenon. I'll pay you good money. Where can I find one?"

"A phenomenon? What's that?" the peasant asked.

"A human monster. A rarity."

The peasant replied, "I don't understand."

"My sister gave birth to a monster, a girl with an enormous head, but someone stole it. I've been following the thief, but he is crafty."

"Ah! I haven't seen that, but people are talking about someone, a young boy, but you don't wanna mess with his grandfather… Easier to find one in the Capital City."

The man with the tie said, "I come from there…" He was going to say something else, but the watery surface disappeared, and Lázaro felt the first beat of his heart.

Lázaro was at the bottom of a dark hole. He stood and yelled, "Help!"

Someone removed a canvas from the top of the hole; the light rushed in and blinded Lázaro momentarily. He lay at the bottom; pieces of rocks and dust covered him. He'd crushed the boulder. His grandfather's face appeared at the circular entrance, well above Lázaro's head; he threw down a lasso. Lázaro tied it around his waist and his grandfather lifted him. At the top, his mother was kneeling in prayer, her eyes swollen and reddened. As soon as Lázaro set foot on the ground, his grandfather extended his arms, as though protecting himself.

"Lázaro's been resurrected!" Leonor said and ran to meet Lázaro, but he raised a hand and she stopped.

"Grandpa," Lázaro said, but Señor Villamayor didn't respond.

His grandfather retreated and said, "I don't mind. I don't care. I'm not you."

"Grandpa," Lázaro repeated.

His grandfather continued, "No, I told you already. I am not you. I don't have to see anything. I don't have to remember."

"Grandpa, are you all right?"

His grandfather kicked the air. Lázaro retreated to avoid a kick in the head.

"Get away from me. I said I'm not you. If you want to eat, work. That's what I did when I was your age. I don't want to go back to that city."

"Wake up, Grandpa. Wake up. It's a nightmare!"

His grandfather was panting. He looked everywhere. "Where am I?" he said, shaking his head.

"Here, Grandpa. Here!"

With a broken voice, Señor Hipólito Villamayor said, "I saw myself when I was a child."

Lázaro grabbed his grandfather's hand, but Señor Hipólito Villamayor pulled away from him and said, "Get away from me, you devil."

Lázaro lowered his head.

"No, you're not the devil. It's a miracle," Leonor said. "Did you see God?"

Lázaro didn't answer.

The next day, they sat at the dinner table and Lázaro's grandfather announced: "Lázaro and I are going to the Capital City."

"Can I come?" Leonor asked.

"Of course not," her father replied.

The day before their departure, Leonor packed their luggage: light cotton shirts, old pants, rough leather boots, cow leather belts, underwear, a worn-out suit for her father, and a new suit for Lázaro that looked like an apprentice had made it.

That night, Leonor put Lázaro to bed. She kissed him on his forehead and said goodnight. She was about to blow out the candle, but Lázaro said, "I know you're not my real mother."

"What did you say?" she asked. "Who told you that?"

"Nobody. I saw it."

Leonor gasped. "When?"

"When I was dead," Lázaro said.

"What did you see?" Leonor asked.

"I saw two pictures."

"An album?"

"I don't know… I was a baby and a woman had me in her arms. You were behind her, and she had a letter in one hand."

"It's impossible! What did the letter say?"

"'Name my son Lázaro.'"

"But you don't know how to read!" his mother said.

Lázaro thought for a moment.

"Nonsense. Maybe you were dreaming. Yes, you were dreaming, my sweet little angel," she said and sighed deeply, the candle at the level of her face.

The flame of the candle sounded as if it were sputtering miniature bullets.

Chapter 5

Lázaro awoke to the sounds of the rain hitting the roof; he opened the bedroom door. The scent of the jungle, mixed with the aroma of freshly brewed coffee, had traveled up the stairs. He came out to the corridor. Dark clouds hovered like crows. Lázaro got dressed and bounded down the stairs.

His grandfather roared, "God damn it, it shouldn't be raining now."

His mother was saying to his grandfather, "Father, please, postpone the trip one or two days."

"No. We're leaving right now, come hell or high water," her father replied.

The foreman had just arrived completely drenched; Lázaro's grandfather barked some instructions. Leonor ordered a servant to bring the single suitcase; as they walked out of the house and through the garden, Leonor tried to protect Lázaro with an umbrella. When they reached the stone arch, she bent to hug him. "Be well, mi angelito."

Lázaro kissed her on the cheek and asked, "Mom, what would you like me to bring you from the Capital City?"

She put one hand to her chest. "A heart from the hearty-heart shop," she said, touching Lázaro's chest with the other hand.

"All right, I'll bring you a corazón de la recorazonería," Lázaro said.

"Come on!" Señor Villamayor said, "we have to leave now. It's not like we aren't coming back!"

For a moment, it stopped raining. "It's about time," Señor Villamayor said.

Leonor bent and kissed Lázaro on his head.

Before Lázaro, his grandfather, the foreman, and a peon walked into the cane forest, Lázaro turned his head; Leonor's frog hairpin sparkled. She turned around and ran toward the house.

It started to rain again.

"Not again, this damn rain," Lázaro's grandfather blurted.

They made their way down to the river on a couple of horses; a mule carried their luggage. Two Indians were waiting for them at the river in a dugout with an awning. One of the Indians placed the suitcase in the canoe. Grandfather and child sat under the awning, next to the luggage. The Indians started to paddle, while the foreman and the peon got lost in the distance. Lázaro couldn't see the river bank; it was dark and the wind blew rain against his eyes.

They traveled for several hours until sunlight passed again through the clouds, the river merged into another, and it stopped raining.

Lázaro's grandfather said, "We can't see the opposite riverbank. I told you this river has no end. If we don't stick close to the bank, we could get lost."

The Indians kept close to the riverbank while they followed the current. Turtles rested on fallen tree trunks and dove into the water as the dugout passed by. Herons flew.

At the end of the day, they arrived at a village by the river and spent the night in a house.

"Whose house is this?" Lázaro asked.

"Mine."

The next day, they both rode on a mule while the Indians followed barefoot. The jungle became denser and the sky disappeared, obscured by the canopy of trees. The Indians followed the mule while parrots and monkeys screamed. The mule advanced at a slow pace until it stopped suddenly; it tried to retreat, lifted its front legs to stand on the hind ones.

"Grandfather!" Lázaro yelled. Grandfather and child almost fell backward. A serpent had crossed their path; one of the Indians advanced, machete in hand, and cut off the head of the snake.

"What did you do, idiot?" his grandfather yelled.

The Indian looked at his grandfather first and then at the snake. The snake's blood dripped down the hand of the Indian. Lázaro turned his head automatically in the opposite direction.

"Are you afraid of snakes also?" his grandfather asked.

Lázaro shook his head. "Grandpa, are you going to put this snake in a flask, too?" he asked.

"No. The dumb Indian ruined it. He cut its head off."

Lázaro turned to look at the snake's blood, but animal blood did not have the power to conjure death for him, unlike human blood.

They stopped at another house in a village with no more than a dozen houses.

"Is this house yours, too, Grandpa?"

"Yes."

While grandfather and child slept in hammocks inside the house, the Indians slept on palm-tree mats set on the tamped earth, in a shed.

With the first crow of a rooster, Lázaro woke up. Through sleepy eyes, he saw his grandfather put a pair of chairs on the Indians' backs, securing them with leather straps. He sat Lázaro on one chair and fastened him there with a leather belt. He ordered the other Indian—taller and stronger—to bend, so he could sit on the chair. He flexed his knees and rested his feet on the footrest. His grandfather said, "Indians are more sure-footed than mules."

As the sun rose, the mountains in front of them stood like an enormous wall. They started to ascend. From his perch, Lázaro watched their shadows following the bumps and cracks on the rocky wall. "Look, Grandpa, we look like spiders! Look at my hand," Lázaro said and moved his fingers like the legs of a spider.

His grandfather looked at him and shook his head.

When they reached the summit, the heat of the sun was gone. Child and grandfather stood at the top of the mountain, the ocean below, the Indians behind. Lázaro held his grandfather's hand. "Grandpa, the ocean is beautiful, it looks like a bowl full of bluish soup!"

"You and your weird comparisons."

The Indians set up a tent using the dugout's awning. Lázaro and his grandfather slept wrapped in heavy wool blankets, while the Indians covered themselves with jute sacks.

The next day, just after dawn, they started to descend, skirting precipices.

Two days later, they reached the valley on the other side of the mountain and entered a town with paved streets, and houses covered with stucco painted in bright colors. They walked to the town square, in the middle of which a man sold remedies to get rid of intestinal parasites.

Señor Villamayor told the Indians to wait for them until they returned from the Capital City in about two weeks, and gave each man twenty pesos. The Indians looked at the bills and then at Señor Villamayor, back and forth.

"What? You've never seen bills like these?" Señor Villamayor asked.

The Indians looked at each other and shook their heads. In their broken Spanish, they said they were used to coins.

Señor Villamayor showed the bills to a passerby and asked him, "Sir, is this good money or not?"

The passerby smiled, "Sir, what do I have to do to make this money?"

"These Indians don't want to wait for us," Señor Villamayor said, pointing at the pair.

"For this kind of money, sir, I'd wait for you for a whole month," the passerby said.

A small crowd surrounded a ladder bus—the first of its kind in the country, somebody said. The chassis had been imported from the United States.

A young boy invited passengers to get in. Señor Villamayor and Lázaro climbed aboard and sat on wooden benches with other passengers, who carried all sorts of living packages: hens, a cat that cried incessantly, two puppies, and several squealing piglets. Sacks of herbs and fruit released their scents.

"I'd kill those little piglets," Señor Villamayor said.

As soon as the vehicle started to move, the road released a storm of dust that did not end until the end of the trip.

They passed through villages and towns. The landscape changed. The more trees disappeared, the more people appeared. After almost two weeks, the bus crossed over a stone bridge and stopped in the middle of the Capital City. They got off the bus. Señor Villamayor was wearing a worn striped suit, a straw hat, two faded shirts, one on top of the other, and muddy boots. Lázaro was wrapped in a blanket stained with mud. Dogs sniffed around piles of garbage on the sidewalks. Women and men wearing mostly black hats walked on the streets. Señor Villamayor asked the first passerby where they could stay, and he directed them to a pension, but on their way to find it, they found the Hotel Europa, a two-story building. Señor Villamayor said, "It has to be the best hotel in the city, it's elegant."

"Get out of here," the hotel's clerk told them.

Señor Villamayor took a cloth bag out of his pants pocket and threw a big roll of bills on the counter.

The clerk went to an adjacent room and came back with a woman.

"Sir, you need new clothes to stay here," the lady said. "If you want, I can send somebody to buy you new clothes."

"Who are you?" Señor Villamayor asked.

"I'm the owner."

Señor Villamayor grabbed one of Lázaro's hands and pulled him to the entrance door.

A group of well-dressed people came in and skirted them.

"The guests are arriving!" the clerk exclaimed.

Lázaro's grandfather ran back to the counter, pulling Lázaro with him. "Come on, Lázaro. These mestizos are not going to intimidate us."

The guests stepped aside, avoiding the pair again.

The clerk argued with Señor Villamayor until he agreed to wait in a room off a back patio. The woman left and came back with a man. Señor Villamayor gave him some money; the man left and a maid brought coffee and cookies.

Grandfather and child waited until the man came back with the new suits for each of them. They bathed and changed into the suits in a room adjacent to the patio, and returned to the front desk.

"Sir, would you like a bathroom with cold or hot water?" the clerk asked.

"Hot water, of course."

Lázaro felt stiff and trapped in the suit. His grandfather complained as well. "I cannot stand this collar, it's so stiff!"

Lázaro's new shoes made him slide on the floor that reflected the beam of light from the chandelier.

"Grandfather, they don't have candles here!" Lázaro exclaimed.

"Yes. We have electricity," the clerk said.

"What's electricity, Grandpa?"

"Electricity is…" Lázaro's grandfather thought for a moment. Tiki-tak, tiki-tak, their shoes tapped on the floor. "Electricity is… like… a midget with a thousand hands and the power of a giant. Like this," he said and pinched one of Lázaro's arms.

"Ayayay!"

They climbed the stairs one floor up and slept on beds next to each other.

The next morning, they went downstairs, had breakfast in the dining room, and left the hotel. It was cold. Lázaro and his grandfather wore ruanas on top of their suits. Lázaro had never seen so many people in a single place, and he followed passersby with his sight until they moved around a corner, or blended into a more distant crowd. A vehicle passing in front of them made Lázaro's heart jump.

"Grandpa, what's that?"

"A trolley, I believe that's what they call them."

"Can we ride it?"

"Maybe later. We have things to do."

In another two-story building around the corner, they found the office of the physician the hotel owner had recommended during breakfast. "Doctor Miguel Canales, Médico de la universidad de París," Lázaro's grandfather read.

The doctor asked them to come into the examination room.

"This child suffers from a strange disease," Lázaro's grandfather said.

"Please, tell me…" Doctor Canales said.

A picture on top of the doctor's desk caught Lázaro's attention. Two nuns stood surrounded by sitting women. Several of the women had strange faces that looked like cats, or tigers, or monkeys.

When Doctor Canales asked about Lázaro's parents, Lázaro paid attention.

"His mother is fine," his grandfather said.

"What about his father?"

"He died."

"How come? If I may… Any inherited disease?"

Lázaro paid attention.

"A… snake," Lázaro's grandfather hesitated, "a snake bit him in the nuts."

The doctor frowned and said, "Please, take the child's clothes off."

"He can do it himself."

Lázaro took off his clothes except for his undershirt, his underwear, and his socks.

Doctor Canales examined Lázaro. First, he listened to his heart and lungs, then he palpated Lázaro's stomach. He looked into his pupils with a flashlight, asked him to stick out his tongue, hit him with a little hammer on the knees and elbows, touched him with a feather all over his body, and then pinched the child on one of his big toes.

"Don't you feel anything when I touch you here?" Doctor Canales asked while he pinched Lázaro's toe even harder.

"No," Lázaro lied; he wanted to show the doctor he was strong and didn't flinch.

Doctor Canales asked about Lázaro's skin condition. His grandfather hesitated before saying Lázaro's skin changed colors like a chameleon. Doctor Canales scribbled some notes on the chart and said Lázaro had to be isolated.

"Why?" Lázaro's grandfather asked.

"He's got leprosy."

"What?"

"Yes, this is an incurable disease," the doctor said. "There's a lazaretto not far from here, Agua de Dios—"

Señor Villamayor got up, grabbed Lázaro's hand, and took him out of the office without saying another word.

Lázaro asked, "Grandpa, what's a lazaretto? It sounds like my name."

Lázaro's grandfather headed for the stairs but he stopped. "Jesus Christ! We went into the wrong office. Look, this is the right Doctor's name."

Next to Doctor Canales' name was another name: Doctor Perilla.

They went back and knocked at Doctor Perilla's door.

"My grandson is not a leper," Lázaro's grandfather said as soon as the doctor opened the door.

"I bet you went into the wrong office," the doctor said.

On a wall, there was a life-size line drawing of a skeleton standing in a life-like pose. Its jaw rested in one of its hands, while it contemplated a skull placed on a pedestal. On another wall, next to Doctor Perilla's desk, hung a poster with a frontal view of a skeleton with all the bones in the body labeled.

This doctor diagnosed Lázaro with epilepsy and explained that the disease could possibly cause mental retardation, which would hinder Lázaro's future.

"We'll have to wait and see what happens. Hopefully, he'll be able to learn how to read and write," the doctor said. "I'd like to see him back in a month."

"A month?" Lázaro's grandfather howled. "It would take us almost a month to get back to where we live."

"All right then, in four months."

The doctor wrote a prescription and gave it to Lázaro's grandfather. In return, Señor Villamayor took out a couple of bills and paid the physician.

Señor Villamayor read the prescription and stuck it into one of his pockets. "I knew it," he said, "these doctors know nothing," he said and left the room with Lázaro.

They walked along the street and came to the Plaza de Bolívar. Women and men were dressed in black. Several black cars were parked in the middle of the plaza. A black child, dressed in dirty raggedy clothes, carried bricks in a basket.

"See that child? I began to work when I was his age. No one took care of me," his grandfather said.

"Grandpa, what happened to your mother?"

"She died."

"And your father?"

"I never knew him."

"How come?"

"Do you know about yours?"

"Yes, a snake bit him in the nuts."

Lázaro's grandfather laughed. "Let's go find the hospital. I know it's not far from here. There's got to be more doctors there."

They continued to walk a couple of blocks until they found a building that had an enormous iron door decorated with crosses. They went in.

"This hospital has changed a lot," Lázaro's grandfather said.

"Have you been here before?"

"Yes, a long time ago."

They walked along a hallway with black and white tiles on the floor and came to a courtyard. A nun, who came from a long and narrow corridor, approached them.

"Do you need help?" she asked.

"We came to see a doctor, Sister," Señor Villamayor said.

"For you?"

"No, for the child."

"What's wrong with this beautiful child?"

"Everything is wrong with this beautiful child," Señor Villamayor said.

Lázaro lowered his head.

"But he looks so strong and healthy," she said, "look at those beautiful eyes." The nun looked at Lázaro's grandfather and laughed. "Like yours."

Lázaro lifted his head and smiled. The nun took them to an office and left them with a secretary. Before the nun left, she looked at Lázaro, winked, and bent to whisper in Lázaro's ear:

"I know you're a good boy. I'm sure there's nothing wrong with you."

The secretary requested one peso for the consultation and told them, "Go back to the courtyard, turn to the right, and continue walking down the corridor until you find office number one-zero-one."

The corridor had windows and doors on one side, and on the opposite side a wall painted in light green. The scent of alcohol mixed with camphor and formaldehyde saturated the air.

"Grandpa, it smells like the snakes you have in the bottles," Lázaro said.

A scream of pain came from behind one of the doors, startling them.

"Help me, help me. Don't let me die," someone yelled.

Lázaro stopped, but his grandfather pushed him forward. "Mind your own business."

They continued along the corridor, turned at a corner, and came upon another courtyard. This one was smaller. Four children played. Two ran after a ball; one stood, so thin that he looked like a skeleton. The last one was just sitting; he had an enormous bald head. The courtyard smelled of urine and feces. Lázaro stopped again.

"Leave them alone. Didn't I tell you to mind your own business?" his grandfather said.

One of the boys kicked the ball and it hit the child with the enormous head. The child swayed and fell, his head bouncing on the tiles like a balloon filled with water. Señor Villamayor pulled Lázaro by the hand to move him onward.

"If you start helping others, it'll never stop, they will never leave you alone. Come on, let's find that room."

They found the doctor's office. In a small waiting room, a mother and boy sat in one corner, and a girl with both parents sat in another corner. Lázaro and his grandfather sat and waited for their turn. Lázaro swung his dangling feet. The girl wouldn't stop staring at him.

"Grandpa, that girl wouldn't stop looking at me."

His grandfather said, "I hate your baby talk. When are you going to talk like a regular boy?"

After a while, Lázaro and his grandfather were the only people left in the waiting room. A voice from inside the doctor's office said, "Next, please."

They stood up and entered the room. A doctor greeted them and, pointing at two chairs, said, "Please, sit down."

The doctor asked Lázaro's grandfather what the purpose of the visit was.

"There's something wrong with this child," Lázaro's grandfather said and proceeded to explain the situation as best as he could.

"So, he shakes?"

"Yes."

"How often?"

"Sometimes once a month, sometimes every week. Sometimes, nothing in several months."

Lázaro whispered in his grandfather's ear, "Don't forget to tell him that nobody can lift me, and that I make holes in the ground, and that I change colors like a chameleon."

"What did you say?" the doctor asked.

"Nothing," Señor Villamayor said.

"Do you want the doctor to think we are crazy?" Señor Villamayor whispered back in Lázaro's ear.

"I hope your secrets are not relevant to the illness that afflicts this child," the doctor said, and looking at Lázaro asked, "Do you pass out?"

"Yes," Lázaro said.

"For how long?"

Lázaro looked at his grandfather.

"Sometimes seconds, sometimes minutes, sometimes hours."

The doctor proceeded to perform an exam similar to the one the last doctor had done. When he finished, he wrote a prescription and agreed to see them in five months.

They went into the corridor. Señor Villamayor read the prescription. "Who knows what these poisons are," he said.

Lázaro needed to go to the bathroom. They asked a nurse and she guided them to a metal door in a corner with a sign that read Sanitarios. Señor Villamayor went in with Lázaro. When they came out, they went back to the courtyard. The children were not there any longer.

"I'm going to find the pharmacy. Sit on that bench over there and wait for me," his grandfather said, "and don't move."

Lázaro sat on the bench and waited. A couple of people passed by. He stood up and walked in the direction his grandfather had gone, but he came back after several steps and sat again. He waited. He stood again and started to walk. He proceeded along the corridor, toward where they had heard the scream. A room with the door ajar drew his attention. He peeked in. A very old and thin woman lay on a bed. Her white hair was neatly styled in a long braid that encircled her head. Her face was so pale.

"Hello," Lázaro said.

The woman tossed.

"What are you doing, señora?"

She mumbled something.

Lázaro stepped inside the room and closed the door. The room smelled of herbs and alcohol.

"What are you doing, señora?" he repeated.

"Don't you see, child? I'm dying."

Lázaro thought for a moment. "I die, too," he said.

The woman looked at him and kind of smiled.

"You're right, you'll die, too."

"No, I've been dead several times… whenever I see blood."

Lázaro moved closer and stood next to her bed. "But I resurrect."

She opened her eyes. "Oh, I understand. You're a fainter."

Lazaro was going to explain further, but she asked him: "What's your name?"

"Lázaro."

"Lázaro? Who gave you that name?" she asked and closed her eyes, but she opened them again. "I had a son who looked like you. He had one eye of one color and the other of another."

"My grandfather is like that."

"And what's your grandfather's name?"

"Hipólito Villamayor."

Lázaro heard quick steps outside and his grandfather's voice calling him.

"I'm here," Lázaro raised his voice as he hurried to open the door.

The woman said hastily, "Don't open that door," but Lázaro had already opened it.

Lázaro said, "Grandpa, this lady is dying," and he moved close to her bed.

"Didn't I tell you to wait for me on that bench?"

Lázaro stood next to the woman.

"Let's go," Señor Villamayor said.

The old woman was shaking and started to cry.

Señor Villamayor looked at her. "Sorry, ma'am. We're leaving."

"You have to remember, Hipólito," the woman said.

Señor Villamayor looked at her once more. "Do I know you?" he asked.

"She said she had a son like us, with different colored eyes," Lázaro said.

Señor Villamayor looked at the woman again, "Let's get the hell out of here," he said, grabbing Lázaro's arm.

The old woman grabbed Lázaro's other arm.

"Let the child go, you wicked woman," Lázaro's grandfather yelled.

"No," she said.

"Who is she, Grandpa?"

"Nobody," his grandfather said.

"Nobody?" the old woman said, and sat up with an effort on her bed panting. "I'm his mother!" she said.

"All this is your fault. You made me come here. You're cursed. You should die forever," Lázaro's grandfather said.

"Let me go, señora," Lázaro said, lowering his head.

The woman let go.

Lázaro started walking toward the door, looking at the floor.

"Please, forgive me," the old woman said.

Lázaro stopped and looked at them. "Forgive her, Grandpa."

"Shut up, devil," his grandfather said.

"Have mercy. Don't you see he's a child?" the woman said.

"Mercy? Did you have mercy when I was a child?"

Lázaro walked by his grandfather as though he were passing next to a jaguar, his trunk inclined away from him, but he saw a pan filled with blood by the bed. Fresh blood.

He took one step and died. No voice called him. No tap on his shoulder. No pressure around his body.

When he opened his eyes, he'd made a hole in the floor. Half of the woman's bed was on top of him. She was motionless. His grandfather helped him to get out of the hole, but the old man's eyes were red as though he'd been crying.

"Is she dead?" Lázaro asked.

His grandfather nodded.

"I understand now," Lázaro said. "Go and look in that drawer." He pointed at a nightstand table.

His grandfather went, opened the drawer, and took out something.

Hanging from his grandfather's hand, a delicate golden chain with a baby tooth, oscillated.

"This used to be mine," his grandfather said. "A spoil of war."

"I know," Lázaro said.

Chapter 6

Lázaro and his grandfather went to see three more physicians, and by the end of the week, Señor Villamayor filled the prescription that the first doctor had ordered, written by the hand of the last. Afterward, they stopped at a hat store. After trying on several hats, Lázaro's grandfather bought a felt one.

"The only good thing about this city is that you can buy things you can't find anywhere else," he said. "This hat was made in Italy."

Two weeks later they were back in the town where the Indians were waiting for them. The Indians scanned them from top to bottom, circled them a couple of times, and spoke between themselves.

"God-knows-what-the-hell they're talking about," his grandfather said.

"They said we look like different people," Lázaro said.

"How do you know that?"

"I understand a little."

One of the Indians was wearing a shirt and pants, but he was barefoot; the other wore a loin cloth.

"You look different, too," Lázaro told the Indian who was dressed, speaking in the dialect of the Indians.

"You baby talk, and yet you speak like them?" his grandfather said. "What did you say?"

"I said… that they are… very good Indians because they waited for us."

The Indian who wore the shirt and pants pointed at the felt hat and took out a bill from one of his pockets. Señor Villamayor laughed, "No. This hat is not for sale."

The Indian took another bill. Señor Villamayor dismissed him with a gesture of his hand. "Tell them there's more money at the end of the trip."

Lázaro, Señor Villamayor, and the Indians started their trip back to Sirirí.

It rained and rained again.

"Rain, rain," the Indians said, between huffs and puffs as they climbed the mountain carrying grandfather and child on their backs. They spent the night at the top of the mountain. The next day, they started the descent; the Indians sunk in mud up to their knees while grandfather and child rode on their backs. The harder it rained, the slower the Indians moved, and the angrier Señor Villamayor became.

Lázaro's grandfather started to whip the Indians almost the same way he whipped the mules.

"Grandpa, don't whip the Indians," Lázaro begged.

"Shut up, niño. These Indians don't feel a thing. Come on, fast, fast," he barked at them.

Finally, they got on the mules and rode once more, toward home again.

In the river, the Indians had difficulty paddling against the current. As the dugout made its way, they saw that the riverbank had changed because of sliding mud, and the waters were darker and angrier. Lázaro didn't recognize the landscape and he wasn't sure they were going back the same way they had come.

"I'm not sure, but I think the first town we stayed in has disappeared," Señor Villamayor said.

The group couldn't continue their trip up the river; the dugout threatened to capsize in the strong current.

For four days, they walked along the shore, close to what had been the bank of the river. On the fifth day, they started to go up a small mountain and came to a spot where few trees remained. A dog stood on a branch at the top of one of the trees. Lázaro's grandfather said, "How on earth did that damn dog get up there?"

Lázaro said, "It swam." The tree had a mark up to where water and mud had risen, close to the foliage.

They found puddles and more puddles. Finally, they arrived at the site where their house had been, but the house wasn't there, only rubble, yet the mountains were there, where they had always been. Señor Villamayor and Lázaro zigzagged through the debris. To move about was difficult; they sank into the ground as if stepping into quicksand.

Lázaro went ahead. Among the wreckage, he found half of a torn photograph: It showed Señor Villamayor standing next to a carved wooden pedestal with one of his elbows resting on it. It reminded Lázaro of the skeleton on the poster at the doctor's office in the Capital City. The other half of the picture was lost. Lázaro put the half picture in his pocket, waited for his grandfather, and then held his hand tightly.

"Grandpa, what happened?" Lázaro asked.

"A fucking avalanche," his grandfather said while he continued to walk. He tripped on a piece of a banister and almost fell. "Damn! See? This is what happens when one goes where one shouldn't go. And you're the one to blame."

Lázaro covered his ears.

Grandfather and child wandered aimlessly.

"Where's Mom?" Lázaro asked.

His grandfather didn't answer.

Lázaro asked again.

"She wasn't your mother," he said. "Don't ask anymore."

Lázaro let go of his grandfather's hand and walked away. His grandfather followed, but Lázaro was faster. "Come back here!" he yelled, but Lázaro kept walking. "I said come back here," Señor Villamayor continued to yell, while trying to maneuver around the debris.

Lázaro kept going. Before his grandfather could reach him, Lázaro came upon a big puddle, almost the size of the garden. The remnants of the stone arch inscribed with "DEN"—the last three letters of what had been "EL EDEN"—rose above the water. A huge tree had fallen: its roots at the edge of the puddle clenched like the claw of a beast, its trunk directly above the water like an outstretched arm, its foliage in the middle of the puddle, like the soft hair of an armpit. Lázaro stepped on the trunk and started to walk across it.

His grandfather shouted, "Lázaro, for God's sake, come back! You're going to fall in the water."

Lázaro continued to walk, keeping his balance and stopping at the end of a big branch growing from the end of the trunk. A swarm of flies surrounded something covered by a piece of canvas in the water. A fetid smell came from it. Some flowers floated nearby. Lázaro lay on top of the trunk and reached with a hand to lift the canvas. A head, almost bald with some tufts of hair here and there, was raised above the water; an emerald hairpin in the shape of a frog hung from a lock of hair. Most of the face was gone, one eye was missing, and maggots writhed in the sockets. From the edge of the pond, his grandfather yelled Lázaro's name again. Lázaro didn't answer; he ignored the stench, reached to grab the hair pin, and put it in one of his pockets. His chest heaved. Lázaro's tears fell on top of the head. He looked around; the water seemed threatening: monsters could come up to the surface at any minute, the mountains could fall down and bury him any time, the branch of the tree next to him could turn into a snake and bite him at any moment, the sky could fall and crush him, his grandfather could punish him, kill him, or worse, abandon him.

"Lázaro…" his grandfather said standing on the trunk of the tree.

Lázaro lifted and turned his head. "Is she?" he asked.

"Let's go," his grandfather said, extending his hand.

They went back to the edge of the pond and continued to walk away. They passed the rotten body of one of the dogs, boiling with maggots. Beyond the dog's corpse some flower bushes had survived the avalanche and the flood.

"Was she dead?" Lázaro asked.

"Didn't you see the head?"

The Indians had left without saying a word. Lázaro followed his grandfather through the debris. He wondered if their house still stood, intact, somewhere else, even though the mountains were still in the same place… The desolate terrain was proof that something terrible had happened here.

"It's getting dark. Let's look for a dry spot where we can spend the night," his grandfather said, grabbed the tarpaulin, set it on the ground, then the sacks the Indians had used to sleep on, and set them on top of the tarpaulin.

Grandfather and child sat on top of the sacks and the tarpaulin. Señor Villamayor stuck his hand in one of his pockets, took out a caramel, and offered it to Lázaro.

"I'm not hungry," Lázaro said.

His grandfather put the caramel back in his pocket and took out a blanket from one of the suitcases. Lázaro lay down and his grandfather covered him.

A swarm of mosquitoes found them. A cricket landed on Lázaro's face and startled him. His grandfather brushed it away.

"Good night, Lázaro," his grandfather whispered and lay next to Lázaro.

It was still dark when Lázaro woke up. He walked to the river, sat on a rock by the edge, and wrapped himself in the blanket.

"Mom," he said.

The river rumbled.

"Mom-mom-mom-mom-mom," he yelled until he was out of breath and started to sob.

He felt a weight on top of one of his shoulders and looked up, scared.

"Lázaro," his grandfather said, standing on the rock. Behind him, the sky was dark.

"Where's my mom?"

"She's dead."

A dark shadow came flying at his grandfather, making him lose his balance.

"Damn bats!" his grandfather yelled.

Lázaro grabbed his grandfather's hand, but the man's weight jerked him to his feet. They were going to fall in the river. His grandfather released Lázaro's hand and fell in the water. Lázaro stood on top of the rock, motionless.

The river continued its rumbling.

Lázaro went back to the spot where they had been sleeping. His grandfather had left the caramel on top of the canvas. A snake slithered near the caramel.

"Don't move."

Lázaro didn't move. The snake disappeared. Lázaro turned around. His grandfather was drenched.

"Let's go back to sleep," his grandfather said and stripped off his clothes.

"Grandfather, when I saw her blood, I found out she wasn't my mom," Lázaro said.

"Forget about it."

"I want to know who my real mother was."

"Do not stir muddy waters."

"And I'd like to know also who my father was."

"I-am-going-to-say-this-only-once," Señor Villamayor said. "He could have been any motherfucker who happened to wander by. Your mother was a whore."

Chapter 7

It was almost midnight. Araminta's body was lying on the table. What a barbaric way to reveal a life, Lázaro thought: cutting into a body as a means to recover a lost story. But he had been a spectator, until now. The pain was something new—at least the physical pain. He wondered if he could endure it; he knew that, as with his temporary deaths, it was precisely that—temporary.

Araminta's eyes had lost the luster of life, looking like worn-out marbles; they were fixed on some point in the distance. Lázaro imagined he stood between that point and her dilated pupils. What if she could see him? Had her brain stopped working at the same time her heart had stopped beating?

Lázaro could have sworn she was smiling. He took a clean cloth, dampened it with water, and cleansed her face with tender strokes. Then he placed a wooden block between her shoulder blades, causing her arms and neck to fall backward, while her chest was pushed upward.

Autopsies had rules, protocols, and patterns. Lázaro was a methodical man. Her cause of death would be listed as: penetrating trauma to the chest (death by a bullet). What did the bullet injure? To judge by the wound and the angle of entry, it had injured the lung, but not the heart. He reconsidered. In this autopsy, he wasn't there to find a cause of death, but to let Araminta tell her story: there was something she wanted him to know…

With the scalpel, he made an incision in the shape of a Y on her chest until he reached the umbilicus.

He lifted the skin and peeled back the muscles, revealing her rib cage. The ribs, part pearled cartilage, part yellowish bone, looked like bars holding prisoner the lungs, the heart, the trachea, and the esophagus. He cut the ribs on both sides of the sternum with a pair of sturdy scissors that produced a cracking sound with each cut, like the bite of a dog on a bone.

He reached for her heart, but his hand didn't obey his command. He felt a subtle push as though the hand sensed the heart did not want to be touched. Lázaro resisted, but it was useless. His hand stopped in midair, reluctant to obey. Anarchic Hand Syndrome—the hand acted on its own, as though it had an independent mind. The scalpel extended the incision, and the blade cut the scant fatty tissue until it reached the recti muscles. At that point, his hand recovered its freedom. He cut around the umbilicus until the scalpel reached the pubic symphysis. He opened a small hole between the recti muscles and put the scalpel aside. He stuck his finger inside the hole, lifted the muscles, and tore out the fascia—a layer of strong whitish tissue—like he was ripping a piece of fabric, to avoid perforating the intestines.

The intestines poured forth. A mass of entangled snakes.

He separated the intestines and unearthed the stomach. With one hand he lifted the stomach, and with the other he cut into it over the major curvature. Air escaped and the sound resembled a whistle. A mixture of mucus and yellowish fluid tinged with blood leaked out. The folds inside the stomach became more prominent as it deflated. He passed his fingers over the internal surface, the rugae.

Some say that destiny is written in the skies, in the tarot cards, in ancient books, in cigar ashes, in the prints that a burnt hair leaves at the bottom of a crock, or in the dregs left by chocolate at the bottom of a cup.

The stomach sounded like a deflating bagpipe. ÑEEH!

The dentist, his wife, and Araminta were standing behind a table loaded with food. The dentist took a ripe plantain, stuck out his tongue, engulfed the plantain, and started to chew.

"Yummmy, this plátano is so goooood," the dentist said. His voice resembled the bagpipe, somewhat nasal.

"Happy birthday, Señorita Araminta!" he continued.

He masticated and talked at the same time; the sounds were disturbing.

The dentist's wife sniffed at the air like a dog and looked at the table filled with fried plantains, sausages, roasted veal, soft baked yucca, and crunchy pork skin. She took a plantain and ate it.

"It isn't as goooood as you say..." She was about to continue, but the dentist walked away. She looked at her wedding ring, then at Araminta, but when she turned to look for the dentist, he was already lost in the crowd. She hurried after him and the crowd swallowed her, too.

Araminta's sister came out of the crowd. "Come on, let's go! The photographer is going to take your picture!!" she said.

In a corner of the patio, a photographer unpacked his heavy black camera and set it up on a wooden tripod. He inserted a silver plate in a slot between the camera in the front and a black hood that hung on the back of the camera. He had a display board with samples of his pictures. Couples, their smiling faces enclosed in twin hearts above inscriptions that read Te quiero; black and white photographs; hand-colored photographs; and different motifs to make the photographs stand out. Some of them were decorated with gold dust.

Several children gathered around the photographer, who was pleading with Araminta to pose for a picture. He looked at Araminta through the camera's lens and with one hand in the air gave her directions. "Señorita, move your head a little lower. No, no, that's too much. To the right. No, no, to the left. Yes, that's it. Now you, please, young man, step out of the picture. No, no, don't put your hand like that, señorita. Correct, that's it, perfect." After a few seconds, he announced: "Done."

At the sound of people applauding, Araminta set both hands on her chest.

Chiquita came to hug her sister.

"Chiquita, I hate having my picture taken," Araminta said. "I don't like those eternal moments between the smiling and the click of the camera."

A group of people gathered around the photographer, waiting for him to develop the picture. The photographer stuck his hands under the black hood for several minutes.

"What are you doing, sir?" one of the children asked.

"Magic. You'll see," the photographer answered.

With his hands under the hood, he moved his arms until he took out a white sheet of paper and put it in a bucket of water. A crowd had flocked to see what was going on. They waited some more until the photograph came out to light. The crowd laughed and exhaled Ohs and Ahs.

"Let me see," Chiquita said.

The photographer dried the picture using a white towel and handed it to her.

"Oh, Araminta, this picture is beautiful," she said.

The photographer took a bunch of pictures from a box and arranged them forming a fan. Among the pictures already taken was one of Araminta and her father behind the table loaded with food.

"I want to see all the pictures," Chiquita said. "No, better, let's take our picture," Chiquita said.

In that moment, a string quartet started to play a bambuco. Araminta's father appeared, grabbed Araminta's elbow, went to the center of the patio, and the two started to dance. The guests applauded.

The music ended and Araminta went to sit next to her sister. On top of a table, there was a mound of gifts. They unwrapped one; it was a hand mirror with a tortoise shell comb and a hair brush. They unwrapped a small one. It was a small wooden box containing several lipsticks.

Her father grabbed the box, threw the contents on the ground, and crushed the lipsticks with his shoe.

Kill. Ñeeh. Boom. This voice was a composite of the two sounds: the bagpipe and the drum.

"You're not the type of woman who wears lipstick," he said turning his back, his voice sounding like the mix of a bagpipe and a drum, too.

Araminta and her sister went to the kitchen. The maids were busy cooking. The fire licked huge pans and big pots. The aroma of dulce de leche was distinctive.

The kitchen disappeared when he inhaled, and he was back in the autopsy room; the air was a mix of formaldehyde and fresh flesh. With one finger, Lázaro touched a small reddish ulcer in the lesser curvature of the stomach.

In the stove, a circular pile of firewood was about to disappear, and an old maid ordered one of the helpers to bring more logs. Before the helper vanished through the back door, she told Araminta: He's waiting for you.

The sun extended its flamed fingers in the late afternoon sky, and the air blew, and the trees swayed, releasing their floral scents. Araminta walked away, stopping several times to look behind.

The dentist was standing in front of the pond. Araminta hesitated for a moment but the dentist invited her to continue with a movement of his hand. She advanced, her silk shoes bending the grass, until she stopped at a point where the dentist could touch her by extending his arm. The breeze carried the citrus scent of his cologne, mixed with the smell of his armpits. The dentist reached for her chin and kissed her on her lips.

Araminta transformed into a fragile transparent pink rose. In the center, her lips surfaced.

The dentist's lips got closer.

The rose dissolved in his mouth like an ice cube thrown into the fire.

The dentist drank the last drop of liquor from the glass, threw it over his shoulder, and lifted Araminta's skirt. She closed her eyes. Everything disappeared. Time elapsed. It could have been a second or an hour.

The smell of semen and alcohol impregnated the air.

Araminta opened her eyes again. She was on top of the dentist who grinned, his lips wet with Araminta's saliva.

Araminta's father's voice called from the distance. The dentist lay flat on the ground to avoid being seen, while Araminta stood up and ran to meet her father. "What were you doing?" he asked.

"Nothing."

They spoke for a moment and then Araminta went back to the house. At the kitchen door, a woman wearing red lipstick and a colorful scarf on her head asked Araminta, "Do you want to know your destiny?" She had a cup of chocolate in her hands and held it out for Amarinta to take. "I can see the future by looking in your cup," the woman said.

"Who are you?" Araminta asked.

"The chocolate cup reader," the woman said.

Araminta drank the chocolate, lifted the cup in the air, moved it in a circular fashion three times, as the chocolate cup reader had instructed her, and then turned it upside down, on top of a plate.

"We have to let it dry," the woman said.

They waited, and then the reader looked inside the cup.

"What do you see?" Araminta asked.

The woman continued to look into the cup.

"What? What do you see?" Araminta asked again.

"It's funny, I see you standing in the middle of a bunch of brown cows."

"No! I don't want to take care of my father's cows!" Araminta exclaimed.

The woman looked inside the cup again.

"Are you sure?" Araminta asked.

The reader wrinkled her nose, "But these are weird cows, it looks like they are standing on their rear legs," she said.

Araminta snatched the cup from the woman's hands; the chocolate had stained the porcelain cup, but she couldn't discern any cows. She went to the sink, opened the faucet, washed the cup, and offered it to a maid, "Fill it again," she said.

The maid filled the cup with more chocolate.

Araminta drank the chocolate. "Read it again," Araminta said offering it to the chocolate cup reader.

"This is not a game," the reader said, shaking her head.

"I said, read it again!"

"It's bad luck…."

Araminta threw the porcelain cup against the floor.

Lázaro shook his head and was back in the autopsy room. Araminta's stomach was fully deflated among the intestines, silent now. He set the scalpel on the slab and sat on the stool. He had also seen a chocolate cup reader once. He'd performed the ritual: drank the chocolate, moved the cup in circles three times, and set it upside down on a plate as it dried. The chocolate cup reader had looked at the cup for some time and then said, "I don't understand. I don't see any good or bad future for this child. It's as though the poor boy is already dead. Poor little thing."

Chapter 8

The next day after returning from the Capital City to find the devastation the avalanche had left, Lázaro said, "I want to go back to the city."

His grandfather shook his head.

Someone was coming from the distance.

"Mom!" He tried running toward the approaching figure, but he sank up to his knees in the mud. He tried to free himself but he couldn't. His grandfather had to come and pull him out.

The figure got closer.

They waited.

"Josefina!" Lázaro yelled.

Josefina was covered in mud.

"Where's my mother?"

Josefina shrugged and started to cry. The mud on her face came off in streaks as tears rolled down her face.

"Of course, it had to be you," Señor Villamayor snarled.

"Josefina, where's Mother? Is she dead?

Josefina said nothing.

"What are we going to do, Grandpa?"

"We'll wait. Maybe the government will send some help."

"Josefina, where's Mother?" Lázaro asked again.

Josefina's voice cracked. "Everybody is dead."

"Everybody, except you," Lázaro's grandfather said.

Lázaro, his grandfather, and Josefina walked for four days to the pastures where Señor Villamayor's cows still roamed. He sacrificed a cow, kept the best cuts for himself and Lázaro—which he salted using the salt blocks he had hidden in a locked room behind a patch of trees—and sold the rest to hungry peasants. Since they had no money, he kept a ledger. Then they went up the mountain to oversee the coffee plantation.

"Thank God, we're not completely ruined," his grandfather said.

"We'll stay here, we will sell some cows, ship some coffee to the Capital City, and we will rebuild the house."

After a week, riding three horses, grandfather, Josefina, and Lázaro returned to where the house had stood. The jungle had started to advance, replacing the ochre stain the flood had left.

Peasants approached. "Patrón, please, help us," they pleaded.

"Tell that to the government. We'll see if they show up. I bet they don't even know we exist," Señor Villamayor told them. "If you want to eat, I'll sell you some meat, but I know you don't have any money, so you're going to sell me your land."

More peasants came, and they agreed to sell their land.

Lázaro turned melancholic and begun to search for his mother. He still had hopes she hadn't died and ended up looking for her in the cracks in the ground, the crevices of rocks, indentations in the trunks of the trees, among piles of rubbish, peeking in puddles of water, until he found a clear stream that had a rock in the middle that looked like a grotto.

He made a clay figurine, put it on a small altar he built out of branches and flowers, and kneeled. "God, please, help me find my mother." He remembered the prayer Leonor used to make and added, "Please, get rid of Lázaro's temporary deaths, also."

The house was rebuilt, a one-story brick house painted in yellow. Lanterns hung from the walls. A gravel pathway led to the house through the middle of the garden and encircled a tree full of orchids. There was a cobblestone patio in the front and meadows on the sides. A low stone wall encircled the hacienda that rose into an archway at the entrance. Two words were carved in the archway: EL EDEN.

The front door led to an enormous living room. The dining room followed, with a table for sixteen people. The kitchen followed. Next to the kitchen were the help's quarters, outside of which was a vegetable garden, and a basin to wash clothes. The servants had dug a new pond. Past the pond, a wild cane forest was reviving.

Lázaro continued searching for his mother, in secret, but instead of finding her, he found a green rock. He went to the altar and placed it in front of the clay figurine.

On his way back home he found another rock, more brilliant. He put it in his pocket and continued to walk. At home, he passed by his grandfather, who was sitting on a bench under the tree with orchids; his grandfather called him over, took a candy out of his pocket, and offered it to him. In exchange, Lázaro took the rock out of his pocket and gave it to him.

Señor Hipólito Villamayor looked at the stone in his palm and smiled, the hairs of his moustache sticking out.

"Where did you find this rock?"

Lázaro pointed in the direction of the grotto.

His grandfather bent forward and whispered in Lázaro's ear, "Don't tell anybody."

"Why?" Lázaro whispered back.

"After all, every cloud has a silver lining," his grandfather said, getting up from the bench. His voice was strong and energetic as usual. "At least something good came out of that continuous searching of yours."

With the help of a servant, they found nine more green rocks in over a week. His grandfather said they were emeralds. The closer they got to the mountain, the more emeralds they found. By the end of the month, they'd found the seam, and Señor Villamayor hired two workers, who built a tall barbed wire fence.

"Why do those men have guns?" Lázaro asked.

"To protect us," Señor Villamayor said, and he paused. "If anything happens to me… If I die—"

"What if I die first, Grandpa, once and for all?" Lázaro interrupted.

"You'll never die, and someday, all I own will be yours, but for now, we need somebody to help us," his grandfather said.

A huge iron and wood chandelier, a bronze bed, a painting, and hand-carved window frames arrived from Mexico. The footboard of the bed had an eagle with a snake in its beak. The painting showed Jesus Christ semi-nude surrounded by darkness.

A man arrived from a distant land at the same time. He was not as old as Lázaro's grandfather, but he wasn't young, either. Lázaro didn't understand the language the man spoke. He spoke in a funny way that reminded Lázaro of the Indians, but different, and he used his hands to make gestures as though he was playing charades.

"Monsieur Abélard knows a lot about emeralds. He'll teach us," Lázaro's grandfather said.

Lázaro sat next to them while they looked at the stones with an instrument.

"What's that?" Lázaro asked.

"A magnifying eyepiece," his grandfather answered.

"What for?"

"To look inside the emeralds."

When they were not using the magnifying eyepiece, Lázaro went around examining all sort of things. "Grandpa, there are things inside other things we cannot see with the naked eye," he said.

"Yes. Inclusions."

Monsieur Abélard liked to talk to himself, and Lázaro paid attention.

And one day, Lázaro said the first word the foreigner understood without difficulty: "Émeraude."

"Très bien," the foreigner said. "Do you want to learn this language?"

Lazaro nodded.

Monsieur Abélard took out a little booklet with pictures, and pointing at them, asked Lázaro to repeat after him. Then, they went all over the house pointing at things and naming them in both languages.

Before Monsieur Abélard left, six months later, he asked Lázaro, "Òu est ta mère?"

Lázaro made sure his grandfather wasn't around and said, "Je ne sais pas." He refused to say his mother was dead.

Señor Villamayor sat at his desk in his office, the picture of Jesus Christ behind him; holding a newspaper in his hands he said, "The damn government didn't say anything about the avalanche, but they're talking now about the emerald mine."

"Is that why all those people are coming to town now?" Lázaro asked.

"Yes. They're coming like packs of hungry dogs—What am I saying? I am talking like you! Soon I am going to start baby-talking."

Soon there were more houses, a church, a municipal house, stores, a pharmacy, and a bar.

Lázaro went back to the shrine he'd built and found a group of people praying to the clay figurine he'd made; they swore it was the replica of a saint who made miracles happen, but it was a shame that someone had stolen an emerald the saint had put in the grotto; otherwise more and bigger miracles would be happening. Did anyone know who had stolen the emerald? If they found who'd done it, they were ready to lynch the thief. Lázaro walked away from the crowd in disgust.

Out of habit, he looked down and a semi-buried rock caught his attention. He unearthed the rock with difficulty; spears of quartz made it prickly; it was big enough that it fit the palm of his hand and he couldn't clasp it.

He washed the emerald in the stream. As the mud and debris washed away, the rock shone. Lázaro lifted it up to the sun. Inside, like miniature planets he had seen in a book, inclusions—like his grandfather had said—floated in the rock's green solid ocean. He knew he held a fortune in his hands.

On his way back home, Lázaro found a piece of a sack and wrapped the rock in it. He passed under the stone arch, crossed the garden, and went inside of the house. One of the rooms had a wooden door with a lock. He opened the door. A wave of formaldehyde shocked his nostrils. The room was a mess—there were empty flasks, flasks filled with formaldehyde, a row of shelves along one wall, and an armoire on the opposite wall. Only one flask contained a serpent. His grandfather had started his serpent collection anew. Lázaro lifted the flask with both hands and shook it. The serpent levitated and sank in the liquid. He put the flask back and walked among bricks, pieces of wood, a pile of sand, several cement bags, and several cans filled with white paint sitting on the floor. A cement table stood in the middle of the room.

With a hammer and a chisel, he carved a hole in the wall next to the armoire, hid the rock in the hole, and sealed it with clay.

He went to look for three servants and asked them to slide the armoire. The workers obeyed without questioning. The hole was now hidden behind the armoire.

For the next two years, Lázaro went to the market once a week with two of the maids. Sometimes his grandfather went along with them. The selection of clothes sold at the market expanded along with the fruits and vegetables. The peasants wore new clothes, but they looked more like peasants than ever.

His grandfather ordered the purchase of the first incandescent lamp for the house. Lázaro went about carrying the lamp at night and sat next to his grandfather while Señor Villamayor read the newspaper.

The radio arrived a few months later.

Señor Villamayor hired more body guards.

"We need an army to protect us," his grandfather said. "People would kill one person for a small stone."

Lázaro's grandfather continued to make trips; some of them lasted for days, the longest a month.

"You're not dying anymore," his grandfather said after returning from a trip. "I'm not going away for another six months. It's time for you to learn about this business."

That afternoon, Lázaro went to the patio; it was hot; he took off his clothes and stepped into the outdoor shower next to the basin. A very thin and pale worker was filling a bucket with water. After a coughing spell, he spat a dense ball of phlegm mixed with blood at Lázaro's feet; in between them, the blood swirled.

"Niño Lázaro, come," someone called and tapped him on the shoulder.... Lázaro trembled. He knew he was going to die and felt as though someone had stabbed him with a knife in the middle of his chest. He gasped, and his heart stopped.

The interminable fall came.

The worker was standing in front of him, but he looked different. "Come, Niño Lázaro," the worker repeated, but his mouth didn't move. Lázaro looked around. The worker was not on the patio, and this was not his house.

"What happened?" Lázaro asked the worker.

Again, he heard an ear-piercing sound.

"He cannot see you." Ramiro was behind Lázaro.

Lázaro started to run away, but he didn't advance one inch, so he stopped. Ramiro was standing in front of him. He looked different as well, cleaner, his hair was shiny, and he had gained some weight.

Lázaro murmured something apprehensively, but no piercing sound came to hurt him. "Please, forgive me. I didn't do it on purpose," Lázaro said.

"I know, silly," Ramiro said, laughing.

"Why are you here?" Lázaro asked, still panting.

"Because of my godfather," Ramiro said, pointing at the thin worker.

"Let's go," Lázaro said.

"I can't."

"Why?"

"'Cause I'm dead."

Lázaro looked at Ramiro's godfather. "Is he dead, too?" he asked.

Ramiro nodded.

"But he was alive just now," Lázaro said.

Ramiro's godfather said something.

"I cannot understand," Lázaro said.

"That's cause he's talking dead language."

"Can you speak it?"

"Yes, I told ya, I'm dead."

"Forgive me, please," Lázaro said.

Ramiro smiled. "I don't think I'm gonna see ya again."

"Why?"

"I don't want to play no more, I'm tired," Ramiro said and vanished without saying good-bye, but his godfather remained.

Lázaro's grandfather appeared.

"Grandpa," Lázaro exclaimed. The piercing sound came like a red-hot needle.

Lázaro remained silent, covering his ears.

"I need you to do me a favor," his grandfather said to the worker.

"Yes, Patrón."

"Tell Lázaro I am his father."

"Why is that, Patrón?"

"It's a white lie. He doesn't have a mother now. And I know he feels alone."

It smelled awful: putrefaction and formaldehyde combined. Lázaro's eyes hurt as the light pinched them; he'd woken up in the serpents' room. He had a terrible urge to cough and vomit at the same time. A fetid ball of phlegm came out of his mouth. Something tickled in one of his nostrils. He snorted. A maggot came out of his nose. He tried to move, but he couldn't; his body hurt all over, and it was covered in pustules. In some places, the skin had melted, leaving portions of rotting muscle exposed. He was swimming in a fetid liquid that a sheet of plastic had collected underneath. More maggots tickled inside his ears.

He started to burp and vomited a yellow-green liquid.

Josefina came in with a handkerchief covering her nose and mouth. She tried to vomit, but she looked at Lázaro and her face transformed: Her eyes seemed blacker, and she didn't look so childish. She removed the handkerchief and spoke in a voice that although monotonous, was stronger. "The patrón will never accept me as his daughter. I know you're the only one that matters to him. I am going to look for my mother."

Her voice was painful in Lázaro's ears. He couldn't utter a word.

"He said he was sure you were going to come back from this horrible thing, and he asked me to stay here, as much as I could, so I could tell him when you'd resurrect. That's what he said."

Josefina told him his grandfather had summoned a doctor and the doctor had said Lázaro was dead; he'd been dead for a month, this time. Completely dead.

"Get up, Niño Lázaro! I'm going to tell your grandpa."

His muscles didn't obey.

"I'm gonna tell your grandfather," Josefina said and left the room.

Lázaro's grandfather came into the room with Josefina; he held a handkerchief over his nose and mouth. He approached Lázaro and stood looking at him. Lázaro tried to smile, but only a mouthful of saliva came out through an orifice in one of his cheeks.

Josefina threw up in a corner of the room.

"Leave," Señor Villamayor ordered Josefina, "and bring back a towel, a bucket of warm water, and soap." He turned to Lázaro, "I don't know what I'd have done, if you hadn't resurrected."

Lázaro tried to speak, but a wheezing sound came, carrying more fetid air.

"Don't talk. You'll be fine, you'll see," his grandfather said.

Josefina returned with the requested items; his grandfather started to clean Lázaro's body. One of his tears fell on Lázaro's abdomen. Lázaro flinched. His grandfather wiped the tears off his face with the sleeve of his shirt.

"Get out of here!" he reprimanded Josefina.

Once she left, he said, "We're going to take a very long trip. There's a doctor on the other side of the world, a specialist in occult diseases," his grandfather said.

Lázaro looked at his hands: the nails that had fallen off had begun to regrow.

Chapter 9

Three years had elapsed since the trip to the Capital City. Lázaro was eleven. Two servants struggled to get the two big steamer trunks onto mules. The size of the trunks indicated grandfather and child would not be back for months. Josefina followed them to the arch and embraced Lázaro; she carried a scent of fried onions. She told him to be safe while traveling over an ocean she'd heard was treacherous.

Before they went very far down the slope, Lázaro turned his head; Josefina's hand waved at the top of the hill, like an ear of corn in the wind.

They traveled across the jungle in a bigger boat that didn't need Indians with paddles. The jungle, which previously had been so dense, now had huts dotting the shoreline. They didn't have to ride on the Indians' backs because there was a trail for the mules.

They rode along the trail until they reached the town across the mountain, where Señor Villamayor and Lázaro boarded a train to the Capital City. They spent the night in another, fancier hotel, the Hotel Regina, which smoothed a corner with its round façade with iron balcony railings. They bought the tickets at the Continent De Perea & CIA agency for the sum of one thousand pesos each. First class.

"The next time we come back to this city, we are going to get lost. This city has grown so much," his grandfather said before they boarded another train that would take them to a port on the Caribbean.

The train advanced. Through the window, the landscape changed. They traveled along precipices, pastures, coffee plantations, arid terrain, almost-deserts, sugar cane plantations, and another enormous river that was not quite as large as the one in the jungle. People with different attire appeared and disappeared through the train's window. The train stopped in several towns. The way people talked had also changed. Same language, but different accents. Dogs and children ran after the train. The children screamed and laughed; the dogs barked.

When they finally arrived at the port, six days had elapsed. A pier advanced into the ocean and got lost in the distance. The shore was almost a desert with scant bushes covered in dust.

Cows, donkeys, and dogs roamed among the pedestrians. The tallest building was two stories, and on the unpaved streets, lamps alternated with vendors.

Lázaro said, "Grandpa, the people here are very dark, like the child we saw in the Capital City."

"Yes, they came from Africa."

"Where's that?"

"On the other side of the world."

"That's where we're going?"

"No. We're going to Europe."

Floating in the water by the concrete pier, the American Hamburg Line transatlantic steamer looked like a monster ready to ingest them. The three caravels sailed by Cristobal Colón would have looked like insects next to this steamer. Lázaro remembered reading about the ancient men who had imagined the world flat and the ocean overflowing into an infinite abyss.

The passengers showed their tickets and disappeared one by one through the steamer's mouth, sorted by class: First class, which included Lázaro and his grandfather, upstairs; the rest, downstairs below the water line.

The ship set sail at night.

"This ship is like a big city that floats," Lázaro said.

"You and your weird way of talking," his grandfather said.

Lázaro imagined the ship would trail the routes that whales had followed for centuries.

"I don't feel well. I think I'm going to be sick. Bring me a bucket," his grandfather said.

He vomited. "We shouldn't have done this trip, I knew it," he said in between heaves.

Lázaro sat next to him in their stateroom and cleaned his grandfather's face with towels. His grandfather looked like a different person, with a pale face, vitreous eyes, his power to impose gone.

"Grandpa, I can call the doctor, if you want."

His grandfather said no.

The next morning, somebody knocked at the door. It was a man asking if they needed something.

"My grandfather is sick."

The man left and came back with a doctor.

Señor Villamayor refused to be seen, so the doctor gave Lázaro a bottle with a dropper. "Give him five drops in the morning and five drops in the evening," he said.

The medication worked partially.

The ship docked in a humongous city whose buildings pierced the sky.

Lázaro told his grandfather, "This is New York."

"Yes? How do you know?"

"The captain told me. And that's Lady Liberty."

At the next port, they couldn't disembark because the ship had been declared unsanitary. Several other passengers had been attacked by fevers, vomiting, and diarrhea. People said it was cholera.

The next day, Lázaro's grandfather stopped vomiting, but he slept for hours only to wake up when one of the servants brought him chicken, broth, and bread. He looked pale and wasted. "We shouldn't have come, I knew it," he said again.

Lázaro didn't waste time and began exploring. He could take an elevator and go from one deck of the ship to another. Sometimes he got lost trying to find his way back to their stateroom, but someone would always help him find it.

His grandfather started to feel better, but still, he preferred to remain in the stateroom. One day he came out with Lázaro, and they saw what looked like a funeral.

"Somebody's dead," Lázaro's grandfather said.

Lázaro wanted to get closer.

"You go, I'll wait here," his grandfather said, "but be careful, it might be cholera."

Lázaro went over.

The captain presided over the funeral procession. The crew was dressed in their best uniforms, and the dead body—placed on a plank—was wrapped in white linen, a weight attached to the feet. A young lady stood in a long black skirt, her eyes red and swollen. She had a dog on a leash. It looked like a miniature lion. Several people surrounded her. She leaned toward the body and lifted the shroud from the face.

"Be careful," the captain said, "you don't want to get sick."

Lázaro glimpsed the face for one second. That was enough. He could have sworn he was the man with the tie who'd been looking for the phenomenon. The man he'd seen with the fisherman when he'd died in the hemorrhagic dengue epidemic.

The lady with the dog retreated, and the sailors pushed the body off the plank and into the ocean. It floated for several seconds before sinking, leaving behind a stream of bubbles.

The lady walked away. Lázaro followed her. She blew her nose with a handkerchief.

"He might resurrect," Lázaro said.

She stopped and turned around. "At the end of the time?" she said, and continued to walk away, pulling the dog by the leash.

The following day, Lázaro found the lady and the dog sitting on a deck chair. He sat down next to them. The dog jumped onto his lap. He smiled.

"He seems to like you," she said.

The dog licked Lázaro's face.

"Yes, definitely, he likes you," she said, and looked Lázaro in the eyes. "Child, you have the strangest eyes I've ever seen. Are you a gypsy?" she asked.

"What's its name?" Lázaro asked.

"Sultán." she said.

"Like a man from Arabia?"

The woman said yes, but he had the impression that she didn't know what he was talking about.

"Have you been there?" she asked.

"No, but I read it in a book."

"How old are you?"

"Eleven," Lázaro said. "Who was the dead man?"

She lowered her gaze and said, "My brother."

"Had he been to the jungle?"

"I believe so, why do you ask that?"

"I saw him in the jungle."

"I wouldn't be surprised."

The dog returned to the woman's lap.

"He was looking for a phenomenon," Lázaro said.

"And how do you know that?" she asked standing quickly. The dog jumped to the floor.

"He told me."

"When?" she asked, alarmed.

"Last year."

"He was looking for my daughter, probably, but he never told me... I'm going to look for my daughter."

"Where?"

"She must be somewhere in France. The man who kidnapped her sold her."

The dog started to bark. "Hush," the lady said. "Now, if you'll excuse me, I have to go, Sultán is hungry." She disappeared, leaving a trail of perfume.

The lady and the dog reappeared the next day.

"Hello," she said while the dog played with Lázaro. "I don't even know your name."

"Lázaro."

"My name is Lucinda. Where do you live?"

"Sirirí."

"I have no idea where that is."

"A village in the jungle."

"I imagine that's where you saw my brother."

Lázaro nodded. "Your brother sold her."

"How do you know that?" she asked alarmed.

"I saw him in a hospital…"

She started to cry.

"My brother was a scoundrel… God forgive him." Lucinda pursed her lips, got up, went to the railing, and looked at the vast ocean. "I'll find her wherever she is."

Another day, she asked Lázaro, "where are you going?"

"Paris."

"Try not to say where you're from. I always say I'm from Spain," she said, feigning a Castilian accent.

"We're going in search of the specialist in occult diseases," Lázaro said.

"Really? Why?"

"Because my grandfather has a strange disease."

"I don't think I have seen your grandfather," she said, forgetting the Castilian accent.

"He likes to hide."

"Why?"

"He doesn't like people. But he owns a lot of cows, a coffee plantation, and an emerald mine."

"Really? An emerald mine? I think I've heard—" The lady crossed herself. "God forgive him."

"He doesn't forgive anybody," Lázaro said.

She sighed. “Lord have mercy on us.”

“He doesn’t have mercy, either,” Lázaro said. “Grandpa says I’m the devil.”

“Oh, that man!”

“He says I’m a monster.”

“My God, that man is the devil indeed,” she said and fell silent for a while until she said, “I’ve known a monster. Not all monsters are bad.”

Lázaro took his grandfather to the ship’s library; since he “didn’t like the gossip the steamship’s newspaper published,” he picked a book. Lázaro picked another one.

The library door opened and the lady with the dog entered.

“Grandpa, look, that’s the lady with the dog. Her brother died.”

“Don’t say anything. I don’t want to talk to anybody,” his grandfather said.

Lucinda and the dog approached them.

“Madam, this is my grandfather,” Lázaro said.

She didn’t offer her hand. “Señor Villamayor. My name is Lucinda Tapias,” she said. “And your grandson is not the devil!”

Lázaro’s grandfather pinched him on the arm.

“Ayayay!” Lázaro exclaimed.

“Don’t you go telling everyone what they don’t need to know.”

“No specialist in occult diseases is going to be able to cure you,” Lucinda remarked, and left.

“Now you’re lying?”

After another week, they disembarked in Marseille, a tranquil city with buildings that seemed to come out of the rocky terrain. More trams. Vendors. Carriages.

“We have a couple of hours before we board the train. Do you want to see something amusing?” his grandfather said.

“Yes.”

“Let’s look for the Place Castellane.”

It was a human zoo. People were exhibited in cages, like tigers; they reminded Lázaro of the Indians in the jungle. A bunch of people surrounded the cages. What would everyone do if he had a temporary death in front of them? Applaud? Stone him?

A group of people huddled together inside a cage. Lázaro could swear they were a family.

"I don't want to be here any longer, Grandpa," Lázaro said.

They were about to leave when Lázaro saw a child with eight arms.

"An octopus child," Lázaro said.

Next to the octopus child, a boy with an enormous head cried silently.

"Grandpa, look, the boy with the big head from the hospital!"

Just as he was saying it, Lucinda made her way through the crowd and starting yelling, "That's my daughter, my daughter, oh God! Somebody help me!!"

"I thought it was a boy!" Lázaro said.

"Let's get the hell out of here," his grandfather said.

"Please, Grandpa, help her," Lázaro begged.

"I told you. Mind your own business," he said, grabbing Lázaro by the arm and pulling him away.

They boarded a steam engine train that had a ceiling full of paintings. Lázaro thought of a new word he'd learned: luminosity. The train took them to Paris, passing by little towns, vineyards, streams, ponds, castles among them. They arrived in Paris on a sunny day in the middle of June. At la gare d'Orléans, the physician they had been referred to was waiting for them. He greeted them in French.

"Are you the specialist in occult diseases?" Señor Villamayor asked.

The man looked at Señor Villamayor and smiled. "Je suis le docteur Bernard."

"I don't understand," Lázaro's grandfather said, exasperated.

"Yes, he's the doctor," Lázaro said.

"How do you know?"

Lázaro said nothing.

Doctor Bernard sent them on their way to the Hôtel Regina without saying one more word.

The naked statues that adorned Paris, bathed in the sunlight, made Lázaro wonder what he looked like when he was dead. People said he looked like a statue.

"The statues are naked," Lázaro observed.

"Yes. Imagine the kind of city this is."

The Seine made Lázaro smile. A baby river, he thought. And the trees were like toys compared to the trees in the jungle. It took them over an hour to travel from the station to the Hôtel Regina.

"This hotel has the same name as the one in the Capital City," Lázaro remarked.

The Hôtel Regina was a luxury seven-story Art Deco building, recently built.

Once they were settled, Doctor Bernard said good-bye with a smile and a wave.

At Doctor Bernard's office the next day, Lázaro spoke haltingly in French. Señor Villamayor nudged him. "Porqué hablas este idioma?" his grandfather asked.

"Lo aprendí con el experto en esmeraldas," Lázaro said.

Doctor Bernard asked, "Where did you learn French?"

Lázaro hesitated, "At home." He tried to remember more words. "An emerald expert teach me," he said.

"Taught me," Doctor Bernard corrected.

"An emerald expert taught me," Lázaro repeated.

"Good. It will be easier to communicate," Doctor Bernard said.

His grandfather sat writhing and clasping his hands.

"What did he say?" he asked.

"Nothing."

"Nothing? Do you think I'm stupid?"

Doctor Bernard requested some documents, among them a letter a physician had written. He read the letter and eyed the other documents.

"Doctor Perilla was one of my students," he said and proceeded to examine Lázaro.

Lázaro observed how the doctor examined him, comparing Doctor Bernard with the many physicians who'd previously examined him. Doctor Bernard was meticulous. But so were the others. There was something about him that made Lázaro like him.

"This doctor isn't doing anything different from all the other physicians, we're wasting our time," Señor Villamayor said.

Doctor Bernard reclined in his chair behind his desk surrounded by diplomas. Lázaro stood and looked at them—the seals, the golden calligraphy.

"Those diplomas are the validation of my life, the proof of my knowledge," Doctor Bernard said.

"What did he say?"

"He said the diplomas are a proof of his knowledge, the validation of his life."

"Tell him he better not try to fool us, or I will cut off his nuts."

"Your grandfather is a severe man, isn't he?" Doctor Bernard asked.

Lázaro nodded.

"What did he say?" Doctor Bernard asked.

"He said he hopes you can help us."

"We will be running some tests," Doctor Bernard said.

"What did he say?"

"He will run some tests on me."

"Please, tell me exactly what it is that's happening to you," Doctor Bernard said.

Lázaro relaxed in his chair. He did not mindlessly recite his symptoms as he had done before. He articulated the words, one by one, so Doctor Bernard could understand. But still, he did not say everything.

"Are you sure you're not embellishing your symptoms?" Doctor Bernard asked.

"No."

Lázaro still didn't tell him about the sudden and exaggerated increase in weight. Much less about his journeys into the past of people whose blood he had seen.

Lázaro's grandfather stood up. "If you don't tell me what's going on, I'm leaving right now. And don't lie."

Lázaro told Doctor Bernard he was going to explain to his grandfather what he had said. And so he did, in a way that he knew would appease his grandfather. Everything seemed to fit within the realm of a seizure disorder, the shakes, the loss of consciousness, and the changes in skin color—epileptics turned purple from lack of oxygen.

"Did you tell him that you rotted for a month?" his grandfather asked.

"Yes," Lázaro lied.

"And what did he say?"

"He has no explanation."

Lázaro thought that Doctor Bernard was a gentle old man; the nature of the two men presented a study in contrasts. Doctor Bernard was like one of those monkeys that fit in the palm of the hand, while his grandfather was a wild boar, or maybe a dangerous snake. Seeing his grandfather in distress made him feel something in the middle of his chest; his grandfather could be vulnerable, too.

"Don't worry. He said he's going to help us," Lázaro said.

"Are you sure he's the specialist in occult diseases?" Lázaro's grandfather asked.

"Êtes-vous le spécialiste des maladies occultes?"

"Mais non. Je ne suis pas."

"Yes, he is," Lázaro lied again.

"All right, we'll see if it's true," his grandfather said.

Doctor Bernard told Lázaro something.

Señor Villamayor looked at Lázaro.

"He said we have the marks of the jungle," Lázaro said.

"What does he know about the marks of the damn jungle?"

Doctor Bernard told Lázaro he wanted to see them the following day.

They walked past Notre Dame, through the Square de la Tour St.-Jacques, and along Rue de Rivoli to the Hotel Regina. They were on the other side of the world, and this world was… luminous.

The ritual of questions, exams, tests, was repeated every day for a week.

A new medication was available: The drug was known as Luminal—illumination. Light. Luz. Lumière. Bromide, the medication that they had used before, was poisonous, but barbiturates like Luminal had begun to be used, and Doctor Bernard hoped that this marvelous medication would allow him to avoid sending the afflicted to asylums. It had worked in many other patients he had treated.

The proximity of their hotel to the Louvre had delighted Lázaro, but under the influence of Luminal, he lost his desire to do anything. Regardless, his grandfather took him to the Luxembourg Garden, Montmartre, and a bookstore close to the hotel, where his grandfather wanted to buy Lázaro a children's book.

Another day, Lázaro saw his grandfather running his hand over the wall of their room.

"Isn't it soft, Grandfather?" he asked, lying in bed without moving a finger.

"Yes. I wonder where they get the silk."

"Damasco."

"Where did you learn that?"

"I read it in a book they have down in the lobby."

"Where's Damasco?"

"In Syria."

"How come you know those things?"

"I went to the Bibliothèque Mazarine."

"I thought you were with Doctor Bernard. Why didn't you tell me? Show me the library."

"I don't feel like doing anything."

"It's the damn Luminal. We need to get back home. We need to leave Paris. I want to go now."

"Doctor Bernard hasn't said we can go."

"Who cares what he says. I don't give a damn."

"But—"

"You made me come here. You're making me do things I don't want to. You're turning me into somebody else."

"I thought we came here to find a cure for my disease."

"We came here to find the specialist in occult diseases and he doesn't even exist!!"

Lázaro and his grandfather stayed in Paris for two months. Doctor Bernard observed Lázaro and adjusted the dosage of the Luminal so the child would not be sedated. He was content that the child had not experienced any "seizures." To him, the medication was working as expected. Señor Villamayor and Lázaro were to go back home and follow up with the fellow Doctor Bernard had trained. They said goodbye and Lázaro and his grandfather left with a bag full of medical documents.

The night before their departure, Lázaro heard his grandfather get out of bed and leave their room. He followed him. Señor Villamayor went up to the hotel's top floor. One of the bellboys was there, and extended his arms when he saw Señor Villamayor. Lázaro thought for a moment that the person he had followed was not his grandfather. Not this affectionate person who was stroking the bellboy's hair. What Lázaro saw after made him run downstairs to their room.

Lázaro woke up the following morning to find his grandfather sitting on his bed, looking pensive.

They took the train back to Marseille. The transatlantic steamer was ready. They showed their tickets. A man at the entrance made sure they were on the list. Lázaro asked if there was a Lucinda Tapias on the list. There wasn't.

People on the ship spoke different languages. Two nuns were on board. One of them did not speak.

"Is she mute?" Lázaro asked.

"I don't think so," his grandfather said. "Some nuns elect not to speak."

"Ever?"

"Ever."

"So, one can tell them secrets that will be safe with them?" Lázaro said.

"Secrets?"

"Yes, secrets. Do you have any, grandpa?"

As soon as Lázaro and his grandfather stepped off the ship back home, Lázaro saw one man stab another. The voice that called him was terrifying, agonizing, painful. He barely had time to remember the human zoo in Marseille. He was afraid and ashamed as he fell into the entrails of earth.

When he opened his eyes, a ladder had been put into the hole, and Lázaro climbed out. A crowd surrounded him. They cheered and applauded.

"I will kill the first one that moves," Lázaro's grandfather said, pulled a gun from one of his pockets.

Somebody yelled, "Dracula has returned."

"Stupid, don't you see the sun?" somebody else yelled back.

Lázaro showed them his teeth and hissed; most of the crowd retreated. And there was a clamor, like a universal confession in which all the voices went up in the air and nobody could discern what had been said.

Two bodyguards escorted them away. His grandfather had arranged their return and had anticipated the unforeseen. He always anticipated everything.

Chapter 10

They took the train to the Capital City. There, Señor Villamayor hired a teacher, and the three of them rode in an automobile from the city to the town at the base of the mountain. They crossed the mountain on mules. A small steamboat took them close to Sirirí.

Lázaro also spent the days with his grandfather learning how to keep the business' books, supervising the mine, making trips to the coffee plantation, overseeing the cattle farms, tending to horses. He also had daily lessons with the teacher, who requested books and books from the Capital City that he'd never read and had always wanted to, he confessed to Lázaro. Lázaro read them all as well.

One afternoon, when they were returning from a meeting with a foreigner who was interested in buying an emerald for the crown of a queen in a remote land, Lázaro and his grandfather stopped at a pond. Lázaro took off his shirt, pants, and shoes, and went into the water. His grandfather sat by the bank.

"When I was twelve, like you are now, I left the capital city," his grandfather told Lázaro.

With his head above water, Lázaro paid attention.

"I went to the plains, beyond the mountains. There, I met a man who took me under his wing. He was like a father to me."

Lázaro swam closer to his grandfather, moving his hands and feet like a dog.

"I learned all I could about horses and cows. He had the finest horses, stallions, although some of them were so wild that we had to castrate them."

"Castrate?"

"Yes, cut their balls off."

"Ouch. What for?"

"To pacify them."

Lázaro floated in the water looking his grandfather directly in the eyes. "What's pacify?"

"To calm."

"How about castrating you, to pacify you?" Lázaro said.

"Would you like a belting?"

"No. What happened?"

"The man with the horses loved a woman who had been sent away by his family so she wouldn't marry him."

"Like one of those loose women at the bar?"

"No. What are you talking about?"

"Whores."

"Who told you that?"

"Carmen, the maid. She told Josefina and me a story about a man who loved a whore."

"Don't say bad words, do you want to hear my story or not?"

"Sorry, Grandfather."

"He sent me to Spain. They had sent her there with the Carmelitas Descalzas."

"Carmelitas Descalzas?"

"The nuns who never leave their convent and go barefoot."

"Why do they go barefoot? Don't they have any money?"

"Because they want to. Are you going to let me finish the story?"

Lázaro nodded.

"Because they want to serve the poor. What a waste!"

His grandfather took off his shoes and socks and submerged his feet in the water.

"I found the woman he had sent me to look for, but she was dead. Tuberculosis. So, I brought her skeleton back to him. I stole it for him."

Lázaro floated on his back and brushed his grandfather's feet with his.

"And what did he do?"

"He gave me gold and named me his heir, like I'm going to do with you."

"I don't want money. I want to be like the Carmelitas Descalzas. A servant."

"Over my dead body."

Lázaro pushed his grandfather's feet with his and slid away in the water.

"I've realized when you revive, people around you confess…. The last time you died and then resurrected, the mob started to confess. You've made me remember things I don't want to. And I saw things from my past…"

"I see things, too."
"About me?" asked Señor Villamayor alarmed.
"No, Grandpa."
"What do you see?"
"I see things that happened to people."
"What people?"
"The people that bleed."
"You'll never see my blood then. I vow it."

Chapter 11

In the autopsy room, the night continued passing slowly. Lázaro looked at his pocket watch, a remnant from his grandfather's belongings. It was past two o'clock in the morning. The story that was being revealed had something in common with all the stories he had witnessed. He had seen everything, from the mundane to the bizarre. Human beings were capable of anything and everything; even those revelations he least expected did not surprise him any longer. Human interactions were predictable—for the most part. There were common threads in the human experience: birth, death, love, hate, happiness, suffering, wealth, poverty, triumph, deception. The past built identities, anchors that forced people to continue being the way they are. And memory was just reaffirmation, even if what we remember is not what really happened. Memory isn't always reliable. Hope could be then found in amnesia, to start anew, with no memories.

Lázaro thought all of a sudden that the stories he had witnessed during autopsies were really just partial stories. On some occasions, the full spectrum of a life had started to show itself from the very beginning, but even then, a whole life was too much for a single one of Lázaro's temporary deaths to reveal; and there were no second chances… once a story started to be revealed, it didn't matter where it ended. The end was the end, he couldn't access that world ever again. Lázaro had never had the opportunity to see an entire life. Perhaps the autopsy of an infant would enable him to.

He'd found cures for mortal ailments that had been misdiagnosed; he'd solved mysteries that had tormented the recently deceased. He'd explained some elusive causes of death; he'd understood cause and effect… all because of his temporary deaths. He was only twenty-four, but the temporary deaths had given him the advantage that comes from years of experience. He felt as though he had lived an eternity in those twenty-four years. It is said that the devil knows so much because he's old, not because he's the devil.

As though it were detached from him, his hand moved toward Araminta and scanned her body until it stopped at the thorax. He lifted the ribs, as if lifting the hood of a car. The purplish lungs were deflated; the left was intact, the right lay in a pool of blood. Shreds of pleura, the semi-transparent membrane surrounding the lungs, clung to the ribs. The bullet had fractured two ribs and perforated the right lung and right pulmonary artery. Air and blood had entered the pleural space and constricted the lung, strangling her and exsanguinating her. He stuck a finger inside the hole the bullet had made.

Araminta's father passed next to him. He retreated instinctively.

The man's face was more discernable than before. The nose was in the middle of the face, the lips centered, without any unusual features. He could have been anyone. He could have been any motherfucker… Lázaro tried to remember where he had heard that before, but he couldn't. It was then he realized the man did not have eyes; still, he moved as though he could see.

Araminta whispered, "He believes he's the king," and as she said it, her father metamorphosed into a king carrying a bull whip instead of a scepter. She curtsied and bowed. He strode away. His crown and cape sparkled in the afternoon light. She followed him and grabbed his cape.

"What do you want?" her father asked.

"I don't know."

"You better figure it out. What you need is some time away from your enabling sister. You need to think," he said, and pushed her away. Araminta fell to the grass.

Kill him, the lungs said. It was the voice of a flute…. FIIB.

"What I want is something I don't have," Araminta said. Her voice had a tone that resembled a flute.

"What don't you have? Her father's voice also resembled a flute. "I've given you everything I could. You have food, shelter, clothes. What else do you want?" The last word had lost the flute tone.

Araminta didn't answer.

"Pack your bags. You're leaving tomorrow," he said.

"Where am I going?" she asked in tears.

"Auntie Delfina's."

"She doesn't like me."

"Go figure it out."

Chiquita waited for Araminta with a valise in her hands. "You'll come back, you'll see," she said.

The sound of a claxon pierced the air.

Their father was sitting in the back of a car.

"This is what happens when you spoil women. The next time, you're going to ride on a mule," he said.

Araminta got into the black car that looked like a colossal insect with vitreous eyes. She sat next to her father. The engine roared. She turned the chrome crank to roll down the window. The wind made her hair flow while the car meandered along a yellow ochre path through the jungle. A cloud of dust followed. They crossed over a wooden bridge and stopped in front of a villa. Her father stepped out of the car first and she followed, carrying her luggage. They walked through an iron gate with peeling paint to a garden with a statue of the Virgin Mary in the middle. Narrow cement pathways riddled with cracks and intruding weeds converged in the center. Flowers were planted as if their seeds had been kernels scattered for hens.

A tiny woman standing on one of the paths asked, "What are you doing here?" The woman's voice was irritating, like the highest tones of a flute.

"Good afternoon, Auntie Delfina. Who takes care of this garden?" Araminta asked.

"No one."

"No wonder. It's horrible. Sorry, little flowers," Araminta said while she caressed the roses.

"She's crazy, like her mother," the tiny woman said to Araminta's father.

"You're just jealous because she was prettier than you are," he said.

"Don't think I am stupid. It was your fault my sister killed herself."

"Don't pay attention. Your aunt, Delfina, is just silly," he told Araminta.

"I would rearrange it," Araminta said, and pointed at different plants: "You here, you there, umm, no, better over there." The plants moved where Araminta told them to.

"I need you to take care of her for a while," Araminta's father said.

Delfina said, "Why would I do that?"

"You need company. Any company. Perhaps, this way, you won't miss your husband so much."

Auntie Delfina started to cry. "You're right. I feel so lonely. I can't believe he's dead."

"I told you not to marry an old man. After a while, you won't even remember that old creep."

"You've always been with young women, and you're alone," Auntie Delfina said between sobs.

"Poor Auntie Delfina, I'll be your companion," Araminta said. "I can take care of your garden, and your hair. I'm good at it. I love your hair, I bet it's very long, like my sister's."

Auntie Delfina's hair was in a tight bun.

Auntie Delfina said, "Thank you." She turned to her brother. "I'll try, but she's like her mother, you know," she said, and she burped. "Excuse me." Burp. "Excuse me." The scent of garlic and cumin rose in the air.

Auntie Delfina started to pace back and forth.

"She looks like a wind-up doll," Araminta whispered into her father's ear.

"What did she say?" Auntie Delfina asked.

"Do not say one more word," her father said, and looking at Auntie Delfina he continued, "I don't want any men around her. Do you understand?"

"Of course," she replied. "Who do you think I am? La Celestina?"

He ordered the chauffer to take his daughter's valise inside, said good-bye, and got back into the car.

Araminta and her aunt waved from the entrance of the house while the car disappeared.

"I'll teach you something. You need to be occupied," Auntie Delfina said.

"I'm not going to be your maid," Araminta said.

"Of course not. I like your attitude. Keep that up and you'll go far," Auntie Delfina replied and walked inside the house. Araminta trailed.

She brought a bag and took out several skeins of Calabrese thread. Araminta sat next to her, and so the lessons started. In the beginning, Araminta lost patience easily, but the more her skill developed, the more she relaxed. Once she got the hang of it, she could use a crochet hook to twist the thread with precision. She made collars, cuffs, and hems, the thread twisting around her finger like a rope around a convict's neck—now loose, now tight, now gone.

"Ropes, ropes, ropes. There are so many kinds of ropes. We create them. And then they choke us, and sometimes they even kill us." The flute voice was choking.

"What else do you want me to do, Auntie Delfina? Can I go to the village?" Araminta asked.

"I promised your father I wouldn't let you out of the house."

"What do you think I'm going to do?"

"One never knows."

"If you stay inside the house, you'll never remarry," Araminta said.

"I don't want to remarry."

"Life's too short," Araminta replied.

"You don't know anything about life."

The skeins of Calabrese thread disappeared one by one, while a pile of hems, collars, even a skirt appeared in a basket in the living room.

"What else do we do?" Araminta asked. "I am bored."

"I don't know."

"Don't you get bored?"

That same afternoon, they finally went to the village. They walked along the market and saw clay pots.

"I have an idea, let's do clay dolls," Araminta said.

"I'm not going to dirty my hands."

The dentist was there, a bit farther on, among fruits and vegetables, his wife by his side. He took off his hat and greeted them.

"What a nice surprise to see you in town," he said. "One of these days, I'll come to vist."

The sound was composed of three tones; one of them was the drum, ***Boom***, the other, the bagpipe, ***Ñeeh***, and the last, the flute, ***Fiib***. The sounds made up a language he understood perfectly.

One night, Araminta heard a noise outside her window.

BOOM. ÑEEH. FIIB.

She got out of bed, parted the curtain, and looked through the window. The light of the moon bathed the dentist, who stood next to a rose bush, one leg in front of the other, with the tip of his foot touching the ground. He took his hat off and smiled. She stood quietly in her beige gown, her long hair in front of her breasts. The dentist got closer.

"Let me in," the dentist said almost soundlessly.

She read his lips without difficulty.

"No."

Sunsets and dawns came and went. Araminta sat on a stool in front of a battered wooden table with a bucket of water on the ground near her feet. To one side on the table was a pile of clay. To the other side was a row of little dolls of different kinds, from babies to demons.

"Why do you make these monstrosities?" Auntie Delfina would ask.

"I don't know. I think they're beautiful."

In the bedroom, in the kitchen, in the garden, in the parlor, Araminta sat alone with her aunt.

More and bigger monstrosities appeared. The brick oven no longer produced bread, just monsters.

"Why do you keep making these monsters?" Auntie Delfina insisted.

"I don't know."

More sounds of pebbles bouncing off the window at night.

The dentist put his lips against the window.

Araminta didn't know why, but she pressed her lips against the glass.

FIIB. FIIB, the flute said first. The stomach and the brain whispered, ***ÑEEH. ÑEEH... BOOM. BOOM.***

The dentist came in when she opened the window.

The days flew by. One night, Auntie Delfina found her standing in front of the curtains, arms extended.

"What are you doing?" Auntie Delfina asked.

"I am a somnambulist," Araminta said, "didn't you know?" She started pacing past the window.

"I don't like your sleepwalking. Your father never said anything about it. Besides, you don't like anything, you don't like the food, you don't like the servants. I swear you are hiding something."

"What? A man? Why don't you look under my bed?"

"I don't know. I'll call your father."

"Call him."

"You'll see."

"I'm not afraid."

Araminta's father arrived at the house and sat with Auntie Delfina and Araminta in the parlor.

"It's time for her to go home," Auntie Delfina said. "I feel fine now."

"What happened? Did she do something?"

"She went to town by herself and she got lost."

"That's a lie!" Araminta said. "She went with me."

"How dare you—"

"Enough. You're coming back home with me," Araminta's father said, and dragged her to the black car that traveled on the interminable yellow ochre road once more. The strong winds of August howled while Araminta turned pale and stuck her head out the car window to throw up.

The car went under the stone arch and stopped in front of their house.

Araminta got out, ran inside the house, and went up to the second-floor balcony, where she rested her elbows on the railing. Her sister trailed behind her.

"What happened?" Chiquita asked.

"Nothing," Araminta said, left the balcony, and walked down the corridor, followed by a dog. She went down the stairs, came into the kitchen, and looked at the boiling pots. She pulled kernels from cobs and went to feed the hens. Her sister trailed.

"What's wrong, Araminta?" Chiquita asked several times. Araminta didn't answer.

The cycles started again: Araminta knitted and crocheted with fast movements; she flung the skein aside and went to the river to gather some clay. More monsters kept coming alive. She sat back to back with her sister. She cried. Her sister followed her to the pond filled with colored fish. They crossed the garden back and forth. Araminta ignored the flowers. No dialogues. No monologues. Her sister watered the plants.

"What's wrong, Araminta?" Chiquita kept asking.

"I want to go away from here, to wherever nobody knows me, to the other side of the world," Araminta said.

"We could escape," Chiquita said.

As the sisters talked, they ran through different landscapes: They picked their way along the bank of the river, bushwalked through the middle of the jungle, walked up and down an enormous mountain, crossed a suspension bridge, ascended the almost-vertical wall of a precipice. Opening the front doors of several strange houses, they moved through unfamiliar rooms, exited out the rear, and closed the back doors behind them. They walked through a labyrinth with no end, wandered in an unknown city and got lost in a crowd….

When they were done running through the series of scenarios, Araminta, panting, said, "I cannot do it, I hate the jungle, the bugs. I'd rather die!" She began to run while moving her arms, as if attempting to fly. At the same time, the sound of flapping wings brought Lázaro back to the autopsy room. Through the little window, he saw the silhouette of the tree swaying in the wind; suddenly it sprouted nocturnal flowers: a flock of potoos had perched on the branches. The potoos emitted sounds like human voices saying poor-me-one.

On a metal table next to the slab, his hands were pressing the lungs. He lifted them; the indentation from his hands lingered on their surface for some time. He waited. Silence. He waited a bit more. Silence. The story had come to a halt….

He wondered if the story would be the same if she were alive and telling it. Organs didn't lie. The stories that were engraved in the cells, in the tissues, in each organ, were true. But his access to them was always only partial. His temporary deaths were bouts of intermittent consciousness. He had seen the world of the dead as a composition of images, some of them crystal clear, and some of them foggy. Pieces of truths were what he had seen. But just because he hadn't seen an entire life, it didn't mean the story was a shallow one. Humans lied. The dead didn't.

The left lung showed the indentation her heart had made on its surface throughout the years. Lázaro put his fist in the dent. It fit perfectly. If you hold your hand in a fist, that's the size of your heart.

Chapter 12

Two years after the trip to Paris, three letters arrived from there. Señor Villamayor took two and handed Lázaro the third. The stamp on the envelope caught Lázaro's attention: a woman wore a giant hat over a green background. Lázaro opened the letter: in it, Doctor Bernard declared that he had found another patient whose symptoms resembled Lázaros', and he'd made some advances in curing the disease. He'd been experimenting with a new treatment that could benefit Lázaro.

His grandfather began to read one of the other letters.

"Who's the letter from?" Lázaro asked.

His grandfather's eyes grew wide. "Oh God. What's happening?"

One of the servants came into the room, glanced at Lázaro and ran away.

"What's going on?" asked Lázaro.

"Go look at your face in the mirror."

Lázaro stood up, went to the mirror in the living room, and looked at his face; he didn't see anything unusual: smooth hairs were appearing above his upper lip. He had just turned fourteen years old and was now his grandfather's height. His grandfather had followed him and was standing behind him, pale.

The teacher who had just arrived, dropped his jaw.

"I hadn't realized I was growing a moustache," Lázaro said.

"Don't you see?" his grandfather asked.

"See what, Grandpa?"

"Your face is transparent."

"I don't understand. What do you mean?"

"I can see your muscles," Lázaro's grandfather said and took Lázaro's hands. "I can see your bones." Señor Villamayor opened Lázaro's shirt and gasped, "I can see your heart, and your lungs…."

Lázaro lowered his head and saw the muscles in his chest, which had started to develop, but he didn't see his heart.

"I don't believe you," Lázaro said.

"Do you see the same?" Señor Villamayor asked the teacher.

The teacher nodded and said trembling, "I'm leaving."

"Go fuck yourself!" Señor Villamayor said.

That night, he went into Lázaro's bedroom. "We will go back to Paris," he said. "I've been thinking about this for a while. We'll kill two birds with one stone.... We'll see Doctor Bernard.

He says he has found another patient like you."

He handed Lázaro the letter from Doctor Bernard.

"And since it takes twenty tons of meat to feed the passengers on each trip across the ocean, we'll sell them the beef. I've also heard from Monsieur Cartier, who wants emeralds. He wrote this letter." He handed Lázaro a second letter. "So we'll take some emeralds. At least something good will come from this trip. But if Doctor Bernard's new treatment fails, this will be our last trip."

"What about the third letter?" Lázaro asked.

"Nothing important."

The following day, Lázaro read the letter. It was Aristide's.

He packed his suitcases in silence, and went to the serpents' room. The room was lined with shelves of transparent flasks, each containing a snake, and a cement table in the middle of the room. This time he didn't need the servants to help him move the armoire; he pushed it aside and dug the emerald out of the wall. It was covered with cobwebs, dead insects, and dust. He cleaned it. His hands were bigger than when he had found the emerald; still, it almost covered his entire palm. He wrapped it in a silk handkerchief, went to his room, and put it in one of his suitcases.

They left a month later, on a Monday. Lázaro wore a monk's robe and a mask to hide his transparency. This time, a bigger boat with an internal combustion engine took them down the river. The jungle had been cut down to facilitate the passage of men, so it took them half the time to get to the Capital City, where they purchased tickets for the ocean liner. The railroad system had improved and the trip from the Capital City to the port only took them three days. Señor Villamayor's cows had arrived ahead of them, and were ready to satiate the immense appetite of the ships; he had already shipped the emeralds to Paris.

They brought two trunks filled with dress suits, dinner coats, cuffs, dress collars, suspenders, dress ties, and patent leather shoes. Lázaro had one trunk, filled with more robes. And this time Señor Villamayor had come prepared with Glonoine to ward off seasickness.

When Lázaro removed his mask to show his face to the man who was checking the tickets and identification papers, the man almost fell over backward. He called another man and soon there was a crowd around Lázaro.

Señor Villamayor gave the men forty pesos and said, "Get us out of here. Right now!"

The steamship with its four smokestacks, and innumerable windows that looked like scales on a humongous fish, was filled with passengers from all over the southern hemisphere.

Nineteen days later, as they neared the old continent, Lázaro's skin became opaque again. His grandfather blamed him for this: "For God's sake!" he yelled. "What's Doctor Bernard going to see? What are you trying to prove?"

"Nothing. You were the one who said to come back to Paris. I am simply, obeying."

They arrived in Marseille. Neither of them mentioned the human zoo. They took the train, arrived in Paris on a sunny day, and went to the Hotel Regina. Aristide, the bellboy from their previous trip, was standing at the Hôtel's entrance, in front of the revolving doors, one foot in front of the other and one hand on top of his hip, smiling. He looked in tune with the Art Deco style of the hotel.

"Bienvenue, Monsieur Villamayor," he said.

Señor Villamayor smiled as he walked by.

"Bonjour, Aristide," Lázaro said.

"Bonjour, monsieur," Aristide said, and escorted them to the front desk and then to their room, one floor below the top.

The next morning, they met Doctor Bernard in his office at the Hôpital Hôtel-Dieu. The latest treatment for epilepsy, he told them, was rattlesnake venom.

"Rattlesnake?" Lázaro's grandfather yelled, shaking his head. "We have plenty of snakes where we live. Coral snakes. Pit vipers. Not to mention poisonous frogs and spiders. Tell the sonababitch I could have let you be bitten by a damn snake right at home."

Lázaro told Doctor Bernard, "Grandfather says if you need more snakes, he can arrange to get them to you."

"You're not lying, are you?"

Doctor Bernard asked why his grandfather seemed so flustered. Lazaro told his grandfather that Doctor Bernard apologized; he was going to try once more. If the treatment didn't work, he wouldn't insist further.

That, pacified his grandfather.

Doctor Bernard admitted Lázaro into a private room on the ground floor of the Hôtel-Dieu to start the experimental treatment. Besides Lázaro, there were three other boys and four girls.

They gathered once a day. They were divided in two groups. One group got infinitesimal doses of venom, the other a placebo, Doctor Bernard explained.

Once a week a nurse gave them the medication without knowing who was getting what, and she drew their blood, which was sent to the lab. Lázaro asked many questions. Doctor Bernard told him he was comparing the composition of blood from the two groups, and invited him to look at the slides under the microscope in the lab.

Lázaro had been careful to avoid staring at anybody's blood, but the excitement of seeing the slides made him disregard the danger that seeing blood posed for him. He approached the microscope… Through the lens, the world of blood revealed itself for a second. He heard a loud crack. He was in a different mood than usual when it began; he was unafraid; he started to fall into the earth; he was no longer in the hospital room but at the human zoo in Marseille. Lázaro hadn't seen this cage, but he recognized the boy with fish skin, one of the kids who was receiving the treatment. The boy was with the girl with the enormous head. They were in the same cage. A sign stuck to one of the bars read: À Vendre. For sale.

When Lázaro opened his eyes, he was at the bottom of a hole. A wooden shelf and many glass receptacles—most of them broken—lay on top of him. He was clutching the microscope against his chest. Doctor Bernard was standing in the doorway. Had he advanced into the room, he'd have slid down the slanted floor and landed on top of Lázaro.

They used a ladder to get Lázaro out of the hole.

A mob had gathered outside the room and blocked the door. They talked about a miracle. They talked about the devil.

It was late at night when Lázaro was moved to an isolated room beyond the garden.

"Well, now you know," Lázaro's grandfather told Doctor Bernard.

Doctor Bernard asked Lázaro to tell his grandfather he had nothing else to offer. "I wish there was a specialist in occult diseases," he said.

Lázaro translated.

Lázaro and his grandfather were preparing to return home.

They went to the restaurant at the Hotel Regina, Le Pluvinel. An old man accompanied by a middle-aged lady sat at a table by the fireplace. A pâte de verre lampshade produced an aquarium-like light.

Lázaro and his grandfather sat on the other side of the fireplace.

The old man observed them. After a while he stood and walked towards them, limping and using a cane.

"Good evening," he said.

Lázaro's grandfather raised his thick eyebrows and looked at him.

"Do you really not recognize me?" the old man said.

"Who's that man?" the lady asked from her table.

The old man made a gesture as though trying to tell Señor Villamayor not to speak, but Lázaro's grandfather said, "Let's get the hell out of here." He stood up and pulled Lázaro to his feet.

"That voice," the lady said. "Hipólito?"

Lázaro asked: "Who are they?"

"Nobody."

"You said the same thing when we met your mom at the hospital."

"Hipólito, let the boy stay," the old man said.

"So, you are indeed Hipólito Villamayor," the lady said. "Aren't you?"

"Are you blind?" Lázaro's grandfather said, and started to walk away.

"It's all right. I'm not going to say anything bad in front of the boy," the old man said.

"I have nothing to hide," Lázaro's grandfather said.

"Then let's have dinner together," the old man said. With a motion of his hand, he invited them to sit.

"Grandpa, you have nothing to hide," Lázaro said, and took his grandfather's hand to prevent him from walking away. They sat. The table trembled. There was a sound of metal and crystal, a vibration that faded, and then, silence.

"The last time I saw you, you were almost your son's age… fourteen?"

"He's my grandfather, and yes, sir, I'm fourteen," Lázaro said.

"I see, I got confused because of your eyes," the old man said.

The lady said, "He must be the son of—"

"What do you want?" Señor Villamayor said.

The lady gave Lázaro's grandfather a hateful look.

"Have you met my parents?" Lázaro asked.

"No," said the old man, putting a hand on top of his wife's. "I was surprised when the bellboy told me there was a gentleman staying here by the name of Hipólito Villamayor, from our country, I thought it was just a coincidence," the old man said.

"Why didn't you tell me?" the lady said to her husband.

"I didn't want to upset you," and continued: "It's been what, fifty years since the last time I saw you?"

Señor Villamayor was silent. A waiter came to ask what they wanted to drink.

"The world is a handkerchief," the old man said, looking at Lázaro's grandfather. Then he turned his head and looked at Lázaro. "I met your father in the Capital City when he was a child."

Señor Villamayor got up to leave.

"Don't worry, I'm not going to say anything disturbing," the old man said quickly.

"Grandpa, is he the gentleman you brought the skeleton to?"

The man laughed. "A skeleton? I'd like to hear that story."

"All right, tell it then, if you are so eager to do so," Lázaro's grandfather said, and sat down again.

Another waiter had come back with menus.

The lady said, "No, Hermenegildo, he's just a child."

"I was awfully good to you, wasn't I?" the old man said to Señor Villamayor.

"Too good," the lady said. "I hope this meal won't give us indigestion."

"I have an iron stomach," Lazaro's grandfather said.

They all fell silent. More diners came into the restaurant.

The man started with potage de legumes, Lázaro had oysters, Señor Villamayor ordered Pavé de saumon grillé, which he barely touched, and the lady had ratatouille.

Lázaro wanted to ask more questions about the skeleton and the trip, but his grandfather's eyes had that dark look that kept him silent.

"We're going back home tomorrow," the man said.

"I wish you a safe trip," Señor Villamayor said, and snickered.

The lady thought for a moment, looked at the old man, and scowled. "The Carmelitas Descalzas convent is not in the plains anymore, and these days, nuns are able to see their loved ones," she said. She looked at Lázaro. "But just in case, one of these days, go to the Carmelitas Descalzas convent, you may find—"

"Nothing," Señor Villamayor said.

"I don't forgive you," she told him.

"Who cares," he said.

"I have lost the capacity to recognize faces, but I still remember all that you did. And above all, your voice."

"What did you do, Grandpa?"

Nobody answered.

The woman left first.

Lázaro's grandfather stood up, followed by Lázaro. They walked out of the dining room and into the lobby with its black-and-white checkerboard floor, passing by the Louis III armchairs and the brown front desk with the 'Concierge' sign on top of it.

Señor Villamayor told Lázaro, "I don't know how you do it, but you don't fool me. Are you bringing all these people back from the past to confront me?"

They rode the elevator and walked to their room.

Lázaro was beginning to understand. He was some sort of excuse, a channel through which the past returned to reveal something to those who surrounded him. He understood he had a responsibility and he shivered; he didn't want it.

Señor Villamayor opened the door to their suite.

Lázaro didn't sleep that night. The next morning, he stood by the open window in the hotel room, looking out at the Seine River. Such a different river from the one back home. In the distance, the steeple of Notre Dame reached for the sky. The blowing wind parted the curtains. Someone was knocking at the door. He imagined hearing the sound of the elevator doors opening like an accordion, going into the elevator, the doors closing, descending. They'd hear the sounds of their footsteps on the marble floor in the lobby; they'd smell the scent of flowers in big vases, they'd see the marble vault with a lion statue on top, a classical-style bust on the fireplace mantel, they'd hear the sound of his grandfather's pen signing the bill. Then they would take the cab to the train station.

Señor Villamayor went to open the door. A porter took the luggage; Lázaro was still by the window.

"Hurry up. We're leaving now, come on," his grandfather said.

Lázaro looked at his grandfather and thought of him as an old tree in the jungle, strong, tall, stiff, its bark difficult to cut with an ax. He knew his grandfather had done everything possible to help him get rid of his disease. He began to tremble.

Señor Hipólito Villamayor looked around the hotel room, at Lázaro, and then through the window to the outside. Finally, he walked toward Lázaro and set a hand on top of one of Lázaro's shoulders.

"Come on, let's go."

Lázaro crossed himself.

"What's going on?" his grandfather asked.

"I am staying, Grandfather. I won't go back with you." Lázaro grabbed the balcony railing as though it were an anchor.

"Are you kidding me? Let's go."

"I'm not going back, Grandfather. I'm staying."

Señor Hipólito Villamayor pointed with his right index finger at Lázaro's face. The bristles of his moustache were paralyzed, his lips tight.

"What? You're coming with me."

The air in the room grew denser. Lázaro looked straight into his grandfather's eyes.

"No, Grandpa, I said I'm not going back."

The wind blew and the curtain furled in between grandfather and grandson. Señor Hipólito Villamayor brushed the curtain aside with his hand as though getting rid of a fly.

"Why are you doing this?"

At that moment the bellboy, Arístide, arrived at the door. "Todo listo?" he said. He was smiling, but in a second his smile disappeared. "What's going on? Did you tell him? Did you tell him I'm coming as well?"

Lázaro looked at his grandfather through watery eyes.

"You don't belong here," his grandfather said.

"I know, Grandfather. I don't belong anywhere."

"Who's going to take care of the businesses? What if anything happens to you?"

"I'll be all right, Grandpa, you'll see. And you'll be all right too."

"Do you want to sell emeralds here?"

"No."

"So, what the fuck you want to do?"

"I don't know. But something is telling me don't go back."

"You will be sorry," Señor Villamayor said.

Lázaro knelt and tried to kiss one of his grandfather's hands, "Forgive me, Grandfather," Lázaro said lowering his head.

A blow to Lázaro's head made everything go dark. The darkness must have lasted only a couple of seconds, because when he could see again, his grandfather was standing in the same position and Aristide was still by the door. The only difference was that Lázaro himself was now lying on the floor.

"Why did you do that?" Aristide asked his grandfather.

Lázaro stood up clutching his head. He was dizzy. He felt unsteady.

Señor Hipólito Villamayor grabbed him by the lapels while he put his hands on his grandfather's chest.

"You'll obey anything I command," his grandfather roared.

"Not this time, Grandfather. Forgive me, please."

His grandfather shoved Lázaro across the room with violent force. They crossed the room sliding on the marble floor. A macabre dance. Lázaro felt he was a puppet; they collided with a small stool, a glass coffee table, causing a vase full of flowers to fall to the floor and explode. His body kept moving at high speed propelled by his grandfather; they crossed the bathroom door till his head slammed into the marble wall.

The impact felt as though somebody had cut his head open with a smoldering knife. His vision blurred and he couldn't see half of the room. He barely heard the sound of his lapels being ripped off. His grandfather was on top of him on the marble floor, grabbing his neck with his calloused hands. It was as if an army of bees had entered his throat. He tried to defend himself, but his hands wouldn't move.

Aristide yelled, "Arrêtez, Hipólito, arrêtez!"

Behind his grandfather's head, Lázaro saw Aristide trying to pull his grandfather off him. His grandfather's fist came up and smashed Aristide's nose. Aristide screamed and his face disappeared as he fell backward. His grandfather stood, his polished shoes next to Lázaro's face. He heard more footsteps as several men pulled his grandfather away.

Aristide knelt close to Lázaro. "Are you all right?" he asked, blood dripping from his nose.

His grandfather yelled, "No, stay away from him. He mustn't see your blood!"

Lázaro tried to move again, but he couldn't. He couldn't feel his arms or legs. He looked at Aristide's bloody face as he called, "Monsieur Lázaro, come!" Inside his head was a bonfire; he heard the marble floor crackling.

"The floor is collapsing!" somebody yelled.

The feet surrounding Lázaro scrambled to retreat.

Lázaro's head sank into the marble floor as though it were the soft surface of a pillow.

"I already know, Grandpa," he said. And his heart stopped.

Chapter 13

He opened his eyes.

"Il est vivant! Lázaro s'est réveillé!" someone said.

He laughed. Or he thought he'd laughed.

"How are you feeling?"

"Light and happy," he said, but the words came out garbled, as if he was chewing a big bone.

"What are you saying? I don't understand."

"Light and happy," he repeated, but his voice sounded strange and unrecognizable. He wanted to shake his head, but he couldn't. He lowered his gaze and saw that his neck and thorax were immobilized inside a hard shell. He remembered some strange animal, somewhere… He couldn't remember the word….

Turtle.

"What happened?" he asked. Again, his own words were incomprehensible to him.

"Can you talk?"

He was drooling and tried to move his hand to wipe his mouth, but his hand didn't respond. He wanted to remember something, but he couldn't.

"Poor boy."

"Where am I?" he asked.

"What did you say?"

"Where am I?"

"God, you can't talk."

The person who spoke was a woman. "You've suffered a terrible injury."

A man came in.

"Lázaro has woken up," she said.

Who's Lázaro? The name sounded familiar.

The man came closer.

He was sick to his stomach and started to gag.

The man called, "Nurse, nurse."

A woman came into the room.

"Remove the gastric tube," the man said.

She came closer, pulled a long thing out of his mouth, and cleaned around it.

He vomited and had a feeling that this was a repetition. Sometime in the past he'd done the same thing. But when? And where?

He fell asleep without wanting to.

He woke up and something was in front of him. He tried to remember what it was called, but he couldn't find the word.

The same woman he'd seen when he first woke up looked in the same direction and said, "What are you looking at?"

She was chubby and short.

He didn't respond. She'd said he couldn't talk.

"That?" she asked and pointed in the direction he was looking at.

He moved his head up and down.

"It's a tree."

He remembered a place with many trees, but where?

"I'm going to open the window," she said, and went to open it. Her words bounced around in his head like an echo. Fenêtre. Fenêtre. Fenêtre.

So, it's a fenétre. Window. Ventana, he thought.

Something in his nose tickled. He inhaled but his armor forced him to stop. He remembered the word scent. He remembered a garden somewhere; he'd stood in the middle of that garden and he'd knelt to grab something… a weed. The weed released a scent. The scent was strong, like the scent of cleaning liquid; one scent reminded him of another, alcohol, and another, formaldehyde, and another, piss, and another, shit.

Yes, I am in a hospital, he thought.

And another scent slid in.

The chubby woman was in front of him with something in her hand. "Soon, you'll be able to eat an orange," she said.

Of course, the scent of oranges.

He'd once had a slingshot that had been made for him from the branch of an orange tree, and it had never lost its scent. He would rub the slingshot between his hands and set it close to his face before firing. But who had given him the slingshot? He couldn't remember.

He fell asleep again. Against his will.

They said two months had passed since the incident. That he had made a hole in the floor and ended up in the bathroom of the lower floor, inside the tub filled with water. They said his name was Lázaro. He kept remembering pulling a weed and then he remembered when the weed snapped. He froze. The sound reminded him of a swing hanging from a giant tree at the edge of a precipice.

"NOO!" he yelled.

"What's wrong?" the chubby woman asked.

He looked through the window. The sky was gray. He remembered a blue sky with clouds of birds of so many different colors. Some birds would fall from the sky, struck by the rocks that he shot with dexterity. One more, one less didn't matter, until a blue bird fell at his feet. He picked the bird up. The bird trembled in his hand; he threw it on the ground and gasped.

"NOOO!" he yelled again.

"What are you saying?"

"I killed a boy," Lázaro said.

"What? I don't understand."

"I killed a boy."

"Poor boy. I cannot make out a word you're saying."

The ease and happiness he'd felt before any memories came back were gone. He didn't want to remember anything else. He wanted only new memories that began on the day he'd woken up in the hospital in Paris. He didn't want memories from distant lands. He tried to stop his mind, but his mind was a turbulent river. He had spent his life traveling from one place to another, meeting hundreds of people that he knew well, intimately. Who knew someone better than the one who witnessed their lives in the way he had? How many years had he been alive? Fifteen? That's what someone had said.

Another month passed. Time had turned into a rubber band: sometimes it stretched, sometimes it recoiled. He kept remembering the weed. He tried to dig the root out, but it held the earth as though attached to its very core. He froze again. He remembered a strange disease that somebody said afflicted him, but what disease was it? Somebody said someone had died… He did remember the phrase—temporary deaths—and he threw up.

His memories were like books lined up on shelves at a library. The first rack contained a row of books about scents. Dulce de leche. Rotten cadavers. A slingshot that smelled of oranges. Hospitals. Boulangeries.… The next row was full of thick black books with so many stories he'd witnessed during his temporary deaths. He remembered that he had tried to get rid of his illness, like when someone shakes a rag to get rid of the dust.

The next row was comprised of books of bargains he had made. He stopped killing the birds despite the rage. Instead, he'd walked barefoot on thorns. He'd crawled over rocks, hands and knees bleeding. He knew he was far from a saint, but he'd tried to become one. But the illness would not go away.

The subsequent row had several books: the books of hope, thin books that became thinner with every flip of a page.

Only one book occupied the next row: the book of denial. He'd tried to ignore his temporary deaths and pretend they didn't exist; he'd thought that he had imagined or dreamed everything, but people's faces reminded him that they feared his presence the same way he feared the sight of blood.

In the last row, another single book had been dropped carelessly: the book of shame, a book whose pages stuck together, so that he had to almost rip one away from the next to turn it.

And on the floor, among the garbage, lay another book, the book of resignation. He lifted it. Its pages were stiff and heavy. He threw it at the shelves. A book in the row of scents fell and bounced on the floor while the shelves swayed from side to side dangerously.

Lázaro remembered that his grandfather had made the slingshot for him.

The bookshelves teetered perilously, while the book of ambivalence appeared to levitate.

The last book, the book of anger, had pages that burst into flame when he turned them; but instead of burning up, the book grew thicker, stronger, its flames brighter. And it burned all the other books.

Doctor Bernard said that Lázaro's spinal cord had swelled inside the vertebral canal. He had turned back into a helpless child who had to learn how to walk, how to talk, how to eat.

In his young man's body, he endured a second infancy, with the impotence of legs and arms that he could not control. The cast Doctor Bernard had put him in from neck to pelvis was like a rusty suit of armor.

His temporary deaths, to some extent, had prepared him for this.

Disobeying his grandfather had turned him into a wreck.

He ordered his limbs to move, but they didn't. His arms lay limp at his sides like dead appendages.

He wanted liberation, lightness, the end of his temporary deaths.

As each visitor passed by his hospital door, he hoped it would be his grandfather. His heart would beat fast, but in the end, it was always someone else. He wished his grandfather would walk through the door and tell him that everything was fine, that he could go back home and do and be whatever he wanted to do and be. He wished his grandfather would come to rescue him, just as he'd always done.

He wanted to write a letter to his grandfather asking for forgiveness, but he couldn't, and he wouldn't ask somebody else to do it for him.

He remembered his luggage.

"Where's the trunk? Where is it?" he asked apprehensively.

"Calme-toi, calme-toi. C'est bien, tout c'est bien," Doctor Bernard said. "The luggage is safe."

So they had understood, finally.

"Please, bring it, I want to see it," Lázaro declared.

Madame Bernard came back the next morning with a man carrying the trunk. They didn't have the key so they had to force it open.

Lázaro recognized his grandfather's scent.

Since Lázaro couldn't sit, Madame Bernard took out a neatly folded shirt. Lázaro didn't know whether to cry or laugh. Indeed, Madame Bernard had in her hands one of his grandfather's shirts.

She took out a pair of pants.

Madame Bernard said, "Mais, si je croi qu'ils sont les vêtements de ton grand-père."

Yes, they were his grandfather's pants, and some other things, among them a pocket watch.

Lázaro started to laugh. He imagined that his grandfather, upon discovering he had Lázaro's trunk, would curse, would throw the clothes in the air. He'd find Lázaro's book, Pasionarias, álbum para mi madre muerta, he'd tear the pages from the binding, and then he'd find the emerald, and he'd laugh. After all, his grandfather was the lucky one.

Chapter 14

Lázaro's lips trembled when he saw his reflection on the surface of the object in front of him. He remembered the name of the object with difficulty, espejo. The word came to his mind in French as well, miroir.

"You're such a handsome man," Madame Bernard said.

Behind the mirror, Madame Bernard made him laugh when she stuck her tongue out.

She was the one who was there when he bent a knee, then bent an elbow, and then lifted his head. She danced in front of the window, sliding her feet on the black and white tiles with each of Lázaro's triumphs, and when he was able to sit in a wheelchair she almost jumped out the window with joy.

When Lázaro left the hospital, the cold was gone and the summer heat had arrived. His legs, which had been like strong tree trunks before the accident, looked like twigs now.

He went home with the Bernards as if it was the natural thing to do. Two men lifted the wheelchair up the steps to the main door of the house. Sophie, the Bernards' daughter, five or six years older that Lázaro, welcomed him with a stern smile. One of the servants pushed the wheelchair behind the Bernards. The wheelchair slid on the marble floor while Lázaro remained silent.

He was given a room on the first floor with enormous windows, a fireplace, and a wall full of books.

After a few days, Sophie came to the room with oil paints, brushes, a canvas, an easel, and started to paint Lázaro's portrait without saying a word.

"Drawing you is like doing still life," Sophie said, and asked "Don't you feel anything?"

"Pinch me."

Sophie continued to paint portraits. She observed Lazaro from different angles, walking around his wheelchair. One day she stopped behind him. Lázaro had his robe partially open. Through his pajamas, she saw his erection. She let out a little scream and left the room. Lázaro heard her steps in the distance and looked down. There was something that wasn't completely dead after all.

Sophie started to help the maids and her mother tend to Lázaro. She'd grab his hand and guide the trembling spoon so he could have soup. She'd lift glasses of water to his lips. She'd wash his hair. She'd comb his hair and shave the stubble from his face.

"At first, I was jealous of you, but now I'm glad I'm no longer the center of attention in this house. I've regained some freedom," she said.

The afternoons passed; the healing continued. Lázaro reread the classics, or allowed himself to become suspended in time and attacked by his thoughts.

Sophie did four more portraits, numerous sketches, and a jungle scene based on photographs she had and conversations with Lázaro. She was trying to free herself from the influence of Realism and embrace monsters, as Bosch had done. She came every day to Lázaro's room and showed him the paintings.

With time, Lázaro's movements softened; he no longer moved like a robot. Sophie started to venture into abstraction. Cubism had taken over Paris. Lázaro smiled, seeing colors and shapes that looked like leopards flying across the sky of her canvases. Or moons with breasts.

"I would like to travel to your country someday," she said.

"I might never go back."

"I imagine the women are exotic."

"Yes, they are." Lázaro smiled. "Do you like women?"

"Yes. Do you like men?"

He thought of his grandfather; if someone as macho as he liked Aristide, any man could be interested in another man.

"I am not interested in men, not in that sense," he said.

Sophie continued to paint in Lázaro's room where they had more conversations. Eventually Lázaro was able to get up from the wheelchair, but slowly, like an old man.

One afternoon he stood up, tottered past the kitchen, and came to a room whose door was ajar. He looked inside. Sophie was sitting on a chair. A young maid sat on her lap, legs wide open, one of her breasts bared. Sophie tilted her head back; the maid kissed her on the mouth; Sophie kissed the woman's breasts and licked her nipples. Sophie extended her neck, arched her back, and the chair tipped and fell backward. On the floor, they laughed.

Lázaro tried to turn, but lost his balance and grabbed the door. Sophie and the maid turned their heads fast and saw Lázaro standing in the doorway. The maid gasped and tried to cover up while Sophie laughed out loud.

"You got here without using the wheelchair?" she said between laughs.

Lázaro nodded. "I'm sorry," he said.

"Don't be silly," Sophie said. "I am not ashamed of nudity, nor liking women."

The maid dressed quickly and left the room.

Sophie was pure and genuine. She wasn't ashamed of anything. He on the other hand was ashamed of everything. He was ashamed of being at the mercy of this family, he was ashamed of having been abandoned, he was ashamed of his two different color eyes, he was ashamed of his illness.

"My father said the day you could walk, he'd remove the cast," Sophie said.

That same day Doctor Bernard ordered Lázaro's cast removed. Lázaro's chest was covered in white dust and his muscles were gone.

At night, when everyone was asleep, he went to the library and opened an anatomy book. The veins, arteries, and nerves, reminded him of the roots of weeds he used to dig out of the earth. The bones reminded him of plant stalks, and the organs reminded him of flowers. Where would he find the seed of his disease?

A drawing of a skeleton contemplating a skull reminded him of the doctor's office he'd gone to visit when he was a child in the Capital City. One doctor had said he was a mentally retarded kid. Another had said he was a leper. Perhaps he would like to be a leper. At least then he'd have a common disease. But in the end, like leprosy, his temporary deaths had turned him into a pariah.

His hands trembled. He imagined the blood inside the bodies. How long does it take for blood to coagulate inside a dead body? If he could survive his encounters with blood, would he be able to understand, to find a cure for his disease? Doctor Bernard had said scientists were on the verge of new discoveries that would explain phenomena they'd deemed incomprehensible before then. This was the twentieth century; everything was being discovered.

From the book, a piece of folded paper fell; he picked it up and read: Anatomy is destiny. Sigmund Freud.

Chapter 15

A few days later, after dinner, Doctor Bernard and Lázaro sat in the living room, as they had done so many times before. They sought each other's company. Doctor Bernard was a fatherly figure, and perhaps he saw Lázaro as the son he'd never had. Some evenings they would sit in silence; others, they had brief conversations; and when they least expected it, they would talk for hours. Lázaro listened to Doctor Bernard's stories about his patients, about his medical students, the learning, the teaching.

"How long does it take for blood to coagulate inside a dead body?" Lázaro asked.

Doctor Bernard stopped reading the newspaper and lifted his eyes. "I really don't know," he said, "but I've heard some corpses bleed during autopsies."

Would he die seeing a cadaver's blood as he did when a living person bled?

"I'm curious.... I was thinking about death. What do you think about death?"

Doctor Bernard put aside the newspaper. "Before you, or after you? Are you asking me that question because of what happened to you in the hospital and the Hotel Regina?"

"Yes."

"Have you died many times?" Without waiting for a reply, continued, "everything I believed has crumbled now. I do not know what to believe anymore. You've left me in limbo. I did not believe in God, but now, I see you, and I cannot stop thinking about God. I had gotten used to death, but now..."

"To me, death is a repetitive act," Lázaro said.

There was a long silence.

"Why do I die repetitively? What's to blame for my fake deaths? Is it my mind, or my brain, or something else?"

"I don't know. Who could?"

"Do you think we could find the cause of this disease? Is there a way you could test me?"

"We've done so many tests/"

"Another experiment?"

"We've tried, and failed."

"I know you've helped other people become doctors. Can you help me? I want to study medicine," Lázaro said. "Yes. I want to understand what's wrong with me."

"You say it because you're desperate. You might not find the answer."

"At least I would have tried."

"You'd have to pass the baccalauréat exam."

"Do you think I am incapable?"

"No. But you could be stepping onto the sacrificial stone. Those who deviate from the norm are attacked mercilessly."

They remained in the living room for some time in silence until it was time to go to bed.

Doctor Bernard said, "Lázaro, you've become like a son to me, you know that. I would do anything for you." He stood up and put his hand on Lázaro's shoulder.

"There's a human zoo in Marseille…" Lázaro said, standing up.

"I know about it. I rescued one of the children."

"You've rescued me too…" He was going to shake Doctor Bernard's hand, but the doctor embraced him. Lázaro wanted to pull back, but doctor Bernard said, "Good night, son."

Lázaro was taller; he lifted his arms and felt the roundness of the older man's back, and rested his cheek on his almost-bald head. A rock where he could rest.

Doctor Bernard started to walk away. But before he went up the stairs he said, as though to himself, "I've known two physicians who had diabetes, I've known another who was an epileptic; I even knew one who suffered from psychogenic deaths. But I've never met one who made a hole in a marble floor."

Lázaro stood in the shadows. His chest moved in jumps. He remembered the night in the jungle when he felt his grandfather's arm on his shoulder. It could have been different. He could have sat and discussed his plans with his grandfather. They could have talked about which city to send him to for his medical studies. Santa Fe de Barquetá? Puerto de Indias? Boquerón? Or perhaps somewhere in Europe, where he'd been getting his treatments. Eminent doctors had been trained in France, Italy, and the

United States. Why not Boston? His grandfather was rich. Lázaro could go anywhere he wanted. But they'd never discussed Lázaro's plans; it had always been what his grandfather wanted.

In the first letter he'd written to his grandfather, his handwriting looked like twisted wires. He'd torn it up. He wrote another letter, and another, and another, and tore up each one. In his most recent letter, the words stood tall, strong, and well defined, as they had been before the accident: Dear Grandfather, please forgive me, I miss you. I am going to return. I will be your accomplice. I'll take over your businesses.

He tore that up too and wrote yet another: Grandfather, I will return to find out the truth. Even if you have to die.

He never sent it.

Chapter 16

September arrived. The leaves on the trees were turning yellow.

For the first time, Lázaro climbed the staircase without assistance, as the Bernard family and the maids watched from below. On the second floor, there was a spacious hallway with several rooms. The Bernards and the maids followed him. He walked slowly to the end of the hallway and stepped out onto a balcony. Everyone clapped.

A month later, his muscles had recovered their full strength. But his room remained on the first floor. He suspected the Bernards were afraid he would open a hole in the floor and fall to the first floor, if he had another of those strange attacks. In the Hotel Regina, he and his grandfather had been staying in a room on the seventh floor when he fell through. He'd landed on the floor below and stopped there. So maybe the Bernards' fear was justified.

He'd never had a formal education; if he wanted to become a physician, he would have to finish high school.

Another month later, Lázaro went to the consulate with Doctor Bernard to request the birth certificate required to enter the Lycée Janson de Sailly to finish high school.

The consul asked about Lázaro's parents. He said they had perished during an avalanche and a flood in Sirirí. The consul said he remembered the town because of the emerald mine.

"How did you end up in Paris?"

"He had a terrible accident and his grandfather left without him," Doctor Bernard said.

"Did he abandon him?" the consul asked.

"It's a long story."

"So, you're going to be responsible for this boy?" the consul asked.

"Of course," said Doctor Bernard.

Lázaro answered the questions about where and when he was born: Sirirí, December 31, 1910, at midnight, so it could be January 1, 1911 as well.

"What's your full name?"

"Lázaro de Jesús Villamayor."

"Villamayor and? Aren't you the son of Hipólito Villamayor?"

"No," Lázaro said.

"Just Villamayor? Are you an illegitimate child?"

"What kind of a question is that?" said Doctor Bernard.

"A legitimate question," the consul said, and issued the birth certificate. "You should go back home, a lot of foreigners are coming here and the French don't like it," he said in Spanish. "This is no longer a safe land. I'm leaving soon."

A month later, Lázaro began to attend the Lycée Janson de Sailly. The students had already formed groups and he jumped from group to group without making close friends. The consul was right: more than once Lázaro overheard students saying to each other, "He's not French." But one of the teachers, a middle-aged woman, discovered Lázaro was a gifted student and took a liking to him. Soon, other teachers followed.

He invented stories about his origins, his family: his father was an Arab who sold horses, his mother was a Turkish princess; but he never mentioned his temporary deaths. Assiduously, he studied physics, chemistry, biology. The occasional sound of a plane in the sky seduced and terrified him at the same time. How would it feel to be suspended in the air, weightless?

After three years, he finished high school.

As a prerequisite for entering medical school, Lázaro had to do a preliminary year, a baccalaureate course.

He studied more assiduously. In his room, in front of the window that faced the garden, Lázaro sat at his desk, among his books and notebooks filled with notes. The hours passed by. He read the work of ancient and contemporary philosophers who questioned the purpose of life, the evolution of thought. Sometimes he fell asleep on top of his books. Some other times, he lay on his bed. History on his chin, religion on his chest, philosophy on his forehead—his hair splayed on the pages—and geography at his feet. Doctor Bernard or his wife would touch him on the back, or would lift him by the shoulders. To bed, to bed; he longed to be a small child again, so they'd put him in bed and kissed him goodnight on his forehead. Goodnight Lázaro, sleep well, rest, they would say before they closed the door.

The invention of the microscope had revealed an invisible domain; new techniques showed the presence of elusive particles—viruses—

responsible for diseases like yellow fever, typhoid fever, influenza. Lázaro wondered if the origin of his temporary deaths was some kind of infection, a particle swimming in his blood that multiplied during each temporary death. Diseases that had been fatal were now defeated with new medications, and the discovery of hormones—infinitesimal substances—had explained ailments that had previously been mysteries. Diabetes had a cure now. Was his illness caused by a hormonal imbalance? New inventions replaced old options. The horse-drawn omnibus had disappeared and more cars now crowded on the streets. He felt hopeful: so many new things were being invented and revealed that it wouldn't have surprised him if they did find an explanation for his strange disease… and a cure.

He took the baccalaureate exam—the exam that Napoleon had implemented for any French person who wanted to pursue higher education; the written portion lasted four hours, the oral section, 45 minutes. He passed with highest honors.

When the medical school year began, Lázaro became nervous at the thought of dissections. Would he die when he saw the blood of the dead? He'd read that blood coagulated thirty minutes to an hour after the heart stopped, and that, as Doctor Bernard had told him, when autopsies were done on the day of the death, some corpses bled. Does my blood coagulate when I'm dead?

Lázaro and the rest of the students, almost a hundred, walked through the door into the dissection room for the first time. After a silent moment, they started to talk and the room filled with the sounds of their voices.

There were other foreigners in his medical class, including an Ecuadorian who barely spoke French, three Asians who spoke it perfectly, four Americans; and five women, all French.

"Bonjour, mon nom est Jacques," a male student said, his wavy hair in harmony with his handsome face.

"Bonjour, je m'appelle Lázaro," he said, and they shook hands.

"Where are you from?" Jacques asked.

After Lázaro's answer, Jacques laughed, "I'm sorry. You will have to show me where that country is on a map."

"South America."

One of the women walked over and extended her hand. Lázaro stood up.

"Je suis Genevieve," she said and leaned against Jacques.

The class mingled and people exchanged names and brief histories.

The Ecuadorian asked Lázaro and Jacques, "Have you been to El Prado?"

Lázaro said, "No. What's that?"

"A special place for fun," the Ecuadorian said.

"Where is it?" Lázaro asked.

"In the quartier Latin, on the left bank," Jacques answered.

"What's there?" Lázaro asked.

"I'll tell you later," the Ecuadorian said and winked an eye.

Genevieve said, "We already know."

"Come on. Let's drink some wine after class," the Ecuadorian insisted.

"I'm not going," Lázaro said.

"Don't you like women?" the Ecuadorian asked.

"Mind your own business," Genevieve said.

The Ecuadorian stared back at Genevieve and hissed, "Puta mierda, cabrona!"

Jacques imitated the Ecuadorian's accent.

Lázaro laughed.

The Ecuadorian turned around and left.

"He's a pest. I can tell," Genevieve said.

"I've been to El Prado," Jacques said. "If you are in need of a woman, let me know," Jacques laughed.

"He doesn't need your help. Look at him. He could have any woman he wanted."

Lázaro reddened.

"Besides, aren't you afraid of syphilis?"

Jacques said, "Who cares? There's no problem. Syphilis is no longer a threat, we have Salvarsan 606."

"Do you two know each other?" Lázaro asked.

"No," Jacques said.

"Yes," Genevieve said.

Lázaro chuckled.

She said, "We come from the same town."

"All foreigners who come to study in Paris are rich. Are you one of them?" Jacques asked.

"Leave him alone," Genevieve said.

"Come on, you bourgeois, confess. Do you have any siblings? Do you have any pictures? What does your mom look like? And your father?"

In an amphitheater-type room, a table in a corner of the stage area was full of body parts: disjointed extremities, intra-abdominal organs, a rib cage scraped to the bone to expose its contents—the lungs, the heart. A torso with its skin hanging over the edge of the table, like a drape, completed the still life composition. Another torso had the abdomen opened; the aorta had been torn and the coagulated blood reminded him of the contents of a sausage. There was no fresh blood in the amphitheater. Lázaro's heart stopped racing.

Rows of wooden desks ascended in front of the stage; the smell of formaldehyde made the air difficult to breathe. Some of the students took handkerchiefs out of their pockets and covered their noses. A blackboard with data scribbled in chalk leaned against a wall.

Hanging on a wall were anatomy illustrations depicting brains and fetuses in wombs, as well as photographs of dissections. In one of the photographs, several students wore long gowns. In others, some of the students wore regular suits. An armoire with books stood against the opposite wall.

Around an empty table in the middle of the stage area were several wooden stools.

Through an almost-hidden door, a man dressed in black entered followed by a man pushing a stretcher. The room fell silent.

The man in black introduced himself—Claude Clément, Professor of Anatomy. He had a white beard, a white handkerchief in one of his pockets, and he wore glasses.

He invited the students in the last row to approach the stretcher. Among them was Lázaro. Professor Clément stood on one side the stretcher while students gathered on the other.

On the stretcher was a canvas sheet stained with dried blood, grease, and the remnants of other organic matter. Under the sheet there appeared to be a human body. A mountain range: a peak where the feet were, a valley in the abdomen, a plateau at the head.

The silence was palpable.

Clément looked at the students. He placed the palms of his hands on the edge of the stretcher.

"Welcome to your first anatomy lesson," he said. "Herodotus of Alexandria was one of the first men to dissect bodies. Vesalius, who wrote De humani corporis fabrica, was also a cornerstone in the evolution of dissections; without their legacy, we probably wouldn't be here, at the University of Paris, dissecting bodies."

Clément paused and scanned the crowd.

"When one face death, one wonders if there's some type of equilibrium in life."

This got Lázaro's attention.

"Henry Adams said, 'Stable equilibrium is death'. But is there such a thing as 'stable equilibrium'? Shouldn't he have said 'temporary equilibrium'?"

Lázaro's eyes and ears were wide open.

"I believe that at the moment of death, for an instant, no energy is generated; no energy is expended. At this brief moment a perfect equilibrium is reached. After that, everything is decay.

The anatomy professor took a moment and continued: "But thanks to formaldehyde, we're now able to stop decay so that bodies will remain more or less intact so we can dissect them."

Lázaro remembered the snake room.

He took out a handkerchief, removed his glasses, exhaled on the lenses, and cleaned them with the handkerchief. As the students silently looked on, he put his glasses back on his face and returned the handkerchief to his pocket. "Four hundred years ago, the English physician William Harvey discovered the circulatory system, thanks to his expertise in dissection and his knowledge of anatomy. Ever since then we've come a long way. Facts that in the past we thought were set in stone have been refuted. Beliefs have been overturned. What seemed unreachable has become tangible. Life is no longer a matter of faith, but one of proof.

Lázaro thought that for some reason, he didn't have faith.

"Nonetheless, what William Harvey said in the 17th century remains true today: 'All we know is still infinitely less than all that remains unknown.'"

Hope swelled inside Lázaro's chest. Hope and faith were two very different things.

"And now, we are going to discover the world of muscles and tendons and organs, those delicate structures that make us ponder how much we have in common with other animals."

With one swift movement he swept the canvas aside and uncovered the body that lay on the stretcher.

It was the body of a six-year-old child.

Lázaro thought of Ramiro. They'd never found his body. Some said he had escaped with a convict; others said he'd gone to the Capital City and didn't want to return, he wanted a better life, he wanted dentures.

Lázaro had not been able to say good-bye to Ramiro, so when another child drowned, he had joined the funeral procession. He followed the entourage without his grandfather's permission. A child carried a stick from which long colored ribbons hung. Several other children each grabbed the end of one of the ribbons. Two men followed, carrying the casket on their shoulders: one in the front, the other in the back. They arrived at the grave, set the coffin on the ground, and lifted a little window on top of the coffin that let the child's face be visible. The last view. The definitive farewell. His mother, a toothless woman, cried in silence. Her two rachitic braids hung over her shoulders, tied with pieces of cloth.

Clément asked the students to gather around the body.

Lázaro pictured Ramiro and trembled. His heart raced. He wanted to run away. He turned his head and looked for the door. He had imagined Ramiro innumerable times, like a ghost, trying to find his way up the cliff to reach him. His legs felt weak but he leaned forward. From behind, somebody pushed him and he fell on top of the corpse. The boy's nostrils were filled with cotton and his eyes, only inches from Lázaro's, looked like those of a dead fish in the market. Still, their oval shape seemed like a door to a world where perhaps God was waiting. Lázaro swore the child was smiling.

The auditorium laughed.

Professor Clément stared.

Silence returned.

"Who did it?" Clément asked.

Silence. Somebody pushed the Ecuadorian forward.

"Did you do it?" the professor asked.

"No, I didn't," the Ecuadorian said.

Jacques stepped in. "Yes, he did. I saw it."

Clément slapped the Ecuadorian on the face and yelled, "Get out of here! And don't come back, ever!"

"No, please, Professor Clément," Lázaro said.

"Why not? He humiliated you."

Lázaro thought for a moment. "He did me a favor. I am not afraid of the sight of a dead child anymore."

The auditorium laughed again.

In the afternoon, they attended a class on how to use the microscope. The Ecuadorian never came back.

At the beginning of the course, there were complete bodies, intact. Dissections were journeys of discovery, in which Lázaro traveled through mountains of muscles, traversed rivers of arteries and veins, trailed nerves, and unearthed bones. He learned the names of the anatomical structures: clavicule, artère carotide, cerveau, sinus frontal. Rib cages were caverns. Bones were alabaster sculptures. La crâne. Organs attached to surrounding structures looked like exotic fruit peeking from the bushes, and the heart, trapped inside the rib cage, was a wingless bird. Cœur. Heart. Cor. Corazón. He repeated the word. It was as pure as crystalline water, but with a softness that broke his heart.

He was able to remain standing over a cadaver for hours to dissect an artery, a vein, or a nerve, making minuscule turns with the scalpel.

"We've never had anybody do such detailed work, Monsieur Villamayor," Professor Clément said.

Lázaro thrived amid the cadavers and books. Along with anatomy, he would learn physiology and natural history. They experimented in the preparation rooms: using an electric battery, and soaking the cadavers in saline solution, they could make them dance like marionettes.

The work was grueling, and the students had to assimilate an enormous amount of scientific information. Others succumbed to the pressure of learning it all. Rumor was, a student had been found walking down the street in the nude, reciting the muscles and nerves of the body.

The three friends routinely got together to study in Jacques' room in the Marais, but Jacques and Genevieve inevitably paired off, and Lázaro ended up in a corner, staring intently down at the book on his lap while trying to block out the sounds of love coming from across the room.

During one of these so-called study sessions, Jacques looked at Genevieve and whispered something in her ear. She looked up at Lázaro and beckoned him to join them. He smiled, thanked them, and left the room.

By the end of his first year, Lázaro had become attached to the corpses. Most of them had been beheaded, with torsos open to expose the viscera, and arms and legs cut to uncover muscles, bones, arteries, nerves.

The prospect of having to face the living and their fatidic blood the following year disturbed him.

On the last day of class, he bent over the cadaver he had cut open at the abdomen. He wanted to remove the liver, so he stuck one of his hands underneath the cupule formed by the diaphragm muscle to find the hepatic pedicle; using his other hand, he intended to grab the knife on the table to his right, so he could cut the phrenic ligament, but it was too far away. He tried to free the hand grabbing the pedicle, but it was stuck. He felt a little pull, as if something inside the dead body was pulling his hand. He turned his head to see if anyone was watching. Jacques and Genevieve were dissecting the feet.

He pushed down on the rib cage with his other hand to help free the stuck hand, but he felt another pull, this time stronger. Then another pull came, softer, and two gentle touches, as though someone were petting his hand.

He panicked. He pushed against the body with all his might, one foot on the edge of the table to gain more stability.

Jacques looked at him. "What are you doing?"

Another tap on his trapped hand.

He murmured, "Let me go."

Genevive asked, "What did you say?"

Another tap. A bit stronger.

"Let me go, now!" he ordered.

Jacques and Genevieve looked at each other. "What?" Genevieve asked.

His body twisted as though someone were bending his arm.

"What's the matter?" Jacques asked.

The grip on his hand was stronger now. His fingers ached. He stopped struggling for a moment, and the pressure on his hand decreased.

He tried to pull his hand out with a single strong movement. His hand moved a couple of centimeters and then a strong force pulled it even farther inside the body.

A grave voice, almost human, said, "Stop fighting." It reminded him of a musical instrument, but he didn't know which one—perhaps a piano? Something solemn and at the same time soothing.

Though the students at the nearby table were absorbed in their work, Jacques and Genevieve had stopped theirs, and were staring at Lázaro.

"Did you say something?" Lázaro said to them.

Genevieve yelled, "Oh my God!"

A strong wave of heat flooded Lázaro's body.

The professor looked at Lázaro and opened his eyes wider, "A bucket of water. Get a bucket of water!" he yelled.

Smoke was now rising from Lázaro's chest and arms. The scent of burnt flesh obliterated the smell of formaldehyde.

Jacques yelled, "My God, Lázaro is burning!"

Someone threw a cold bucket of water on top of him. The water froze into icicles as it made contact with Lázaro's skin, and at the same time bullae started to form.

"He's burning!" somebody yelled.

"No! He's freezing!!" another voice yelled.

"Get a blanket!" the professor yelled.

A strong force thrust him away from the dead body. He fell onto his back and slid along the floor for several feet until he bumped into a couple of stools. One of them caught fire. The other one froze.

Everyone retreated.

Other students came to see what was happening.

"Did somebody set fire to him?" one of them asked.

"Help me, please," Lázaro moaned.

"Get away from him," another voice yelled.

Lázaro wallowed on the floor.

Somebody threw a blanket on top of him, but nobody dared to get closer.

"Help me, please," Lázaro repeated over and over, and with every 'help me,' his voice became weaker, until he was moving his mouth without emitting a sound. Time slowed, and he could discern every movement around him. He could hear every word that was said, even if several people were talking at the same time.

The stool fire was extinguished.

The students and the professor circled him, like crows in the sky.

Lázaro stood up and walked toward the door, smoke still coming off his body, icicles hanging from his hands and ears. The students cleared a path for him. He looked at one, who opened his mouth and said, "If I could finish that bastard, I'd do it in the blink of an eye."

"Which bastard?" somebody asked.

Lázaro advanced and looked at another student, who said, "I confess… I like innocent girls; they turn me on… Their peach skin…"

He continued to walk. Many turned their eyes away from him, but one didn't do it fast enough and caught Lázaro's stare.

"I asked someone to kill a beggar, so I could practice on him…"

Lázaro stopped.

Nobody moved.

Another student turned to look at Lázaro, but Lázaro averted his eyes, and continued to walk without looking at anyone. When he reached the door, he turned around. All the students were facing the walls.

He left the Île de la Cité and wandered along the Seine. He turned on Quai des Tuileris and stopped by the Hotel Regina to ask for Arístide.

Arístide had left the country. A long time ago.

It was past midnight when Lázaro returned to the Bernards' residence. Doctor Bernard, his wife, Sophie, Genevieve, and Jacques were waiting for him.

When Doctor Bernard spoke, his words were mixed with the scent of cognac: "This is what I was afraid of… They were terrified. They said they had never seen anything like it."

"We were worried about you," Madame Bernard said.

Lázaro wanted to cry, but he couldn't.

Jacques said, "What kind of disease is this? Is this a kind of a miracle? Can you talk to God? Do you see the devil?"

Lázaro remained silent.

"We know you're not an evil man," Madame Bernard said.

"I am an anomalous man," Lázaro said.

"I hope you understand. Of course, this is very strange," Doctor Bernard said.

"Fascinating," Jacques said.

"And where are your burns? I see nothing," Genevieve said.

Lázaro looked at his hands. The bullae had disappeared; soot covered the clothes that hung from his body in rags. He rubbed one hand against the other. His skin was like a baby's—soft.

"Do you want me to leave this home?" Lázaro asked.

The Bernards looked at each other. Madame Bernard shook her head no. Sophie did the same.

"They will ask us to testify," Doctor Bernard said.

"They will treat him as though he didn't have hands, or legs, like a cripple," Sophie said.

"Enough. It's late, let's go to bed," Madame Bernard said, and stood. "If you want to stay, you are welcome," she told Genevieve and Jacques.

Lázaro removed his burnt clothes and put them in the trash. He lay awake for hours. He thought of disappearing forever. Everything depended on charity now.

Sleep came crawling, advancing across the floor on its long nails, scratching the marble.

In the dream, he was walking through an expansive field of grass, and found his own body on the ground, semi-decomposed. A mob stood by his putrid corpse. They laughed. Lázaro turned around and started to run, and the crowd followed him. He tried to escape, but everywhere he turned there was someone laughing. He woke up gasping for air.

He didn't get up until late the next morning.

At lunch, they all sat together in silence. Lázaro felt there was no other remedy but to leave.

"Did you read the news?" Doctor Bernard asked.

"What for?" Sophie said. "Did Jack the Ripper return?"

"Sophie?" her mother scolded her.

"What are you going to do?" Doctor Bernard asked.

"I am a danger to all of you," Lázaro said.

"We all hide something. Lázaro showed it to us yesterday," Jacques said.

"I don't," Sophie said.

"You're the only one," her mother said, rolling her eyes. And looking at Lázaro said: "You gotta be strong, patient. You gotta have faith."

"You're right," Lázaro said, "I'm going back…"

"To your homeland?" Doctor Bernard asked.

"No, sir, to the hospital."

Chapter 17

The sounds of the jungle slid inside the autopsy room through the small window: crickets, owls, frogs. It was now thirty minutes past three in the morning. Lázaro moved his hand in between Araminta's diaphragm and her liver. The diaphragm, a dome-shaped muscle, felt like a canvas that separated the thorax from the abdomen. The liver's surface was smooth and slippery, like a rock that had been submerged in a river for a long time. Ligaments anchored the liver to the abdominal cavity. He grabbed the scalpel and cut them first. With one hand over the liver's dome, he cut the hepatic artery, the portal vein, and the ducts that drained the bile. The liver was freed at last.

Using both hands, he cradled the liver and lifted it out of the abdominal cavity. The metal table next to the slab was already crowded with the lungs and the brain, so he set the liver on the slab itself, next to the body. Now he wrapped his hands around the liver and held it.

Silence.

He waited. More silence.

He picked up a knife and cut through the center of the liver. The tissue offered little resistance. Inside, the blood vessels formed a massive tree. He cut the cystic duct while he pinched the neck of the gall bladder; the sound of something breaking startled him. ***CLIING!*** Bile leaked through the stump, green and thick.

Araminta was kneeling at the edge of a small pond where colorful fish swam and vomited. She sat on the grass, wiped her lips with her hands. Her face had lost its pink tone and was now greenish, like bile. The fish began to die. They floated on the surface like abandoned vessels, immobile; one eye looked at the sky, the other at the bottom of the pond. They rotted. A stench rose like green thick mist. Algae took over the pond.

"If it's not the liver, it must be parasites," Auntie Delfina told her. "I'll call the doctor." Her voice although impregnated by the tone of the flute, had the dominant sound of a cello.

"No, Auntie, please, no!"

***Cliing-Cliing*.**

"Why not? You're sick."

"I don't want father to know."

"Why?"

"He'd make me go back to the house again."

The voices in the rest of the dialogue were completely human.

An old doctor arrived at Auntie Delfina's house. He put his medical bag on the bed and asked Araminta what was going on.

Araminta said: "I am sick to my stomach."

"And what else?"

"I feel something down there."

The doctor hesitated. "When was the last time you had your period?"

"I don't remember."

The doctor asked her to lie down on her bed and examined her abdomen. "Please, remove your underwear."

"Why?" Araminta asked.

"I believe she is pregnant," the doctor said to Auntie Delfina.

"That's impossible," Auntie Delfina said.

"No. I don't want to," Araminta said and crossed her legs.

"I will send somebody to look for her father," Auntie Delfina said.

"I need to examine you," the doctor said and put on latex gloves.

Araminta started to cry. Auntie Delfina asked her if she wanted for her to remain in the room.

"Please," Araminta said and removed her underwear slowly.

Auntie Delfina turned around to face the garden.

The doctor grabbed a vaginal speculum.

"No, please," she said, but something was pushing between her legs.

"I knew it," the doctor said.

She screamed in panic and lay down. The doctor parted her legs using his elbows.

A vertiginous spell came over Lázaro; he turned his head away from Araminta and tried to grab something to stop his fall; the light went out and his sight went with it.

He didn't know how much time had elapsed, but when he could see again, Araminta was sitting on the bed, leaning against the wall, looking down with scared eyes at a cluster of translucent and bloody bubbles between her legs.

"I've never seen anything like this," the doctor said. "It looks like a mass of bloody grapes."

"Am I pregnant?" Araminta asked.

"No," the doctor said.

"Would I be able to have children?"

"I think not."

"Is she still a virgin?" Auntie Delfina asked.

The doctor said, "I think so."

"Poor thing, she's so pale."

"Give her plenty of liver to eat. She has anemia," the doctor said.

"What should I tell her father?"

"Tell him her menstrual cycle was off," the doctor said, and pulled out a small bottle.

"What's that?" Auntie Delfina asked.

"A tonic."

"What for?"

"To make her stronger."

A sharp sound against the window and Araminta covered her ears with her hands to ignore the tap-tap of pebbles on the glass, and the whistling that came from behind the pine fence.

"Did you hear something?" Auntie Delfina asked.

"Nope."

"Niña, you're deaf."

"And you blind."

"And you crazy."

"And you stupid."

"You're going home soon."

"Who cares? I'm not going to miss you."

"We'll see."

The chauffeur arrived to pick Araminta up at the end of the week; she looked like a ghost. He didn't say a word.

As soon as Araminta got out of the car, her sister ran to help her.

"What happened to you?" she asked.

"I'm full of parasites," Araminta replied. "I've been throwing up worms. Remember Joselito? I pulled a worm out of my nose, just like Joselito. Remember the flasks filled with worms the medicine man shows in the town square?"

"Shut up. Who knows what else you're going to say! Did you see the doctor?"

"Yes, I did."

"And what did he say?"

"He said I'm full of parasites."

"Why do you always lie?"

"I'm not a liar. You are."

"I know something is wrong. What is it?"

"Nothing."

"If you don't want to talk, so be it."

Araminta laid down on her bed. She grew restless. She took out a small photograph of the dentist she carried in her brassiere. His hair was sleek and neatly combed and he wore glasses with thick lenses. She kissed the picture and hid it again; she took it out and threw it on the floor; she stepped on it; she picked it up; she hid it again.

"If you don't let me go back with Auntie Delfina, I won't eat any more," Araminta said.

"Stop that game. She doesn't want you there," her father replied. "You will go with the nuns. Your aunt knows the Mother Superior. I've heard of several good señoritas who have gone to the convent. Let those nuns deal with your madness."

Kill him.

"Once you're in the Carmelitas Descalzas convent, you'll never get out alive," he said.

Kill him. The drum, the bagpipe, the flute, and the cello had joined their voices in a potent clamor.

Boom. Ñeeh. Fiib. Cliing.

Two months passed. Araminta helped the maids with their chores, cleaning the mirrors, sweeping the leaves from the patio, squeezing the fresh pulp of the fruit, watching the milk boil on the stove, feeding the chickens with corn kernels.

So it was. Auntie Delfina fell and broke one of her legs; now she requested Araminta's company. Repetitive cycles: Araminta in the car with insect eyes moving along on the road, the yellow road meandering through the green jungle. The villa with the statue of the virgin, and the garden that looked a bit less chaotic this time. During her aunt's convalescence, once again, the dentist's lips appeared against the window glass. Araminta forgot the perils of love and opened the window.

After a couple of months, on a Saturday afternoon, without warning, her father showed up with Chiquita.

While their father and Auntie Delfina spoke in the parlor, Chiquita and her sister went to the garden and sat next to the statue of the virgin.

Chiquita asked alarmed, "What's going on? Did you cut yourself?"

"No. Why do you ask?"

"What do you have there?" her sister asked.

"Where?"

"On your chest."

Araminta looked down at her chest. "Blood! I must have cut myself!" She ran off to the bathroom to clean the wound. Chiquita ran after her.

He swore he had seen the picture Araminta hid in her bosom was glowing, but now he saw pure red blood—but he wasn't dying.

The floor gyrated again. Vertigo. Araminta and he were gyrating.

Chiquita went to Araminta's bed and whispered in her ear, "The Carmelitas Descalzas will be here next week. That's why Father brought me with him."

"I will kill myself before I go with them," Araminta shouted. "I would be buried for life."

Boom. Ñeeh. Fiib. Cliing. Kill him. Kill him. Kill him.

"Help me. Chiquita. I made a mistake," Araminta said, and sobbed. "I'm pregnant."

"I'm coming with you!" Chiquita said. "Did you tell the child's father?"

"What for?"

"Maybe he can help us."

"No, he left for the city. He was a poor peasant."

"You're lying again."

"No."

"You cannot go to the convent! Sooner or later, they are going to find out. What are we going to do? Father is going to kill us."

"I am going to escape. Or I am going to kill myself."

Araminta appeared with a knife stuck into the left side of her chest. She collapsed to the floor, the knife pulsating with the rhythms of her heart, fast at first, then slow, until it stopped. She stood, went to the river, and threw herself in the water with a rock tied around her neck. She came out of the water, like a dolphin, stood on top of a rock, bit the end of a revolver, and the back of her head burst open.

Araminta and her sister embraced each other.

Araminta said, "I'm going to the Capital City, before he kills me. Will you come with me? He won't find us there."

"He'd find us," Chiquita said. "But anyway, before we even got to the city, we'd be lost in the jungle. And the river, you've always been terrified of the river. You don't even know how to swim.... If the wild beasts don't kill us, the bandoleros will.

Boom. Ñeeh. Fiib. Cliing. Kill him.

"I'm going to kill him," Chiquita said.

"How?" they said, looking at each other. Araminta began to speak.

Araminta's father fell like the trunk of a tree, knocked down by a lightning bolt, while Araminta stood at the end of the corridor, holding a gun.

For a moment he thought she had killed her father, but the appearance of an enormous ship through a cloud of fog interrupted this thought.

"How much would the trip cost?" Araminta asked.

"We could ask for help from someone who would betray our father," Chiquita said. "Or we could look for a buried tin can filled with money and dig it up. I saw him asking a servant to dig the hole."

"We could shoot him in the back while he rode his horse, or set the house on fire while he's asleep, or give him some poison, or..."

"A dart. Let's get a poisonous frog," Chiquita said.

"That will only paralyze him."

"You're right, we'd have to shoot him several times... A poisonous snake? A coral snake will do it. I've heard they are highly venomous."

They said farewell to Auntie Delfina, and as soon as they set foot back in the hacienda, they asked one of the servants to get a coral snake.

"What for?" the servant asked.

"None of your business," the sisters said almost in unison.

"I only want to warn you, be careful," the servant said. "If you play with fire..."

He returned the following day with a wooden box.

Araminta stayed several meters away from the box.

Chiquita gave the servant one peso and took the box to hide it.

That night, the sisters watched as one of the maids took the usual cup of coffee up to their father in his room.

"Do not close the door, leave it ajar," Chiquita whispered.

The maid turned; she was about to say something, but she left the door open and went down the stairs. They waited a couple of hours and went to peek into their father's bedroom.

They watched him take a sip and then set the cup down on the nightstand. He put down the newspaper that he always read before falling asleep. Their father blew out the candle. They waited some more and went in. Chiquita led, carrying the wooden box. Araminta came in behind her on tiptoe and closed the door. Chiquita took the lid off. In the darkness, they could just make out the snake slithering on the old man's bed. Their father didn't move. The snake disappeared under a fold in the blanket.

"Let's wait until the snake bites him," Chiquita whispered.

They waited for a while.

"The servant is going to accuse us," Araminta whispered.

"We will be far away—"

They heard a scream.

Chiquita took a handkerchief out of one of her pockets.

"Who's there?" their father asked, his voice sounding pained.

"We heard the scream and we came quickly," Araminta said.

"Something bit me," he said.

"Where?" Chiquita asked.

"Here, on my chest."

Chiquita came closer and started to prick her father with a dart; her father defended himself with his hands.

"What are you doing?" he yelled.

"What happened?" a voice from downstairs shouted.

Chiquita signaled to Araminta to go to the door while she covered her father's mouth. He tried to pull her hand away but he was already too weak.

Araminta opened the door a crack. A maid was approaching. "He's having a nightmare, that's all," Araminta said. "Go back to your quarters, go back to bed, everything is all right."

"Are you sure?"

"Yes, everything is all right," Araminta replied, while Chiquita continued to cover their father's mouth.

The maid was silent for a moment. "All right, then I'll go back to sleep, good night."

"Good night."

The maid's steps got fainter, then there was the sound of a closing door.

Araminta closed the door to her father's bedroom. "I didn't know you were planning on using the frog poison," she said.

"Just to be sure," Chiquita said.

"Where's the snake? I don't want to get closer," Araminta said.

They looked at their father. He was limp.

"That's it," Chiquita said.

The sisters ran out of the house. As they reached the patio, the dogs started to bark. Araminta looked back at the house. A light came on. The sisters continued to run in the direction of the river. The dogs followed them, barking, wagging their tails. Araminta turned her head. Behind the dogs, three men were chasing them. The distance between the sisters and the men grew shorter and shorter. Up ahead was a suspension bridge across the river. The bridge was so narrow and unsteady that they couldn't run on it, so they walked. Even so, with every step they took the bridge swung harder. Araminta looked back. The men had reached the near edge of the bridge. One of the men was carrying a rope that had been tied into a lasso. He threw it. It wrapped around Chiquita's body like a snake jumping from one tree to another. She tried to grab the sides of the suspension bridge, but the man tightened the lasso and she fell backward, making the bridge roil even more. Araminta held on to the sides of the bridge with all her strength and closed her eyes.

He saw blackness. Please, open your eyes, he begged.

As though she'd heard him, Araminta opened her eyes.

The men rushed the bridge and grabbed both of them.

Four more men arrived, carrying their father on a chair. He looked like a cripple, twisted and spastic. With his nose, he gestured to one of three men.

The sisters were panting; the dogs kept barking.

"Why did you try to kill me?" the father said in a languid voice. "The servant gave you a ground snake that only kills rats, you dumb girls. And the poison dart? I already took the antidote! Haven't I given you everything you needed?"

Araminta started to cry.

"Grab her," their father demanded. The bodyguards grabbed Araminta by her long hair and pulled her down to the ground.

"That's the way. Now you'll see," their father said.

The voice sounded so close that he looked around for their father, but instead, he saw that his own feet were dangling from a chair, and felt his lips forming the words their father was saying. Somehow, he was inside the old man now.

"Please, don't hurt her. Don't hurt her," Chiquita said.

Rage filled him. And he was astonished to find that he was also thrilled. Who am I? He couldn't even remember his name.

Araminta was on the ground. He felt not one iota of tenderness for her. Adrenaline ran through his body.

Their father said, "Put me close to her." They did, and he placed one of his feet on Araminta's belly.

"Stop!" Chiquita yelled. "Let us go. She's pregnant."

Their father hesitated. "I knew it," he said. His voice was sad. With uncoordinated movements, he managed to take a gun out of his holster.

Their father's body constricted him like coils of snake flesh.

Chiquita fell to her knees. "Please, don't kill her."

Being inside their father's body had made him inert. Useless. Incapable. A marionette. But it didn't matter. He was more indifferent than ever.

One of the dogs licked the father's hand, the one that was not holding the gun. The sensation made him jump inside the other body. The father pulled his hand away; the dog looked at the man and jumped back, growling. The father kicked the dog. Within a second, the dog charged and bit their father's hand.

The pain ran through his hand as though the dog had bitten him.

The gun fell from their father's other hand as he screamed in pain.

"Kill the damn dog," he said.

One man took a handkerchief from his pocket, another helped him wrap the hand, while a third picked the gun up from the ground. The dog escaped as though he understood the imminent peril.

The bodyguard with the gun aimed at the sisters, who started to walk back to the house in silence; the other two bodyguards carried their father.

As the group passed by the pond, their father told a bodyguard, "Get a servant. And get the horses ready too."

A colorful fish jumped out of the water and landed close to the entourage. The fish shook; its mouth opened and closed as though it were screaming. Asphyxia. Fish floated on the surface of the pond. Flies crawled over floating cadavers, their wings creating a rainbow of decay.

The sisters were obscure silhouettes. The echo of their father's words bounced, distorted. A soliloquy. But he wasn't able to understand, the words happened too fast, too many words at the same time. He let himself fall, rest. His hands were heavy, like anchors. He shook his head and he saw his own hands again; he looked around and there was no one else in the garden with him. The cello voice was quiet.

He fell asleep for five seconds. When he opened his eyes, the two sisters were walking. On top of Araminta's back, a transparent amber mass seized Araminta with invisible fingers, like a tumor. It covered her head and made her neck bend until she almost fell forward. She managed to center the tumor on her back and balance the weight on her shoulders, but with each step the tumor moved, making her stumble. She looked like she was about to fall, but she regained her equilibrium and continued to walk; several steps later, she stumbled again.

Chiquita tried to help her sister, but she was not capable. She was carrying another mass, different, whitish. Smoke in a jar, or milk in a glass.

He looked at the amber mass, composed of different textures and hues in different shapes and sizes. There was something beautiful and terrifying in it, as though it hid the eggs of monsters, or a terrible creature that could break free at any moment to destroy everything. Something inside it boiled like water.

"What is that?" he asked.

"Her pain," the cello voice said. And he understood. He was, too, a man composed not only of his own memories, but others' as well; he hadn't thought any of them could leave scars on the body. Was he too carrying an amber or milky mass that he couldn't see? Or would his pain look different?

He remembered his name again, Lázaro.

The autopsy room was still here, in front of him, with its brick walls. He looked at his pocket watch. It was four in the morning.

Chapter 18

Lázaro was to take physics, chemistry, pharmacology, and toxicology during his second year. No exposure to patients, no contact with fresh blood, so he could deter another episode that would draw people's attention. He was twenty.

Jacques and Geneviève returned at the beginning of the school year as well. They attended lectures on diseases, ways to diagnose them, treatments, and prognoses. They walked along the Avenue des Champs Élysées. Lázaro told them it was named after the Elysian Fields, the place of the blessed dead in Greek mythology.

"Lázaro, you know more about this city than we do."

He smiled.

"Have you seen the catacombs?"

"No."

"I'd love to work in the amphitheater."

"You and the dead."

He had the impression that Jacques and Genevieve had become one.

The first time they went to the Place de la Concorde, Lázaro said, "They executed people here, in the times of the guillotine."

"That I know, Lázaro," Genevieve said and laughed.

That year Lázaro, Jacques, and Genevieve were practically inseparable. They sat near each other at lectures in the hospital, he visited them in the Marais where they lived, and they visited him at Doctor Bernard's. They drank coffee at the Place de la Concorde and they went to Montmartre to talked with painters and poets. A couple of times Sophie came with them; she'd find a friend, and disappear for a day or two.

By the end of the second year, the temporary deaths had abandoned Lázaro—he hadn't had one in twelve months. Memory faded and everybody around him had almost forgotten about it, but he knew that in the past they had vanished for some time only to reappear with a vengeance.

During the third year, Lázaro was to study medicine itself as well as legal medicine. Danger. Hospital work was bloody work. It was going to happen again. Up until now, nothing could've prevented his deaths, as far as he knew, except avoiding the sight of blood. But there was no world devoid of blood.

On rounds at the hospital, doctor Dubois would stand on one side of a patient's bed and the students on the other, with the patient in the middle and medical jargon floating everywhere.

"This patient has cardiomegaly, I mean, an enlarged heart. I know this because the point of maximal impulse is low. It would normally be located at the level of the seventh intercostal space, but here it's deviated to the left. You can see it. We can palpate it, too," he said, and set the palm of his hand on top of the patient's chest; his hand pulsated with the rhythm of the patient's heart beats. The patient's neck veins were so distended that his throat looked like the trunk of a tree encircled by vines, and his eyes had a slight yellowish discoloration.

"The cause of an enlarged heart is hypertension. Uncommon in a man his age."

The patient fixed his sight on Lázaro and smiled. There was something familiar in the man's face; his swollen eyelids gave him the appearance of a toad.

Professor Dubois continued explaining the mechanism by which the heart became enlarged due to hypertension. He spoke about multiple failures: renal failure, heart failure, respiratory failure, hepatic failure. Everything seemed to be a failure.

As his first encounter with blood approached, Lázaro fretted. As usual, he hoped this would be one of those times when, despite seeing blood, he didn't die. The patient was a seventy-year-old man who had been brought to the hospital from the site of an automobile accident in which his arm had been almost completely severed. Lázaro was able to hold the man's head while the professor ripped the man's shirt open to expose the arm. Nothing happened. Lázaro didn't die.

During another routine morning round in the hospital, all the students gathered around Doctor Bernard, who was sitting on a chair next to the bed of an infirm patient. He was instructing them about signs in patients with liver failure.

He took the patient's hand and showed the students its flapping movements, called asterixis. The bile had spread into the moribund patient's blood and impregnated his skin, which was almost fluorescent yellow; the flesh had gone, his skin stuck to his bones, except at his abdomen, which was distended and criss-crossed by a web of veins ready to explode.. His face looked like a skull, and his eyes were two yellow balls immersed in the sockets.

"Am I dying?" he asked in a voice that seemed to emanate from a ghost. There was silence. Before anyone could say something, the patient said, as though the realization had hit him all of a sudden, "Oh my God. I'm dying!"

Doctor Bernard lowered his hand.

The patient vomited onto his own chest and distended abdomen. The disgorged matter was mostly blood. Lázaro watched with watery eyes; he heard the patient's voice, now crystal clear, calling him.

"Lázaro, come."

Lázaro's heart stopped. He looked around, trying to find someone or something to hold onto. There was a nurse standing by the door with a metal tray in her hands. She smiled at him. The floor cracked. There was no point in resisting. He let himself go. The nurse, Doctor Bernard, the patient, the students disappeared, and Lázaro slid into the temporary death like a leaf carried out by a wind.

The patient was in the midst of a throng. Lázaro walked in the middle of it, closely observing the faces, inhaling the scent of everybody, touching them without touching them. There was something very pleasurable about it that he had not experienced while alive. While alive he was terrified of being touched, as though the stone he became when he was dead could be drilled with a single finger, destroyed, turned to dust.

When he opened his eyes again, he was standing in a hole among pieces of marble, the patient's bed, and the patient, who was pale and rigid by now. The room was on the ground floor and he hadn't fallen on anyone below and killed them. The afternoon rounds had ended, and Doctor Bernard was sitting on a chair by the edge of the hole. Genevieve and Jacques were sitting next to him, she with a book on her lap. Lázaro thought about closing his eyes again and pretending to be dead until they got tired and left. They reminded him of his mother; she had been there next to him for most of the temporary deaths in his childhood.

Someone had tied a rope to a leg of a heavy armoire in the patient's room, and dangled the other end into the hole. He grabbed the rope and started to climb out.

Neither Genevieve nor Jacques nor Doctor Bernard said a word. She set her book on the chair and offered Lázaro a hand as he climbed out. She seemed an automaton. Lázaro had noticed that when he resurrected, people around him were in some kind of trance, as though some revelation had occurred that had left them astounded. As she was squeezing Lázaro's hand with her right, she grabbed Jacques' hand with her left, while he in turn grabbed Doctor Bernard's hand. Lázaro's three friends then made a series of comments, a litany, their words forming a chain as their bodies had just done, as if they knew what Lázaro was thinking.

Genevieve: "Lázaro, poor thing, we need to help him…"

Jacques: "…he's fragile, even if his body turns to stone…"

Doctor Bernard: "…even if he makes holes in the marble floor…"

"…even if he makes us look ordinary…"

"…he's just a poor boy who needs care, he's been abandoned."

Doctor Bernard must have told them, Lázaro thought.

"No," Doctor Bernard said, "I didn't tell them."

"He didn't tell us," the lovers said almost in unison.

They were speaking in Spanish, in the Tupian language, and laughing.

As though Lázaro wasn't standing before them Doctor Bernard said, "I had a strange dream. I dreamed I was walking in the Bois de Vincennes and I found my own body, decomposed, but my eyes were not mine, they were Lázaro's. Then a mob came after me, and I had to step in front of them to defend me, because I knew they thought I was Lázaro, not me."

He added that he had been a strong force in ending the reign of the clergy over the hospitals. He had turned away from religion at an early age, that's why he had become a physician, that's why he wanted to understand deviations from the norm, that's why he wanted to understand the nervous system; he believed the clue to so many misunderstandings of humans lay in the central nervous system. He wanted to unearth secrets in patients the same way Lázaro did.

Genevieve flinched. Lázaro looked at her; she seemed to have come back from a deep sleep. As did Jacques.

When Lázaro asked her about the conversation they had had moments ago, after she helped him out of the hole, she said she didn't remember a thing. He asked Doctor Bernard. He didn't remember either. Neither did Jacques.

All over the hospital, there was distress. The professors felt they were setting foot on uncertain terrain and they wanted Lázaro to be expelled, even deported. A recently appointed manager asked who was going to pay for all the damage.

Doctor Bernard reported this to Lázaro one night in his living room. He was concerned about the holes—what if Lázaro could kill someone on the floor below? Still, he had defended him.

"I told them, 'Over my dead body,'" he said to Lázaro.

Lázaro couldn't avoid hearing the comments here and there, usually when he entered a room abruptly.

"Can you imagine? Eleven men were not able to move him."

"Seemed like he was stuck to the floor. So strange."

"Yes, unbelievable, and after that, the poor man he was looking at died."

"Maybe he killed him; who knows what he's capable of."

"They shouldn't let him touch patients; he could be dangerous."

"Come on, the poor man was already sick, practically dead. He couldn't have killed him; on the contrary, he freed the poor man from his misery by helping him die."

He was walking down a hallway when a nurse came out of one of the rooms.

"Monsieur Villamayor," she said.

Lázaro stopped and turned around.

"Yes, Madame."

He recognized her; she had been the one standing by the door holding the metal tray and smiling at him.

"I want to tell you something."

Lázaro listened.

"Forget what they say. No matter what, I believe in you, I've seen the way you talk to the patients, the way you touch them. And I am not talking about physicality. Sometimes they tell me things. They say you are a savior, that you've helped them, like no one else has, just by listening. No matter what they say, don't give up. You've touched me as well"

Lázaro lowered his head.

One day in the bathroom, he found graffiti on the wall:

Lázaro Villamayor est un fils de pute

Maybe he will die forever one of these days. Let us wait.

Another day, attending a birth, he saw a gush of blood come out of the mother. He closed his eyes quickly. To his left, he heard a thump. He turned his head and opened his eyes, looking for the source of the sound. He saw a fellow student, an otherwise robust man, lying on the floor. He had fainted at the sight of the blood. One of the nurses ran and brought a handkerchief saturated with salts to his nose. The student opened his eyes.

So, like Lázaro, others fainted at the sight of blood. But, unlike Lázaro, this student got used to the sight of blood and stopped fainting. He didn't open holes in the floor either.

Neither Jacques, nor Genevieve, nor his classmates, nor Doctor Bernard knew of Lázaro's nighttime adventures. After dark, he walked the bridges under the yellow glare of the streetlights, and ambled over the wet streets that had been built stone by stone. He had heard people say that the Eighteenth Arrondissement was "forbidden area," a hotbed of thieves and assassins, and at night that is where his feet took him.

There, he discovered people wearing rags over rags, with putrid teeth, living amid a horrid stench, one on top of the other. The houses had smoke-blackened stone facades.

A butcher he passed on the street recognized him from the hospital. In the previous century, they'd have been colleagues. Soon, several men and children surrounded him; they sniffed the air like wolves. A blond child asked for money.

"Who are you and what are you doing here with your fancy clothes?" a woman with shoes full of holes asked. "Would you like to spend a good time with me?" She grabbed Lázaro's hand and he pulled it away. Her hand felt sweaty, sticky, oniony.

"Leave him alone, he's a doctor," the butcher said.

"Ah! A fancy doctor," the woman said and spat on the ground. "We have enough with the priests."

Men pushed him away. Women stood at a safe distance, where they could see him and he could see them. Children came closer. They surrounded him, and unlike in his most recent temporary death, being encircled by a throng left him feeling anxious, breathing fast, looking everywhere. He was a rat surrounded by hundreds of rats.

A ten-year-old girl came with a raggedy doll that she resembled. She said her name was Magda and asked his name. Children didn't frighten him. He crouched and said, "Lázaro." She laughed.

Once the children became acquainted with him, the adults realized he was not a hunter, so they allowed him to sit around their fires, or invited him to come into their homes. He went up decaying stairs, heard screams, and smelled the vapors of boiled potatoes and onions that escaped through the hinges and half-open doors. He faced the stench of clogged communal bathrooms. He heard more screams, mixed with the scent of liquor, and the sounds of languages he had never before heard.

He did not have to understand the words to comprehend the anger, fear, and pain. He heard echoes of slaps, sobs, cries, curses, which escaped through windows and doors.

He went with the children, who kicked disintegrating balls in the streets and carried muddy dolls. They shifted the dolls in their hands to grab his fingers. He sat on rooftops to see who could catch the moon first.

He had begun to help, offering rudimentary treatment, gaining their trust. Poverty was similar everywhere. Surrounded by the music of different languages, under the influence of the changes in seasons, amid the magnificence of the city, he found this poverty more melancholic than the poverty in his native land. Here, the remaining opulence of the centuries before the war was in stark contrast with the run-down houses. Back home, a shack in the middle of the jungle was just another plant growing out of a fertile land.

Then it happened. He was going to rescue a five-year-old boy who had gone into a large ring sewer, climbed on top of a ball used to clean the sewer tunnels, and fallen. Lázaro hesitated. "Is he bleeding?"

"No," an older boy said. "He told him to go there," and pointed at an adolescent whose face was full of acne craters.

Lázaro walked into the sewer cautiously, it was the reign of typhoid fever, it was the mouth of earth, and he knew the earth had an appetite for him. The floor was covered in dirty water and as he advanced, darkness descended. When his eyes became used to it, he saw the boy coming to him, limping. The boy had a long, bleeding gash on his knee and was struggling to walk. Somebody laughed.

When he came back to life, the boy was caressing Lázaro's face. He was standing in dirty water, surrounded by the stench of urine and feces, and he hadn't made a hole. He wanted to laugh, to cry. He took the boy's hand and stepped out of the sewer.

"You turned into stone," the boy said.

The child's parents, stood at the entrance of the sewer and reprimanded their son for not coming out with them; they had been terrified by the sight of Lázaro turning to stone. They were now screaming in the muddy street. Neighbors opened their windows and doors and came out of their homes to see what was happening.

"Turn the lamps on, quickly. We don't want darkness around this man," the parents said. But they realized the child was holding Lázaro's hand, unafraid.

He set the child on a barricade and asked for clean water and soap. He washed the wound. The barber brought a needle and thread. With stoicism, the five-year-old tolerated the cleansing and the passage of the needle through his skin,

One evening, a good-looking woman approached him as he strolled through the neighborhood. Her beauty disappeared as soon as she opened her mouth. She had no teeth and a stench emanated from her mouth. She asked him with a thick Russian accent to see her husband, a carpenter, who was shitting blood. But it couldn't be right then. She had to work; her job was a nocturnal one.

The next day, Lázaro went to the hospital in the morning for medical rounds. He was carrying a bottle of water. He stood between Jacques and Genevieve and poured the water between his feet, making a small puddle, and then stepped in it. Genevieve and Jacques looked at him.

"I'm testing something," he said.

He then looked directly at the bloody piece of cloth wrapped around the foot of the patient in the bed nearest to them.

In the afternoon, he went up the cobbled street in Montmartre to tend to the carpenter. Among his medical instruments he carried the bottle of water. The man was lying under a blanket on a filthy bed in a room by a back patio and Lázaro sat down next to him on the bed; his wife insisted on giving the man a glass of wine while she blubbered and staggered. Lázaro checked the man's pulse, set the stethoscope on his chest, his abdomen. He palpated the abdomen without lifting the blanket. The man moaned. His stomach was rigid, hard as a rock. Lázaro spilled the water, stepped on the puddle, and removed the blanket from the patient. The man was floating in a pool of blood. Lázaro slipped into the other world. And he saw. And he heard.

When he came back to life, the man had died and his wife was sobbing, her toothless mouth open. He hadn't made a hole, and it seemed this temporary death had been shorter than usual. The images had passed so fast, and yet he had retained everything, as if an entire year had passed with all its seasons in one second. It didn't seem much different from the previous temporary deaths: all was stored in his memory. He told her what the carpenter had not told her while alive. The woman was surprised to know she had been loved. She cleaned the snot with a dirty rag and threw the bottle of wine. She wanted Lázaro to help her find a 'decent' job.

Lázaro crossed the Sacré Cœur cemetery. Beyond, the others, with their tall hats and golden pocket watches, roamed in their gardens along the

Seine, adorning the bridges and streets of Paris with their elegance and glamour. Sentinel statues of Pegasus, lions and eagles, bearded men, beautiful women with perfect lips, delicate hands, voluptuous breasts and inviting nipples, angels with garlands of flowers and flowing hair gathered to testify that the nature of stone could be changed. He felt pleasure again imagining all the statues had gathered around him to protect him. After all, there was beauty in the weight of the stone.

Chapter 19

Lázaro had doubts; he'd always been skeptical and had discovered that professors could be wrong; he was learning a science that had sprung out of the Middle Ages and the Renaissance, but he didn't trust it completely… it hadn't provided answers for him so far.

Doctor Dubois presented another patient who'd come from a distant land; the patient had asked Lázaro to come closer and he had whispered something in his ear. Jacques and Geneviève asked him what he had said.

"Nothing important," Lázaro said. He needed to be alone to do this task, and that night at almost 12 a.m., as he had done so many times during the day, he passed under the archway with the words LIBERTÉ ÉGALITÉ FRATERNITÉ carved into it, and entered the grounds of the sleeping hospital. Inside the entrance was a courtyard garden, at the far end of which rose a building that resembled the Parthenon.

He turned right; his steps echoed along the corridor. He came to the building where the infirm slept, pushed the wooden door, and walked in. He climbed a spiral staircase to the second floor. Dim lights on the wall followed the changing angles of the steps and shone down on the ornate handrail, casting a shadow on the staircase.

On the second floor, he looked side to side; a nurse walked along the corridor, turned a corner, and was out of sight.

Like an angel who had descended into darkness, Lázaro entered a large ward where patients slept on beds organized in two rows. Amid the sounds of snores, breaths, belches, flatus, and the squeaking of mattresses, patients tossed and turned.

He went to the bed of the patient that had whispered in his ear something in Spanish, and that he wasn't sure he had understood. He was next to a window. The bluish light illuminated him. Lázaro moved closer. The patient was breathing with difficulty, and despite his swollen eyelids he managed to look at Lázaro. His legs had swelled to gigantic proportions. He had come from a distant land, and in a patient who was 31, as this man was, the cause of hypertension was a mystery. Indeed, nobody knew the cause of high blood pressure in most patients. Idiopathic, they called it. This man had ended up developing heart failure.

"So, you know my grandfather," Lázaro said.

He nodded and with difficulty, he spoke. "He sent you something," he said.

Lázaro waited for a moment until the patient regained his breath.

"What?"

"Don't you recognize me?"

"No. Your face is so swollen."

The patient chuckled. "Last time I saw my face in a mirror, I didn't recognize it either," he said.

The patient took a series of quick and shallow breaths.

"I'm Manuel. I've worked for your grandfather since you were a young boy."

"Manuel, of course, I remember," Lázaro said, and held one of Manuel's hands.

"He said, 'Let him see your blood.'"

Lázaro thought for a moment.

Manuel languished. "You don't want to make a hole in the floor and wake up the others?"

Lázaro had brought his bottle of water. He poured some on the floor and stepped in the puddle.

"Is there anything else you want to tell me?" Lázaro asked.

"You'll find out, niño Lázaro. Do your thing."

Using one hand, he wiped one of Manuel's fingers with a cotton ball soaked in alcohol and pricked it with a lancet. A drop of blood welled up like a miniature rose.

Lázaro's heart began to slow. Vertigo. He heard Manuel's voice, strong and clear, "Venga, niño Lázaro. Don't be afraid."

His heart stopped. The earth did not constrict him as if Manuel's embrace lacked strength.

He landed in the middle of the jungle. The trees breathed like an enormous green lung. Lázaro smelled the earth. Manuel was lying in a hammock. An insect landed on his face, close to his lips; its body resembled the bark of a tree. Lázaro remembered its name: the kissing bug. Using its long labrum, it sucked up Manuel's blood.

For the first time, Lázaro saw the world invisible to the naked eye, but not to the microscopy eye. Like a fish swimming against the current, a parasite swam from the insect's stomach and entered Manuel's blood. The parasite, like a human settling in a deserted land, inhabited Manuel's body, proliferated, built enormous structures in his intestines, on his liver's surface, attacked his spleen, and enlarged Manuel's normal heart until it was the shape and size of a soccer ball.

Lázaro's grandfather came into the hut.

Lázaro forgot he was dead and hid behind a chair.

His grandfather gave Manuel two rolls of bills and a wooden box.

"You'll receive the rest of the money when you bring the box back."

Manuel nodded.

"Tell Lázaro to remember the snake room," Señor Villamayor said, and put a small flask that contained a serpent in formaldehyde into the wooden box. "He must be at the hospital Hotel-Dieu. Tell him this box is like the armoire in the serpent room." He handed Manuel the box.

Lázaro came out from behind the chair. His grandfather was already disappearing.

Manuel's face was almost blue and glowed in the darkness. He was shivering.

"Thank you," Lázaro said.

Manuel murmured, "Did you find what you were looking for?"

"Yes. You have Chagas disease. I just read something about it, I'm afraid we don't have a cure."

Lázaro paused for a moment.

"Where's the wooden box?" he asked.

"Underneath the pillow."

He moved Manuel's head to the left and lifted the pillow. The box was there.

Manuel smiled and closed his eyes. The skin of his face became transparent. Lázaro saw the facial muscles, as though he had dissected them with a scalpel. Manuel's shirt, without buttons, let his chest show. His heart was an enormous ball. The two remained in silence for some time. Two shadows in darkness.

Lázaro opened the wooden box and took out the flask that held the serpent. He set the flask on the nightstand, crushed the box with his feet, and found the envelope that had been hidden in it. He read the letter. It was his grandfather's will, in which he named Lázaro his sole heir.

Manuel stopped shivering; his breath became shallow and irregular; guttural sounds came out of his mouth, and he looked up.

"I'm ready," he said.

Lázaro continued to make rounds and regularly see patients. He continued to study assiduously. As he learned medicine, he began to understand more about the elusive nature of his temporary deaths. Like Chagas disease, so far, they didn't have a cure. Chagas disease presented with some commonalities: enlarged heart, enlarged liver, but each patient was different: some of them died soon after the diagnosis, others continued to live. His temporary deaths behaved as if he were more than one person. The common features were death, his body turning stone-hard, and his skin changing colors. But there were also many variations. He had become rotten once, transparent another time; yet another time he'd been both on fire and literally freezing. Also, he didn't die every time he saw blood. But when he did die, he'd usually hear a voice just before dying that invited him. But sometimes he didn't, and he didn't know why. Furthermore, even when their voices did grant him permission to see their lives, some patients nevertheless resented his presence, as though he were trespassing on a world they didn't want to reveal. There was no uniformity to his temporary deaths, and little logic.

More learning came; Jacques and Genevieve were by his side. The diurnal temporary deaths receded. So, in order to see more about patients with difficult cases than he was able to do when alive, he began checking on them during his own private nocturnal rounds.

In his deaths, Lázaro saw the patients' pasts. Then, when he was alive again, he asked them to tell their stories. Most confessed, and they admitted to experiencing some sort of catharsis.

"Doctor," one woman said, "I let my father die in his bed, and I didn't do anything to help him. He was a bastard. I left before he took his last breath, and I laughed."

Lázaro didn't have to imagine her story; he had already seen it with his own eyes. The bed, the nightstand, the crucifix. He had smelled the urine and heard the man yelling for a sip of water; his yells had echoed deafeningly in Lázaro's head, followed by the woman's laugh.

"Thank you, Father, you've lifted a weight off me."

"I'm not a priest," he said.

"Sorry, Father—I mean, Doctor. You have no idea how relieved I feel."

Some patients remained silent, reluctant to speak, but they opened their eyes wide and hid under their sheets when Lázaro told them what he knew.

"Who told you, Doctor, who told you that?"

Even if the patients were murderers. In sickness, close to death, their souls turned softer and more pliable.

The sight of blood gave him the freedom to enter the world of the past, but once he had come back to life, he couldn't go back again with the same patient, no matter how many times he stared at their blood. After one temporary death, the door to a person's past was closed to him forever.

Then, six months went by in which he did not experience a single temporary death, although occasionally, even in their absence, his X-ray vision revealed diagnoses his professors had missed or misinterpreted. Depending on the severity of what he saw, he remained silent or he challenged them. When he did, they asked how he came to be making such asseverations, and he kept silent, until the life of a six-year-old was in jeopardy. Nobody believed Lázaro when he said the little boy had only one kidney, and also an abscess in the right hepatic lobe.

In the lecture hall, packed with students, disheveled professor Garnier—known among students as The Drill-Master—asked: "How do you know this?"

"I know it. We need to drain his abscess."

"He'll die if we do it."

"Maybe, but it's also his only chance to survive."

"We're not doing it. If he dies, it's your fault."

Lázaro went to look for Doctor Bernard, who said: "He must be in a bad mood. I bet he lost gambling." He hesitated, but then sent someone to look for a surgeon.

The little boy died with an open wound on his right flank, colored like an orange, dried as a prune.

Doctor Garnier said to Doctor Bernard: "See? He killed the little boy."

"Please," Lázaro said to Doctor Bernard, "let's do the autopsy."

The surgeon moved aside and Lázaro finished opening the body with the scalpel as if cutting through the belly of a salmon. On the opposite side of the table, Doctor Bernard, Jacques, and Genevieve watched his skilled movements.

Lázaro unearthed the liver and followed the anatomy of the lobes with his knife. The abscess was there, just as Lázaro had said it was, and the remainder of the autopsy revealed Lázaro's other prediction to be true as well: the boy had only one kidney; the smell of fresh blood and the putrid scent emanating from the abscess localized exactly where he had said it was lingered filled the room.

Standing over the corpse, Doctor Bernard asked, "How did you know?"

"I saw it," Lázaro said.

"How?"

"I can see like an X-ray machine."

"How is that possible?" Genevieve asked.

"Because of my temporary deaths, I'm sure."

"Is that what you call them?" Doctor Bernard asked.

Lázaro nodded.

"I wish I were like you," Jacques said.

Doctor Bernard, his gloves still stained with dried blood, said, "If you open holes in the floor, and set yourself on fire, and make people confess their innermost secrets… I guess we should not be surprised that you can also diagnose people by seeing their internal organs through their skin."

"What is this all worth if I didn't save the little boy? What's going to happen now?" Lázaro said.

"What if we all become useless because of you?" asked Jacques. "That would be something."

"The discovery of X-rays has been of enormous help to medical science, but you can do even more than an X-ray," Doctor Bernard said. "Drs. Desault and Bichat encountered resistance here, in this 'Hostel of God,' during the previous century."

"Exactly! But they weren't the devil," Doctor Garnier said, opening the door abruptly. The Drill-Master was so drunk that for a moment the smells emanating from the corpse were drowned out by the whiskey smell of his breath.

"Are you? Are you the devil?" Jacques asked, and laughed.

"If all the devils in the world were like you, we'd be in a much better place," Genevieve said.

The following day, after the students waited for him for a couple of hours, Doctor Garnier finally arrived, and they gathered around a patient. Doctor Garnier explained, "This patient has gastric cancer. We can palpate the mass here." He pointed at the epigastrium and, looking at the students, he asked for a volunteer to palpate the upper portion of the abdomen.

While the volunteer palpated the abdomen, Lázaro realized he was seeing inside it without having died or opened a hole on the floor, just as he had seen the boy's kidney. A slimy dark mass was obstructing the stomach's outlet. He looked beyond the mucous to realize that it wasn't a tumor.

"It's a trichobezoar!" Lázaro exclaimed. A hairball.

"How do you know this? By any chance, do you have X-ray vision?" Doctor Garnier said.

An awkward silence followed.

"Let's call Doctor Hartmann," Lázaro said.

"You might be the angel of death, but I'm still your teacher. I can fail you if I want to."

"If I'm right, the patient needs surgery, correct?" Lázaro asked.

"Perhaps, but not because of a hairball."

A student went to look for Doctor Hartmann, the Chief of Surgery in the hospital.

When Hartmann arrived, Lázaro said, "Please, Doctor Hartmann, notice the bald patches on his head. He's been eating hair for years."

Doctor Hartman examined the patient's head, auscultated, palpated the abdomen, and said, "Let's do it. If he's right, we can present this case at the next congress of the surgical association."

Doctor Garnier said reluctantly, "Fine. I need proof."

That same day in the afternoon, the students followed Doctors Garnier, Hartmann, and Bernard, along with Lázaro, to the operating room.

The patient was put under with nitrous oxide. The operating room was crowded, as though a circus spectacle were about to take place.

Doctor Hartmann, scalpel in hand, opened the abdomen. In moments, Doctor Garnier was livid and the students speechless. Genevieve, Jacques, and Doctor Bernard were smiling. Some of the students left while others remained.

The next morning, Doctors Bernard, Hartmann, Dubois, Garnier, and Lázaro, gathered in a conference room, along with Doctor Emmanuel Montpellier, a notable and rich physician Garnier had brought.

"You will expel Monsieur Villamayor," Doctor Garnier told doctor Bernard.

"Over my dead body," he said.

Lázaro looked at Doctor Montpellier and just like that, he saw a small tumor in the pituitary gland.

"Doctor Montpellier, you have been losing your peripheral vision, right?"

Doctor Montpellier was taken aback. "How do you know?"

"Precisely. That's why we're here together today," Doctor Bernard said.

Doctor Montpellier chuckled, fidgeted, became silent.

They waited for him to say something; he turned to face Garnier. "Doctor Garnier, we understand that this situation is not easy for you. It's one thing to be brilliant, like Addison or Hodgkin, but it's another to see tumors with a simple look.

"He's brainwashed you, too!" Doctor Garnier said in dismay. "All he wants is glory. He's come to destroy our order. Don't you see? The janitors now pretend to know more than us, giving medical opinions to patients and families. They believe they can do that because Monsieur Villamayor can do all those things they say!"

Garnier burped directly into Doctor Bernard's face. His yellow teeth appeared behind a forced smile, and he laughed shrilly, pretending to be jolly.

Doctor Montpellier asked. "Can you cure me?"

Lázaro said, no.

"See? Is it worth to have those useless powers? Garnier said and burped directly on doctor Bernard's face, showing his yellowish teeth while he laughed noisily.

"Please, try to remain unnoticed," Montpellier said.

Lázaro wanted to laugh. That's precisely what he had desired all his life: To be unnoticeable.

"Now nobody will know whom to believe," Garnier said with resignation.

Lázaro asked, "May I see your blood, Doctor Garnier?"

"What for? Your powers are useless," Doctor Garnier repeated, gave him a hateful look, turned around, and left.

Diagnosing pleural effusions had long been a matter of auscultation and percussion over the patient's thorax; experts could detect medium-to-large-sized tumors using these techniques. But nobody except Lázaro could diagnose small lesions that would not even show up on X-rays.

He knew people talked behind his back; when he least expected it, in the middle of lunch, or when walking to class, he overheard people talking about him. The remarks would vary according to the mood, the time of the day, the weather, the speaker. One day, sitting at a table by himself in the cafeteria, he heard the following conversation among a group of students and professors eating lunch together at the table behind him, none of whom noticed he was nearby:

"Suppose someone else like him appears."

"And what if other miracles start to happen? Because this is a kind of miracle, isn't it?"

"Yes. That's what it appears to be. But what if it's a hoax?"

"Shouldn't we be testing him? Something that could explain his illness."

"What should we test? His blood? His brain? His eyes? What kind of test? Maybe the microscope could help us figure out if his blood is not really human blood?"

"Miracle or not, he's a threat to the medical community and maybe to patients. Who knows what else he's capable of? Perhaps he can make us do things we don't want to, or turn us into animals."

"Could it be endemic to the mysterious jungle he comes from?"

"I don't care what he does or he doesn't do. I don't want him here!"

"Yes, I agree." "I agree." "I agree."

"Cowards!" Jacques and Genevieve said.

"If he leaves, I'll go with him," Doctor Bernard said.

"You can't do that," one of his colleagues said.

Doctor Cherubin said, "We cannot ignore that he is an excellent student. If we let him continue, and pretend that his powers will help us to advance science, perhaps this matter won't go any further. After all, he's not doing anything we can't do. We, too, can now see inside the body, thanks to X-rays."

Doctor Espaillat said, "Yes, we are now seeing what used to be invisible to us. Not only via X-rays, but also the microscope."

"Maybe a miracle will happen and we will be rid of him," said a defeated and frustrated faculty member in a low voice.

Another said, "We could send him to the new pathology building, that's far from here, he'd be isolated."

"We could kill him," said someone, a voice he could not identify, and he didn't dare turn around.

"And who'd do it?" said a voice almost inaudible.

That night, Lázaro went to La Place de la Concorde for coffee with Genevieve and Jacques.

"As aberrant as I am, I believe I have a place in this world," Lázaro said. "I don't know if I have come to disprove something, to challenge systems, beliefs… I don't fully understand, but what's happening to me now happened during the Inquisition as well. What people do not comprehend, they condemn. Here in this place, they guillotined people."

The Eiffel Tower stood against a clear sky. Lázaro took a sip of coffee and bit a croissant.

Jacques kissed Genevieve, then turned to Lázaro and said, "We wanted to tell you something."

"I hope it's something good."

"Oh yes."

Genevieve said, "I'm pregnant."

Lázaro smiled.

Genevieve and Jacques laughed.

"My mother is coming to help us with the child," Genevieve said.

Lázaro kept expecting the patients to be upset by his temporary deaths, on those rare occasions when they happened. But so far none of them seemed to mind, as long as somebody paid attention to them. This was, after all, a charity hospital. And thanks to water, he had stopped making holes in the floor.

The professors, occasionally, were confounded by a case they saw on their rounds. In those instances, they reluctantly consulted Lázaro, who often was able to solve the mystery. It was a difficult time for authority at the Hôtel-Dieu; the other students didn't know who or what to believe.

In the presence of patients, when Lázaro didn't have anything relevant to say, he was quiet, preferring instead to listen. His patients appreciated this. He studied the clinical subjects as everyone else did, and even without the powers of X-ray vision that sometimes came to him whether he died or not, he was able to see beyond the patients' flesh through their words, their gestures, the way they looked. In short, he demonstrated his own humanity by treating his patients as humans.

As with his temporary deaths, the more he knew about medicine, the more it revealed its elusive nature to him. The more he learned, the more questions he had, and the fewer answers he found. He could diagnose a tumor, but neither he nor anyone else knew what had caused a tumor to appear.

He completed his clinical hours, and at the end of each year, he took the tests. There were other students who knew more about the minutiae of medicine, those who surpassed him with their ability to memorize, but he passed the tests, and at the end of the sixth year, he began to work on his thesis. With the help of Doctor Bernard, he set up a clinic in the eighteenth Arrondissement. There, he developed programs to treat patients with syphilis using salvarsan, and to treat rickets in children using the recently discovered vitamin D. His writings stressed the importance of the Paris School of Medicine and the contribution of notable physicians like Xavier Bichat.

He was offered a job at the Ministry of Health, but he declined. He could have applied for an internship, the most precious goal among all soon-to-be physicians, or he could have started on the pathology path, but he didn't do either.

On the evening of their graduation, Lázaro, Genevieve, and Jacques gathered in the Bernard family living room along with the Bernards. The new doctors held in their hands the pieces of parchment that represented their degrees in medicine. The golden calligraphy and the seals were proof of their endurance and persistence. Genevieve held her son in her arms as well. Lázaro had become their boy's godfather.

While they chatted, ate, and drank, Lázaro looked around; all the objects told the story of this family—the sculptures, the tapestries, the paintings, the marble floors, the lamps, the glass, and porcelain vases. Lázaro's eyes turned glassy, and he lowered his head.

"I have to go back," Lázaro told the Bernards and his friends.

"Why?" Doctor Bernard asked. "If your grandfather had wanted to keep in touch with you, he would have come to look for you."

"We knew it," Genevieve said.

"Yes, this little friend is a wanderer," Jacques remarked.

"We will visit," Genevieve said.

"That would be nice," Sophie said.

"Will you come back?" Madame Bernard asked.

"I will repay all the good you've done for me."

They fantasized about going to the exotic lands, including Doctor Bernard.

"Would you take our son with you?" Jacques asked.

Genevieve hit him on the shoulder.

"Yes. He forgets everybody."

"Right. That's why he's going back to his home land."

"I remembered when you showed me your country on a map," Jacques said and laughed.

"I have something for you. Shall we?" Doctor Bernard picked up a leather bag from his desk and handed it to Lázaro. "You'll need this," he said.

Lázaro opened the bag. Inside was a set of dissecting instruments, a stethoscope, a sphygmomanometer, a reflex hammer, a thermometer, an ophthalmoscope, and an otoscope.

"On second thought, you probably don't need them," Doctor Bernard said. There was a pause, and then they all laughed.

Madame Bernard kissed Lázaro on his forehead. "I want to give you a Victrola."

"A box of music," Lázaro said.

A maid brought the Victrola. It was much smaller than others Lázaro had seen. Lázaro kissed her on both cheeks.

"A friend made it; it will keep you company, and you won't forget us."

"And I want to give you this," Sophie said, handing Lázaro a portrait she had painted of him when he'd first come to stay with them. "You were still life. Now, I can almost see your wings. Your eyes were narrower. Now they are open as though you were already seen those landscapes you talked about. Even the way you walk is different." She thought for a moment. "Almost like your grandfather."

A maid came in and announced that a Doctor Garnier was at the door. He wanted to speak with Lázaro.

Lázaro and Doctor Bernard looked at each other with curiosity.

Lázaro rose calmly and went to speak to Doctor Garnier, who looked more disheveled than ever. Without saying a word, the Drill Master extended his hand. Lázaro thought he was offering it as peace treaty, but then he saw what the doctor was holding: a lancet and a cotton ball soaked in alcohol.

Chapter 20

Once the Wright brothers gained flight for the first time, the course of the world was altered forever. Now that planes had started to cross oceans, Lázaro could fly for the first time. It was the fall of 1939.

The plane took off from Marseille with a sound of thunder that shook the passengers' entrails. From above, Lázaro saw the countryside: the earth had transformed into a puzzle of squares and lines.

For a man who could weigh a ton during his temporary deaths, it was a miracle to be floating like a leaf released from the branch of a tree. It crossed his mind that if he had a temporary death at that moment, the plane could fall to earth like a bird hit by a stone, and he would kill the nineteen passengers who were traveling with him.

A man of about forty sat next to him, traveling by himself, just like Lázaro. His Arian head sat on an athletic torso. They exchanged a gestural greeting. The infernal noise produced by the engine all but prevented conversation.

The man interrupted Lázaro's thoughts: "Traveling where?" the man yelled.

Lázaro couldn't make out the words.

The man yelled the question again.

Lázaro detected an accent. "Where are you from?" he yelled back.

"Germany. And you?"

"Sirirí."

The German's eyebrows lift. "Where's that?"

"In the middle of the jungle."

"My name is Hans Völlert."

"Lázaro Villamayor."

The yelled conversation was painful. Lázaro closed his eyes and cleared his throat. He was already uncomfortable sitting on the wooden chair, and the dreadful sound of the engine and the cold inside the plane didn't help, either.

Planes couldn't hold enough fuel for long trips, so they started in Paris and made their first stop in Dublin to re-fuel. There, Lázaro asked the German, "Where are you going?"

"Havana. Do you live in Paris?"

"I did."

Lázaro was overwhelmed by ringing in his ears. "Purpose of the trip?" he asked.

"I am looking for someone."

The next morning the plane took off from Dublin and they flew to Reykjavik.

"I'd like to see the aurora borealis," Hans said.

Lázaro imagined the dancing lights in the sky.

"What did you do in Paris?" the German asked.

"I recovered from an accident."

"What kind of an accident?"

"I broke my neck."

They left Reykjavik the next morning. The plane was again in the air: the rattling noise, the hardness of the uncomfortable chairs, and coldness.

From Iceland, they flew to Nuuk. They refueled the engine. The torture continued. The plane took off with a deafening sound and rattled. Coldness. Hard wooden chairs. Neck pain.

After a couple of hours, Hans yelled: "Greenland is the largest island in the world and yet it doesn't have a lot of people. I should have remained there."

The infernal noise didn't cease.

From Nuuk, they took off for Halifax. More rattling. Tiredness. More coldness. Lázaro, Hans, and the other passengers were covered in blankets.

"What do you do?" Hans asked.

"Nothing."

While they were on the ground in Halifax, another short conversation ensued:

"We're exactly halfway between my homeland and the North Pole," Lázaro said.

"Where's your home?"

"Right on the Equator. The land of primal impulses."

"That sounds exotic. I deem the jungle mysterious." He paused. "Maybe I should go there to die." Hans confided almost in a secretive way, "I suffer from a strange disease."

Lázaro's heart skipped a beat.

"What kind of strange disease?"

"One that defies nomenclature."

"Try me."

After a moment, Hans said: "In the end, life is a mortal disease. We all have to die… Sooner or later."

The next morning the plane was again in the air. Torture in Hades.

They flew to Boston without speaking. Eyes closed, pretending to sleep.

Another night, another short conversation on land:

"Every year, there's a marathon here," the German said.

"Are you an athlete?" He looked as if he was.

"No, I was born with this façade."

Lázaro shifted in his seat, ready to endure another takeoff.

From Boston, they flew to Baltimore. Lázaro's ears rang constantly.

"I am good at guessing," the German said when they landed and the plane stopped. "And you? What's your gift?"

"Guess."

"I guess you're a lonely man."

"I guess you can do better than that."

"I guess you are afraid of death."

"You're pulling my leg. Who's not afraid of death?"

"And if we have more than one life?" the German said, and continued without pause, "I guess you're an orphan."

"That's better," Lázaro said. "I am good at making holes in the ground."

Hans was pensive. "Are you an undertaker?"

Lázaro laughed.

From Baltimore, they flew to Atlanta. The airport was in the middle of wide-open land surrounded by grass where cows roamed.

From Atlanta, they flew to Miami.

"There's a casino here in Miami, the Smith's casino. Do you want to go there for a drink?"

"I don't drink," Lázaro said, "and I don't gamble, either."

They walked along the beach and Hans stopped at a religious shop and bought a rosary made out of rose petals. They continued to walk until they arrived at Smith's Casino, where men in tuxedos and women in dresses with square shoulders populated the room.

"Rum punch, please," the German said, as they sat side by side on stools at the bar.

Lázaro had a Coca-Cola and remained silent as the Dorsey Brothers Orchestra played.

"We're going our separate ways in Havana," Hans said.

"I need to take a ship or a boat to Boca de Buritaca," Lázaro said.

"Boca de Buritaca? I need to go there, too!"

"I thought you were going to Havana."

"I didn't think you were going to such an unknown part of the world."

"Finally, I guess you're not a good guesser," Lázaro said.

They laughed.

Among the sounds of conversations, the music, the clanking of crystal glasses, and the sliding and tapping of dancing feet, Hans' voice reached Lázaro's ears: "I'm going to the desert in search of a nun…"

Lázaro's ears perked up.

"They say she performs miracles."

"So, you believe a miracle is going to cure you of your strange disease?" Lázaro asked.

Hans nodded and looked directly at Lázaro's eyes. "Do you know the term for two different-colored eyes?"

Although Lázaro knew, he remained silent.

"Heterochromia."

"Are you a doctor?" Lázaro asked.

"Yes."

Instead of saying he was a doctor too, Lázaro asked, "What kind of strange disease do you suffer from?"

"One you wouldn't believe," Hans said.

"Try me," Lázaro said.

"I bet you haven't seen anything like mine."

"Try."

Hans was silent for a moment. "I can see the future," he said.

"I can see the past."

"Your talent is memory then. How far back can you remember?"

Lázaro said, "I don't know if it's my first recollection, but every time I think of the past, I cannot avoid remembering living people covered with mud."

"How far is the desert from Boca de Buritaca? I've never heard of it," Lázaro said.

"In the Guajira peninsula," Hans said. "I heard something about the Wayuus. They are at war with the people who stole their land."

"It's always been like that. Same thing with the Indians in the jungle; I hope one day they finally win."

From Havana they set sail at night on a medium-sized boat. The next morning, they opened their eyes and watched as the port grew closer.

The scent of the land of primary impulses seemed to grow stronger; that familiar scent Lázaro had never forgotten, even when he was passing by a fragrant boulangerie or patisserie, or passing through a group of people emitting the aroma of perfumes.

A small crowd waited on the dock for the ship's arrival. Lázaro's heart jolted; he thought he had seen his grandfather in the crowd, but when he looked again, he wasn't there. He felt empty, and then, moments later, relieved.

As soon as they stepped onto land, the travelers received bad news. An earthquake had destroyed the main road and the railroad to the Capital City; repairs were expected to take months. The river was the only other option, but pirates had been attacking the boats and killing people.

The small crowd reacted like an amorphous mass: in some spots there was overt movement, almost an explosion, in others quivering, and in others, paralysis.

"When will the railroad be repaired?" a gentleman asked.

"Who knows," a woman next to him said. "You know how things are in this country."

"Oh my God. How could this be possible?" an old woman asked, "I don't want to die far away from my husband."

The sun had started to rise in the sky, and the Indians started to arrive, ready to carry the passengers' luggage. Hans was trying to make arrangements to travel north, but he was having difficulty communicating with the Indians. Lázaro tried to help, but he didn't understand their dialect, and the Indians spoke in broken Spanish.

An Indian dressed in a shirt, trousers, and leather shoes said, "Go north? Desert and cross border."

"Is it a good idea to cross the border?" Hans said.

"Go south, take boat along river, cross back. There, boat take you north, you get next port."

The Indians had brought donkeys in case some passengers wanted to go to the next town to spend the night. Part of the crowd decided to wait for a miracle and some decided to follow the Indian who knew the other route. Lázaro took his two suitcases and joined the small caravan heading north, along with the German. An hour into their journey, a small truck came upon the group, and the most aggressive among them jumped in it.

An Indian yelled to Hans, "Señor! Señor!" and waved for him to follow him to the truck.

Hans headed for the truck. Lázaro yelled, "Good luck!"

"Same to you!" Hans yelled back. "I will find the nun who performs miracles soon. She's my last hope. My days are numbered."

"Where's she?" Lázaro asked.

Lázaro barely heard his reply: "The Nazareth oasis."

"I hope you find her," Lázaro said, and he wondered if he could help him, but a mouthful of dust and the heavy scent of half-burned gas made him choke.

When the dust cloud dissipated, Lázaro saw the truck disappearing behind a dune. It crossed his mind that perhaps, like a cat, he too had a certain number of lives. But how many?

Chapter 21

Lázaro sat on a rickety bus that undulated like a worm along a dusty terra-cotta road. On his left, white piles of salt bordered the ocean that ended in a distant blue line; on the right, his eyes met the desert. Ahead, in the distance, ocean and desert fused, while a pink cloud of flamingoes crossed the sky.

The bus sputtered to a stop and the driver announced, "I've run out of gas."

A wave of blame poured over him.

"Dumbass," somebody said.

"It's gotta be a leak in the tank," the driver said in his own defense. "I swear I put

enough gas in yesterday. We'll have to wait for somebody to pass."

"Unbelievable," a woman said.

Lázaro asked if there was a village nearby.

"Yes, ahead. You'd have to walk along the shore," the driver said, "but it's a long walk."

"How far is the Nazareth Oasis?" Lázaro asked.

"Ayayay, that's really far, very far up north."

Lázaro took his two suitcases and walked away from the bus. He walked along the coastline for about an hour. By then, thousands of luminous eyes blinked in the celestial vault. The moon painted a cone of silver light on the surface of the ocean. He sat on the sand, took out a canteen, and gulped some water.

He stood, grabbed his suitcases, and continued to walk for another hour, until the shadow of a solitary tree appeared in the distance.

He got closer. It was an almost desiccated tree, with hens perched on its branches like plump feathery flowers.

He lay down on the cool, soft sand, rested his head on one of the suitcases, and covered himself with his linen jacket. The wind swirled around him and created small sand storms that left him coated in glitter.

When he opened his eyes, an Indian boy was looking at him. Behind the boy's face, the sky was beginning to ignite. Lázaro got up and shook his head; the sand fell back to the ground in minuscule streams.

The little boy told him something in wayuunaiki, a dialect that Lázaro could not understand. He replied in French, instinctively. The little boy started to laugh and grabbed one of Lázaro's hands, trying to pull him away from the ocean. Lázaro took his suitcases and followed him. They walked a short distance until they came to a hut. A skeletal tree gave off an equally skeletal shadow; under the tree, a rudimentary bench sat in front of an arbor where, over a plank, a fire came up through three rocks and licked a skillet. Next to the skillet, a kettle that had turned black from thousands of uses gave off the scent of coffee. To one side of this outdoor kitchen, a hammock hung.

A Wayuu woman, her face painted in colors, wearing a long colorful dress, came into the kitchen carrying a thick bundle of twigs on her head. As soon as she saw Lázaro, she froze. The little boy said something. The only word Lázaro understood was mamá. The woman said something also.

"Buenos días," Lázaro said.

A Wayuu man wearing a guayuco came out of the back room. The guayuco reminded Lázaro of Tarzan's loincloth. That was the only thing the Indian man had in common with Tarzan.

The woman and the man exchanged words in their language and then looked at Lázaro. The woman spoke in broken Spanish that Lázaro had difficulty understanding. She took some eggs and cracked them in the skillet. Lázaro's stomach growled, reminding him he hadn't eaten in more than a day.

The woman took the skillet away from the fire and grabbed two clay plates. In one she put a portion of the eggs, and filled a cup with freshly brewed coffee, gave it to Lázaro. He devoured the eggs and took a first sip. The woman put the rest of the eggs in the other plate, and she, the man, and the little boy ate from it without hurry.

The man took one of Lázaro's suitcases and opened it. He tried on one of Lázaro's shirts, a pair of pants, and shoes. His ample feet didn't quite fit, so he took the shoes off and extended his arms. Lázaro smiled. The man looked like a scarecrow. He looked at his feet and continued to speak in his dialect. He kept Lázaro's shirt, took the pants off, and threw them back in the suitcase. He noticed the Victrola, took it out, and examined it. Lázaro was about to show them how it worked when the little boy opened the other suitcase, took one of Lázaro's books, and opened it. He studied it for a moment and then he ran to show it to his parents.

The image in the anatomy book depicting all the muscles in the body seen from the front scared them as though they had seen a phantom. The man looked at Lázaro and spoke to the woman, pointing at the book. He walked around like a dog sniffing the air. The woman told him something and then took the little boy by the hand and went inside the hut.

Lázaro was about to leave, but the little boy came running after him, and the mother came running after the little boy, and the father after the mother. The little boy hid behind Lázaro; the mother and the father stopped in front of Lázaro. They gesticulated and yelled at the boy, who wouldn't give up the shield of Lázaro's legs.

Lázaro lifted the boy in his arms. The man and the woman took a couple of steps backward and started arguing. Lázaro extended his arms, offering the boy, who resisted, arching his body and kicking the air. Lázaro set the little boy down on the ground and sat on a wooden bench in front of the hut. The woman stood near the entrance. The boy went to one of the suitcases, took out the leather bag Doctor Bernard had given Lázaro, and dropped it on the ground. Several medical instruments fell out. The woman and the man hurried inside the hut, pulling the little boy with them again.

Lázaro folded his clothes, picked up the shoes, put them back in the suitcase, and packed the instruments. He was about to leave again when the little boy came running after him, once more followed by his parents. The boy hid behind Lázaro yet again; the mother and the father looked at each other. The woman went back to the kitchen and the man started to walk along the shore.

Lázaro and the boy sat on the bench, and soon they were out in the sand, playing with shells.

The man returned carrying several fish. The woman got up from the hammock and started preparing the fish. When lunch was ready, Lázaro started to devour the fish, but almost choked on a fish bone. The Indians laughed.

After lunch, the woman pointed at the hammock while she stared at Lázaro. Lázaro declined, inviting her to take the hammock, but she brought a palm mat and lay down next to the man; the boy lay next to his mother.

Lázaro lay down in the hammock.

When he awoke, he found the little boy had taken out the stethoscope from the medical bag and was playing with it. Lázaro signaled for him to come closer, put the stethoscope's ear tips in the little boy's ears, and set the diaphragm on the little boy's heart. The little boy took a moment to listen, smiled, and set the stethoscope on Lázaro's chest. Lázaro directed the little boy's hands to an area where he knew his heart would sound stronger. The little boy listened and laughed; he climbed into the hammock and fell asleep on top of Lázaro, listening to Lázaro's heart.

Lázaro looked in the direction of the ocean. Little crabs ran away from the hens near the shore.

On the mat, the Indian mother, still with her eyes closed, groped for the boy. When she did not find him, she opened her eyes. Her little boy was sleeping in Lázaro's arms. She sat for a moment. Lázaro was about to say something, but she lay down again and embraced her husband.

Two days later, when the sun was at its zenith, a ranchero passed by the hut on his horse. When he saw Lázaro, he stopped his horse and said, "Buenos días, señor."

"Buenos días," Lázaro replied.

"Excuse me," the man said, looking at Lázaro from head to toe. "I haven't seen you before. Where are you from?"

"Sirirí."

"That far?" The man extended his hand and introduced himself.

The Indians saw the ranchero and went into the hut. The little boy stayed outside, playing with a battered toy car.

Lázaro asked the ranchero if he knew where to buy a tent. The man hesitated. "That's not gonna be easy, but let me see what I can do," he said.

The man took his hat off, said good-bye, and started to ride away.

Lázaro ran after him and took out some money from one of his pockets, "How much would it be?"

The man held the horse and said, "You're the second foreigner I've seen in the last week. Señor, that money is no good here. See you later."

Two weeks later, the man reappeared with a military tent. "I bought it from a fisherman," he said and threw the tent to the ground.

"How much is it?" Lázaro asked.

The canvas was mottled, greenish, and brownish. Folded, it was the size of one of Lázaro's suitcases and it weighed a ton.

"It wasn't that much. The man stole it from the army."

The man had a bulge in the front of his neck. From below, Lázaro thought it was a goiter, but he didn't remember having seen it during the previous encounter.

"This damn neck is killing me," the ranchero said.

Lázaro thought twice about speaking up, but said, "Can I examine it?"

The ranchero looked at Lázaro and took a moment. "The shaman did nothing," the ranchero said as he got off the horse.

As Lázaro got closer, the bulge in the center of the man's neck, on top of his thyroid gland, looked ready to burst.

He palpated the mass and said, "That looks like an abscess. I'll try to help you."

He got the leather bag, took out a surgical knife and a pair of rubber gloves. As best as he could, he requested that the woman set a pot filled with water on the fire to boil. He put the knife in the water and the gloves in one of his pockets. The fire surrounded the pot and the water broke into feverish bubbles.

"Are you a doctor?" the man asked.

Lázaro nodded. Yes, one who dies at the sight of blood, Lázaro said inside his head.

"Thank God," the ranchero said.

Lázaro spread water on the sand, but it disappeared quickly. He went to the shed and spilled more water in the tamponed earth, but the same thing happened. He let the scalpel cool, brought a wash basin, poured water into it, and stood in the water, but the wash basin broke. He then brought the Indian woman close to the man, and as best as he could, he showed her what she had to do. He took the knife and showed her with repetitive movements how she should puncture the abscess.

The man said, "Why don't you do it yourself? This Indian woman will kill me."

The Indian woman took the knife, but she wouldn't move.

Lázaro encouraged her to incise the bulge, but she refused.

"Like this." Lázaro took her hand close to the bulge and moved it up and down.

The man looked at Lázaro and then at the Indian woman. "Why don't you do it?" the ranchero begged. "I don't understand. Are you a real doctor?"

Lázaro didn't answer; he stood still. The knife was half of an inch away from the swelling.

"Please, do it," Lázaro said.

The woman wouldn't move, so Lázaro grabbed the knife, looked carefully at the site where the incision should be done, turned his head away from the ranchero, and pushed the woman's hand holding the knife.

The man yelled, "Ayayayay! That hurt!"

Lázaro, took the rubber gloves out of his pocket, closed his eyes, groped for the ranchero's neck, and squeezed the bulge.

The man yelled, "Oh my God, I feel something moving!"

Lázaro heard a thump, the ocean, the wind, the man spitting on the sand, and the Indian boy crying.

The man said, "She passed out."

The woman lay on the sand.

The ranchero was behind him now.

"Something is moving inside my neck, I swear!" he exclaimed.

Lázaro knelt and took the woman's hand to check her pulse. "She will be fine," Lázaro said, trying to console the little boy.

"Now what?" the man asked.

"Press on the bulge, as hard as you can."

There was a pause, and then Lázaro heard the ranchero laughing. "Doctor, it's a worm. I had a damn worm in my neck."

Lázaro turned around. On a white handkerchief, a worm half the size of his pinky finger contorted. Black hairs at one end gave it the look of a monster.

"Thanks so much, Doctor. You can have the tent. You don't have to pay me," the ranchero said.

The Indian woman moaned and sat on the beach.

"How long are you gonna be staying here?" the ranchero asked.

"Not for very long, I hope. I'm heading to Nazareth," Lázaro said.

"That's where the other foreign doctor went too, I spoke with him, he was on his way," the ranchero said.

The woman got up and went inside the hut. Her husband followed her, and the little boy followed them.

"Did you talk to the foreigner?" Lázaro asked the ranchero.

"No. I haven't seen him since then, but I heard he's waiting for the Carmelitas Descalzas."

"I thought they never left the convent."

The ranchero shrugged.

Lázaro gave the ranchero some gauze and instructions about how to clean the wound. The man thanked him again, said he was going to tell other rancheros that there was a doctor around, and mounted his horse. "I still don't understand… Are you afraid of blood?" he asked and left.

Lázaro set up the tent next to the hut. The next patient after the ranchero was an Indian man. Nobody asked for credentials. The Carmelitas Descalzas were late and nobody knew when they'd show up.

With the shaman, the midwife, and the charlatans who came once a month selling remedies to expel parasites, tonics to cure anemia, creams to heal skin lesions, and potions to attract unrequited love, Lázaro shared the labor of assisting the Indians. He accepted hens, eggs, goats, and someone gave him a cow to pay for his services. The goats he consumed with the Indian family, or sold. He gave the cow to the couple; the little boy loved its milk, and whenever he could, he crouched underneath it to suck the milk from the tit.

The Carmelitas Descalzas, including the nun who performed miracles, didn't come, and Lázaro began to wonder if he should head south to look for his grandfather, but the railroad strike continued. Was he waiting for the Carmelitas Descalzas, too?

The ranchero came back almost two weeks later with a bunch of plantains and a dog. Lázaro could barely see the site of the incision on his neck.

"What do the nuns do at Nazareth?" Lázaro asked the ranchero.

"There's a leper place over there. The nuns go there every year to help them."

"A leprosarium?"

"Something like that."

"And the nuns?"

"The strikers won't let them pass."

"Who?"

"The plantation workers."

"What do I have to do to go to Nazareth?"

"If you wanna, I can take you there."

"Aren't you afraid of the lepers?"

"I'd leave you close by," the ranchero said.

"What am I supposed to do with the dog?" Lázaro asked.

"It's a present, to keep you company."

"Thank you. What's its name?"

"Bobito," the ranchero said.

Lázaro laughed and said, "I hope he's not really that dumb."

Chapter 22

The sound of a barking dog outside the autopsy room startled Lázaro. It was almost three o'clock in the morning. The night kept advancing. He washed his hands with soap and water and wiped his forehead with a clean handkerchief. Now he remembered everything. It was a good thing he had lived anesthetized, because the nun's story was opening a hole in his heart, a mix of pain, sorrow, and anxiety.

He prepared himself for the next organ.

The light of the candles flickered on the shiny surfaces of the intestines, like the sun illuminating the mountains. Areas of light, areas of shadows, a desolated body. The organs had been grouped like children and when they were summoned, they were coming out to play hide and seek. His hand dug inside her abdomen until it found the spleen. Using the scalpel, he separated it from the stem.

Nothing. Silence.

He sliced it into two halves to push the story forward. The organ reminded him of a pomegranate. When he heard the voice of the spleen, the autopsy room disappeared. The voice was childish, like the sound of a triangle.

JIING!

He heard the sound of jingling keys mingled with the voice of the triangle, and the story continued…

He didn't know where he was. It was dark, and he could smell urine, feces, and mold, with a pungency as when those scents concentrate in a small space. Somebody opened a door, and a torrent of light blinded him for a moment.

It took a moment to discern; Araminta and Chiquita were sitting in a brick room, their heads together like conjoined twins. They shielded their eyes with their hands; their movements were slow, painful, weak. They looked so different, emaciated. They must have been starving for a long time. They looked like specters.

Araminta's abdomen bulging against her dirty robe almost made him cry. Cases of resilience made him want to cry. But he couldn't.

He heard someone coming. A bodyguard and a woman were at the door.

"Auntie Delfina. It's Auntie Delfina," Araminta said with a feeble and broken voice.

Aunt Delfina remained on the threshold of the door; a handkerchief covered her nose and her mouth. Her eyes were wide open.

"If I had known he'd do this to you, I wouldn't have told your father. I'm sorry," she said, and started to cry.

"The Patrón said you can return to the house," the bodyguard said, and helped the sisters to stand. More servants came to carry the sisters.

Auntie Delfina said, "I'm sorry. After begging and begging, I was able to convince your father! He let me come here to help you."

Auntie Delfina, the sisters, and two bodyguards walked away from the one-room brick building. They walked between patches of drying coffee beans on the ground.

"He said he hoped you were carrying a boy," Auntie Delfina said.

The same car with the same insect eyes waited for them and took them to the villa down the same ochre road.

Some time passed.

When the sisters reappeared, they had changed: Rosy cheeks, clean clothes, clean nails. They walked around the garden, they watered the plants, they talked to the flowers, they pruned the plants, they named more flowers. They talked about the unborn child.

The story came to a halt on its own. He waited for the spleen to continue, but it did not say anything else. He made another cut in one of the halves of the spleen.

Nothing.

He proceeded to search with his hand behind the bladder. The uterus was attached to the lateral pelvic walls by broad ligaments that looked like pinkish wings. The uterus bent forward, like a fallen angel. He cut the ligaments, freed the uterus, and took it in his hands, the ovaries hanging over the sides of his hands like wilted flowers.

LARII!

The voice of the uterus resembled the sound of a harp. It was celestial. He wanted to sleep, to rest.... These amnesic episodes were like resting pastures in the garden of Eden.... That word reminded him of something, but he didn't want to remember.

Araminta lay on a bed among red velvet pillows; opposite the bed, the doors to the balcony were open and the light and the warmth of the sun came in. In a corner of the room, a pot filled with boiling water and eucalyptus leaves produced a pillar of vapor. Araminta's face was pearled with sweat. A woman was at the end of the bed encouraging her to push. Chiquita was at the head of the bead, with a towel, wiping Araminta's forehead.

"Push. Puush."

Araminta's breathing became louder, faster, and it stopped.

"It's a boy!"

The baby screamed.

The midwife tied the umbilical cord with a clean thread, cut it, and handed Araminta her baby.

She held the baby and kissed him. He stopped crying. The midwife encouraged her to breast-feed.

From the corner of the room where he was standing, he experienced a flash of heat that ran from the top of his head to the bottom of his feet. A subtle column of smoke rose from the fluids of labor and spread across the room to mingle with the vapors of water and eucalyptus leaves.

Araminta looked at the baby and said, "I hope Father will forgive me."

The midwife told the maid, "Clean the baby and wrap him in a blanket."

Chiquita and the midwife helped Araminta to sit in a chair.

The maid did as she was told and when she finished, she looked at the midwife.

Araminta said, "Give the baby to my sister."

Chiquita took the baby in her arms.

"Take care of him as if he were yours," Araminta said.

Somebody knocked at the door. A masculine voice said, "Is it a boy or a girl?"

"It's a boy," the midwife replied.

Their father opened the door, "Give it to me," he said.

The sisters' and their father's faces reminded him of someone, but who? They seemed so familiar, and yet, plenty of times during his temporary deaths, he had thought the same. The need to know makes us see what we want to see.

Chiquita gave the baby to the midwife, who gave it to their father, who left the room. A bodyguard with a shotgun was waiting outside. Everyone followed. They crossed the patio, a portico, and arrived at a fish pond, where their father held the baby by one foot and yelled "Did you think a boy was going to do the trick?"

"Give me my baby!" Araminta yelled.

The bodyguard put the shotgun on the ground and, extending his hands, said, "Patrón, don't do that. I will take care of the boy."

Araminta's sister lunged for the shotgun and grabbed it, "I am going to kill you!" she yelled.

Their father held the baby in front of him. Wherever Chiquita aimed with the gun, he would hold the baby as a shield.

"Grab her!" the father ordered another servant.

The second servant snatched the shotgun from Chiquita's hands.

The father swung the baby over the pond; the baby made a splash and sank. Moments later he reappeared in the middle of water lilies, covered by their roots, floating, crying.

Araminta was paralyzed staring at the water, but Chiquita dove into the pond, rescued the baby, and stood in the middle of the pond, water up to her breasts, the newborn in her arms, water lilies surrounding them. "What kind of monster are you?" she asked.

With the first rays of the sun, the sisters went out onto the balcony. The mountains appeared in the distance like the profiles of hidden princesses in faraway kingdoms. The veranda, the cobblestone patio, the pond where colored fish had once swum among rocks and aquatic plants, the lemon tree, the stables, the chicken coops, the fence, and the road all seemed unreachable.

Araminta looked down at the baby in her arms, she wanted to cry, but her breasts had become full and milk was starting to leak. "I am not going to make this milk sour," she said, and wiped away the tears that were rolling down her cheeks. The baby sucked her nipple….

As he held the uterus in his hands, a gentle electric current ran through his body and he fell asleep standing.

Araminta's father's voice woke him up. He was with her and the child in the room; the child had grown two or three inches and had more hair on his head.

Araminta's father told the young maid, "Take good care of the baby. I don't want him to miss his mother." He paused and told Araminta, "Get ready to leave."

Araminta started to write something on a piece of paper.

He wanted to read the words, but the page was blank; his sight became blurry, as though he were opening his eyes under water.

Kiillll….

Boom. Ñeeh. Fiib. Maass. Jiing. Larii.

His memory came in waves, sometimes a wave came close, sometimes a wave retreated; he was some kind of vessel at the mercy of a strange tide that pulled him in a certain direction... He wanted to scream in unison with the orchestra of organs, but something inside him was made of concrete, like a wall. He trembled. The something cracked; he'd seen cracks in other people's walls, which sooner or later would fall down and crumble into a dust that the lightest of breezes would make disappear.

Chapter 23

The ranchero left Lázaro and Bobito at a prudent distance from the Nazareth oasis. A small river crossed through the middle of a circle of adobe huts. Some of them had little square holes in the walls that served as windows. Nobody came outside, but Lázaro knew the lepers were observing him. A dog came out and barked at Bobito. Both dogs showed their teeth, smelled each other, then parted ways as Lázaro kept walking. He could see a brick building in the distance. The ranchero had said the health dispensary was unmistakable, and this was the only brick building in sight. Lázaro turned his head. From a hole in one of the huts, a disfigured face emerged for a second, almost floating, then retracted like a coil.

Lázaro walked through the front door of the health dispensary and found himself in a small deserted waiting room. He put the suitcases on the floor in the entrance hall; he wished he could get rid of them, they felt like anchors, but he needed most of their contents. He sat on a chair. Bobito lay at his feet.

Hans walked in the door Lázaro had come through. Before Lázaro had a chance to say hello, Bobito growled.

"I see you have a new friend," Hans said. His face, which had been pale, was now bronzed.

Lázaro smiled and petted Bobito. Bobito relaxed. "A nice present," he said.

"I heard you were a doctor. You didn't mention that."

Lázaro didn't respond, instead, he said, "The workers are still on strike; they won't let anybody pass beyond Cuchilla San Lorenzo."

"I might have to leave the Nazareth oasis then," Hans said.

"How is it to work here?"

"I feel I am one of the lepers," Hans said.

So that was that invisible connection between Hans and him. "Do you really believe in miracles?" Lázaro asked.

"Some things don't have explanations."

He had found someone with whom he felt close. "You don't look sick. I thought your disease was a matter of life and death," Lázaro said. "That sounds grave."

Hans hesitated.

Lázaro asked, "Can I stay here, at least for tonight?"

Hans nodded. "I'll help you with the luggage," Hans said, and grabbed a suitcase. Bobito growled again. Lázaro hushed him.

"Why didn't you say you were a doctor?" Hans asked.

"I'm still getting used to it."

The doctor's quarters were at the back of the dispensary. On the way, they passed the infirmary and a couple of exam rooms. In one of them, a leper lay on a cot; one of his hands, which lay on top of the sheet, looked like a hammer, devoid of fingers. A Wayuu woman with no deformities sat beside him. Hans spoke with the leper. The time had come for the man to return to his home. The man thanked him and began to pick up his things.

The following morning, they had just sat down to have breakfast when they heard an uproar outside. Lázaro and Hans ran out. A man with leprosy stood by the entrance to the infirmary with a baby in his arms. "Please, save him," he begged.

"Come in!" Hans ordered.

Hans looked at Lázaro. "Do you want to help me?"

Lázaro nodded.

Hans went inside, followed by the father with his baby and then Lázaro.

"Put him on the stretcher," Hans said.

"What happened?" Lázaro asked.

"He was cursed by the evil eye," the man said, still holding the baby.

Lázaro took the baby and set him on the stretcher. Hans went to get a bottle of saline off a shelf. The baby was limp, his face pale, his lips purple, and he was hardly breathing. Hans took a needle out of a metallic box used to sterilize instruments.

Lázaro grabbed a stethoscope that hung from a nail in the wall and put it onto the baby's teeny-tiny chest.

Mortal silence.

"For how long has he been like this?" Lázaro asked.

The man didn't know.

Lázaro encircled the baby's thorax with his hands and started compressions while Hans started to search for a vein in the baby's scalp.

Lázaro stopped the compressions and tilted the infant's head back, put his mouth on the baby's mouth, and started to breathe into the baby's lungs. He stopped and put the stethoscope on the baby's chest again.

Again, mortal silence.

He resumed the chest compressions alternating with respirations.

The bottle of saline dripped furiously, like a sudden rain. Lázaro looked at the baby's scalp. No evidence of blood. Hans has done a clean job, Lázaro thought with relief. After another minute, they stopped and looked at the baby. He was still limp. They resumed. After another minute, they stopped again.

Lázaro put the stethoscope on the baby's chest once more. He nodded with relief.

Slowly, the baby came back to life. The bottle of saline continued to drip fast. Lázaro offered the baby to his father. He cradled it in his arms and started to cry.

Hans tried to cover his eyes. Lázaro recognized that gesture, the feeling of impending peril. Hans started to shake, his skin started to change colors, like a chameleon. Lázaro opened his eyes wide.

Lázaro anticipated that Hans would sink, but instead he levitated. Lázaro grabbed one of Hans' hands to anchor him, like a child holding the string of a balloon; Hans didn't pull him up. He floated like a leaf in the gentlest of breezes.

Lázaro checked Hans' pulse. Hans was dead. The father was in some sort of a trance, his eyes fixed somewhere in the distance. Lázaro moved his hand in front of the father's face and he didn't react. Lázaro released Hans into the air and blew on him. Hans undulated in the air like a feather.

He guided the father, who was holding his baby, to an adjacent room, while pushing the wheeled pole that the saline bottle hooked to; the father let him push him. Lázaro asked him to lay the baby in a cradle; he obeyed, and Lázaro slowed the dripping of the saline bottle.

The father's tears had crystalized and shone like marmite. He didn't remember anything.

The sun was about to die an orange death. Lázaro was sitting on a bench near the entrance of the health dispensary with Bobito by his side when Hans came out of the infirmary. Half an hour must have elapsed.

"You're not going to ask me?"

Lázaro shook his head no.

"You are a strange man," Hans said, and sat next to Lázaro, "I can see the future," he said.

"Now I understand why you're waiting for the nun who performs miracles. It must be terrifying to know what's going to happen."

A group of women passed in front of them carrying pots and pans on top of their heads, leaving a food scent trail.

"I'm hungry," Lázaro said.

"Let's eat something light. Tonight, the Mother Earth festival commences," Hans said, "and there's going to be plenty of food."

"What if your nun never comes?" Lázaro asked.

Hans sighed. "I'll find her. Sooner or later."

Bobito licked Lázaro's hand. "He's hungry, too," Lázaro said.

"Aren't you curious about the future?" Hans asked.

"No. I'm more interested in the past," Lázaro said.

Hans was pensive for a moment and said, "But the past cannot be changed."

"And the future?" Lázaro asked.

"I can change it," Hans said.

"Did you change the future of the man and his little son?"

"No."

"Why?"

"He already had what he wanted."

"He didn't have any desire? Not even for his little son?"

"No."

"What about the infant?"

"He still doesn't know what he wants."

"Why do you want to be cured?"

"Because I know I have only one more life left."

"How do you know that?"

"I saw it once. I used to cry easily. I saw how many lives I had left, and I don't want to die now…"

"You said you could change the future. Why didn't you change yours?"

"Mine is the only future I cannot change… But I could change yours?"

"I never cry," Lázaro said.

Ancient ladies with long braids and wrinkled faces, dressed in their colorful best, sat by the fire; some lepers observed from the distance. A table had been set away from the fire; it was full of food: mouton, turtles, yucca, arepas, lizards, chickens. People could eat as they pleased.

As the mothers sat next to each other in a circle, elbow to elbow, shoulder to shoulder, they allowed Lázaro and Hans to sit inside the circle.

"Sons, sons, sons," they chanted.

The children and younger women watched from outside the circle. Chicha, an alcoholic beverage made from corn, was passed around. Lázaro drank. It was sweet, sour, thin and murky. Soon all the celebrants were dancing as though possessed, and Lázaro felt he had become someone else. He lay on the sand, arms and legs outstretched.

The mothers brought two young Wayuu women inside their circle. Their long black hair seemed part of the night around them. Lázaro was in a euphoric state, unknown to him before now. Perhaps this is like opium… Indians played drums and flutes. The mothers touched his head, his feet. He got up and started to dance with one of the young women.

More men and women came in and the circle was broken.

They continued to dance for hours until the fire was about to die out.

At last, the drumbeats and the sounds of flutes faded, and dancers started to fall to the ground. The mothers, one by one, retreated to their huts.

Hans came closer. "Where's your dog?" he asked.

Lázaro looked around. He wanted to say: He must be somewhere. He doesn't like noise. I'm going to look for him. Good night, Hans, but the words were incoherent, like when he had woken up in Paris after breaking his neck.

Lázaro zigzagged away to look for Bobito. He heard somebody following him and turned around. It was the young woman he had danced with.

Hans smiled and winked.

Lázaro continued to walk until the young woman caught up with him. He stopped and she stood in front of him, the sweet smell of liquor wafting from her mouth. He heard his heart beating in his chest. She came closer until her breasts touched his chest. An urge called him from the depths. He took her by her hand and rushed to the beach.

He unbuttoned his shirt and threw it away. He inhaled the air suffused with the scent of her hair, her breath, her skin. She kissed him with wet lips. She unbuckled his belt, and his pants dropped to the sand. He lifted one leg, and then the other. He removed his underwear, his socks, his shoes.

She pulled her colorful tunic and freed one shoulder, then the other; the tunic fell from the precipice of her breasts. Lázaro ran his tongue in circles around her nipples and then sucked them with an expertise he didn't know he possessed; the woman arched her spine, offering her body, and he held her at the waist with one hand. They almost lost their balance. The young woman laughed as they lay down on the sand. Her breasts fit into the palms of his hands. She kept arching her back. He kissed her from her neck down to her toes. He slid inside her and pushed deeper, impaling the cave full of pleasure.

The night darkened; the sound of the ocean faded and Lázaro felt his body become an incandescent ball; he was traveling at the speed of light, a comet looking for the edges of the universe. The young woman grabbed his behind and pushed and pushed against his hips. She trembled. He trembled.

He was still on top of her when he heard a whimpering. Bobito was standing right next to them. The animal had sleepy eyes. Lázaro tried to scare him away, but he resisted. She laughed. She grabbed Lázaro's penis again, ready for more pleasure. He was enthralled looking at the curves and the softness of her skin when a trickle of semen mixed with blood seeped down the roundness of one of her thighs.

The moonlight intensified.

Bobito ran as though someone had chased him with a stick.

There was no time to react. Lázaro tried to roll aside, but it was too late. He felt a touch on his shoulder; he heard a tremulous voice calling him. He cringed at the sound of a crack; the branch of a tree snapped, a twig broke.

The departure was painful. He fought tooth and nail not to die. He tried to grab onto something that would stop his fall… but this felt like sliding through an opening and into a septic tank. This time the earth didn't embrace him. There was a small rock to hold onto, and his hands grabbed it, but the rock came loose. He wanted to cry.

The landing left him almost breathless. Up above him, the young Wayuu woman stood on the sand, singing. He didn't understand the words, but the song sounded like a requiem. She was crying, and Hans was looking at her.

"But I want to have a baby with him," she said.

"You'll die. This time I can't change your future," Hans said. "There's something about him that doesn't let me do it."

"I don't believe you," she said.

Lázaro opened his eyes and gasped. Crushed bones, splattered entrails, and spilled blood covered the sand, as though an enormous rock had crushed the woman. He stood. Blood clots and pieces of bone fell to the ground.

"I should be dead, not her!" he wailed. "Why didn't I let Hans foretell my future?"

Bobito reappeared wagging his tail, whimpering. He hesitated before getting closer to Lázaro and grabbed a juicy bone from the body with a string of a muscle attached to it. Lázaro snatched the bone and tried to kick the dog, but Bobito ran away.

Lázaro set the bone and then the tunic on top of the body. Although he knew the futility of the act, he covered the body with sand.

He walked to the quarters. Hans wasn't there. Lázaro took his suitcases and left.

The desert grew desolate before his eyes. When he walked on the dunes, he could see the brownish movement of the Carmelitas Descalzas herd in the distance. At least Hans would get his wish, he thought as he scurried, like a murderer, just before the sun started to ignite.

Chapter 24

Lázaro walked for the entire day and half the night through the desert, dragging his two suitcases without knowing exactly why he didn't abandon them. He had been a man marked by death. His shadow looked languid and feeble. His feet throbbed, as though he was walking on two beating hearts. He took out the canteen and gulped some more water. Bobito, who had been following him at a judicious distance, came closer and drank from the cup of his hand. His linen shirt and pants had blood stains everywhere.

"I am a murderer, a monster. There's no escape," he said aloud and wiped the sweat off his forehead with his forearm in one single, harsh movement, but it wasn't the sweat that was obliterating his sight, he was crying.

Bobito barked. Lázaro looked at him. Bobito barked again. Lázaro knelt and Bobito licked his face. Lázaro didn't move; the dog barked again and started to walk. Lázaro followed.

A thick layer of clouds covered the moon. Lázaro knew the ocean was not far away because he could hear its distant sound. He wanted to wash off the blood.

Finally, they came to the ocean. Bobito watched as Lázaro submerged himself fully clothed. Afterward, they continued to walk until they heard a car's engine approaching from behind. He didn't see any lights. By the sound, he knew the car was getting closer, yet he did not look, ignoring the danger. Bobito barked and barked. A cloud parted and the moonlight shone on them. Just before hitting him, the car swerved and almost tipped over. He felt a rush of wind and sand. Someone cursed; several voices joined the cursing and faded into the distance, along with the sound of the engine.

That car should have killed me, he thought. He lifted his eyes to the sky. The light of the moon appeared again. He heard a whimper and lowered his eyes. In front of him, Bobito lay. The dog tried to stand, but his entrails threatened to come out of his belly. Lázaro cringed.

"Don't move, Bobito," he whispered and leaned over to examine the dog.

Bobito's eyes were sadder than ever. Lázaro stroked him on the head and he licked Lázaro's hand. The blow had injured the ribs and the muscles, but intestines and other organs seemed intact. Lázaro thought the dog had a chance. He washed the sand from the wound, took out the medical bag, picked up a needle holder, a needle, and a thread. The dog tried to bite him a couple of times, but Lázaro closed the wound and wrapped it with his shirt. The dog's eyes were now serene. He rested on Lázaro's lap.

Some lights and the sound of another vehicle startled him. The dog paid attention, too. The truck stopped and a stocky policeman asked Lázaro his name. Lázaro did not answer. Several men stepped out of the truck.

"Don't you hear? What's your name?"

Lázaro didn't answer.

Another policeman asked for identification papers. Lázaro didn't move.

"He's deaf," the stocky policeman said, "or so he pretends," and hit Lázaro with a wooden club on his back.

Lázaro fell to his knees. Bobito growled and barked at the policemen, then stopped and whimpered.

"Kill the dog," one of the men said.

Lázaro formed a shield on top of the dog to protect him.

"He has to be a smuggler. They think they can do whatever they want," another policeman said, and kicked Lázaro on his butt. He flew a couple of inches and landed on the sand, his cheek against the cool surface. Redemption. Physical pain at least. Bobito attempted to bark, but whimpered again in pain.

"Didn't I say kill the fucking dog?" the man said.

While one of the men opened Lázaro's luggage, another aimed at the dog.

"Please, don't kill the dog," Lázaro said.

The policeman saw the medical instruments, and said, "This one robbed a doctor."

Two policemen grabbed Lázaro and threw him in the back of the truck.

"Give me the dog," Lázaro said. Bobito bit the leg of the closest policeman.

A shot and a whimper were heard. The night grew darker as he felt a blow to his head.

When Lázaro woke up at the police station, they'd found his medical diploma, his identification papers, and some photographs that proved he was a doctor.

"Sorry, it's not every night we find a doctor roaming like a smuggler," the police chief said. "This is the land of smugglers."

Lázaro noticed the chief was a tall man with a nose that resembled the beak of a parrot; he had green eyes and fair skin. He waited for Lázaro to say something.

Since Lázaro continued to be silent, another policeman asked, "What's wrong with you, doctor?"

The chief leaned against a wall. Another policeman grabbed a dirty rag and tried to wipe the stains of grease left from someone's meal on a table.

"Where's the dog?" Lázaro asked.

"Sorry," the police chief said, swiping one of his fingers from one side of his neck to the other.

"I killed a woman," Lázaro said.

All the policemen turned to look at Lázaro.

"How come?" somebody asked as the roosters began to crow in the distance.

"By mistake?" one of the policemen asked.

Another said, "Come on. Don't make fun of us, doctor. You look mad, but doctors don't kill people."

"Yes, I did, I lay on top of her and I crushed her," Lázaro said in a calm voice.

The policemen laughed; the chief toyed with a toothpick he had in his mouth.

"No way! You're not that heavy," the stocky policeman said and all of them laughed again.

"The problem is that you drank too much. Take a shower and you'll see. You'll feel better." The captain leaned toward Lázaro in an almost secretive way and said, "We have no time for minor things here. We're after smugglers." He paused. "Who did you say you've killed?"

"A Wayuu woman," Lázaro replied.

"An Indian woman? Doctor, those Indians are feeble. They die if someone blows air in their faces." The chief spat on the floor and told a policeman, "Take the doctor to the bathroom so he can take a shower."

One of the policemen got up, guided Lázaro to the bathroom, and handed him a clean towel, a bar of soap, and a razor.

He undressed. A curtain of water fell in front of his eyes. He opened and closed his mouth like a fish; and the water filled his mouth and then overflowed, following the course of gravity. He wished water and soap were enough to wash away his sins until they disappeared somewhere in the sea. The razor they had given him looked just like one of his grandfather's—shiny and sharp, with a tortoiseshell handle.

The sound of a train woke him up; he opened his eyes. White walls surrounded him. He lay on a hospital bed; his wrists were wrapped in gauze stained with blood. He peeked under the gauze. The wounds had been sutured poorly.

After a while, somebody opened the door, a nurse. She smiled and said she was glad he was feeling better.

"How do you know?" Lázaro asked.

"I can see it in your face," she said.

"Can you read faces?"

She laughed. "I was just checking to see if you were all right. The policemen brought you to the health dispensary."

"I want to go to the bathroom," Lázaro said.

"The bathroom is around the corner."

Lázaro tried to get up, but his head spun.

The nurse motioned him to lie back down. "Do you know Wayuu use suicide as a form to punish someone?" she asked.

He reclined in the bed. She fetched a bed pan, gave it to Lázaro, and left.

There was no blood available to transfuse him, so the nurse provided him with iron pills.

"Where's the doctor?" Lázaro asked.

"We're waiting for one. Nobody wants to come out here," she said.

"I thought I heard a train."

"Yes, finally the strike's over."

He spent four days recovering at the health dispensary. On the fifth day, he shaved his beard and put his clothes on.

The nurse pointed to his suitcases. His identification papers were there, as well as the medical diploma, the bag with the medical instruments, and the Victrola.

A black man helped him with the luggage.

The health dispensary was next to the railroad tracks, and Lázaro waited for the next train at the shack that served as the station. When it arrived, he climbed into the last car, which was almost empty. The train advanced, expelling its vaporized breath. Insignificant towns passed by the window, almost in slow motion. He saw the occasional house, or a woman carrying water from a well. Some people waved at the train, some dogs barked and ran after it, followed by children. Lázaro rested his head against the wooden window frame. The air felt hot. Flowers that had grown by the mercy of nature were wilting. He looked at the sky, where vultures soared, the sign of a death somewhere on the ground, and the palm trees' tops were still in the absence of wind. Everything was covered in dust. His lips were dry. He tried to wet them with his tongue, but the chalky taste made him want to spit.

The train stopped in a small town and passengers rushed to get on. The almost empty train car suddenly became crowded.

Children with containers full of fruit yelled, "Mangooooes, one ceeeent. Watermelooon haaaalf."

Lázaro bought a piece of watermelon.

A hefty well-dressed woman with a vibrant silk scarf covering her head sat down across the aisle from Lázaro. She had a full-moon face and the appearance of a respectable matron.

The train continued its climb through the mountain range. The air grew cold; he was freezing in his linen suit. He opened one of his suitcases and took out another jacket, and a sweater, and put them on.

The scent of egg made him stare at a passenger eating one. He was ready to snap up a morsel that fell to the floor. The matron set a piece of cloth over her lap, took some sausages and bread out of a colorful knitted basket, and turned her head. "Young man," she said with an ample smile. "Would you like something to eat?"

Lázaro hesitated.

She encouraged, "Come on, don't be shy, I saw the way you were looking at the food," she said and almost immediately she covered her mouth with her hand.

Lázaro smiled.

"Sorry, I have a big mouth," she said and placed some of the food onto another napkin and handed it to Lázaro.

Lázaro extended his hand.

The matron saw the gauze wrapped around his wrist and asked, "What happened?"

"An accident."

"Really?" she said and looked at the other wrist and gasped, "Don't tell me, niño. No wonder you look so pale," she said, and again, covered her mouth with her hand. "I bet you're hungry. We've been traveling for almost a day."

"Thank you, Madam..."

"Iguarán. My name is Rosaura Iguarán. Would you like some coffee too?" She took out a thermos and poured steaming coffee into a cup. From another thermos, she added milk. Several people, including Lázaro, looked at the containers with curiosity.

Lázaro devoured the meal and drank the coffee.

"Was the coffee too cold?"

"Not at all, thank you, Madam."

"And what's your name?"

"My name is Lázaro."

"And your last name?

"Villamayor."

"Don't tell me—"

"Yes, he's my grandfather."

"Hipólito Villamayor? The one who owns the emerald mine?"

Lázaro nodded.

"Oh Lord, I've heard terrible things about him," she said and covered her mouth yet again.

A full stomach and the rocking movement of the train helped Lázaro to fall asleep.

Screams startled him.

"Somebody, help!"

He had difficulty seeing; it was dark, but the voice crying for help seemed to be coming from the middle of the train.

"Please, somebody, help!"

Lázaro ran toward the voice.

In the darkness, he discerned a figure, a woman pointing frantically at a seat.

Lázaro got closer. A prepubescent girl lay limply across it.

"Please, tell me what happened." Lázaro asked.

The woman babbled but managed to say, "She woke up hungry and asked for something. I gave her a chunk of meat and she started to choke."

Passengers started to crowd around them. Somebody lit a flashlight. The little girl was almost blue.

"Niña, niña!" Lázaro called.

She didn't respond.

Lázaro opened the girl's mouth, "I need the flashlight," he said.

The hand with the flashlight came fast.

He looked inside the girl's mouth.

Lázaro saw what was obstructing the girls' throat, so he stuck his finger inside, curved it, swept the chunk of meat free, and threw it on the floor.

He put his mouth on the girl's and blew; the girl's chest expanded. Then he listened to her heart. There were no sounds. He set his hands on her chest and pressed. His wrists hurt. Her chest sank and recoiled.

The woman yelled, "My daughter is dead!"

"For how long has she been like this?" Lázaro asked.

Nobody answered.

He raised his voice, "How long?"

There was complete silence. Lázaro resumed the chest compressions despite the pain in his wrists; after the tenth compression, the girl shook and arched her back. Lázaro had read about opisthotonos. It's tetanus, he thought. The girl's back continued to arch until Lázaro heard a break. And she was gone.

Her mother emerged from the crowd like a phantom. She knelt and embraced her daughter. The crowd froze. The woman wept. Somebody had turned on another flashlight. Rosaura Iguarán handed the mother a handkerchief. Someone lit a candle.

"So, you're a doctor," Señora Iguarán said.

"A useless one."

Somebody lit another candle, somebody else lit another, and somebody else another.

Lázaro's wrists were bleeding.

Mrs. Iguarán took Lázaro's hands and said, "You did what you could."

"I believe she died of tetanus."

The crowd went back to their seats.

Through the window, the day was coming alive. The sun rose in the sky, making visible the invisible. Colors painted the sky: yellow, orange, blue, white. A white heron interrupted the stillness.

The train stopped. The mother and the dead daughter were removed from the train, the passengers' heads, looking back at them, lined up in the train windows.

"The railway workers are on a strike again. We can't go on," bellowed the train's conductor. Rumors spread that the strikers had blocked the tracks again with large, fallen trees.

Passengers wandered around the stopped train like corralled animals.

Lázaro didn't go hungry; plenty of people were willing to share their food. They sat, staring out the windows, eating from bags, dozing, wrapped in blankets.

Later, vendors came from nearby villages to sell food to the stranded passengers.

The children continued to play while the adults talked. The adults yelled at the children. The children wouldn't listen.

"It looks like everybody has forgotten about the dead girl," Lázaro said.

"Nobody knew her," the Mrs. Iguarán said. "We all forget about the dead."

"I don't seem to be able to shake death."

"Why did you do it?" the matron asked, looking at his wrists.

"Because I couldn't cry."

"You're so young. Anyhow, I'm glad you're alive."

Mrs. Iguarán wanted to know more about Lázaro. She fanned her face with a Spanish fan. He remembered a wine bag his grandfather had in which a Spanish lady dressed in a polka dot dress hid half of her face behind a fan.

"Where's your grandfather?"

Lázaro sighed. "I don't know, I guess he's still in Sirirí."

"When was the last time you saw him?"

"A long time ago."

"My grandson is the Minister of Health. If you're looking for work, I'm sure he will help you."

"Thank you, Señora Iguarán."

"Please, call me Rosaura."

"Very well, Doña Rosaura."

"Niño, you make me feel very old. Forget the Doña," she said and laughed. "And where have you been all this time?"

Lázaro hesitated. "Paris."

"I cannot believe it! I always wanted to go there."

"It's easier now that we have airplanes."

"Have you traveled by plane?"

"Yes."

"Oh no! Not me. I would never get on one of those things."

"A kid who was listening said, "The doctor has been on a plane!"

Soon several people had gathered around them.

"Please, tell us something about Paris," the matron said. Lázaro could see in her eyes that she was ready to fly, although she had said never.

Chapter 25

Five days later the strike ended, the track was cleared, and the train continued its journey. It was February 1, 1940. The train arrived in the Capital City two days later. A chauffer was waiting for Mrs. Iguarán on the station platform. "How was the trip?" he asked while he picked up the luggage.

"Fine," the matron answered.

Lázaro had difficulty recognizing the city. The plaza, which through his child's eyes had been enormous, was now just big. Streetcars rolled amid a horde of cars, and dogs skulked through piles of garbage.

They reached one of the far edges of the city. The matron's house was protected by a row of trees and a tall wrought-iron fence.

A Wayuu maid came to the door and greeted Mrs. Iguarán; the maid had almond eyes that reminded Lázaro of the woman he had crushed.

The matron asked the maid to help Lázaro settle in one of the rooms upstairs. He took his valises and followed her.

After a short time there was a knock at his door. He opened it.

"Doctor, la Señora Iguarán dice que baje a comer."

Lázaro followed the maid down to the dining room.

After dinner, he followed her to the second floor. The bedroom was cold. He put on a pair of pajamas the maid had left on top of the bed, next to a black suit Lázaro supposed belonged to the grandson.

The light of the moon illuminated the window; the shadow from a tree outside waved in the wind like a gigantic monster. The light of a car passing on the street made the monster run from one side of the wall to the other. Next to the nightstand, there was a calendar. His birthday had been a month before, and he hadn't even remembered it.

The next morning, he took a shower, dressed in the black suit, and went down for breakfast.

Mrs. Iguarán was sitting at the table in the dining room.

"Good morning, Lázaro. I spoke with my grandson, and he said he'll be waiting for you."

Lázaro inhaled the scent of coffee and said, "There's no better coffee in the world."

They ate a hearty breakfast, a mix between the styles of the coast and the mountains.

"The driver will take you downtown. Do you need any money?"

"Oh no, not at all," Lázaro said, despite having little money.

"I always give money to charity," she said, and again, she covered her mouth.

Lázaro laughed. He got up and went to the door. "So long, Doña Rosaura."

"Again 'Doña.' Why are you so formal? There's no need."

She was right, his formality was a kind of stiffness, as if he had a metal bar inside his body that wouldn't let him bend.

As they drove downtown, he saw many businesses flourishing. Shoe-shine stands crowded the sidewalks; vendors pulled carts selling roasted peanuts, or sold candy from small boxes that hung from their necks.

Lázaro wanted a haircut and shave. They stopped at a barber shop. The barber, a middle-aged man with a prominent belly, grabbed the strop attached to the chair and sharpened the razor's edge with long gentle movements; the razor sounded like it was trying to hush someone, shsh-shsh. His grandfather had a similar strop for sharpening his razor, and sometimes to lash him.

The razor slid across Lázaro's skin, sounding like small explosions one after another in rapid succession, like the sound of a scalpel cutting into the scalp.

Mrs. Iguarán's chauffeur was waiting for him outside the barbershop.

They came to the same hospital's entrance where he'd gone with his grandfather years before.

Inside the hospital, Lázaro asked the guard for Señora Iguarán's grandson's office. Lázaro crossed a hallway with black and white tiles and came to a courtyard. Lázaro stepped into Doctor's Iguarán's waiting room. A secretary sat behind a desk piled with papers. Lázaro introduced himself.

"I'll let Doctor Iguarán know you're here."

He sat on a chair next to a window through which he could see a patio in the distance. The secretary had the features of a mix between white and Indian, about Lázaro's age.

Doctor Iguarán opened the door, Lázaro went into the office, and gave the doctor his medical diploma and a letter Doctor Bernard had written.

"So, you went to medical school in France?"

"Yes, sir."

"I don't know many doctors who trained in Europe. These documents need to be translated. How did you end up studying in France?"

"My grandfather went to do some business and he took me with him. I stayed."

Doctor Iguarán looked at him through his glasses. "So, your grandfather is Villamayor, my grandmother told me, the one with the emerald mines."

"Yes."

Doctor Iguarán looked at Lázaro with curiosity. Before he could say something, Lázaro said: "I'd like to go down south."

"Sirirí?"

Lázaro answered quickly, "No."

"You can go anywhere you want. You can stay here, too. My grandma would be delighted." He pointed to a map on one of the walls. "There's a list of towns with health dispensaries too, if you'd like."

Lázaro stood up and looked at the map.

The next morning, he woke to the sound of a couple of knocks on his door. Señora Iguarán and the maid were waiting for him with a cup of coffee.

"This room smells funny," the maid said.

"Niña! I am the one with the big mouth, not you!" Señora Iguarán said. "But I agree, the scent reminds me of something, but I cannot tell."

The maid said, "I know what it is, Señora Rosaura. It's jasmine, the flower of death."

Chapter 26

Each body he'd dissected had revealed something that was in itself a lesson, and Araminta's body was like a map that was giving Lázaro meticulous directions.

Lázaro took out both kidneys; they were the shape of beans and quite rubbery. He cut them open as if they were oysters, revealing a cavernous red area at the periphery that gradually transformed into a whitish and smooth surface in the center, the renal calices. The ureters hung down like flower stems.

A mix of a small amount of urine and blood trickled out of the renal calices.

PIINK!

The precise cuts had unlocked the kidneys' voices, which sounded like a violin duo.

"After the baby's birth, it rained and rained for several weeks…"

He readied for the next part of the tale.

Araminta went to the balcony and shouted. "Sister, look the rain is piink!" Her voice was now impregnated with the tone of the violins.

Puddles formed on the ground. The red roses became redder, the pink gladioli deepened their color, and daisies turned pink.

"God must be crying tears of blood," Araminta said. "The world is close to the end."

Chiquita came to the balcony and exclaimed, "Oh my God, you're right. I thought you were having another of your crazy spells."

Araminta's father shouted from the patio, "A bloody rain is not going to make me change my mind. If the world is coming to an end, let it end."

How many times had he tried to interfere as he witnessed people's lives, but to no avail? He knew any action he attempted would be futile, but when Araminta was cuddling the baby, he tried to get her attention. He tried to knock the bowl out of Chiquita's hand while she fed Araminta. He stepped in front of one of the maids as she came down the stairs, but nothing happened. He, who had always desired anonymity, now wanted its opposite.

The sisters came into the room and sat on the bed side by side, Araminta holding the baby.

The wooden floor in the corridor screeched. Their father pushed the door open and strode into the room.

"Today is the day," he said. "Today is the day. I want to be sure there is no misunderstanding. I don't care where you go as long as you never come back."

Boom. Ñeeh. Fiib. Doom. Jiing. Larii. Piink.

Kill him, please! The voice had become universal.

Araminta said, "I hope God kills you right here, or that a lightning bolt cracks you in two." She paused. "Or that your heart just stops, or that you'll swell up and explode. I'd pick up the pieces of flesh from the walls, the entrails from the floor, the pieces of brain from the doors, and I'd feed everything to the dogs."

The symphony of voices had become silent, and Araminta's voice sounded like a normal voice. No vibration of the violin strings.

He looked around and couldn't see their father, but he was in front of the sisters. His finger pointed at her in a menacing way… and he realized he was inside their father again, like a matryoshka doll. He fought to get out, but he was trapped; the man's voice resonated in his head. "You thought I'd forgive you?" Their lips moved in synch. A symbiotic pair.

Araminta cried, "Please, Father, I'll agree to be locked inside the brick room again, but please, don't take my son away from me. I'll sleep outside in the pigsty, or share the mats with the dogs… Please do not make me leave without the child. I'll do whatever you want."

Being inside their father was disorienting…. Something he'd never imagined…. Maybe that's what they called empathy, being in someone else's shoes. These new feelings he was experiencing gave him pleasure. Kill him. Destroy him. Immolate him. Nobody was going to miss him. The anger had been unleashed and it was… soothing. Lázaro's rage grew, a foreign sensation. It wasn't only his rage, but also the father's, two potent rages, and yet, all inside of him, as though he were a new person.

"You should have thought of that before. It's too late to repent," the symbiotic pair said.

"Jesus forgave María Magdalena," Araminta said.

"You're right. Jesus liked whores."

Lázaro wanted to bite his tongue, but the tongue felt heavy, unresponsive.

Kill the bastard. Inside their father's body, the organs' voices had weakened.

Araminta wept while rocking the child in her arms. "Forgiveness… prudence… a constant drop can make a hole in a rock… persistence," she said looking at her sister. "You told me that."

"Who cares about forgiveness, prudence!" Chiquita said, "forget about it!"

"Give him to her," her father said pointing at a young maid.

Araminta turned away from her father, protecting her child, and continued to plead. All was useless. She finally handed the baby to the maid.

The maid took the baby and started to walk away, but she stopped. "Patrón! Something is wrong with the baby!" the young maid said, a look of horror on her face.

"What's going on?" the symbiotic pair asked.

"He stopped breathing!" the maid said.

Araminta grabbed her son, who was turning purple. "Please, you're going to kill him," she said.

"He's going to die!" Chiquita cried. Araminta handed her sister the baby.

The baby started to breathe.

Araminta went down on her knees. "Thank God. Please help me, give me strength. If you want me to leave, I will," she prayed.

"Get up," her father ordered, "get out of my house."

She got up and started to walk away, like a cow making her way through a narrow corridor inside the slaughterhouse.

Chiquita tried to follow her, but the bodyguards formed a wall that would not fall.

They left the house, her father first, the bodyguards following. They continued to walk past the pond, the orange trees, the Castilian cane forest, until they reached the river. A feeble suspension bridge hung above the roiling water.

He was trapped in the story. He'd been trapped in all the stories he'd witnessed.

Kill him, kill the bastard, the universal voice continued, but it didn't have any effect on him any longer. Indifference.

Araminta grabbed the ropes on the sides of the rickety bridge, balancing like a clumsy acrobat until she reached the other side.

While she walked away with hesitant steps, her father yelled at the top of his lungs over the roar of the river, "If you come back, you'll be sorry!"

Araminta ran along the path that disappeared into the jungle; the muddy road turned into a dense carpet of leaves. As soon as she set one foot on the ground, the other one was ready to jump; she imagined a multitude of snakes ready to strike, tarantulas that lay on the trunks of the trees, bats that flew straight for her neck. She ran, fell, got up, and fell again a hundred times, but she didn't stop running.

When the last rays of the sun disappeared, she stopped. She was alone in the jungle at night. There were no monsters, or tarantulas, or bats, but a swarm of mosquitoes that drove her mad. She couldn't stay still; the swarm overtook her, seeking the warmth of her blood. She started to run again, but in the darkness the giant trees were almost invisible and she bounced from one to another.

"Slow down, slow down," the benevolent giants of the jungle murmured.

She fell and rolled in the mud. There, she found solace, her heart beating like the heart of a frog trapped in a jar.

The next morning the bugs had disappeared. She walked without direction until she found a small stream. She was aware that she could drown even in this small body of water. She bathed, holding onto a branch. When the mud washed off, she looked at her hands, her legs, her body. Her skin was criss-crossed with marks left by branches, thorns, roots, falls. She had turned into a canvas, like Jesus Christ on the day of his death. In a single night she had turned into one of the specters she feared: the Llorona. She sat on the trunk of a fallen tree and cried. She had all eternity in front of her; she was dead and this was the inferno, the price for all of her sins.

She waited for someone to appear and save her, but no one did. She drank water from the river, knowing she shouldn't. Diarrhea came and left her even more exhausted, then hunger came. She had seen the dogs digging for iguanas' eggs. She followed the marks that iguanas left on the sand and dug until she found their eggs.

Her stomach, used to warm milk flavored with cinnamon, the tender flesh of slow-cooked chicken, fragrant tea, had to endure the torture of eating raw things. She didn't have a fan to mitigate the muggy heat. She cried beside the river, afraid of the water, her breast milk flowing as the tears ran down her cheeks. Her milk dried in a matter of weeks. Not so her tears.

One day, instead of finding eggs, she found the rough and spiky surface of an iguana's tail. The sand moved as the iguana tried to escape. She jumped back and ran down the river beach. It was when she ran that she cried the most; she imagined her son was close, and ran with her arms extended in the air.

She found the tails of the iguanas more often than their eggs, and in this way she lost her fear of lizards. Soon, hunger and desperation turned her into just another jungle beast, and she pulled an iguana out of the sand by its tail, a monster twisting in anguish. She set it on a piece of driftwood. The iguana tried to escape and she smashed it on the head with another piece of wood. The iguana started to shake and she continued to smash its head, its tail swinging with each blow, until it was a mass of macerated flesh. An impulse from within her told her to eat the entrails and the eyes.

It stopped raining and didn't rain again for months. The flow of the river decreased. Extensive areas of white sand appeared as the water retreated. Araminta's skin grew thicker. She learned the plants she could rub on her skin to repel mosquitoes. A small waterfall provided safe water. She looked for flesh to eat; she caught fish that had been trapped in small pools of water, and avoided bats she found in caverns. She also tested all sorts of leaves and herbs in meager amounts, until she was sure they were not poisonous. As beautiful as the frogs were, she knew they were bathed in venom. A long stick crowned with leaves, moss, roots, feathers, scales, scared away the occasional jaguar.

She thought about going back for her baby, but she knew her father would be vigilant.

In the calls of the brightly colored birds, in the monkeys' yells, she thought she heard her baby's cries. The softness of Spanish moss reminded her of his skin; she saw him in the pebbles at the bottom of clear streams: little petrified dolls.

When her mind quieted, she learned the location of navigational stars, and she decided it was time to go back. She was not afraid of the darkness any longer. She followed the river for weeks until she found the suspension bridge. She moved like a panther and ended up behind the stone wall that surrounded the garden. She waited to see if her sister and the baby were still in the house. The dogs didn't recognize her at first and started to bark. Hush. Hush. They sniffed the air until they recognized a familiar scent; they got closer and started yapping and wagging their tales.

When night fell, she climbed to the balcony. The doors were closed. Araminta tapped on the window glass. Her sister was sitting in front of a mirror, undoing her long braids. Araminta blew on the glass and wrote her name backward. Her sister turned around and covered her mouth with both hands. Araminta lifted one of her hands gently. Her sister got up, went to the balcony door, and opened it, looking in all directions.

"Is that really you, sister? I can't believe it. I thought you were dead,"

Chiquita said while hugging her sister. Araminta was lanky, but her muscles had hardened. Both of them cried.

Araminta's hair, which had been as black as coal, had lost its shiny silkiness and turned into an amorphous mass that resembled tar. She was almost nude, her clothes ripped to rags. She whispered, "Where's my baby?"

Chiquita put her finger to Araminta's lips. "Your son is in the next room," she said.

"Bring him, please," Araminta begged.

"Come inside, but stay put. If anyone knows you're here, they'll send for Father."

Araminta waited until her sister came back with the baby and held him with extreme care, afraid that she would hurt him.

"How old is he now?" Araminta asked.

"Eleven months."

"I thought years had passed!"

"Shhh. If somebody hears, we're lost."

"Are you coming with me?"

"Father's going to come after us like a dog, and he will find us. I'm sure he'll bring the Indians. They know the jungle better than anybody else."

"I didn't see any when I was lost," Araminta said.

"You didn't, but they saw you, I'm sure."

Araminta rocked the baby and sang a lullaby. Tears formed little roads on her dirty face, but she smiled.

He felt an enormous desire to cry. But it remained stuck in his throat.

"How did you survive in the jungle?" Chiquita asked.

"I grew crazy. That saved me."

"You've always been crazy," Chiquita said; they smiled for a moment.

The sisters were fleeing with the baby in a dugout, following the current and paddling for days. They prayed together. They followed the meandering current. Food was scarce and the baby cried and cried.

In the distance, they heard shots and voices.

They paddled faster. Looking behind them, they saw two small blurred objects. As the object grew bigger, they became two dugouts filled with men, approaching fast. The sisters were paddling a losing race. More yells. They paddled with the last strength they had in their veins. Then they stopped. The infant was crying frantically. Their father, three bodyguards, and the Indians surrounded the boat and forced them to move closer to a small beach of brown sand.

"Get out of the boat," their father ordered.

The sisters didn't move.

He got out of the boat and stepped on the sand; two Indians followed. Araminta jumped out of the dugout and kicked her father in the genitals. The Indians laughed while the old man doubled over; two bodyguards seized her. Their father straightened up and punched the closest Indian in the face.

"Get out of the dugout!" he yelled at Chiquita.

Chiquita didn't move, so three more Indians disembarked and fetched the infant. The water was shallow. Chiquita followed them to the beach.

Their father gave the Indians several pesos and a gun. Chiquita, the child, the old man, and the three men got into a boat and paddled back the way they came, while the two Indians in the boat with Araminta paddled in the opposite direction.

She begged the Indians to go back. The Indians laughed and spoke in their dialect. One of them took out a little animal skin bag with some kind of dust and blew it into Araminta's face so fast she didn't have time to turn her head.

A black curtain descended. Silence and darkness.

Chapter 27

Señora Iguarán told Lázaro someone wanted to speak with him over the phone.

"Who is it?" Lázaro asked.

"Señor Hermenegildo Cabrera," she said, handed Lázaro the phone, and disappeared behind a door.

The name sounded familiar.

"Hello."

"Doctor Villamayor, you might not remember me, but we met in Paris. Your grandfather was with you."

"Yes?"

"We had dinner; your grandfather was there. Hotel Regina. At the restaurant Le Pluvinel. My wife was there, too. The lady who couldn't recognize faces."

Lázaro said, "I remember."

"The minister of health told me you went to his office today. He also said he had an envelope the secretary forgot to give you. How's your grandfather?" Señor Cabrera asked.

"I don't know."

"Does he know you're here?"

"No."

"I know where you're going. I'm going in that direction, sort of. I can give you a ride."

The next morning, Señora Iguarán said good-bye to Lázaro as Señor Cabrera arrived in his car and apologized for not getting out, as his bad leg was particularly sore that day. Besides, his weight didn't help either.

"Come back, m'hijo, whenever you want," she said, and hugged him.

As they left the Capital City, the land started to flatten, as if smoothed by an invisible hand. Señor Cabrera gave Lázaro an envelope, which contained his medical chart and instructions about how to handle certain situations that he would encounter at the health dispensary—mainly, dealing with the two opposing political parties.

They stopped to have lunch at a small stand on the side of the road, and several hours later, the car passed through a tunnel.

"Doctor Iguarán had this tunnel built three months ago, the first one in the country," Señor Cabrera said.

The car continued on its route, leaving a cloud of dust in its path. They drove past interminable pastures with clusters of seemingly immobile cows. On the horizon, Lázaro saw a line of green that met the sky—the jungle.

Sometimes one of them slept. Sometimes both of them slept.

"Did your grandfather tell you that I taught him all about cows and horses?"

Lázaro shook his head.

"Your grandfather was about seven years old when I met him. He was living on the streets in the city, so I took him under my wing. He hated the city. But nobody was like your grandfather. Or maybe I have idolized him. He's done so many things I wouldn't have dared to."

"Nothing would surprise me," Lázaro said. "I know my grandfather was—is—not a saint."

Señor Cabrera raised his shoulders. "Of course, nobody is."

"I don't know if he has killed anyone…" Lázaro said.

"You never asked?"

"No."

"I don't think he's killed anyone, at least not with his own hands," Señor Cabrera said. "But he was a liar."

"We all lie."

"Yes. We have all lied, but there are certain lies. Your grandfather was—is—an astute man."

"I agree. Is that a bad thing?"

"No. Not always."

"I've always justified people's actions," Lázaro said.

He looked at the old man, who had fallen asleep.

People said after Lázaro's birth, his grandfather changed for the better. He had wanted Lázaro to become like him, although he never said it. He'd never said it, but Lázaro knew his grandfather loved him; still, he had left him for dead in Paris. Did he not believe he was going to resurrect as usual?

The chauffer continued to drive.

When they arrived at Señor Cabrera's hacienda, it was almost midnight. Under the bluish light of the night, Lázaro saw an ancient tree by the house. Spanish moss hung from the branches. They went inside.

"What about your wife?" Lázaro asked.

"She died a couple of years ago."

"Are you all right?"

"Yes. I've done what I wanted to in this life."

Lázaro's sleep was interrupted at different times by the bark of a dog, a gunshot, and the screeching sound of some animal he couldn't identify, making the night long.

After a maid served breakfast, he and Señor Cabrera went out to ride horses. The morning sun was gentle, the horse movement calming.

"It's funny. Who'd have thought I'd be here, talking to Villamayor's grandson."

"It's a small world after all."

"That's what your grandfather said at Le Pluvinel in Paris."

Lázaro smiled and said, "Of course, my grandfather didn't want you to tell me the story. I'd like to know your version."

They came to a river and dismounted. They took their shoes off and sat at the edge of the river; the cool water felt refreshing on Lázaro's feet.

"Maybe my version is not the one you're expecting," Señor Cabrera said.

"Your wife said I could find answers in the Carmelitas Descalzas convent. Was she there?"

"Yes. The whole thing with the Carmelitas Descalzas was just a way to dispose of women without having to kill them."

"Was my mother a nun?"

"I don't know who your mother was."

"I'd like to know something about my mother."

"How about your grandfather? Did you ask him?"

"I don't even want to repeat what he said."

"To him, all women are whores."

"Why did you two become enemies?"

"He betrayed me."

A fish nibbled on one of Lázaro's toes and startled him.

"Why did your wife say I could find answers there?"

"Her family. They didn't want me. They sent her to Spain. I wanted to go after her, but I got polio, I couldn't walk for a while. Hipólito went after her; he brought me her ashes and said they were my wife's, and I believed him. I only knew the truth several years later."

"Maybe there she met someone who knew my mother."

"When she was in the convent, she heard a rumor about your mother."

"Your wife didn't say anything else?"

Señor Cabrera raised his shoulders. "Not that I remember. We wanted to forget everything related to your grandfather. Some things do not seem to be relevant in certain times; later on we understand their importance. Besides, everybody has complex histories."

Manatees were swimming in the river.

"They are humongous and gentle," Lázaro said. "Like you." He was surprised he had said it. He covered his mouth with his hand, like Mrs. Iguarán.

"I wasn't always this heavy," Señor Cabrera said and laughed. "Neither was I always this gentle. A gift from your grandfather."

The manatees swam closer.

"What do you mean?"

"Your grandfather castrated me."

Lázaro removed his feet from the water abruptly and said: "Please, no, that can't be true."

Señor Hermenegildo Cabrera looked at Lázaro.

"Why didn't you kill him? Didn't you want revenge?"

"They say castration alters the mind."

The manatees grew closer; the water was transparent.

"I knew Hortensia was in love with him," Señor Cabrera said, closed his eyes, and took a deep breath. "She made me swear I would kill him. In the beginning I was planning to do it, but then everything changed. I started to see life in a different way. After I lost my balls, my anger was gone."

The manatees were within reach. Lázaro got in the water.

"What else do you know about Grandpa?"

"He wandered in the cemeteries, opening graves."

The manatees surrounded Lázaro.

"He said he had realized that after a while, he preferred the company of the dead. He was curious, he wanted to know how they looked inside, but I think he was just after the gold. People used to dump gold inside the coffins."

The manatees fled all of a sudden as though they had understood something horrific.

Chapter 28

Señor Hermenegildo Cabrera's chauffer drove Lázaro to a small port by a river, and from there, a boat took him to another port, smaller than the previous. There, he met the postman who offered to accompany him. Each mounted a mule and started to ride toward the health dispensary. The postman told him stories about ordinary people that made him laugh. After a couple of hours riding through the jungle, they arrived at a town at the foot of a mountain. Lázaro recognized the town, on the other side of the mountain was his grandfather hacienda. The health dispensary was further up, a compound made up of three small white one-story buildings in a clearing.

The postman pointed at a door and said, "That's where the nurse lives. Be careful, Doctor. See you."

Lázaro knocked on the metal door. Nobody answered, so Lázaro knocked again.

"I'm coming!" a woman's exasperated voice said.

She opened the door and looked at Lázaro with curiosity.

"Good afternoon," he said. "I'm Doctor Lázaro Villamayor. The Minister of Health sent me."

She welcomed him with an austere smile. "Thank God. We've been waiting for months." She was dressed in a nurse's uniform and an apron that had one big pocket on each side, both bulging. She was a heavy woman and the bulky pockets made her look even bigger.

Lázaro gave her the letter Doctor Iguarán's secretary had written.

"I see the seals of the Ministry of Health," she said. "Come in, Doctor. You can leave your luggage here. Nobody will steal it."

Lázaro followed her into a large, empty, poorly lit room.

"Most of the doctors leave as soon as they can," the nurse said over her shoulder. While she walked, her buttocks, two mountains, moved up and down rhythmically.

She opened a door to an adjacent room and said, "This is the pediatric section." Lázaro looked into a medium-size room to see three green cribs. In one of them lay a child; he must have been five years old. The other two were empty

"He's got malaria."

The boy was pale with a twinge of yellow. He looked at them with cavernous eyes. Lázaro went in and caressed one of his hands. The boy started to cry. Lázaro picked him up.

"All of them cry day and night. Let me show you the adult section," she said and left the room.

Lázaro placed the child back in the crib; the child clung to him.

After extricating himself, Lázaro followed the nurse but turned around before leaving the room. The boy kept crying while grabbing the bars of the crib.

In the next room, three old ladies lay on gurneys with bottles of intravenous fluids hanging above them.

"More malaria, but also heart problems, infections, and lung issues," the nurse said.

Lázaro waved his hand in greeting; two of the old ladies attempted smiles. One of them looked like a turtle, the other like a mouse, and the third was blind, her white corneas like oysters' shells.

Lázaro and the nurse walked into another room, much smaller than the previous two. In the middle of the room was an obstetric examining table; the metal stirrups, wide open, shone. Another crib was beside it.

"Sometimes we have a lot of deliveries, sometimes none," the nurse said. They went back into the large empty room. Lázaro got a glimpse of a little girl just before she hid behind a door in the back of the room.

"That's where I live with my daughter, Regina." The nurse pointed to the door. "Regina," she yelled, "come out, right now. I want you to meet the new doctor."

Nobody came. The nurse rolled her eyes and said, "Regina is a terrible child."

They headed out of the building; the nurse closed the door. Lázaro followed her through a connecting corridor to another building. She took a ring of keys from one of her pockets, searched for a key, and opened the door. They went into a spacious room with wooden pews lining the walls. They walked toward a door in the corner and went into another spacious room with a desk, two chairs, and an examining table. Beyond an enormous window that faced the jungle, several monkeys swung through the trees.

"That door connects our offices," the nurse said, pointing to a door on the side wall. She walked over to it. "I never lock this door," she said, and pushed it open.

Their offices were similar except Lázaro's had a cabinet containing medical instruments and bottles. An air trap flask lay on the floor, next to the cabinet.

They left the office building. Between the two buildings, to one side of the corridor that connected the two main buildings, was another smaller building. She told him this would be where he slept, and handed him keys.

Lázaro disliked her, he couldn't pinpoint why… perhaps it was the way she enunciated her words while lifting her chin.

"Be prepared for the elections, lots of dead people." She turned around and headed to the corridor. Before she disappeared inside her building, he saw the girl, Regina, peeking through the window next to the door. She must have been six or seven years old.

He took his luggage inside the apartment and closed the door. A mouse ran across the empty living room, through the kitchen, and out a back patio door.

He went into the bedroom and unpacked his belongings. In the middle of the room was a metal hospital bed with a crank mechanism, and next to it a small table. A wooden desk was pushed up against a big window that faced the jungle, where the monkeys continued to perform acrobatic pirouettes.

Lázaro took out his books, the instruments for autopsies, the Victrola, and the painting Sophie had done for him. He hung the painting from the only nail on the wall and set the Victrola and the books on top of the desk.

The back patio was covered in a sea of weeds. He could see the tips of a ruined fence encircling it. A latrine was surrounded by banana trees, and behind the latrine was a brick room. Lázaro tried inserting several keys in the padlock until one of them opened it.

"It's the death room," a child's voice said behind him.

He turned around. A little girl showing big white teeth, an ample smile, and cute dimples, stood there with a tiny dog in her arms.

"Let me guess who you are," Lázaro said.

"Regina, the terrible child," the little girl said rolling her eyes.

"Nice to meet you, Regina," Lázaro said.

"It's the death room," Regina said, pointing.

"Why do you say that?"

"Open the door and you'll see."

Lázaro removed the padlock and pushed the door open. The pungent odor of formaldehyde hit his nostrils. A cement table stood in the middle of the room with a pair of rubber gloves sitting on top of it. A metal shelf held several bottles and a bucket. Lázaro's heart raced. Indeed, it was a rudimentary autopsy room.

Regina's mother's voice interrupted them like the screeching tires of a braking car: "Reginaaaa!"

"I'd like to go in," Regina said, "but my mother doesn't want me to."

"I won't tell anybody, Regina the terrible child."

Regina laughed.

"Nice little dog," Lázaro said.

"Her name is Pepa."

Inside the room, a cabinet held a few rusty old instruments that were dispersed as though somebody had thrown them with disdain.

At the door, Regina turned her head, looked back, set the dog on the ground, said, "Nobody's watching," and stepped inside.

Her dog ran away.

"Regina!" Her mother's voice called again.

"You better go now," Lázaro said.

Regina left running.

The scent of formaldehyde reminded him of two things: the room where his grandfather collected snakes, and the room where he had had his first anatomy lesson almost seven years earlier.

The first week at the health dispensary was uneventful. Lázaro saw one or two patients per day.

"They will come as word-of-mouth spreads," the nurse said. "They don't know you're here yet."

"I'd like you to know something. I suffer from epilepsy," Lázaro said. "Do not try to move or touch me, no matter what you see."

The nurse rolled her eyes.

The dispensary was settling into a routine. Lázaro got up early, took a shower, had breakfast, and went to his office.

Two weeks after his arrival, Lázaro came to the dispensary in the morning to find the postman sitting in the waiting room and greeted him. Moments later the nurse rushed in. "Sorry, I'm a bit late today."

"Doctor Lázaro, I just came to give you this," the postman said and extended his hand, the same way his grandfather had when he gave him candy.

Lázaro extended his own hand with hesitation. "It's not an insect, is it? Or a frog?"

The postman laughed and said no.

It was an emerald.

"Why are you giving me this stone?"

He took Lázaro outside, away from the nurse. "Your grandfather sent it," he said.

The nurse was peeking through the window.

The postman said, "Your grandfather said to show you my hand," and before Lázaro averted his eyes, the mailman took a knife out of his pocket and cut the palm of his hand with it. One second was enough.

"Doctor Lázaro, come," he heard, and he felt the touch on his shoulder. After so many temporary deaths, he knew what was going to happen. He started to sink as he heard the ground cracking; a rough wind brushed over him as he descended into a dark abyss. The ground pressed against him as though trying to squeeze something out of him. He stopped sinking and descended swiftly onto an unpaved road. The postman sat on a rock, under a tree at a forked road. "You've come to the right place," the man said. And there was something calming in his voice. "But it's not the right time. You must be careful."

Lázaro and the postman walked towards each other, the postman with his hand extended. There was an emerald on his palm. Lázaro was taken aback: for a moment he thought the mailman was seeing him, so he reached for the stone, but another man stood in front of the postman. Lázaro froze. It was his grandfather, and he hadn't changed that much.

"Give it to him, and tell him I am waiting for him," the grandfather said. "And when you are in front of him, cut your hand, like this," and with a swift movement, Lázaro's grandfather cut his hand.

The mailman sat on the boulder by the forked road. Lázaro waited, wondering why his grandfather had done that, when the mailman started to look younger and younger until he was a boy. Leonor was by the boy's side. Lázaro's heart jolted. She was younger than he remembered, but he was sure it was her.

A menacing man standing in front of them said, "I'll kill the boy first, and then I'll kill you. There will be no witnesses."

"Step back, otherwise I will light the match," his mother said, grabbed a matchbox the boy was holding in his hands, and added: "You are standing in a kerosene puddle."

There was the smell of kerosene.

"You won't do it," the man said in a dismissive tone, and stepped forward.

"I warned you," she said.

Smoke rose suddenly.

The man screamed in pain, first like a clap of thunder, then like the sound of a slap, and then, like the sound of a dry leaf burning in fire.

The scent of burnt flesh made Lázaro vomit.

His mother, the boy, and the pile of ashes disappeared.

Outside the health dispensary, a small crowd had gathered around him. A priest was spraying holy water over him. The nurse was crouching like a praying mantis.

"Dios mío," she exclaimed. "His skin changed colors, and I tried to hook him to an IV, but the needle broke."

Lázaro climbed out of the hole he'd made. The nurse and the priest retreated. The nurse fell to her knees and started confession. "Bless me father for I've sinned… I've done terrible things…" Someone put his hand on her mouth.

The mailman with the wounded hand was among those who saw what had happened. Lázaro took him to his quarters.

"Señor Villamayor told me to come to see you and to let you know he's waiting for you."

"Did he know what my mother had done?"

The postman looked at him as if taken by surprise. "What did you see?"

Lázaro decided not to speak.

"Do you still have the emerald?" the mailman asked.

Lázaro opened his hand. The emerald had turned into dust.

Patients stopped coming. So, he stayed in his quarters, reading outdated newspapers and his medical books, playing with beetles, listening to Robert le diable on the Victrola, staring at the monkeys in the trees.

Regina's face began to appear and disappear in the window, one day, finally, she tapped on it.

He opened the door.

She came in with a rag doll and the little dog, and like a playful thief she crouched down and hid behind the yellowed semi-transparent curtain.

"Your mother will be upset if she discovers you're here," Lázaro said.

Regina shrugged. "I'm invisible. You can't see me."

He played along and sat on a chair, pretending he was reading a book. He felt a touch on one of his shoulders at the same time Regina said, "Boo!"

Lázaro stood up like a spring. "Why did you do that?" he asked in alarm.

She recoiled in fear. "I'm just playing," she said.

Lázaro said, "No. I'm sorry, I didn't mean to get upset. It's that—" He was about to tell her that before dying, he'd felt a touch on his shoulder, the way she had just touched him, but she headed for the door.

"Where are you? I can't see you," he said.

"I don't want to play anymore. You yelled at me. You scared me. Mother says you're a devil!" She slammed the door.

The next day, Lázaro was standing next to the Victrola listening again to Robert le diable.

Regina tapped on the window. He went to the door, opened it, and stepped aside so she could come in.

"That music is horrible," she said, pointing at the Victrola with one hand and holding her dog with the other.

The voice of the singer was a lament.

Lázaro laughed. "So you're not still invisible?"

"I don't want to play anymore. My mother says you scare her."

Lázaro looked at Regina and made a gesture mimicking a monster.

"You don't scare me," she said, "but my mother said you died and then you were resuscitated." After Lázaro nodded, she continued, "And that she saved your life." Lázaro shook his head.

In the distance, they heard Regina's mother calling. Regina escaped like steam from a pressure cooker.

She came back several more times and sat with Lázaro on the patio.

Nobody else knocked at his door, not even by mistake.

"I'm leaving soon," he told Regina.

"Where are you going?"

"Sirirí."

"Where's that?"

"Far. On the other side of the mountain."

"I don't want you to go. I'll come with you."

"And your mother?"

Regina shrugged.

"And your dog?"

"I'll take her with us."

"Regina! Regina!" they heard the nurse call in the distance. "Where are you?"

Lázaro wrote a letter to the Ministry of Health in which he explained that he had not been able to perform his duties because of health issues. He'd be leaving soon, so no need to send his next paycheck. He was sealing the envelope when he heard a commotion outside. He went to see what was going on.

The nurse screamed, "Help, please! Doctor Villamayor, please, I need your help!"

Lázaro hesitated. What if he refused to help?

Lázaro came out the apartment to find a man bruised all over, lying on a cot outside his quarters. The man was gasping for air.

"What happened?" Lázaro asked.

The patient had fallen from a tree while he was chasing a monkey. Four men and three women stood by him. All the women cried and one of the men paced.

"Let's take him inside," Lázaro said.

They took the man inside the health dispensary and set him on the examining table. Lázaro set his stethoscope on his chest. The man's heart was racing and banged against his rib cage. He listened to the man's lungs and tapped his thorax. The dull sound signaled the man was bleeding inside. Without any doubt, if he didn't insert a chest tube, the man would die.

Lázaro took a plastic tube from the metal cabinet and picked up the container trap on the floor next to the cabinet. He asked the nurse to fill a syringe with an anesthetic. She crossed herself. After he had set the container trap on the floor and connected it to the tube, she passed the syringe to him. He ripped open the man's shirt, went to the faucet, filled a container with water, and spilled it on the place he would be standing; then lifted his arm and asked the nurse to hold it.

"If I have another attack, insert the tube and hold it until I resurrect."

The nurse crossed herself again.

He cleaned the area below the axilla with iodine, numbed the skin with Tropocaine, and made a quick cut between ribs while trying to avoid seeing blood. He froze for a second, but this time he didn't die.

He inserted the tube in the man's chest. Blood and air escaped into the container trap.

As the blood drained from his chest and the lung re-expanded, the man started to breathe more easily and his heart slowed.

Lázaro sutured the tube to the thorax.

The man opened his eyes and started to cry. He reached for Lázaro's hand and kissed it.

Chapter 29

Patients started to come to see Lázaro again. Headaches. Palpitations. Malaria. Vertigo. Colds. Even sadness. Lázaro had another temporary death while delivering a baby. When he came back from the realm of the dead, the nurse was standing close to him with a glass of guanabana juice.

Diseases and events clustered in waves as though following a circadian rhythm. Some days, multiple people came with similar symptoms, as though they had agreed to show up exactly that day. One month brought people with tuberculosis, the next brought deaths from old age, the next month brought births, and the next, elusive diagnoses. Attacks and murders were interspersed here and there.

The temporary deaths were unpredictable. Sometimes a gushing wound didn't make him die, but the same day a pair of scissors would fall on someone's foot, he'd turn his head to see what happened, and the scant amount of blood would be enough for him to die. Not always could he go spilling water everywhere.

The health dispensary's floor had several planks covering the holes left by Lázaro, each hole shallower than the previous.

Before opening the connecting door between her office and Lázaro's the nurse would say, "Watch out. This one has tuberculosis," or "This one is a thief." Sometimes she said nothing.

One day, she came into his office and gave him a yellow card they used for pregnant patients that registered the patient's weight, heart rate, temperature, and blood pressure.

"Her father raped her," she whispered, handed him the card, and walked out.

Lázaro greeted the woman and asked her to sit on the examining table.

"Are you all right?" he asked.

She nodded.

He asked her to open her mouth. He inspected her gums, her tongue, checked the lymph nodes in her neck, listened to her heart and lungs. He pressed his hands against the roundness of her belly. He felt the baby's head and spine. He measured her uterus from the pubic symphysis to the fundus. The baby kicked. He grabbed the monoaural stethoscope, a wooden double funnel that looked like a small trumpet, set it on her stomach, and set his ear on top of it. The sounds of the baby's heart came through. Lub-dub-lub-dub. Finally, he examined her legs and checked her foot pulses. She had incipient varicose veins.

"Everything is fine," he said.

The woman lowered her eyes and smiled in resignation. "Yes, Doctor, everything is fine," she said.

"I'll see you next week," he said and signed the small yellow card filled with boxes to check issues related to the progress of her pregnancy.

The woman got up, said thank you, and left, closing the door behind her.

Lázaro documented the encounter on the medical chart, opened the door to the nurse's office, and asked her how she knew about the patient's rape.

"She told me," the nurse answered. "They tell me everything. She's not the first one, and she's not going to be the last."

The woman came back the following week.

Sitting on the examining table, she said, "My brother is the father of the child," turned her head aside, and covered her face with her hands. "I don't want this baby."

"I thought it was your father."

She had lowered her hands and rubbed them against the cotton sheet that covered the table, as though she wanted to rid them of a mortal sin, and started to cry, a soft cry, almost soundless.

He let the time pass until she broke the silence and said, "I am fine, Doctor, I swear that I'm fine."

Lázaro examined her. When he finished, she got off the examining table, rubbing her hands against her pleated greenish skirt, while her foot pointed down just a second before she slid it inside her shoe.

Lázaro said, "You're due now, you could have the baby at any time. We'll get help from the police."

"My brother's the police chief," the woman said, sliding her feet into her shoes.

Lázaro checked the corresponding boxes and signed the yellow card.

After she left, Lázaro remained at his desk looking at the monkeys.

Night came and the sounds of crickets, frogs, and owls filled the air. Lázaro went to his quarters and lay on his bed. Under the light of the moon coming through the window, he looked at the trees, silent witnesses. He was also a silent witness. Patients told him their stories—from petty crimes to infidelities to things he could not repeat. Some spoke with an ease he found unbelievable, while others struggled to get the words out, as if they were carrying a heavy object up the slope of a hill. Despite hearing the voice granting permission just before a temporary death, once Lázaro was dead, some people hid their faces. Some power in those who bled refused to reveal who they were. Was it a fight between the id and the super-ego? The stories he'd seen were partial tales. To him, they were truths. He'd learned the most when was dead. He'd felt the most when he was dead. Alive, he was somewhat dead.

The following day he went to the police station. It reminded him of the one up north, with policemen in green uniforms waiting for something to happen. One of the policemen greeted him.

"Good morning. Are you the police chief?" Lázaro asked.

"I'm not, but I'll look for him," the policeman said.

The police chief came. "Can we talk in private?" Lázaro said.

"Sure, Doctor. Come, let's go into another office."

They walked along a narrow corridor with yellow stucco walls and stopped in front of a door. The police chief opened it and revealed a small room. It was gloomy and smelled of mold.

"Please sit down."

Lázaro sat in a chair in front of a small desk covered with papers and old newspapers. The chief of police sat behind the desk.

"How may I help you, Doctor Villamayor?"

"I know you're the father of your sister's baby."

The police chief frowned and jerked his head. "Which sister?"

Lázaro was confused for a moment. "The one who's pregnant."

"I have two pregnant sisters."

"I didn't know that."

"I guess you're talking about the unmarried one. She wouldn't tell me the name of the father, because if I knew it, I'd kill the bastard. I wouldn't be surprised if half the town knows who the father is. This is a town of gossips. And I'd be the last one to know."

"But why would she lie, especially about something like this?"

"Everybody lies. You should know that, Doctor."

"You're right." Lázaro felt like a fool. "Are you?"

"What?"

"Are you a liar?"

"No."

"Would you prove it?"

"Yes."

"Give me your hand."

"Are you a palm reader?"

"No. Let me see your blood."

Lázaro took out a bottle of water and spilled it on the floor.

"What are you doing?"

The chief's right hand had only four fingers. Lázaro quickly removed a lancet from his pocket, grabbed the chief's hand, and pricked it, but the chief pushed him away and Lázaro stepped out of the little puddle.

The chief pulled out his gun.

Lázaro saw the gun pointing at his face and a tiny drop of blood hanging from the man's hand.

He neither felt the touch on his shoulder, nor heard the police chief's voice calling for him, and yet, he died. The cement floor felt like quick sand. He waited to step onto the other side, but he stopped sinking. The pressure around his body increased, He was trapped in the middle of a temporary death. He tried to move his shoulders to slide down, but he couldn't. He tried to jump up. All useless. He thought: what if I remain like this forever? Is this hell? Limbo? Purgatory? The pressure around his body eased, and he was ejected, like excrement.

"No more, please!" a voice said. It was dark, but as his eyes grew used to the darkness, he saw a couple engaged in an intimate act. He turned away.

Again, "Please, leave me alone."

"Just once more. Stay put," the masculine voice said, but it sounded distorted.

He faced the couple. A man dressed in a military uniform lay on top of a woman, the one who had come to the health center. The man's face was distorted, but his right hand only had four fingers. At that moment, Lázaro's heart started beating again.

He had cracked open the cement floor and fallen down into a courtyard. Behind the bars, the inmates looked at him with wide eyes. The police chief was looking down at him.

"Now I know," Lázaro said.

"I am the father of the little one," the police chief confessed. "I don't know why I keep doing it, I know it's wrong, but I'd like to change…"

A chorus of the prisoners' voices, all confessing, bounced around in the cells. Unintelligible.

The next time the woman came to the health dispensary, she was in labor. The nurse had told him the police chief was transferred.

"I think he's afraid of you," the woman said. "But before he left, he asked me to forgive him."

She worked through her labor not saying a single word; the only sound was her breathing, which grew louder with each contraction. Lázaro and the nurse were by her side. The nurse asked her if she had thought about a name for her child. She said she didn't know.

Lázaro delivered a boy. The mother wouldn't look at him. The baby had only four fingers on his right hand.

"Before she left, she said the child was for the doctor," Regina said, "and that his name was Arcángel."

"We need to tell the police," Lázaro said.

Regina said, "We'll adopt him."

"Don't even think about it," her mother said.

"Can I hold him?" Regina asked.

"No," her mother said at the same time Lázaro said, "Yes."

Arcángel was a bit heavy for Regina.

The nurse took Arcángel and said, "I'll put him in a crib, and then send a letter to the orphanage."

"No, Lorenza," said Regina.

"I told you never call me by that awful name!"

March and April brought political quarrels, drunken altercations, familial disagreements, and the simple madness of killing. Bodies started to show up on the sides of the roads, in the jungle, revealed by the stench of their decomposition. The villagers said others were left to the jaws of caimans, jaguars, and piranhas.

"I hate autopsies," the nurse said to Lázaro one day in his office, "why do we have to do them? Just to fill out a death certificate." She paused. "The other doctor forced me to help him. I'm glad you don't." She turned around and started to walk away, her hips swaying back and forth, the sound of keys jingling in her pockets. Without turning her head she added, "Thank God, especially when they find the bodies days later… Who can stand that stench?" Then she stopped all of a sudden. "What if I die?" she asked. "Please, don't do my autopsy!"

"We'll put her in that liquid that smells horrible in the death room," Regina said.

"Formaldehyde," Lázaro said.

"Regina!" her mother screamed.

Lorenza, Lázaro almost said.

Chapter 30

It was about four in the morning. The heat in the autopsy room had receded and the air felt fresh. Lázaro's neck hurt. He remembered a dream: He'd been trapped in a spider's web in the middle of a road. He'd tried to advance, but he couldn't. He heard the clicking of the spider's pincers and felt a sharp pain as they sank into the nape of his neck. The pain was unbearable; he screamed, but no sound came out of his mouth. The spider freed him and observed from a distance, as though expecting something to happen. Lázaro touched his neck. There were no wounds. He was afraid, for he knew invisible cuts were the most painful.

He twisted his neck, stretched his shoulders, and continued Araminta's autopsy.

He incised the bladder; the interior surface, crossed by trabeculae, resembled a dense forest with tree branches that had intertwined. His sight was blurred. He waited several seconds and his vision returned, but everything seemed to overlap, one image on top of another: Araminta was lying under a canopy of shrubs with branches overlaying the bladder's trabeculae.

Several men and a woman faced Araminta. Two men lifted Araminta onto a stretcher and started to walk. They came to a clearing with several tents, and they put her on the ground in one of them.

The woman squatted next to Araminta and asked, "Who are you? What's your name?"

She didn't answer.

"Poor thing, she's mad," the woman said, and her voice sounded as though she were talking inside an amphora.

Silence fell, as if an intermezzo during a theater play: people moving around, coughs, throat clearing, voices, laughs, sneezes. And music in the background that rocked him, back and forth sinking him in a stuporous state. Jungle heat in the middle of the day. He let himself go as though living eternally, and he didn't care.

The sounds of rustling, the clicking of scissors, hair falling, reminded him of a barber. His memory was coming back.

"You look like a beautiful boy," the woman said. Her voice resembled an echo, and inside the echo, the distinctive tone of an ocarina reverberated: the voice of the gods of Incas, Mayans, and Aztecs.

DAAII!

The bladder spoke. "She seems like a porcelain vase placed in the corner of a mantel, accumulating dust while life goes on around her."

Time passed, and Lázaro observed as he hadn't done before. Araminta seemed dead and yet he was more alive than ever. He remembered his name now, but he couldn't remember anything else; he knew there was a story before and a future, but he couldn't make assumptions, his mind was locked in the present.

The woman fed her, bathed her, sat her up, moved her, fed her again, and bathed her again. With the progression of actions, the woman's expression changed from a smile to a stern look.

An infant cried.

Araminta shook, and so did Lázaro.

"The vase doesn't know about time until somebody accidentally pushes it off the mantel," the bladder said.

Araminta screamed, "Where's my son?"

The woman signaled Araminta to hush while she sat on her cot, holding a baby in her arms.

Araminta tried to get up but her legs gave way and she fell to the ground.

"Give him to me," Araminta said, "he's my baby."

"Now you talk," the woman said in a low voice. "If you don't shut up, there's gonna be more trouble."

Araminta pleaded, "He's my baby. Please, don't take him away." She crawled closer to the cot.

The woman held the baby in front of her, the umbilical cord still attached to its belly.

Araminta did not understand. She looked in all directions. "Where am I? Where's my child?"

Lázaro understood. He remembered Araminta's story in a second; the next second, the story continued.

The woman hesitated, moved her head slowly from right to left and said, "Look what you've done! You're just a crazy woman. Here, hold your baby."

Araminta knelt. Araminta looked around again and asked, "Where am I?"

"In the jungle, where else? Aren't you going to hold your baby?"

"I don't know. Everything is confusing."

"I need to cut the cord," the woman said.

"Let me see the baby," Araminta said, and lifted herself up onto the cot, next to the woman.

The woman looked at her with distrust, "Go. Look for some scissors," the woman said.

"Where?"

"Outside. Don't let anybody see you. There's a smaller tent to the right, behind a tree. Inside you'll find a first aid kit on top of a table."

"But I can't walk," Araminta said.

"You're useless," the woman said.

Araminta started to crawl out of the tent. Two rows of at least twenty tents each stood in the jungle.

She did as the woman had told her and when she came back with the first aid kit, her legs had awakened.

The woman was still sitting on the cot with the baby in her arms.

"Quick. Cut the cord," the woman said.

Araminta took out a bottle of alcohol and disinfected the scissors. She dampened a piece of black thread, tied off the baby's umbilical cord, and cut it.

"So, this is what's going on?" a male voice said.

Both of them turned. The woman sitting on the cot stood instantly upon hearing the man's voice. The placenta fell to the ground with a plop, and blood splattered everywhere. The man, an Indian, became pale, his mouth unhinged, and he fell to the ground.

"Quintín Lame passed out," somebody said outside the tent.

At least sixty Indians were peering in from outside.

"Men cannot tolerate blood," the woman said.

The Indians laughed. One of them stepped inside and helped Quintín Lame to sit up.

"It's a girl," Araminta said. "Can I hold her?"

The woman handed Araminta the baby and immediately started to rock her. Milk started to leak out of Araminta's breasts. The woman looked at her with wide eyes while Araminta started to nurse the baby.

"You're strange," the woman said, looking at Araminta's engorged breasts.

In the autopsy room, he felt light, almost weightless, and there was a tickle in his chest.

"Do you have a name for her?" Araminta asked.

"No."

"I'm an expert at names." Araminta said and took a few seconds before saying, "Berenice. You should name her Berenice. She's so plump and juicy, like a berenjena."

"Berenice," the woman repeated. "Yes, I like it."

Quintín Lame stood with the help of two men.

"What's your name?" he asked.

"Araminta," she said and started to cry, "I remember everything now. Please, help me."

Araminta looked around. "You're not the army? Are you?"

"Yes! We're Quintín Lame's army," the woman said.

"Jesus Christ, you are the chusma," Araminta said and crossed herself.

Quintín Lame said, "We're here to form an Indian republic." To the woman who'd just given birth he added, "You should cut your hair, like her," and pointed at Araminta.

Araminta raised her hand and rubbed her head. "Who cut my hair?" she asked in panic.

"I did," the woman said, "your hair looked like a mass of worms."

"Help me rescue my baby. Kill my father. He's one of your enemies," Araminta said.

"We don't have time for babies," Quintín Lame said, "there's going to be a bloody war."

Araminta said, "I'll fight for you."

Quintín looked at her. "You're not Indian."

Araminta hesitated. "I could pass for half-Indian."

"Enough!" Quintín said, and left the tent.

Araminta looked outside the tent with Berenice in her arms. The Indians were in formation. Some of them looked like beggars, no shoes; machetes hung from their waists, and not all of them had guns.

Araminta said to the woman in a low voice, "And you think you're going to fight with this army?"

"Yes, Simón Bolívar did it," the woman said.

"What's your name?"

"Chureni."

"I've never heard that name before."

"It means dusk. I come from the north, the Guajira dessert. There's an oasis over there. Nazareth."

When she found out that more than a year had passed since the Indians had taken care of her, Araminta howled like a wolf. Her mind was slipping away, but Berenice's cry brought her back. Berenice was a restless baby and she cried constantly, especially at night. Araminta woke up several times to check on her. The women had set two cots together; Chureni lay on one, Araminta on the other, and Berenice was in the middle, but the baby did not calm down. She slept during the day, when voices and noises were heightened, and at night she cried, which did not bother Chureni, who slept.

Araminta didn't know how many nights she had gone without sleep. While the Indians were out during the day, she lay on her cot. When Berenice lay on top of Araminta's chest, the infant was quiet. When she was in her mother's arms, she cried and cried.

"You should leave and take Berenice with you," Chureni said.

"What about you?"

"I'll stay. I have to fight for the Indian Republic."

"Let's escape together," Araminta said.

"No. You better go back to look for your son."

"My father will kill me."

"Nah."

"You don't know him."

"All tyrants have a weak spot."

Another year passed.

Quintín Lame announced, "The army is getting closer. We're not going to hide any longer, but it will be easier to fight them if we go to the mountains."

"Come with me," Araminta said and grabbed Chureni's hand.

Chureni hesitated. She looked at her daughter and said, "Take her with you. I know you'll be a good mother. Quick, let's take advantage of the uproar."

Araminta held Berenice and started to walk away.

"Go down the river, and be careful of the wild beasts," Chureni said before disappearing.

Araminta hoped somebody would come to rescue them, to take away the closing madness, the enormous grief that threatened to smash her, but neither the army nor Quintín Lame's militia appeared. The dry season had shrunk the river and large sandbars appeared as white islands. She found places where the current was gentler and sat by the edge of the river, her feet in the water, holding the baby.

"There are no piranhas, water snakes, or mermaids with huge eyes and sharp teeth in this river. Do you hear me, Berenice?"

The water became shallow in places and she could walk, the water up to her ankles, from island to island. Then she ventured in up to her knees, then her waist. Always carrying the girl and a tent they used to sleep at night.

The rainy season came and went. The dry season came and went. Araminta used her imagination to build shelters, spears, to carry the fire she found after following the smoke she saw on sweltering days in the hope of finding someone.

Berenice had grown to be—he thought—a two-year-old. She was a good swimmer but still a slow walker.

"Berenice, my love, there are no monsters anywhere, you know that?" Araminta continued repeating.

Araminta grew used to the waters and the waters became used to her. She was able to submerge until her chin touched its surface, while Berenice swam next to her. Araminta tried to float on her back. After innumerable attempts she was able to see the blue sky, and started to venture into deeper waters. She would grab the root of a tree and let herself glide with the current like a leaf until she found another root farther down. Berenice followed her.

She chose calm waters to try to float like a dog. No monsters arose from the depths, no schools of piranhas attacked them, no water snakes twisted around their feet, no mermaids with huge eyes and sharp teeth came out to kill them. She'd get out of the water and sit on the sand and observe the dense green fortress formed by the trees, the yellow ochre water becoming transparent in the cup of her hand. She followed the river for a year; the farther she went, the wider the river became. She was sitting with her feet in the water, immersed in her thoughts, when she saw them.

At first, she didn't know what to think. Maybe there were monsters in the water after all. She backed away from the river. There were pink fins. She had never heard of sharks in the river. She gasped when a monster jumped out of the water in a parabolic movement and disappeared with a splash. Another one followed, and another. In total, there were five creatures. She stood with one hand over her mouth and the other holding Berenice's. Berenice let go of her hand, and jumped, and clapped.

Berenice giggled and jumped in the water. Araminta screamed. The monsters came, at first surrounding Berenice slowly; Araminta was about to jump in the water, but Berenice said giggling: 'Mama' while she splashed the water with her hands and feet. She was taken aback; this was the first time Berenice had spoken.

The monsters retreated, she became still, floating. The monsters approached her again. She touched one on the toothed beak; they emitted sounds as though they were laughing.

Araminta started to laugh. "See, Berenice? There are no monsters in the water," she said.

The creatures swam closer to shore, and she crouched by the edge of the water. They were all pink but otherwise resembled dolphins she'd seen in pictures. "This is not the ocean," she said, "but perhaps I'm wrong. Sooner or later all rivers flow into the ocean."

She searched the horizon for sails or steamers like she'd seen in magazines. She had always imagined what it would be like to take a steamer to unknown places, places where she would be happy. But all she saw was the green line of trees against the blue sky. She tasted the water to be sure she wasn't wrong, but there was no salt in it.

"These monsters must be confused. How did they end up here and where did they come from?" she said, and swam out to where Berenice was, and dared to touch them.

By the end of the afternoon, the pink swimmers were gone.

They saw them a couple of times more; between sightings, a full moon came and went. Sometimes, they walked for days along the beach. At times, they had to walk in the jungle, following the course of the river, and it took them weeks to advance small distances. Sometimes they stayed in idyllic places for about a month before walking again.

The river carried tree trunks and drowned animals. She saw the latter sliding past and closed her eyes. When she opened them, the objects were small points in the distance.

One day, she saw a human body floating down the river. She turned around and distracted Berenice.

Another day, she saw a dugout that drifted with the current. She ran along the bank, dove in, swam after the boat, and took hold of a piece of rope hanging over its side. She almost lost her grip several times, but she was able to pull the dugout to the shore.

Berenice joined her and together they looked inside the dugout. Araminta almost fell over backward: there was a skeleton on the bottom. Also a cooking pot, a blanket, and a machete. She wanted to push the dugout back into the river, but she knew she needed it. The skeleton wore faded rags of what had once been a linen suit and its teeth were scattered over the bottom of the boat. Hanging from its neck, a gold necklace shone.

Araminta grabbed the pot, the blanket, and the machete. The machete was rusty but still had the smell of sugar cane and garlic stuck to its surface. She made several attempts to get the gold necklace, but every time her finger was just an inch from the skeleton, she shuddered and pulled her hand back. She'd never touched a dead body before, let alone a skeleton.

She grabbed a stick and poked the skeleton and the mandible fell off. She felt sorry, terrified. She pulled the dugout onto the shore and left it on the sand.

She unfolded the blanket, which was bleached from exposure to the sun and smelled of mildew. In some parts, a chessboard pattern remained. A pack of cigars and a box of matches fell out.

That night she and Berenice slept, as usual, on a bed of dry leaves under the tent, the blanket covering them.

With the first rays of the sun, she woke up resolute, and found Berenice playing with the bones.

"Mama!" Berenice said, and threw a bone in the water.

"No!" Araminta said, "we have to bury the skeleton, this is not an animal."

Berenice continued playing with it.

"No! Just get the necklace and give it to me," Araminta said, pointing at it with the tip of a stick.

Berenice did as she was told.

Araminta dug a hole in the sand and asked Berenice to bring one bone at a time.

The bottom of the dugout was covered in leaves and dirt.

"Let's clean this out."

They grabbed handfuls of leaves. Halfway through, Araminta found a pair of glasses. She gasped and dropped them to the ground. They had thick, green lenses.

"Mama," Berenice said again; she was holding something bright in one of her hands.

"What's that?" Araminta went for a closer look.

It was a wedding ring.

Araminta read the inscription: Laura López- Heriberto Rodriguez. August 3, 1901.

"It's him, Berenice! It's him!"

Berenice started to cry.

"No, baby, I'm sorry. I didn't mean to make you cry. It's nothing." She cuddled Berenice and wiped the tears from her eyes. There was no doubt. The skeleton lying on the ground had once been the father of her child.

She kissed Berenice on her forehead. "You be careful. When you grow up, you be careful."

"Mama."

Araminta melted at the sound of the word.

That night she tucked Berenice inside the dugout near a fire she had started in the sand using the matches.

"Good night, my sweetheart," she said and threw the blanket over her.

The next morning, she took the machete and carved a rustic paddle from the trunk of a tree. She knelt, prayed, said farewell to the skeleton she had buried, and climbed into the dugout with Berenice. She paddled, following the current of the river.

The following day, they stopped on the far shore. She caught an iguana and cooked it. Berenice sucked at the bones. That night, she made a bonfire and they slept inside the beached dugout covered with the blanket.

Another day passed. "I don't know what am I doing, going further away from my son," she told Berenice. "Perhaps this is the end of the world. The farther we go, the harder it will be to go back, and I need to go back."

"Mama, pletty."

"Aww, Berenice, the pretty one is you," Araminta said and hugged her.

Dawn came, and she dozed, tucked in the dugout with Berenice at her side. They both were nude. There was a sound in the sand. Araminta paid attention for a second. Silence. She turned over and fell asleep again.

The dugout rocked.

Something moved at Araminta's feet and she opened her eyes. The moonlight and the light of the fire shone on an anaconda's eyes. It stopped for a moment at the end of the dugout as it lifted its head.

Araminta tried to scream, but no sound came out of her mouth. Berenice was asleep. The anaconda started to slither over Araminta's legs. Time slowed down to an eternity in the autopsy room and in Araminta's mind. Araminta felt the anaconda slide on top of her abdomen. The snake's head, which was almost as big as Araminta's, was right in front of her face, its bifid tongue almost brushing her nose. The bonfire light glinted off its eyes again. She's sizing me up, Araminta thought. Berenice moved. The anaconda's attention shifted to the little girl. Araminta lowered her head in search for the machete. The anaconda disjointed its jaws and grabbed

Araminta's head—its fangs like a crown of sharp knives, from forehead to occiput. The snake tried to coiled around Araminta's body; her lips were pressed against the cold and scaly skin of the snake. She screamed in pain but the sound was muffled; She tried to grip the snake with both hands, but it was enormous, and her hands kept sliding off.

Berenice's screams sounded faraway, muffled.

The snake tried to pull Araminta out of the dugout, but she was braced with her legs wide against the sides. She groped for the machete. Half her head was in the anaconda's mouth, and the child's screams started to fade as the sound of her temporal arteries pulsating grew stronger inside her head: drum beats announcing her impending death. She was sure her head was about to explode and she was going to die. Berenice was going to die, too. She frantically searched again, but couldn't find the machete.

The anaconda pulled her out of the dugout and wrapped her in its mighty rings. Araminta's lips were pressed against the anaconda's skin. Araminta bit down. The skin was hard. Araminta sunk her teeth deeper and ripped off a mouthful of flesh. The anaconda loosened its grip a bit. Araminta spat the flesh out of her mouth and gasped in enough air to keep her alive. She bit deeper. Beneath the skin, the flesh was like butter. The grip loosened more. Araminta breathed in as much as she could and bit deeper, forming a furrow.

In the death room, he wanted to vomit as the taste of fat and blood filled his mouth.

The snake tried to retreat but Araminta's head was stuck in its mouth. Araminta kept going until she felt bone. The snake shook in useless contractions.

She wanted to move, but the weight of the snake rendered her immobile.

She dragged herself backward until she hit the side of the dugout. She groped again until she found the machete.

As though she were cutting a hefty mane, she decapitated the snake. Without the weight of the snake's body, she felt lighter, but the snake's teeth were still embedded just below her eyes.

She lay in the sand, struggling to see, but she couldn't get the fangs out of her skull. She gave up and collapsed beside the dugout. Blackness came.

She tried to call Berenice but no sound came out of her mouth. Time passed. Blackness. More time passed. She was half alive; she was half dead. She forced herself to stand. The coolness of the night made her feel better.

"Berenice!" she called, but she couldn't hear anything except her pulse in her temples. "It's mama," Araminta said. "Don't be afraid. Where are you?"

The worst of the headache was upon her; she lifted her head and lowered her eyes; she barely could see the sand. She turned around and saw Berenice's feet.

"We're leaving," Araminta said, "don't be afraid.

She set the dugout in the water and stepped inside. Berenice wouldn't come near her, Araminta could see her feet at the far end of the dugout that glided down the river at the mercy of the current.

Araminta fell asleep, completely spent, and when she woke up, she felt the sun on her skin. She was thirsty and her neck, hands, and feet were swollen. The dugout had come to a stop. Araminta leaned over to drink, but the weight of the snake's head made her fall into the water. Her feet touched the bottom of the river.

"Berenice, help me." She lifted her head and, from under the snake's head, scanned the dugout floor. Berenice wasn't in the dugout. "Oh my God! Berenice!" she called.

She heard the sound of a waterfall. Drops of water carried by the wind hit her body. She tried to remove the snake's head for the hundredth time, but it wouldn't budge. "Berenice, Berenice!" she cried.

She felt a touch on her hand, "Mama," Berenice said. The hardness of a branch poked her hand.

She grabbed the branch. She felt a pull, and she followed the pull. As she walked like a blind woman, she fell and stood up several times until she got under the waterfall. She drank the cool water and submerged herself in the water that was cooler than the river's, then she crawled onto the shore, lay in the sand, and fell asleep again.

She awoke startled because something was licking her mouth. She recoiled in panic. Her face was less swollen, and she could see more of the ground if she tilted her head backward. The animal barked. It had to be a dog. The dog whimpered and she felt its tail brushing one of her arms. It lay down next to her; she could feel its warmth, and this made her feel safer than she had in a very long time. But then the smell of the decomposing snake reached her nostrils, and she threw up before fainting again.

When she woke up the dog wasn't there. If a dog was around, people wouldn't be far away.

"Berenice," she called. The child didn't answer. Yet Araminta could hear her moving around.

The stench of the snake's head was unbearable and an oily substance had started to leak down her neck. First the fever came and later, pus dripped down from the fang wounds. She ripped off a piece of flesh that allowed her to see a bit more.

"There must be people around," Araminta said and started walking.

Berenice followed.

A child running along the shore followed by dogs screamed.

People came to see them as if they were freaks from a circus. Araminta and Berenice started to advance and the villagers retreated.

Someone said, "She's the anaconda woman."

Another said, "No, she's the Llorona. And she found her child."

"No, she's just a lost mother," a very old man said, the last to arrive.

"How can you tell?" somebody asked.

"Yes. You're blind," someone else said.

"I can smell it," he replied.

All of the villagers laughed.

And Araminta fainted again.

Chapter 31

Lázaro had been at the health dispensary for almost ten months.

The nurse complained, "Before your arrival, only three or four patients came in through that door in the morning, and another three or four in the afternoon. Now, I have to be here at half past five in the afternoon."

Still, she had everything ready: syringes, scalpels, stethoscope, sphygmomanometer, speculums, suturing kits, gloves, medications.

Once every so often there was a puzzling case that sent Lázaro to delve into his books for hours. If he couldn't help a patient, and if the patient had money, they would go to the Capital City to seek more specialized care. The others remained at the mercy of the natural history of their diseases. He tried to do as much as he could, but after all, he wasn't God.

Lázaro sat at his desk with the office door open. Patients came in with timid steps, like intruders. He got to know them. He recognized them just by hearing the sound their steps made on the floor, by the way their blurred figures came into his field of vision from the corner of his eye, or by the way they changed the scent of air.

One day, around six, just after Lázaro had seen the last patient, the nurse closed Lázaro's door and went to cook dinner.

He remained for a few minutes in that temporary cocoon.

His door flew open and banged against the wall. The pathology book he was reading fell to the floor; the monkeys retreated to the highest parts of the trees.

A woman came in, barefoot. She ran across the room, threw her child onto the examining table, looked at Lázaro with teary eyes, and then looked at the child. She said, "Doctor, help me, please save my child."

Lázaro went to the table. He looked at the infant's chest; there was no movement. He set his ear close to the infant's mouth. There was no breath, but he detected an acrid smell. He set the stethoscope on the child's chest; it was void of sound. He looked at the infant's pupils with a flashlight, but they were two inert circles. The dead baby was about seven months old and was wrapped in a dirty piece of cloth. His skin was so pale and his lips were deep purple, as were his nails.

"He's dead," Lázaro said.

The mother wailed, and the sound bounced off the walls.

Lázaro was silent.

She moved closer to the examining table, stared at the baby, and caressed his head.

"What happened?" Lázaro asked.

The woman looked through the window. The dying light of the day quivered.

"I knew he was dead, I knew it," she said. Then she wiped the tears from her face with the palm of her hand.

The child had some feathers on top of his head, on his chest, and in his cotton diaper; more feathers were wedged in between his little fingers. He looked inside the child's mouth. More feathers. A chill ran down his spine.

"What happened?" he asked again.

"I left him on the bed and went to wash clothes in the river, like I always do. When I came back, he was all purple and limp, covered with feathers."

The generator began to hum in the distance, and the bulb in the ceiling came on. Drops of sweat lay like butterfly eggs on the tip of the woman's nose. Her blouse was discolored. Lázaro took a few steps back and observed her; the front of her skirt was higher than the back, and the skin on her knees was rough and mottled. She was propped against the stretcher, trembling.

Lázaro went back to the table, next to the little one.

The woman asked, "Do you think a bird attacked him?"

Lázaro examined the child. There were no puncture wounds that would suggest the beak of a bird had injured the child, no abrasions that suggested a bird's claws had scratched him. Vomit was splattered all over his tiny chest. But some circular marks on his neck took Lázaro's breath away.

"I need to do an autopsy," Lázaro said.

She muttered, "Why?"

"I suspect it wasn't a bird."

The generator continued to work, like the incessant roar of a monster.

"This was probably murder," he said. "I'll take him to the autopsy room."

She hesitated.

"Do you know what an autopsy is?

The sound of the generator grew louder.

"Do you know what an autopsy is?"

The woman nodded and said, "You'll bring him back?"

"Of course."

"All right," she said.

He picked up the infant's body wrapped in the blanket, cradled it in his arms, and went to the autopsy room. The bulb flickered, the generator quit humming, and the light vanished. Darkness. He wasn't surprised: the generator was unreliable. So, he lit three candles; their dull light danced on the walls. He had never dissected a baby this young before.

He opened the chest, which offered almost no resistance. The infant was soft and tender, like cutting butter. He heard no clear voices, just different sounds that overlapped, perhaps water running, steps, heavy breaths, hens clucking.

He touched the thymus, which at this age was prominent... The voice of the infant was like a whistle, somewhat whiny, screechy. Lázaro couldn't understand the language, and the images were incipient, blurred, but he was able to discern a room in shadows. A shadow lurked in the room. It had a peculiar scent. Lázaro sniffed like a dog. He could smell sweat, tears, genitals, perineum, feet; each of them separately, and yet, they formed a whole. He smelled chicken shit. The shadow took the baby and went somewhere… There wasn't a dark room any more. Distorted sounds of what might have been chickens combined with the voice of a woman.

The woman had a peculiar scent that enveloped the infant as though emanating from the arms of a mother. Oh my God, this child had two mothers, like me, he thought.

She was singing the infant a terrifying story, like a lullaby. He understood.

"My son, she stole you, but I'm your mother," the woman said.

An uncomfortable movement spread pain through his body, as though someone was shaking him, and then he felt a terrible pain around his neck. Asphyxia.

The story ended in a feeble wheeze, like someone was squeezing a bag full of air until it was completely deflated.

Lázaro cradled the baby against his chest. He set him on the slab, sutured the incision he'd made in the chest, cut the black thread, blew out the candles, wrapped the child in the faded blanket, and walked back to his office.

The woman stood and walked toward him.

"Did you do it?"

"Yes."

The woman smiled.

"It's done," Lázaro said, "I know what happened."

"Why doesn't he move?" she asked.

"What do you mean?

"They said you could bring people back to life."

Lázaro was petrified.

"That's not true," he said.

"What did you do then?" the woman yelled.

The faded blanket slid open and she saw the incision.

"What have you done?" she yelled once more. "You cut my baby!" she wailed.

"I thought you knew what I was going to do," Lázaro said, in horror. "I thought you wanted to know what had happened."

"Yes, I wanted to know what happened, but not this way."

The woman was crying now in silence. "And you had to cut him open?"

"Yes."

"There was no other way?"

"No. He was already dead."

She waited.

"You're not his mother. His other mother did it," Lázaro said.

The silence penetrated the air. It was then Lázaro's turn to wait.

"You are a monster," she said. "What am I gonna do now?"

"We need to tell the police," he said.

"We knew she was mad," she said, "but we never thought she could do such a thing."

"She was broken. You took her baby away," he said.

She kissed the baby on the forehead and said, "Forgive me, my son. Forgive me. Please."

She turned to Lázaro and continued, "His mother returned several times, but we didn't let her take the baby back. We swore she was gonna get lost in the jungle, or forget about him."

Lázaro listened to the story. The woman's husband wanted a child by any means. She'd tried so many different remedies but nothing worked. Her husband had started to go out looking for other women. She couldn't imagine a life without him. So, when her sister, the poorest one, who was also crazy, became pregnant, they thought they'd found the solution. She wasn't going to be a good mother.

The sun came out and found them asleep. Lázaro woke up first. The woman lay on the stretcher with the baby by her side, close to her chest. He went to his desk and took out a form. He signed the death certificate and put it in an envelope.

Later on, a policeman came and asked for the woman's name.

"Clara," the nurse said.

The policeman took the woman's statement, asked for the death certificate, and left with the woman, who had the child in her arms. A little bundle, soon to vanish.

Chapter 32

Rumors about Lázaro's abilities traveled through the jungle and beyond, to places where the hidden could not be found, and in their travels, people embellished them—to the point that many believed he was a saint with healing powers. Others thought he was the Messiah, and others that he was the anti-Christ, or the devil himself.

Gone was the monotony that had reigned in the health dispensary because it had become plagued with people who wanted to know what the winning lottery number was, or who had stolen a radio, or if somebody who had disappeared twenty years earlier was still alive. They wanted to know if a spouse was faithful, if there was hope for an unrequited love, if the father of a child was indeed the father. They came to ask for advice on whom to marry, or whether to sell a horse, if they should lend money to a relative who'd promised to repay in three months. Would the relative keep his word? Should they sell a cow and buy a goat or a pig, or a dozen chickens? Should they pack their belongings and travel to a land more promising than this? Was it worth the risk?

Lázaro felt the repulsion of one who loved solitude but woke up one morning to discover a crowd around his bed. It didn't matter how many times he told those in his crowded waiting room that he could not predict the future. They refused to listen.

"Please, go, and seek the chocolate cup reader, or the palm reader, or the hair reader," he'd tell them, desperate to regain normality.

Some hadn't known that hair readers existed and were curious to discover where they could find one. Immediately.

"Don't you know?" a woman asked, as though a hair reader was the most obvious thing one could find.

"No, I don't." The woman turned to see who had spoken, but many pairs of eyes looked at her.

As long as Lázaro didn't sit on his chair, behind his desk, the many newcomers who had arrived did not recognize him. He'd stand in a corner of the waiting room, hidden behind the mob. Observing.

A man in dirty clothes with disheveled hair and a strong scent of onions emanating from his armpits said, "A hair reader pulls a hair from your head. A bit of pain, but not too much."

The people around him listened as he raised his voice and continued, "He wraps the hair in a piece of paper, like the paper inside a cigarette box, and then lights a match and burns the hair on a plate. Then he waits a little bit and unwraps the paper, to see your future."

Seeing he had captured the attention of everyone in the room, the man continued, "I saw my very own lungs in the picture, and I ended up with walking nemonia. Can you believe that?"

A woman with a big bosom said, "If this doctor won't help me, I'm going to see the hair reader." She looked for the exit. But the crowd had trapped her, so she said, "As soon as this room empties out."

A man who had gone blind because of an accident some years before and was keen for a miracle to regain his sight said, "Last year I had to travel for three days to see Brother Juan. I don't even remember the name of the town. I have gone to so many."

"Where was that?" somebody asked.

"He doesn't remember. Didn't you hear?" somebody else answered.

"Are you gonna let me tell the story?" the blind man asked.

"Go ahead. What else can we do?" someone said.

"I went to see Brother Juan," the blind man continued. "Do you know Brother Juan?"

Somebody in the crowd said, "Yes."

"Well," the blind man went on, "the only hotel in town was full, so I had to sleep in a hut with an old couple kind enough to take me in—"

"Ay, this one likes to talk," somebody yelled.

The crowd continued to grow uneasy, but the blind man continued to tell of Brother Juan. "When he appeared in the bullfighting ring, there were at least two thousand people inside, and more outside. He put us all in a single line around the ring and hit us on the head with the palm of his hand while he prayed. It happened so fast, but many who had not walked in years started to walk right there; they dropped their crutches and walked away."

Lázaro had gotten trapped in a corner, behind a multitude of people who pushed him against the wall.

"And you?" asked a voice. "What happened? Did it work?"

The blind man fell silent for a moment.

"I remember waiting in line. Brother Juan had ordered everybody to keep their eyes closed and not to open them until he said so. But I didn't wait long enough and I opened my eyes before he touched my head."

The crowd deflated like a balloon. "Why did you open your eyes?" somebody else asked. "You're blind."

"I don't understand why the doctor doesn't want to help me," the blind man said.

"This doctor is the worst doctor I've ever known," somebody said from the other side of the waiting room.

"Death is part of life, and when it's your turn, it's your turn, and not even the best doctors can save you, no matter what. But a doctor who doesn't want to help people? What kind of a doctor is that?" a woman pressing against Lázaro asked.

Some people understood that the doctor could not predict the future and tried to dissuade the others. "If the doctor says he doesn't have those kinds of powers, we have to believe him. We should go back to asking for help with the things doctors can cure."

The woman next to Lázaro didn't agree. "If he has powers, he should use them," she said.

"What if he can't?" a distant voice asked.

Somebody said they all should go to Sirirí. A replica of a saint had been found years ago, in a grotto, in the jungle, and since then, it had been performing miracles.

"Like what?"

"I don't know," one man said, "but the clay figurine looks like a child who was lost long ago."

Lázaro was shocked from his silence. "I made that figurine years ago! I can't perform miracles. I cannot predict the future." He should have saved his breath. Even though he didn't want to do it, he said, "Go up north, there's a doctor over there, Doctor Völlert. He can predict the future."

Nobody listened.

The town became distorted; encampments everywhere. Some stayed and waited for several days, others left as soon as they realized they had come to waste time and money.

Every morning, the nurse had to fight her way through the crowd to get to her office. She was sorry she'd eavesdropped when the doctor was talking to Clara after her child's autopsy. She shouldn't have told anyone. Now, she didn't even have time to make lunch and take a nap in the afternoon. Patients would come saying they wanted to see the doctor because they had a cold, but then they'd admit they were there for winning lottery numbers. Liars, all of them.

Lázaro would say the same thing every time: "I'm sorry. I don't know. That's not something I can help you with. The more he told them that he couldn't see the future, the more people insisted, to the point that Lázaro couldn't tell the real patients—the ones who needed a cure for real illness—from the ones who believed he was Nostradamus.

He began to dread waking up in the morning and going to work. One of these days I am going to miss something important, and somebody is going to die, and there won't be anybody else to blame but me, he thought.

Because of the crowds, the monkeys had disappeared deep into the jungle, and Lázaro had lost his desire to sit at his desk and look through the window just before dawn.

I'll go, he thought. It's time to look for Grandfather. So one morning, he wrote his resignation letter.

The postman came, fetched the letter, and said in a whisper, "Don't worry, doctor. I'll make sure this goes straight to the Capital City."

"Did you talk to my grandfather?"

"He knows what's going on, but I cannot tell you much. The windows have eyes and the walls ears."

"Did he say something?"

"He's watching over you," he said, and left.

Two days later, in the midst of the afternoon heat, the mailman came back. "Doctor, the pájaros are here, be careful," he said.

"Which birds?"

"The other army."

"I'm leaving," Lázaro said.

"Where?"

"Sirirí."

"Good idea."

"Does he know I'm coming for him?" Lázaro asked.

"Yes. Just leave. Right now. Tomorrow might be too late."

"Am I in danger?"

"We all are in danger."

The mailman left and Lázaro went to his quarters. As soon as he opened the door, a scent hit his nostrils. A decomposed body was lying on his bed. He covered his mouth and nose with his hand.

"Good afternoon, Doctor Villamayor," someone behind him said.

He turned around. Three men stood in his living room; the men's boots were stained with mud.

One man stood next to the door and the other two were positioned next to Lázaro. A watchful triangle.

"Doctor Villamayor, we came to ask you a favor," one of the men said.

"Who are you?" Lázaro said.

"My name is Joaquín Bermúdez," he answered.

"You're not policemen. Are you?"

The moribund daylight that came through the window left them in shadows, and the sound of the generator began to grow in the distance. He was trembling.

Bermúdez laughed. "The police are a bunch of useless pigs, Doctor. The government can't protect nobody, not even their mothers, so, here, we are the law."

The pájaros, Lázaro thought.

Bermúdez continued, "Like I said, I have a favor to ask."

His voice was soft. He was stocky and his eyes were greenish. His baby face made Lázaro feel uneasy.

"We have a problem, Doctor Villamayor, and I hope that you can help us. The favor we need is not a regular favor, Doctor."

"What is it? Are you sick?"

The man laughed again.

Lázaro wished he could run away.

"First, we need to understand each other, Doctor Lázaro de Jesús Villamayor. I'm not sick, but I know that you have helped some people we consider undesirable."

Lázaro's heart raced.

"You're helping people who are not my people…." Bermúdez trailed off, biting one of his nails.

"And who are your people?"

"Doctor-doctor," he almost sang. "Of course, you know who is who." With a quick movement he grabbed one of Lázaro's hands. His pleasant baby face disappeared. Lázaro tried to pull his hand back, but Bermúdez wouldn't let go.

"Give me your other hand, Doctor," he said; his voice had turned husky.

Lázaro refused. He tried to free himself, but one of the men moved closer. Lázaro tried to push him aside, but he took Lázaro's arm and twisted it behind his back.

"I understand you work wonders with your hands, especially when you work with the dead," Bermúdez said as he caressed Lázaro's hand.

Millipedes walked on Lázaro's hand.

"It would be a shame if something happened to your precious hands. Right?"

Bermúdez's man seemed to agree and with the movement of his boss's head, he released Lázaro.

Bermudez continued, "We need to kill one man. Only one. Just one. And then you can tell us what we'd like to know."

Lázaro did not say a word.

"Come on, Doctor. We know that you can talk to the dead."

Lázaro's heart quivered. "Who told you that?"

Joaquín Bermúdez laughed again, but his laughter was feigned. "Everybody knows."

"I won't do it," Lázaro said.

The man took a deep breath. "We'll see, Doctor Villamayor. You have a couple of days to think about it."

"There's nothing to think about," Lázaro replied.

"Oh, yes, there is. We don't want anything bad happening to you or your family."

"I have no family."

The man smiled again and his baby face reappeared. "Don't lie, Doctor Villamayor. Did you forget about your grandfather? We know everything about you and your family. We have friends everywhere, and they can find out all kinds of information."

"I have done nothing wrong," Lázaro said.

"We all have done something wrong, Doctor. Remember a young Indian woman?" Bermúdez said.

Of course he knows, Lázaro thought and continued trembling.

"But that's not really important. Don't you want to know about your mother? Perhaps… your father?" Bermúdez continued.

Lázaro hesitated. "My mother is dead."

"Are you sure?"

Lázaro shuddered.

The man stood up and paced. The other two men looked at Bermúdez, and again, they seemed to be waiting for something to happen.

Bermúdez said, "We can make a deal. I tell you a secret if you give me the information I need."

He pulled an envelope out from one of his pockets and set it on the desk.

Lázaro stared at it, immobile.

"Come on. Don't you want to know what's in the envelope? Aren't you curious at least?"

Lázaro said nothing.

"Fine. We'll see you later, Doctor Villamayor." He made for the door. The other two men followed.

The sound of the closing door reverberated in Lázaro's brain. The envelope lay on top of the table. He didn't want to open it. He picked it up and threw it, aiming at the garbage can. It hit the edge of the can and a photograph flew out. Lázaro got closer. It was an old photograph of a young woman lying against the trunk of a tree. Parts of the picture were blurred and stained as though it had been submerged in mud.

He picked up the envelope. Inside, there was a torn photograph of the same woman, the other half was missing. His hands trembled. He tossed the picture on the floor, but it was useless, it had already left an indentation in Lázaro's retina.

Chapter 33

Lázaro's room had been cleaned to perfection; no sign of a dead body anywhere. Somebody had changed the mattress and covers. The scent of antiseptic still lingered. He took out the torn photograph he'd found when he'd come back from the capital city to find his home had been destroyed in the avalanche. There was no doubt, the photograph Bermúdez had given him was the other half. His grandfather and the woman had been together in the picture. He set the two halves of the photo on the nightstand next to a book by Chekhov, a pen, a candle, the Victrola, and an outdated newspaper. The picture, originally black and white, had turned sort of sepia with the passage of time. The woman in the picture leaned against a mango tree. It was difficult to see the details, so he got a magnifying glass.

The woman had delicate eyebrows, almond eyes, and thin lips that gave her the appearance of a Renaissance Madonna. Her dark hair fell along the sides of her neck in two braids. A little pendant hung from her neck. She wore a delicate, crocheted top and a long skirt that fell to her ankles. She had one foot in front of the other and wore sandals with silk laces rising up her ankles. She smiled as though she didn't like those eternal moments between the smile and the click of the camera.

The picture had a life of its own and began to exert an attraction stronger than the potent magnet that tried to pull him to the center of earth during his temporary deaths. He set the picture on the nightstand again and picked up the month-old newspaper in an attempt to dissipate his mind. The two main political parties, the Liberals and the Conservatives, were experiencing a reconciliation after the War of a Thousand Days, but the teachings of Marx and Engels were polluting the minds of the people, and knowledge of the French Revolution had pervaded everything like a poison. Still there was hope the country would move out of its primeval times.

Lázaro put the newspaper back on the nightstand and picked up the photograph again. If there had been proof that he'd once had a mother, it had disappeared in the avalanche.

He tried to remember the temporary death when he'd discovered the woman he believed was his mother wasn't indeed his mother, but everything was blurred. It had been at least twenty-two years ago. The man with green eyes and the muddy boots had said he knew everything about Lázaro's family. What had he meant? It didn't matter what Bermudez knew, Lázaro wasn't going to bargain with a murderer, especially when the life of someone else was at stake.

Arcángel's cries interrupted his thoughts. He went to the kitchen to get a bottle of milk that a nursing mother had donated that day.

He went to the crib and picked up the baby, who stopped crying as Lázaro fed and rocked him in his arms.

He put the baby down and went to his bed, but falling asleep was like catching smoke with his hands. He had never forgotten he'd killed in the throes of this strange disease that didn't seem so strange any longer. He'd lived a thousand lives in less than thirty years. He'd been trapped in fires and quicksand. He'd learned and relearned the lessons of life and yet, life was confusing; each time he finished learning something he thought he could apply, when the time came, it proved useless. Life was going from mistake to mistake. He knew the past could not be changed. And the future? Was there more than one Doctor Hans Völlert in the entire world?

He lay on his bed under the light of the moon, listening to the crickets and frogs. Who was that woman? What did Bermúdez know about his mother? How had he found the picture? Who had given it to him? No. Bermúdez was playing tricks. People like him could find all kinds of information, or they could fabricate it if needed. They had connections in the government, everywhere. They would do anything to vanquish their enemies. Even if Lázaro did not accept the deal, the man he was supposed to autopsy would be killed. He was not going to save anybody. Perhaps he himself was already a dead man.

He wanted to leave without a trace, to forget about the incident. If he stayed, he'd find out about what happened to his mother, but he'd have to bargain with a murderer.

He could tell Bermúdez that sometimes, a single drop of blood was enough to unravel the world of others.

He sprang out of his bed and paced. He imagined the prisoner, trapped like an animal, hands and feet tied, no way to move, to run, or escape. The prisoner must have been a strong man if they had not been able to make him talk. He could have been betrayed by someone and sold to the man with the muddy green eyes for five pesos, or less. Lázaro had heard about torture, but when he'd done an autopsy on a man who'd been found impaled, he could not believe humans could partake in such barbaric acts.

That man had been about twenty-one years old with no distinctive features. He could have been anyone, but Lázaro had seen that he'd been a compassionate man, and his family never knew what happened to him. Perhaps they were still waiting for him to return. And Lázaro had done nothing.

He knew both sides practiced torture. How could he change humanity's heart? He was not a savior. Sometimes he wished he had the power to annihilate everyone on the planet.

Lázaro grabbed the picture. He remembered Bermúdez and shuddered to think that even those with angelic faces could do unthinkable things. Lázaro could discover everything Bermúdez wanted. But what would stop Bermúdez from killing Lázaro after he gave him the information? Or would they keep him alive so they could continue to kill others for more and more information? There was an insatiable appetite in the human species. His servitude to Bermúdez could last forever—until the other side found out about him. Then it'd be game over.

Lázaro went to the window. The night had turned everything black. He felt death close to him, but this was a different kind of death, and he knew it. He'd gotten so used to his temporary deaths that he'd almost come to believe he was immortal, but the shadow of this permanent death made him shudder.

"I don't want to die forever," he said. But he realized he was helpless.

Were his resurrections acts of his will? He didn't believe they were. If not, then who resurrected him? Life itself? God? An angel? Or was it an act of expulsion, like an angel being ejected from paradise? What was it to die forever: oblivion?

The night moved between reflective dreams and worm-like movements; the next day brought an enormous tiredness. He wasn't surprised when he received a bottle of French wine and a bouquet of flowers. It came with a note, a reminder that read: "Dear Doctor Villamayor, I thought you might find thoughtful a bottle of French wine to celebrate, and by the way, your mother loves flowers. I hope you've had enough time to think. See you soon."

Nausea. His stomach rebelling.

Lázaro packed his luggage, the same belongings he'd had when he'd arrived. His books went in first, then the medical instruments, and then his clothes. He did not take the Victrola. Instead, he wrote a two-word note: For Regina.

He'd leave the same way he'd fled the desert. He thought some people would call him a coward; others would simply do what he was about to do. Wasn't it common sense? He'd started to run a long time ago, and it seemed there was no way to end the running. The first impulse had been so strong that even if he'd wanted to stop, he wouldn't have been able to. Desperately, he thought his grandfather could fight them, save him, but he didn't believe it. Not that he thought his grandfather belonged to either side. Señor Hipólito Villamayor had always been a solitary lion.

Chapter 34

Lázaro replaced the candles that were almost guttered. The wax had melted and spread across the table and splattered onto the cement floor. The light of the moon cast the silhouette of a tree that followed the angles of the autopsy room onto the far-right wall. A flock of potoos making eerie vocalizations perched on the swaying branches. The haunting call sounded like "Poor-me-one."

He waited until the birds grew silent and still.

He looked at Araminta's body. The corpse on the slab had become incomplete, part human, part slaughtered animal.

At the base of Araminta's neck, the thyroid gland caught Lázaro's attention. He touched it.

CLICK-CLICK!

The thyroid gland said something he couldn't understand. He waited. Nothing happened, so he incised the neck, over the thyroid gland, to expose it. He slit the delicate capsule....

The voice impregnated with the clicking sound of the castanets rumbled. "I can smell it."

"Yes, I can smell it," the blind old man said, and another, and another until everybody agreed that it was the smell of a lost mother, and not the smell of a rotten dog, as someone had said... The castanets vanished with the last voice. The villagers followed Araminta, the old man, and Berenice.

They came to a shack on the outskirts of the village. Araminta was delirious. The sounds of the castanets kept clicking and clicking. Berenice cried.

The old blind man opened the door and asked, "Who's going to help us?"

The small crowd looked at him as though he were speaking in a foreign language.

"Help with what?"

"To take the snake's head off her head," the old blind man said.

The villagers left.

The putrid smell intensified. As the old man, groping, started to dislodge the snake's head, the fangs crumbled like rotten teeth falling from a decayed mouth. A piece of flesh plopped to the floor. Berenice retreated.

Finally, Araminta's head was free. It was covered in pustules.

Another intermezzo came. It didn't matter how many times Berenice caressed her, called her 'mama', pinched her, slapped her, Araminta didn't respond. She had fallen into a stuporous state. Some time passed. Berenice had grown taller, at least the height of a head.

One afternoon, the breeze coming from the river, brought a scent of jasmine. Weird, some said, that flower doesn't grow around here.

Araminta sniffed the air. Berenice looked at her and said: "Mama."

Araminta opened her arms.

Other people started to come. Outsiders. Invaders. Someone in the village had discovered a rare animal nobody had seen before, a saber-tooth cat whose teeth allegedly had the power to enlarge penises and breasts.

Araminta's heart sank when she saw the piles of carcasses. The villagers had cut out their teeth and left the rest. A mix between a black panther and a leopard, but the size of an ocelot, with blue eyes, the cats were mutilated and thrown away. Good only for the large teeth shaped like the extinct saber tooth tiger's.

The town had become infused with the scent of the cats. It smelled like jasmine.

"They say that you just put a teaspoon of powdered tooth in water and… you can imagine the rest," people said.

The old blind man said that if they didn't stop murdering those animals, the invaders were going to destroy the town.

Hunters came from distant places to kill the cats and built a camp that divided the town in two. From there, they shipped the powder to the eastern slope of the cordillera, to the plains, to the mountains, and far beyond. Behind them came prostitutes, and an enormous gas tank to supply the demands of the population.

After her head began to heal, Araminta had to shave her head again, in order to fix her hair. The prostitutes thought the look was stylish and they decided to shave their hair as well. Somebody joked that all the women had turned into men.

When somebody asked Araminta where she was from and who her

family was, she made up stories, sometimes plausible, and sometimes outrageous. The prostitutes also reinvented their lives, but they wanted them to be believable.

"My family has money. I don't do this for need," some said.

Others remained silent.

One day, after the afternoon heat had cooled a bit, Araminta, the old man, and Berenice sat inside the hut on old battered chairs and drank coffee. The light slipped through the cracks of the hut.

"We need to do something. We need to stop the newcomer hunters before they wipe out the cats," she said.

"I agree, but I don't know what," the old blind man said.

"I know," Berenice said. She was almost seven by then.

"What?" Araminta asked.

"Let's burn the town," she said.

The old man and Araminta laughed.

Araminta continued to take Berenice to the river. The cat killers had settled as though they had always been in the town. They called her Anaconda and paid her to wash their clothes. The prostitutes did too.

Every morning she came to the river and sat on a rock and washed the clothes on top of another in silence. Berenice swam, collected pebbles, played with other children, or went to school when she pleased.

"Where do you come from?" one of the cat killers asked Araminta.

"From the plains."

"Really? That's where the tooth powder sells best. Don't you wanna sell it? It makes pretty good money. Much, much more than washing clothes." He smiled. Unlike most of the other hunters, his teeth were not missing and they were bright white.

"And how do I get there from here?"

"Good question. You'd have to paddle up the river." He flexed his biceps, his skin was bronzed, his arm hair, golden.

Araminta smiled.

"You have strong muscles too," he said. "I could go with you the first time." He took out a compass. "This can help us."

"I ought to go," Araminta said, "I've finished washing the clothes."

"You seem… refined. What's your real name?"

"Margarita."

"No. Really?"

"Yes."

"Why are you here?"

"Because—"

A boat was passing by. A priest yelled, "You all are going to burn in hell. This is a town of perdition. Anybody for confession?"

Araminta climbed into the boat and started to confess. After a few minutes, she dove into the water and went to meet Berenice who was waiting with the man.

The man said: "Would he marry us," and laughed.

Araminta was serious.

"I was just joking. By the way my name is Roberto," he said and gave her the compass.

The killing of the cats continued, and Araminta found it hard to avoid their cries. They reminded her of the cry of a baby.

She began to talk about her son again, as though she had remembered him suddenly. The old blind man paid attention. Berenice paid attention at first, but when Araminta mentioned she was going to go back to look for her son, Berenice tried to change the subject, or distract her with things she had found: beautiful butterflies, lizards that ran over the water, feathers of bright colors she used to make things that resembled flowers.

The celebration in honor of the Virgen Del Carmen came, and the townspeople drank. It was the end of the day. Araminta left the old man's hut and went to where they kept the cats, in crowded cages where they could barely move. She broke the padlock with a hammer and opened the cages.

"Go. Hurry. You're free to go. Go. Now," she said in a low voice, but the cats stayed inside. She shook the cages, but the cats remained inside, looking at her.

"Go. Now," she insisted.

The cats wouldn't move.

She decided to fetch some water to throw at the cats. They hissed, but remained inside.

Exasperated, Araminta started to walk away from the cages.

The cats followed her.

She ran back to the hut. The sound of people gathered beyond the old blind man's hut and music played by an improvised little orchestra had silenced the cats. The old man woke up to the scent of jasmine saturating the air.

"It's time to go," Araminta said, "I've lived in this town long enough."

"I'm tired of it, too. I don't want to die here. Let's go," the old blind man said.

"Are we going to burn the town?" Berenice asked.

The old blind man smiled, nodded, and extended his hand. Araminta grabbed it, and he squeezed it.

They packed some things that would help them survive: food, blankets, a canvas tent, and the compass. The three of them went to the river, and Araminta helped the old blind man into the Roberto's boat. The cats waited next to the shore.

"Wait for us here," Araminta told the old blind man, and took Berenice to the other end of the town, where the enormous gas tank was.

Araminta soaked a blanket in gasoline and set it underneath the tank.

"I'll do it, Mama," Berenice said.

"No, you've learned enough bad things. Step back," she said, and threw a match on the blanket.

Berenice clapped.

The explosion threw them back into the middle of the yellow-ochre street, and the flare illuminated the town like fireworks. The stars had begun to appear.

"Are you all right?" Araminta asked, getting up from the dirt.

"Yes, Mama."

Araminta and Berenice ran back to the boat. Dogs barked. People came out of their houses and asked what had happened. Araminta and Berenice didn't stop. When they got to the river, Roberto was standing in front of his boat.

"What's the matter?" he asked.

"Quick. We have to leave now?" Araminta exclaimed.

"Why?" Roberto asked.

"Please," Berenice begged.

"Right now?"

"Yes," Araminta, Berenice and the blind old man said in a chorus.

They saw the orange flames rising into the air. The fire was spreading fast, engulfing the palm leaf roofs, the wooden house walls.

About thirty cats had boarded and they barely had space to fit in. The glare of the fire got smaller as they rode the speedboat against the current of the river and away from town.

The scent of jasmine grew as the scent of burned oil vanished.

Araminta sang a lullaby in the boat with Berenice and several cats on her lap. The motor sputtered; the cats purred.

"I don't understand. Why are we taking the cats with us?" Roberto asked.

"Where are we going?" Berenice asked.

"We're going to look for my child."

Roberto asked, "How's this possible?"

"No, mama. I don't want to," Berenice said. "And why now?"

"I can't wait any longer."

Next to her, the old blind man sat. More cats surrounded them. There was no room for anything else. They paddled against the current. They passed a couple of new towns. They saw people taking siestas in hammocks on their porticos, people swimming in the river, people killing more cats.

Berenice told the old man what she saw.

The blind old man said, "These people are just like the people we left behind. Perhaps we didn't do nothing by burning the town."

Berenice said, "Oh yes, we did. You should have seen the fire." She clapped, crossed her legs, and put both hands on top of her knees, her little flowered dress down to her knees, on top of the wooden platform where she was sitting, her little cheap shoes on top of a puddle of water.

"Berenice, what has become of you?" Araminta asked.

"I wanna be like you," she answered.

The madness of acquiring the saber-tooth cat powder had turned little towns into big messy conglomerates of shacks that left a trail of waste in the river. The towns smelled of fire, gunpowder, oil, and garbage.

"It's a shame," the blind old man said, "I remember when towns smelled of earth."

After several days, they came to a place where they could see the mountains again. Araminta took out the compass.

"We have to get to the top of the mountains. From there, I'll be able to see where we need to go," Araminta said.

Roberto said, "Sorry, I cannot continue, this is too much, I gotta go back."

"I understand," Araminta said. "I cannot ask you for anything else."

"I don't know what I was thinking. I hope we will see each other again."

"I'll go as far as this body takes me," the blind old man assured her, while a cat rubbed against his ample, strong, and calloused feet.

They said farewell and Roberto embarked. Araminta gave him the golden necklace that had once belonged to the dentist. Roberto wouldn't accept it.

"Thanks. Can I keep the compass?" Araminta asked.

"Yes, but promise me someday you'll look for me to return it."

As the day advanced, they started to climb. Rain started to fall. The cats remained faithfully close.

Once darkness came and they could go no further, they slept in the canvas tent. The furry bodies of the cats kept them warm. At times, the cats were silent, at times, one cried, which was enough to unleash a series of cries from the others.

They continued their ascent the following day. In the gray sky, cranes flew. The wet cats continued to follow them until sunset, when Araminta put up the tent. It rained throughout the night and into the next day.

"It'll stop raining. It shouldn't be raining no more," the old man said, "I'm afraid this body won't carry me no more."

Araminta kissed him on the forehead.

As they ascended, the landscape started to change; the trees became more scarce and tall wax palms began to appear. They went up and down, following the folds of the mountain, enduring the cold and the rain. Araminta held the old blind man's hand and sometimes carried Berenice on her back. The cats stayed with them. They hunted, and occasionally they'd drop a lizard, a bird, a huge insect at the feet of the humans as an offering.

It continued to rain and the mist of the morning obscured the mountains. They headed west and stopped at a waterfall. The water came crashing down on the rocks and wouldn't let them pass. They could see the path beyond the waterfall, but there was no way around it, there was a sheer wall of rock on one side of the path and a precipice on the other, from which a fall would be fatal. They had to pass under the waterfall to continue.

Araminta said she was going to try to go under it. Berenice cried. Araminta took a gigantic breath and disappeared under the water. When she returned, she said it wasn't going to be easy. Her back was covered in blood. The force of the water had pushed her against the sharp edges of the rock wall.

Berenice wouldn't stop crying. "Mama, I wanna go home," she said repeatedly.

"Which home? Remember? We burnt it," Araminta said.

"It's going to be all right," the old blind man said.

First, she took Berenice, her back sliding against the cutting rock, and came back for the old man, and then for their food supply. The cats rushed after them, but not all of them made it.

Once they were reunited on the other side, the old man, covered with the blanket, was breathing with difficulty. They drank fresh water and filled their containers. Berenice embraced Araminta. She caressed the girl's hair, and they rocked in each other's arms, trembling, while the old man started to cough.

They ate dried pieces of salty meat, carrots, and oranges, then continued to walk.

The cats did what they were supposed to do, hunting birds, rodents, and snakes.

"Oh God, please, stop the rain, please," Araminta begged.

It didn't stop, but they found a cave that extended deep inside the mountain. They slept on dry ground for the first time in days.

The next morning, they started to descend but the earth was as soft as butter. They slid down, grabbing roots and rocks, avoiding falling into precipices only by putting their feet against the trunks of fallen trees. The old man had developed a fever. Araminta wiped his wet forehead in vain. They followed the compass' needle, as the wind made the mist swirl in front of them. Finally, the sun appeared for a brief moment. Araminta took out the binoculars.

"Look. There's a lagoon down there," she said, pointing. Two small rivers fed the lagoon. A town farther along the path appeared. She scanned the surroundings and managed to distinguish a church. She continued to look until she found the arch, and the stone wall. "We found it!"

"What?" Berenice asked.

"My home. My town."

Berenice looked at her, drenched and trembling. "I don't wanna go to that home," she said.

"You go, I'm tired," the old man said.

"I'll help you," Araminta said.

They walked for several hours more, but the old man was slower. Araminta took out the binoculars and looked again. The water had risen. The lagoon looked engorged, like a monster about to vomit. "We have to get there, we have to let them know of the impending peril," she said.

She had to repeat it so the old man would understand. "Don Anselmo, la laguna se va a desbordar."

"You go. I'll meet you down there," the old man said.

"But you cannot see," Berenice said and started to cry.

Araminta served as a crutch for the old man on one side, and held Berenice's hand on the other, guiding them. They fell innumerable times. They walked on the edge of precipices. Sometimes, she carried Berenice. The wax palms disappeared and the jungle trees reappeared. She continued running, falling, always descending. The cats looked like balls of mud.

They tried to avoid places where she thought they could be caught in the path of a flood if the dam gave way.

The old man was becoming sicker. They stopped, covered in mud. The old man took deep panting breaths.

"Why is he that way?" Berenice asked when he started to wheeze and turned purple.

"He's dying," Araminta said between sobs.

The old man looked like a specter.

"Please, don't die," Berenice begged and continued to cry. Araminta hadn't slept in days. They had nothing to eat. She was about to collapse.

There was a rumble, as though the earth was turning inside out.

Araminta collapsed.

"What's happening, Mama?" Berenice asked.

"The lagoon has flooded!" Araminta cried. "The town is going to be destroyed. All of them are going to die!"

They ran toward the side of the mountain, trying to avoid the avalanche, but it was usless. Araminta embraced Berenice and they rolled down the side of the mountain in a great mudslide until they hit the trunk of a tree. She was breathless for several seconds, and when the air returned to her lungs she asked, "Where's he?"

Don Anselmo had disappeared.

Araminta woke up. She must have slept for several hours. Berenice was eating a piece of rotten fruit, and Araminta's head was on her lap.

The avalanche had brought everything down in its path. Araminta wailed with Berenice next to her and surrounded by the remaining cats; she cursed the heavens, her father, her destiny.

When they finally reached the valley, the steeple of the church emerged in the middle of a huge, flat, dark, muddy area.

Araminta fell to her knees. "It's too late," she cried. Berenice and the cats cried with her.

All of a sudden, someone covered in mud ran toward them. She stood up. Berenice and the cats hid behind her. It was a nude man; the thick layer of mud made him look like a moving statue. He stopped for a moment, his eyes wide open. He was shivering and whispered, "Help me! Help me! Help me!" but he continued to run as though he couldn't stop.

Araminta and Berenice walked around what was left of the town; it was difficult to move through all the mud, debris, puddles, and streams. A half-buried bed had a rosary on a pillow. An empty flowerpot lay on the ground. Araminta headed farther away from the mountain. The town had been turned upside down. The rain stopped and a terrible odor had begun to rise.

"It's not that far from here. I know it," Araminta said.

It took them a day to find the cement arch. Araminta recognized the remains of the villa. The water had formed pools, and the remains of the garden held scattered flowers that fought to survive.

"I hope I find his body," Araminta said.

"Mama, don't cry," Berenice pleaded, sucking on one of her thumbs.

"Where is my son? And my sister?"

No answer. Silence descended. The orchestra of human organs had become still. Only a universal emptiness remained, as if there were no space for anything else.

Chapter 35

The generator growled in the distance. Lázaro finished packing his clothes and took his suitcases when someone knocked on his door; his heart jumped. He thought about leaving through the back door, but he heard Regina's voice calling him. He went to the door and opened it. Regina was alone.

"Mother told a man you were leaving," Regina said.

"I'll be back as soon as I can," Lázaro said and crouched down to look her in the face. "Promise me something. Promise me you'll take care of Arcángel until I get back."

"I don't want you to leave," she said as she wiped her tears with the back of her hand, "I'll come with you."

"I'll come back when things get better. I promise," he said.

Regina grabbed his hand; her mother's voice called in the distance.

"Please, you have to go," he pleaded.

A noise coming from the kitchen door made them pay attention.

The postman was almost indiscernible at the edge of the rectangle of light that came from the kitchen.

"Let's go to the river!" the mailman said and came into the kitchen.

Lázaro took one of the suitcases; the postman grabbed the other.

They were about to leave but the nurse was standing in front of them, next to Bermúdez, blocking the exit. Bermúdez's accomplices came in from the living room.

"Regina!" her mother said. "Come over here!"

Regina didn't move.

"Doctor Villamayor. How are you?" Bermúdez said as he advanced.

Lázaro, the postman, and Regina retreated. Bermúdez's accomplices pushed Regina's mother aside and rushed forward.

Bermúdez said, "So, you're leaving, without saying good-bye?"

Regina's mother yelled again, "Regina, come over here!"

Regina didn't move, so her mother tried to get to her, but one of the men raised his arm and blocked her.

"Since you didn't have any intention of letting me know you were leaving, I decided to come for a visit. I sent you a present, and all I get is this? You didn't even appreciate the little piece of information I gave you. Where are you going, Doctor Villamayor?" He cleared his throat. "Where were you going?"

Lázaro inhaled, but there was not enough air in the room.

The silence was thick, immobile. A cockroach ran along the tile floor. Lázaro lowered his gaze and for a moment all of them watched the insect. Bermúdez stepped forward and crushed it. The sound made Lázaro flinch.

"Oh, I'm sorry. You love animals," Bermúdez mocked, and the hairs on the back of Lázaro's neck stood up.

Bermudez advanced and the men behind Lázaro and Regina moved so they all were herded into the living room. One of the men had closed the kitchen door; the main door had already been closed. Regina's body stuck to Lázaro's legs.

"Doctor Villamayor, I'm a believer," Bermúdez said, "I know you know how to get the information I want. I don't know how you do it, but I know you can. You see, Doctor, there are weird things in life." The man paused. "I'm gonna tell you a story. There was once a man who couldn't be killed with bullets, or knives, or machetes, not even fire. It's true. Do you understand? I believe in those things, and I believe in you, but you don't care, you're just gonna run away."

Lázaro wiped his forehead with one of his hands. The night was cooling off, but he was sweating profusely. Bermúdez's accomplices were taking the postman through the back door and into the darkness.

Bermúdez took a white handkerchief out of one of his pockets and handed it to Lázaro. "It's hot in here, isn't it?"

Lázaro didn't move.

Bermúdez shrugged and dried his own forehead, cheeks, around his mouth, nose, and neck, with the handkerchief, "I know your grandfather, Señor Villamayor. He's our friend," Bermúdez said.

Of course, Lázaro thought, and here he was thinking his grandfather could save him.

"Aren't you interested in knowing about your mother?" he asked Lázaro.

Lázaro continued to be silent, immobile.

"What about your father?"

His father had been his grandfather....

Bermúdez looked at one of the other men and pointed with his nose to Lázaro. "Let's go for a walk," he said.

Regina pressed her body against Lázaro's leg even more. "He's not going anywhere," she said.

"Hush up!" her mother begged.

Bermúdez stepped behind Lázaro and said into his ear, "You're not going to listen to a brat. Right?" he said.

"I'm not a brat," Regina contested.

Bermúdez's accomplices had returned; the postman was not with them.

"Where's the mailman?" Lázaro asked.

Bermúdez exhaled a hot mouthful of breath on the back of Lázaro's neck.

Lázaro wanted to jab Bermúdez with one of his elbows, but the hardness of something against his back deterred him. A gun.

"Let's go, Doctor," the henchman said, shoving Regina to the floor.

Her mother ran to help her, but the other accomplice put his foot in front of her and she fell, and slid on the tile floor like a seal.

Lázaro knew this could be a trip with no return for more than just him. He looked at Regina and her mother. Regina looked back, confused; she stood and helped her mother.

"Please, Regina, go home," Lázaro said.

Bermúdez nodded, "Didn't you hear, brat?" he said.

Regina's mother dragged her across the room and they disappeared through the front door.

They had four horses waiting. Lázaro mounted one, and as they left the town and rode into the jungle, the rocky ground turned soft and muddy. They followed a narrow path. Nobody spoke. Lázaro was sure they were going to kill him once they got what they wanted. He imagined the postman was dead by now, although he hadn't heard a shot. He'd said his grandfather had asked him to protect Lázaro. Nobody was going to protect him now.

It was almost seven o'clock; the silver light of the moon illuminated their path. Lázaro looked at the starry sky and listened to the sounds of the jungle.

They continued to ride alongside the river.

One of the men said, "Look, the manatees are swimming."

Lázaro looked at the huge mammals that swam close to shore. The manatees squeaked. He felt an immense desire to cry.

After about an hour of riding, they came to a halt.

Four men and a nun were standing on a small beach. Lázaro guessed which one was the prisoner—he was blindfolded and his face was so swollen he did not look human. Anticipating blood, he shut his eyes. The wind carried an odor of excrement, urine, and blood. Lázaro shivered.

He heard Bermúdez say, "Open your eyes, Doctor Villamayor."

Lázaro didn't. Somebody pushed Lázaro off his horse. He fell to the sand like a cat, on his hands and feet, his eyes still shut.

"Easy with the doctor," Bermúdez said. "Don't you wanna know who's here, Doctor Villamayor?"

Somebody moved away from him.

"It all depends on you, Doctor," Bermúdez said. "Do you want to help me find out where those motherfucking guerrillas are hiding?" Bermúdez laughed. "Come on, open your eyes and pick. Who's it gonna be?" he said.

"You fucking traitor," a man's voice mumbled.

"So, who's it going to be?" Bermúdez said. "Quick, Doctor. Come on, we don't have all night."

Lázaro threw up.

The nun started to pray. Her voice was soft. "Blessed Father, please, protect us. Protect Lázaro."

Lázaro wiped his mouth with the cuff of his shirt.

"See? Somebody cares about you," Bermúdez said. "Come on, open your eyes and pick. Who's it gonna be?" he repeated.

Lázaro's legs trembled, and for a moment he thought they would not support him.

"She's here because she wants to tell you something. Right, Sister?

"Lázaro…" said the nun.

Bermúdez interrupted.

"The priest says he cannot violate the sacred act of confession, but I know he's hiding them somewhere," Bermúdez said.

Lázaro hesitated. How could he decide? He knew someone was going to die first.

"Heavenly Father…" the nun muttered.

"Take this chalice away from me," Lázaro continued as though he were in the garden of Gethsemane.

"Fine! I'll decide for you. Let's see when the nun's turn comes if you remain silent," Bermúdez said.

Lázaro said, "I can do what you want with a drop of blood."

"Are you kidding me?" A gunshot sounded, and Lázaro lifted his hands as though trying to stop it. He opened his eyes and saw the priest falling. Noises came from the jungle, and a cascade of bullets rained over them.

"God, please, protect us!" the nun yelled.

The bullets passed close with a wheezing sound. He pressed his body against the soft, cool sand. More shots came; one of the horses fell next to Lázaro, sending a wave of air and sand against his face. The remaining horses ran in different directions. More shots, people running, voices, and screams.

"Shoot the bastard! Shoot the bastard!" somebody yelled.

The sky was full of stars. The horse had ceased to breathe. Lázaro was still.

There was a new voice. "I think all of them are dead," he said.

Lázaro continued to be still, pretending he was dead. He heard a thump, but still didn't move.

There was a laugh. "Bermúdez is dead. Let's go," the man said.

The horses galloped away and the sound of a motorboat faded in the distance. Lázaro was rising when the nun called, "Lázaro..."

He closed his eyes again, instinctively.

"Doctor Lázaro!" another voice said.

He paid attention.

"Doctor Lázaro."

"Regina? What are you doing here?" he said, his eyes still tightly closed.

"I followed the horses. I heard the shots and hid until they left. Are you all right?"

"Yes."

"Open your eyes," Regina said.

"I can't open my eyes,"

"Why?"

"If I see blood, I'll die."

"Like in the health dispensary?"

"Probably."

"Is that why my mother didn't want me near you?"

"Yes."

"She doesn't know I'm here."

"Regina," Lázaro said. He wanted to reproach her, but at the same time he was happy she was there. "Please, help me. Give me your hand. Where's the nun?"

"Over there."

They headed in the direction of the nun, but Lázaro felt someone grab his ankle and he almost fell.

"Help me."

Lázaro recognized Bermúdez's voice.

"Bless me, Father for I've sinned," Bermúdez said.

"I'm not the priest. You killed him. Remember?" Lázaro said without looking at Bermúdez, but the man continued.

"I know I'm going to die, Father, but even though you would not come into my home, please allow me to come into your kingdom."

"Why would I do that?" Lázaro asked.

Bermúdez said, "Because your heart is big enough to forgive the worst of sinners."

"Be careful," Regina said. "He's all bloody."

Bermúdez said, "Am I hearing an angel?"

"No," Regina said, "I'm the brat, remember?"

Bermúdez vomited.

"He's throwing up blood!" Regina said.

The man vomited again.

Lázaro lifted his head towards the sky without opening his eyes. "I am the resurrection and the life," Lázaro said. "Ego te absolvo."

Lázaro knelt and groped for Bermúdez's body.

Bermúdez grunted. Lázaro checked his pulse. The pulse became slower and weaker. Somehow, Lázaro thought, it was as though he had the man's heart in his hand, until it stopped.

"The nun, take me to the nun," Lázaro said.

"Her chest is all bloody," Regina warned him.

Lázaro knelt next to the nun. She said something, but he couldn't understand what she'd said. Her words were slurred and her voice, weak, so he palpated her face and set his ear next to her mouth. She said, "I know who you are," and took a shallow breath.

"Please, Sister, don't talk, we need to get you to a hospital."

"I've heard you can see people's lives," she said. "Promise me you'll do my autopsy," she said. "I want you to see with your own eyes."

"We'll take you to a hospital," Lázaro said and tried to help her sit up, but his hand slipped on her back, which was drenched in blood.

There was a refreshing breeze. "When I got to the desert, they told me you'd left," she said.

Lázaro remembered the nuns walking in the distance against the sand dunes while he fled.

"Are you the nun who performs miracles?" he asked.

"You are the one who performs miracles," she said.

The heaviness of death settled in his arms.

He continued to hold her for a while. He considered trying to resuscitate her, but he recognized the futility of the act.

"Regina, we need to get back to the health dispensary now," he said.

"Someone's here," Regina said.

A man's voice said, "Your grandfather sent me. Where are the pájaros?"

"There are no birds here," Regina said.

"There's gotta be a mistake," the man said. "These are soldiers. The pájaros were supposed to be here. They were supposed to be dead!"

Regina's mother yelled in the distance, "Regina!"

"Mom, mom!" Regina yelled.

Regina's mother came with another man.

The newcomer accused her, "You said the pájaros were going to be here."

"I swear they told me!" Regina's mother exclaimed.

"So, where are the pájaros?" the man asked.

"I don't know," Regina's mother answered.

"Someone has to know!" the man said. "If you don't tell me, I'm gonna kill your daughter!"

"No! Please!!" Regina's mother implored. "Not her! Please, don't kill my daughter!"

Lázaro's head spun as he heard the click of a revolver.

He opened his eyes.

Regina's mother stepped in between the gunman and her daughter. Time slowed. The sound of the shot was deafening. Regina's mother was falling to the sand, blood spreading across her white uniform blouse. The nurse's finger touched him on the shoulder and her voice called to him. Doctor Lázaro, venga.

The bullet was coming directly at Lázaro, bursting into fragments against his now impenetrable chest. Lázaro made a decision. He'd smashed two people before. The gunman held his hands out in front of him to try to stop Lázaro from crashing onto him. The man's hands were against Lázaro's chest, like an insect's legs. Lázaro leaned on top of the man and heard the crushing sound of the man's ribs cracking, his lungs deflating. The insect had been smashed. One of the man's eyes rolled on the sand like a marble; his face disappeared in the sand as Lázaro plummeted into the depths of another temporary death.

The nurse's face greeted him on the other side. Ready to tell. Her story was fast, just like her talk.

Chapter 36

Lázaro's cheek against the river sand was cold; the other cheek, facing the sky, was being tickled. One of the horses had returned and was nuzzling him with its chin. The horse snorted and a gush of hot air fell on his face. Lázaro was lying on top of the gunman—or whatever was left of him. Underneath him the corpse's blood was viscous, the viscera slimy, and the bones hard and thorny. The eyes protruded from their orbits, the tongue hung from macerated lips, the teeth were scattered, cerebrospinal fluid leaked from an ear, and the brain was an amorphous gelatinous mass smeared on the ground.

Lázaro sprang to his feet. Clots of blood, pieces of flesh, and shards of bone fell to the sand. Regina was several feet away holding her mother's head in her lap. Her eyes were swollen and red; snot oozed from her nose.

"My mother is dead," she said.

Lázaro knelt and took one of Regina's hands. His body ached; he was bruised and covered in pustules. Like in Paris, but this time he hadn't been on fire, there were no ashes, no soot.

The nurse's face was peaceful now.

"Can you bring her back?" Regina asked.

Lázaro shook his head.

Regina caressed her mother's face. "I'm sorry I was a brat," she said, and wiped her nose with the sleeve of her sweater.

"We'll find your father," Lázaro said.

"I don't have a dad."

"Yes, you do. I know where he is."

"You saw him when you were dead?"

"No, but your mother told someone where he lived."

"What am I going to do now?" Regina asked.

"We need to go, Regina," Lázaro said, "I don't have much time."

"Why? Are you going to die again?"

"No, but I need to do the autopsy now, or, I won't be able to know..."

"To know what?"

"She asked me to do it."

"It's my fault."

"No. It's mine. Let's put the body on top of the horse," Lázaro said, grabbed the reins of the horse, and positioned it close to the nun.

"Please, hold the horse still," he said and offered Regina the reins.

She grabbed them.

He knelt next to the nun's body. She had the body of an athlete. He'd didn't look; he'd learned how to see with his hands. He lifted her with some effort, placed her on top of the horse, and secured her with the same rope Bermudez's men had used to tie her.

"What about my mother? Regina asked.

"Bring the other horse," Lázaro said.

Lázaro placed the nurse's abdomen on top of his shoulder and grabbed her legs, just below her enormous buttocks. He pushed hard on his knees to stand. The effort made him pant. He took a couple of deep breaths. The horse snorted and tried to walk away while Lázaro tried to set the nurse's body on top of it.

"Hold it still," Lázaro said.

Regina hung from the reins.

Lázaro's back and neck hurt more than anything else; the blisters in his body had already started to vanish. He finished setting the nurse's body on top of the horse.

"Get the rope from the priest," Lázaro said.

Regina handed him the reins and went to fetch the rope.

Lázaro secured the nurse's body with the rope.

"What about the others?" Regina asked.

"We don't have time."

She walked around the horse to meet her mother's face. "Forgive me, Mom," she said. "I shouldn't have made fun of you with Doctor Lázaro."

They started to walk alongside the river that continued to flow; the light of the moon cut into its surface; the jungle grew darker, almost impenetrable. Lázaro used one hand to hold Regina's, and the other to hold the horses' reins; ghosts in the bluish light of the night. Lázaro was startled several times by shadows and sounds, thinking that the others had come back to kill them.

The river flowed in silence. No manatees were in sight. The moon floated in the water. The sound of an animal cry broke the silence of the night.

"Arcángel! He's alone," Lázaro exclaimed.

"He must be sleeping," Regina said. "He likes to sleep."

At times Lázaro guided the horse; at times the horse guided them.

They came to a stop when they reached the health dispensary. Lázaro checked on Arcángel and tucked Regina under the blankets next to him in Regina's room.

"I'll be back as soon as I finish," he said.

"Do you want me to come with you?"

"No, you take care of him."

Regina put an arm around the little one.

He guided the horses through the clearing, past the latrine, and stopped in front of the autopsy room. He patted them, untied the corpses, and set them on the ground. The horses snorted and the skin on their flanks trembled.

Lázaro walked to the fence, tied the horses to it, and gave them water he'd brought from the well. Then he retrieved the key, opened the death room door, and crossed the threshold.

Chapter 37

Some of Araminta's organs were piled on the metal table, others on the slab. Enveloped by a strong sack called the pericardium, Araminta's heart lay undisturbed in her chest. Untouched. He'd trusted the other organs.... Their stories... For the most part, the organs had revealed truths.... But when in doubt in previous autopsies, he'd always gone for the heart.

Lázaro took a pair of small forceps, lifted the pericardium, and cut it open with scissors. The heart was immersed in a yellowish fluid, like the embryo of a bird. He stuck his hand in to hold the heart, that powerful pump that had sent blood through arteries, arterioles, and capillaries, again and again, to nurture Araminta's most distant landscapes.

In order to detach her heart from its anchors, he had to cut the aorta, the pulmonary veins, and the superior and inferior vena cava stems.

Once the heart was freed, he placed it on the slab, close to one of her hands, and made a complete transverse cut at the ventricular level. He found a puddle of blood inside the left ventricle. He trembled, and the blood stirred as if a ruby had been contained in a sacred vessel.

He heard a bell. A call for a gathering, a call for an announcement, a call for mass, a sacrifice, a solemn knell....

The mighty heart had the voice of a little bell.

BLIING!

The sound was sweet, gentle, and sadness rose within him. He shivered once more, as if an imminent collapse was approaching. He wished he was like other people, people who'd hear stories and remain untouched because they believed they were immune to tragedy. "That will never happen to me," they would say.

Araminta passed close to him, an ancient ghost. The water splashed. She waded into the puddle. A distant heartbeat poked inside his chest. He checked his pulse. He was dead, and he hadn't realized about it. No more jolts.

Ripples formed and extended like fluid fingers as she advanced into the clear water. Her feet tripped over a tilted table, an armoire, a chair until she arrived at an area full of mud and leaves.

She slid on the slippery surface and sank. She resurfaced holding a bloody leg above the water. She moved around the muddy area and arrived at the trunk of an enormous tree where a swollen face, completely unrecognizable, rose above the water. An emerald hairpin in the shape of a frog sparkled. "God, have mercy on us," she said.

She stepped on the tree limb and submerged her arms in the water on both sides of the head as though trying to lift the body, but it wouldn't budge.

She tried several times.

She went back to the muddy waters and lifted the swollen head by its chin.

BLIING!

Another heartbeat jolted inside Lázaro's chest.

Araminta came down the trunk of the tree and approached the body.

"I'm going to get you out of here, sister," Araminta said. "You're trapped."

She dove and tried to move the concrete arch, then the trunk of the tree.

She came to the surface, "I cannot dislodge you," she said. "Please, tell me, where's my son? Where is he?"

The swollen head tried to say something, but a guttural sound came out of its mouth.

Araminta cupped the face with her hands and said, "Sister. My sister."

The head was heavy, leaning forward, the water almost at the level of the lips. Araminta lifted it and gasped; the face had a mole at the tip of its chin.

"Auntie Delfina, I thought you were Leonor. I didn't recognize your face," she exclaimed.

BLIING! BLIING!

Two beats knocked inside Lázaro's chest.

Auntie Delfina started to convulse.

Araminta tried to stop the quivering movements of the head in the water. Auntie Delfina shook like a fish on a hook until becoming quiet again.

She opened her eyes, and her hoarse voice said, "Where am I?"

"Where's Leonor? Where's my son?" Araminta asked.

BLIING! BLIING! BLIING!

Three heartbeats in a row jumped inside Lázaro's chest. Past and present collided. Lázaro feared returning to life. He wished to remain dead.

"I'm sorry, auntie, I'm sorry," Araminta said. "Where are they?"

"I don't know," her voice was weaker and hoarser. "I'm thirsty." It was hard to hear.

Araminta cupped her hand and filled it with water; then she lifted Auntie Delfina's chin with the other hand. Auntie Delfina drank, but water leaked from the corners of her mouth. She took out her tongue, swollen and dry, like a macaw's tongue.

"Is my son dead?" Araminta asked.

The macaw's tongue didn't move.

"Is my son dead?" she repeated.

No answer. Araminta tilted her head so her ear was next to the floating head's mouth.

"Please, tell me, Auntie Delfina, where's my son, and my sister?"

Auntie Delfina was dead.

BLIING! BLIING! BLIING! BLIING!

Four continuous beats hit Lázaro's chest.

Lázaro thought, as though he were Saint Thomas of Aquino. Seeing is believing.

Araminta climbed up again on top of the trunk of the tree and stood; the remnants of the concrete arch inscribed with the last three letters of what had been El Eden—D-E-N—appeared above the water, behind the tree branches.

Araminta yelled, "Láazzaaarrrrooooo!"

Lázaro's heart was running now like an unbridled horse.

For all these years, I thought it was my mother's head too, Lázaro thought.

Araminta moved back to the edge of the puddle and passed by Lázaro. He tried to touch her; the wind stroked his hand. He closed his hand as though he were able to grasp a memory he didn't own.

She grew lost in the distance. He knew she was in search of his body. He decided to go after her knowing the futility of the action, but the autopsy room reappeared, and he was cradling her heart in his hands. He knelt on the floor, like when he was a child playing with marbles.

"Doctor Lázaro," Regina said standing at the door. "Did you find out what you wanted to know?"

Lázaro nodded.

"Was she the lady in the picture?" Regina asked.

"Yes. She was my mother."

Regina came closer and set her hand on top of Lázaro's shoulder.

"Don't cry," Regina said, took the heart from his hands, and set it on the slab. "We both don't have mothers anymore."

Lázaro got up, went to the sink, and washed his hands. He turned around and said, "We have a long trip ahead of us. Please go back and check on Arcángel."

Regina left. Lázaro put each organ back inside Araminta's body. The heart was the last to go.

He took a large, sharp, and shiny needle, inserted the black thread, and sewed the skin, pinching together the separated edges to join them. The needle entered the skin on one side of the incision, making a dimple, and exited on the other side, pulling the skin up like a tent. He created a neat, symmetrical pattern, unlike most, who sewed the skin as if sewing a potato sack.

Her skin was more difficult to sew in some places. Resistant. But not how it was with some corpses, where he had to use the scalpel's handle to push the needle through the skin. There was no correlation between the toughness of the skin and the toughness of the spirit. Sometimes the stories revealed strong characters that had soft skin, and sometimes feeble spirits had the toughest.

He looked at his mother, so peaceful. A repaired doll. He cleaned her with a wet rag. Dried blood, pieces of bone, little balls of fat, rosy threads of muscles, and the last fluids disappeared under his ministrations. He washed her, a long caress, until the last stain of blood had vanished.

The box full of stories was sealed now. The candles were extinguished. The cement floor had cracked.

The birds had disappeared, but the sun lit the autopsy room. All of a sudden, all that had not contained beauty until then seemed beautiful, and all that had been beautiful seemed horrendous. The exotic flowers were sacrificial offerings. The infernal heat and oppressive humidity of the jungle were a potent narcotic to ameliorate the force of the senses....

He made himself finish preparing her, but he wanted to run away and never come back, get lost in the jungle and the river, among the manatees.

He continued his job with the gentleness of a Japanese mortician. He rolled her aside and set a white sheet underneath her. He rolled her to the other side, and wrapped her. A shroud. Her face and hands floated in the whiteness, one hand on top of the other. Indeed, she was a little Renaissance Madonna.

Lázaro took off his apron and went to the door; he extended his arms. The warmth of the sun spread from his fingers to his forearms, then from his arms to his shoulders. He leaned forward and the sun touched his head. He stepped outside and had to close his eyes as a torrent of light saturated his pupils. He set his hands above his eyes like a visor and opened them again.

The monkeys had returned and were playing in the trees. The latrine was still in the corner of the backyard. Why wouldn't it still be there? But he had changed. Despite his rare disease that had brought isolation, repudiation, he had not felt rancor. He remembered the autopsy as if it had happened many years before. His mother had given him the opportunity to feel in a single night what he hadn't ever.

He went to see Regina and Arcángel, prepared a bottle for the little one, and made breakfast for Regina and himself.

They went to the cemetery following the priest, Arcángel in Lázaro's arms and Regina by his side. The priest wore his cassock despite the scorching sun, and a mule pulled the caskets on a wheeled cart. A concert of noises accompanied them: the screeching of wheels, the creaking of wood, the thumping of caskets when the cart wheels hit rocks on the road.

A curious boy and a girl with a stray dog joined the entourage. Lázaro summoned a man who was walking by and offered him some money to help them bury the bodies.

They entered the cemetery through an iron gate that was falling apart. The jungle had trespassed and weeds had spread and fought with headstones and crosses to see who'd win the battle. The boundaries were blurred.

They found a tree covered with orchids, and Spanish moss that hung down like the beards of millenarian gods.

"Here, this is the spot," Lázaro said.

He and the peasant dug into the soft ground, unearthing a primal scent. When they finished they were drenched in sweat. The priest sprinkled holy water, finished his prayers, and left. The boy, the girl, and the peasant followed the priest, and the dog followed them.

They sat by the graves. Lázaro held Arcángel, and Regina held a raggedy doll. They were silent for some time. Before they left, Regina placed the doll on top of her mother's grave. "Good-bye, Mother," she said.

They returned to the health dispensary, which was again deserted. Lázaro, Regina, and Arcángel slept in the same room. Lázaro woke several times, attacked by deadly thoughts: He had killed three times. Two of them could be judged as accidents but the last one wasn't. He had chosen to save Regina. But did it make him any less of a murderer?

When the sun finally rose, he got up, went to his office, unlocked a drawer, and took out a gun.

"Where did you get that?" Regina asked, standing with Arcángel in her arms, watching him from the door.

"The postman gave it to me," Lázaro said. "To protect us."

"Are you going to use it?"

"Yes," Lázaro said. "There will be beasts on the road."

Chapter 38

The return to Sirirí was easier this time. The jungle had been breached with roads that extended deeper and deeper into the green. A shabby bus station had replaced the mules. A clerk behind a battered desk sold tickets. They rode the bus for several hours until it left them on top of a dusty hill. In the distance, at the bottom of the far side of the hill, Lázaro saw the house surrounded by paved stones. The roof looked at the sky with red clay tiled eyes, and a column of white smoke rose from the chimney. Behind the house, the mountain range, had a massive hole in it. Several trucks were parked in a muddy area and the compound was encircled by a tall wire fence.

They had to walk down the hill for almost an hour. Lázaro carried Arcángel on his back, his medical bag in one hand; in the other he carried a suitcase containing some clothes he had packed for all of them. Regina followed carrying Arcángel's bottle and a bag with some food. Her little dog trailed.

They passed through a cane forest and followed the tall wire fence until they came to the entrance. Next to a booth, where two bodyguards looked about distractedly, stood the stone arch with the words El EDEN carved in it. One of the guards had golden teeth and asked who they were. The other one, a corpulent man, remained silent.

"It's Lázaro. Lázaro de Jesús Villamayor, Señor Villamayor's grandson," Lázaro said.

The corpulent man looked at them, said he was going to talk to someone else, and disappeared. The remaining one was eating something from a greasy paper bag.

"I'm hungry," Regina said, "I'd like to eat something."

The man offered her a piece of bread and salami.

"Thank you," Regina said.

She gave half to Lázaro half and a morsel to the dog.

Lázaro saw the small pond and the garden that never knew the absence of flowers. The house looked smaller than he remembered. Geraniums hung from pots on the yellow brick walls.

They sat on a cement bench by the booth and waited. Arcángel was sleeping. Lázaro drank water from a canteen and passed it to Regina.

The guard returned with another man who greeted Lázaro with surprise. "Niño Lázaro, your grandfather said you were dead!"

"But he always resurrects," Regina said.

"Alirio, it's been a long time," Lázaro said.

Alirio asked the guard to open the gate and let them into the compound.

Lázaro and Alirio shook hands.

"Twelve years? Thirteen?" Alirio said.

They passed the pond where colorful fish swam on the surface of the water, opening and closing their mouths among water lilies. They walked on the stone-paved patio, where two trees stood encircled by small boulders.

They stopped in front of a garden and Lázaro said, "Good afternoon, Victor," and inhaled the perfume of a jasmine bush.

"Who's Victor?" Regina asked.

"The jasmine bush. My mother used to talk to flowers."

"Mine, hated jasmine flowers. She said they were the flowers of death," Regina said and started to sob.

Lázaro put his hand in his pocket to find a candy, but instead he found the hardness of the gun; the gun felt heavy, strange, unnatural. Forgiveness and hatred were far apart, and anger and fear were so close together. Would he be able to do it? He had the motivation. And how was he going to get away with it?

"As soon as we're done here, we're going to look for your father," Lázaro said.

"I don't need another father. You're my father," Regina said and grabbed Lázaro's hand.

"Regina… the terrible child," he said and they laughed.

They continued on their way to the front door. Lázaro took his hand out of his pocket and as they walked, brushed some margaritas, gladioluses, and irises with his palm.

"Hello, flowers," Regina said.

"Niño Lázaro, I want to ask the Patrón if it's all right for you to come in now," Alirio said. "I hope he doesn't have a heart attack. I'm not sure but I think he really believed you were dead."

Alirio entered the house and closed the door behind him.

Lázaro looked at the garden; a hummingbird, suspended in the air, drank nectar from an orchid. Arcángel whimpered.

"Arcángel is hungry, too," Regina said. "And Pepa."

Lázaro looked inside his bag for the bottle; they had run out of milk.

They waited for a couple of minutes until Alirio came back. "Niño Lázaro, come in," he said. "The Patrón asked me to search you, but I know you, Niño Lázaro. Besides, why would you need a revolver?"

They went into the house. The familiar scent of freshly brewed coffee surrounded them. He inhaled deeply.

"I'd like some café con leche and bread," Regina said, "and Arcángel needs some milk. What can Pepa eat?"

"I'll ask for something," Lázaro said.

The house hadn't changed much. A tall case clock stood like a guard against a wall, and next to it, an oil painting showed Jairo's Daughter Raised from the Dead.

A vase full of flowers sat on a console table, next to a colorful serpent in a jar. Some petals had fallen on the glossy surface of the table.

They passed by a stand holding several hats (the Italian hat was there), and continued under a stone arch into a spacious room. Lázaro saw his grandfather in profile, sitting on a sofa in front of a rather large window, drinking coffee. Lázaro hesitated; his grandfather's hair was completely white now.

Without turning his head to look at the visitors, his grandfather raised his hand and motioned for them to come stand in front of him. Lázaro, with Arcángel in his arms, went around to the front of the sofa, followed by Regina. He hadn't changed that much: he was still strong, striking, sharp, menacing… beautiful.

"Welcome, Lázaro," his grandfather said. "I knew you were coming." His voice was clear, strong, determined…. It hadn't changed that much either. And it reverberated in Lázaro's brain, waking up memories, good and bad. His legs trembled and for a moment he thought he was going to fall on the floor.

Lázaro, Arcángel, and Regina, with Pepa beside her, stood in front of Señor Villamayor.

"Is he your grandfather?" Regina asked.

"Yes," Lázaro said.

"I don't like dogs," Señor Villamayor said.

"Patrón—" Alirio began, but Señor Villamayor waved his hand in a dismissive movement, and Alirio turned and left.

"Look, two hummingbirds," Regina said.

Beyond the window, two hummingbirds were suspended in the air.

"Are these your children?" his grandfather asked.

Lázaro hesitated. "No, but it is as if they are my own."

Regina interrupted, "He's like my father. My mother was killed. He saved me."

"But you probably already knew that," Lázaro said.

Arcángel started to cry again, and Pepa grew restless.

"They're hungry," Regina said.

"There's milk in the kitchen," his grandfather said. "And they can feed the dog, too."

"I don't know where the kitchen is," Regina said.

Señor Villamayor picked up a bell that sat on a small table next to the sofa and rang it.

Bliing…

The sound pierced Lázaro's heart.

"I came back for you," Lázaro said.

"I was always waiting for you."

Regina said, "Let's go to the kitchen," and took Lázaro's hand. Lázaro didn't budge.

"Yes, go. Find something to eat," Señor Villamayor said.

"Could you call someone to take them out of here?" Lázaro asked.

"Do you want to get rid of them so you can kill me?" his grandfather asked.

"No!" Regina said and started to cry. "I don't want more deaths. I don't like this place anymore. I'm not hungry. Let's go!"

"I'm joking, little girl," Lázaro's grandfather said, inviting Regina to sit next to him by tapping the sofa. "What's your name?" Señor Villamayor asked her while he rang the bell again.

"Regina."

"Salve Regina," he said and rang the bell a third time.

Lázaro took the torn picture from his pocket and set it on the coffee table in front of the couch, next to a copper vase full of purple statice flowers.

"Forgive me," his grandfather said and rang the bell again.

"Yes. Forgive him, please!" Regina said.

"Why should I? He doesn't forgive anyone," Lázaro said.

"Forgive him," Regina repeated. "You can do it. You're not like the others."

Señor Villamayor took a caramel out of one of his pockets and offered it to Regina. She took it. "Yes. He's not like anyone else," he said.

"What about him?" Regina said to Señor Villamayor, pointing at Arcángel.

"He's too little for caramels," Lázaro said.

"I used to give Lázaro caramels," Señor Villamayor said and rang the bell twice more.

Bliing, Bliing.

Lázaro's heart quivered. He remembered the night after they returned from the Capital City to find everything had been destroyed by the avalanche. "That night after the flood when you found me howling on top of a rock by the river, and you put your arm around me. I never felt so secure," he said.

"Look, there are three hummingbirds outside," Regina said. Lázaro and his grandfather looked.

Arcángel wailed louder. Pepa jumped and barked.

"Josefina!" Señor Villamayor called. "Don't you hear the bell?"

Josefina appeared in a doorway as though she had been waiting behind the door. Her hair resembled Leonor's as Lázaro remembered, in a bun.

"Josefina!" Lázaro said. "Do you remember me?"

Josefina smiled. "Of course, Niño Lázaro," Josefina said. "You're a man now, but who could forget those eyes."

"Take the children to the kitchen and fix them something to eat," Señor Villamayor said.

"Yes, please, take the children out of here," Lázaro said.

"I don't want to go anywhere. He's got a gun," Regina said, pointing at Lázaro.

"Please, Josefina," Lázaro said. "The children are hungry."

Josefina didn't move.

"Didn't you hear?" Señor Villamayor said.

Arcángel cried louder. Josefina hesitated, but picked up Arcángel, who wailed harder. "Come, Regina," she said.

Regina didn't follow her, so Josefina turned around and left.

"People said that the reincarnation of Lazarus was getting closer to home," his grandfather said. "I never lost hope."

"You knew where I was."

"I tried to convince myself you were dead forever."

"Many times, I thought I saw you," Lázaro said.

"Sit down," his grandfather said.

Forgiveness was a small push that propelled Lázaro a couple of steps.... He sat on a chair to the right of his grandfather.

Hatred was an enormous push that had propelled him hundreds of miles....

"My mother wants me to kill you," Lázaro said.

"And you?" his grandfather asked.

"Nobody wants you to kill him. Let's get out of here," Regina said. "I'm tired, I want to sleep."

"Are you going to obey a dead woman?" his grandfather asked. "What if she lied? She was mad. If you're looking for answers, go ahead and kill me, and you will find your answers," he said. "I'm ready. I won't lie."

"He doesn't want any more answers," Regina said.

"I don't need to kill you," Lázaro said. "I know what happened in Paris with Aristide."

"So, you saw it..." his grandfather said.

"Go to the kitchen," Lázaro told Regina.

Regina didn't move.

"Look what a life of mistake after mistake has done to all of us," Lázaro's grandfather said.

"Did you ever kill someone?" Lázaro asked his grandfather.

His grandfather shook his head.

"Not with your own hands. Right?"

"He didn't do it. Forgive him," Regina said and sat on the sofa.

Lázaro's temporary deaths had taught him many things. He had seen the endless cycle of atrocities people committed. He'd always wanted to stick his hand in to take them out of the vortex of repetition. He had been able to find goodness in evil, but at that moment, he felt an enormous weight, so heavy it made him tired, and made him want to be dead forever. He'd been assigned a task he didn't want.

Señor Villamayor turned his head again and said, "Strange. There are more hummingbirds outside the window."

Lázaro looked. The birds were agitated, frantic. Green, orange, pink, red metallic colors swirled in the sky.

"I wanted you to be my accomplice," his grandfather said.

"A replica, that's what you wanted. And all I wanted was to be good so that I would be saved, survive this strange disease, not be alone."

The light coming from the window intensified. His grandfather closed his eyes for a moment. "You were always a believer," he said.

"And so were you. You left the jungle for Paris in search of the specialist in occult diseases."

Regina had fallen asleep with the dog on top of the sofa.

"I've changed," Lázaro's grandfather said. "I hope it's not too late."

"We don't change. Why would we need to change? It's easier to be the way we are forever. I feel this familiar feeling, the numbness that had dominated my life. Can I change it? We all are in a repetitive cycle, like Sisyphus. I am tired," Lázaro said. They were almost whispering now.

"I am tired, too. But I'm old..." The old man nodded, "Yes, let's go to sleep, like Regina."

"I've killed before," Lázaro said.

One of the hummingbirds tapped on the glass. Both men looked. A cloud of birds fluttered in the air.

"Why didn't you want the life I was offering you? We both were lonely," his grandfather said. His eyes had acquired a luminescence that Lázaro had seen before in pure souls about to die. "Lázaro, forgive me, please," he said.

"I am like you."

"I don't think so," his grandfather said. "There is something about you that is almost holy." His grandfather smiled for a second and then flinched.

"What's the matter?" Lázaro asked.

"Nothing, I'm just tired."

"I don't want to do it, grandfather," Lázaro said. "But I've spent my entire life observing."

"Don't do it then. You'll carry my death for the rest of your life. Is it worth it? Death will come sooner or later, and then, we all become equal. We will rot the same way. Poor or rich." His grandfather laughed as he put his hand over his chest, like a helpless animal. "I'm ready for you to see my story. If you haven't been able to learn anything yet, you, who have witnessed many lives, I don't know how you would be able to understand," he said.

"We have poor memories, we forget what we can and remember what we don't need," said Lázaro.

The room grew darker, sadder.

"There are so many hummingbirds outside the window," Señor Villamayor said. "I am at peace now, sort of. And I am sorry that you're not." The hummingbirds retreated. The room became illuminated again.

"You're going to die... One way or another," Lázaro said.

"I don't feel well," Señor Villamayor said.

"La Patrona is here! La Patrona is here!" Alirio yelled as he came in the room.

Regina woke up. Through the window, in the distance, Lázaro saw a brown figure approaching fast; it reminded him of the Carmelitas Descalzas in the dunes.

"Who?" Señor Villamayor asked.

"La Señora Leonor!" Alirio said. "She's now a nun."

Lázaro took out the gun. It felt heavy. His hand trembled. Regina started wailing.

"Don't worry, Regina, you'll see he's not going to do it, he just wants to prove something, but it isn't that he's a killer," Señor Villamayor said as he stood with difficulty.

"I've killed before, I told you," Lázaro yelled and lifted his hand with the gun in it.

A bang made Lázaro flinch, and instinctively, he lifted his arm to protect himself. He didn't know what had happened. He thought he had fired the gun because the window had shattered and pieces of glass were flying in all directions with a sound of myriad bells. Lázaro and his grandfather were enveloped in the light and the birds that had rushed inside. The birds flew in every direction, hitting the walls, the decorations, and the people, except for Regina, who rang the bell like a mad child. Chaos reigned as some birds died and the surviving birds found their way back outside. Shattered glass was scattered across the floor and feathers fell like multicolored snow.

Lázaro didn't have the gun in his hands.... His grandfather's forehead was bleeding. Señor Villamayor swayed and stepped forward, his hands reaching for Lázaro's neck. The movement took Lázaro aback. He's going to kill me again, Lázaro thought; his grandfather had his hands on Lázaro's neck. He's going to kill me again.... But this time, his grandfather's hands embraced him. Lázaro felt his grandfather's weight pulling him down. Lázaro flexed his knees and surged forward. The jump of a cricket. The leap of a frog. The lunge of a snake. His grandfather slid underneath him, his bleeding forehead against Lázaro's chest. Lázaro flew in a parabolic movement. For a second, he remembered that he wasn't leaving holes any longer, just subtle cracks. He didn't hear his grandfather's voice calling him. Nor did he die. Or acquire the weight of the moon.

Lázaro landed on the floor, on top of a rug, and slid a couple of feet. When he came to a standstill, he turned his head and jumped to his feet.

His grandfather was on the floor, like a child, immobile, amid dead birds and splattered blood. Pepa was barking frantically.

In a second, Lázaro was surrounded by many people. Some he knew—

Josefina, Regina, Alirio, Leonor carrying Arcángel, and the Ministry of Health's secretary—and others he didn't.

"Lázaro, my son." Leonor leaned forward and kissed him on his forehead. "What have you done?"

"Mom… Araminta wanted me to kill him," Lázaro said.

Lázaro examined his grandfather's forehead. "This is not a gunshot wound." Quickly, he examined the rest of his grandfather's body. There were no other wounds. He cried, "Thank God, I didn't do it." And he cried and laughed at the same time. He hadn't crushed his grandfather. He hadn't crushed him.

Leonor said: "When I saw him taking something out of his pocket, I thought he was going to kill you. That's why I threw the stone at the window. It must have hit him on his forehead."

Lázaro searched in his grandfather's pockets. He found the slingshot his grandfather had made for him. A scent of oranges rose in the air.

Chapter 39

Bodyguards lifted Lázaro's grandfather's body, took it to the serpent room, and deposited it on the cement table in the middle of the room. The shelves had been arranged carefully, and the snakes reposed in their corresponding flasks with tags that classified them.

"What's the secretary of the Ministry of Health doing here?" Lázaro asked Leonor.

"Don't you recognize her?"

"I have no idea."

"Berenice."

"Churenis' daughter?"

"Yes, her mother died fighting for the Indian Republic."

"And Quintin Lame?"

"Oh, he's still fighting."

"Isn't that what we want? Justice? Your sister is dead."

"I know."

"There was a tree with Spanish moss and orchids; she's buried underneath it."

Leonor smiled; her eyes watery.

"I never understood why I dug out weeds," Lázaro said and looked at his hands.

"Are you going to do his autopsy? You'd have Araminta's version, mine, and his," Leonor said.

"I am afraid."

"To discover something you don't want to?"

"No. To see."

Lázaro undressed his grandfather with careful expertise and took out his medical bag while Leonor folded the clothes and set them on a chair.

"Would it take long?" Leonor asked.

"I don't know."

"Do you want me to help you?

"No."

She left the room.

His grandfather's nude body was ready.

He took the scalpel. His grandfather's life was just at the edge of the blade. At the tip of his fingers. And this time, contrary to Araminta's autopsy, in which she was guiding him, his grandfather let him explore as Lázaro wished. No limits. His grandfather's skin was soft and delicate, like a baby's. And Lázaro saw. And he heard. And he knew.

It was the longest autopsy ever. By the time he finished, the roosters had begun to crow. He cried, and laughed, and marveled. His grandfather hadn't been that lonely after all. Women passed, one after another, and in the end, Aristide was with him until it was over. Who'd have thought his grandfather's feet would tell so many stories in succession, freely, as though they belonged to an experienced runner. His grandfather had set him free. His grandfather had set himself free.

Lázaro went to the garden. It had rained during the night. The ground was soft. He knelt and with one hand took the stalk of a calla lily, and with the other cut the stem. He picked several. No roots dug out this time. Just the flowers.

He found a vase in the pantry and put the flowers in it, brought them to the serpent's room, and went to knock on Leonor's bedroom door.

"Come in," she said.

He opened the door and went in. The light was on. He sat next to her on the four-poster bed.

"Mom, are you dead?"

Leonor closed her eyes and smiled. "I was remembering both of them," she said.

"Abelapetaluloonoñoa," he said

Leonor opened her eyes and laughed.

"No chi mera. No chi mera," Lázaro said.

"I'm not going to die," Leonor said still laughing. "I never forgot your baby talk."

He kissed her on her forehead.

"I thought he'd always been the lucky one," Lázaro said. "He always did what he wanted, but during our last trip to Paris, I'd hidden the biggest emerald ever in my luggage. He took my luggage by mistake, and when he realized it wasn't his, he threw it overboard. The emerald sunk with my underwear."

Leonor laughed first.

Lázaro hesitated but followed. And they laughed releasing memories, thoughts, pain.

The day came, rising like a luminous floating veil.

"Grandfather would have liked to lie under the tree with the swing on top of the mountain. He used to go there plenty of times to play with my spinning tops and marbles, and he cared for the sling shot with all his might. It was as though he were grasping the last piece of me," Lázaro said.

"Did you forgive him?"

Lázaro was silent for a moment. "For what he did to all of us?" We all have something to be forgiven for. I killed Ramiro. While he was in the swing, I pushed him down the precipice"

"I Knew there had to be something. You didn't eat for an entire week. killed a man. I set him on fire."

"I saw it, the mailman. I killed a young Indian woman in the dessert."

"I know. When I got to the Nazareth oasis, they told me you'd left. They could not explain what had happened, but I suspected it."

"Did you meet Doctor Völlert?"

Leonor smiled. "Yes. He was waiting for me."

"So you are the nun who performs miracles," Lázaro said.

"Yes."

"I didn't know."

"How could you? They began when I was in the convent."

"What kind of miracles?"

"Not like yours. People embellish things. You should know that."

"I never thought of my temporary deaths as miracles. They've always been obstacles. Opening useless holes… killing. Changing colors, making people confess," Lázaro said with a dismissive gesture of his hand.

"We're our own worst judges. I am like that—I was. When I began to cure people, I couldn't stop thinking the one I had to cure was you, but I couldn't, no matter how much I tried praying, penitence, starving, nothing worked. There was too much distance. I'd heard of healing at distance by praying, but I felt you were still there suffering the burden of your temporary deaths."

"I was alive—for the most part."

"My healing powers are like your temporary deaths, somewhat temperamental, erratic, unpredictable."

"Did you cure Doctor Völlert?"

"No, and that saved you! Before I can cure someone, I sit and write in this strange language that I only can understand. There's always something positive to gain from the act of healing and a consequence, too. That converts me into a judge, it's terrible. It's like I am God deciding if I should do it or not."

Josefina came in with two cups of coffee and left.

"Before deciding to cure Doctor Völlert, I read what I'd written. It was abysmal. The letter to myself said: If you cure Hans, Lazaro will suffer the consequences. So I didn't even tell him I had to choose between him and you, and I let him die. I didn't ask Doctor Völlert to choose."

They take coffee sips as if a pause were a balm to cure some wound.

"So, did he change my future?"

"Yes. I cried in front of him."

"So, would I have killed grandpa?"

"What he said is that by changing one little thing, one can change so much. I had to come here and throw the stone against the glass."

"Are you going to cure me?"

"Do you want me to?"

Regina came with Arcángel in her arms.

Lázaro said, "I want to show you the rock where Grandpa and I used to sit."

Leonor took Arcángel in her arms, and Lázaro grabbed Regina's hand. They stepped off the patio and into the garden. Pepa followed. They crossed the garden that never knew the absence of flowers, walked under the cement arch that stood high, its letters clear, EL EDEN, and continued along the stone fence.

As they walked toward the river, Lázaro thought about his temporary deaths.... They had given him an identity, and now that Leonor could cure him, they could be gone forever. The thought of him being cured made him feel naked.

They came to the rock and sat on top of it. Regina stood and began to play with Pepa behind them.

"When I die once and for all, the temporary deaths will be gone forever," Lázaro said.

Leonor begun to talk, but another voice sneaked in from the depths of Lázaro's entrails: "I envy you, mortal." He was taken aback, he thought Leonor had spoken, or Regina, but the voice was seductive, enveloping, almost soothing.

"Don't you know who I am?" the voice continued.

"No," Lázaro said.

"No what?" Leonor asked.

"Did you say something?" Lázaro asked knowing the futility of the intent.

"I have the letter here. Do you want me to tell you what is written?" she said.

Lázaro kept silent.

Leonor said: "The temporary deaths have a voice now. They exist on their own! It's written here. If we kill them…"

"I don't want to know," Lázaro said.

Alirio came to tell them the priest was ready to perform the service.

The water in the river continued to pass.

Made in the USA
Middletown, DE
22 July 2023

35557145R00165